Liz Byrski is the author of eight novels and a number of non-fiction books, the latest of which is *Getting On: Some Thoughts on Women and Ageing*.

She has worked as a freelance journalist, a broadcaster with ABC Radio and an advisor to a minister in the West Australian Government.

Liz has a PhD in writing from Curtin University where she teaches professional and creative writing.

www.lizbyrski.com

Also by Liz Byrski

Fiction
Gang of Four
Food, Sex & Money
Belly Dancing for Beginners
Trip of a Lifetime
Bad Behaviour
Last Chance Café
Family Secrets

Non-fiction
Remember Me
Getting On: Some Thoughts on Women and Ageing

LIZ BYRSKI

In the Company
of Strangers

PAN
Pan Macmillan Australia

First published 2012 in Macmillan by Pan Macmillan Australia Pty Ltd
This Pan edition published 2014 by Pan Macmillan Australia Pty Ltd
1 Market Street, Sydney, New South Wales, Australia, 2000

Cataloguing-in-Publication entry is available
from the National Library of Australia
http://catalogue.nla.gov.au

Typeset in 11.5/15 pt Palatino by Post Pre-press Group
Printed by IVE

The characters in this book are fictitious and any resemblance to real
persons, living or dead, is purely coincidental.

Quotations from Prime Minister's apology sourced from 'Apology by Prime
Minister Kevin Rudd to the Forgotten Australians and Child Migrants',
Parliament House, Canberra, 16 November 2009.

For my family – Neil, Mark, Sarah, Bill, Jamie,
Sam and Ashley with love

One

London, early February 2009

uby is in the kitchen when the mail arrives. She is sitting at the table in her winter dressing gown and tartan Marks and Spencer pyjamas, and although she hears the clatter of the postman pushing letters through the slot and the soft thwack as they land on the doormat she stays just where she is. Her usual enthusiasm for the mail is the stuff of legend and her staff frequently tease her about it. Sometimes she thinks it's the first step in role reversal, they're preparing to become the elders of the tribe when she starts to lose it. Not that she minds this, in fact she finds it quite endearing and plays up to it by deliberately demonstrating other eccentricities on which they can pounce with glee. As she has no intention of declining into dementia for a long time yet, and hopefully never, she sees no harm in indulging the younger generation with some amusement at her expense. She does have a childlike enthusiasm for the mail; where others dread crippling power bills, parking fines, requests for donations or news of death and destruction, Ruby anticipates good news of old friends, fresh connections and interesting possibilities.

There is a moment of silence after the mail drops, then a ring at the bell. Jim, who has been delivering the mail for decades, always rings to let her know the post has arrived, but still she doesn't get up.

It's pleasant here at the kitchen table with the comforting heat of the Aga on her back, her feet encased in ugg boots. Ugg, Ruby thinks, is a good name because despite the warmth and comfort they are fiendishly ugly, and have a worrying look of slovenliness about them, but now they seem to have become a fashion item. Not long ago, as she thumbed through *Hello* magazine while getting her hair trimmed, she'd come across a photograph of two pale, waif-like models with straggly hair wearing floaty cheesecloth dresses with ugg boots.

'How ridiculous!' Ruby had said, holding up the magazine so that Amanda, the hairdresser, could see it. 'If it's hot enough to wear cheesecloth it's too hot for fur boots.'

'That's the fashion these days,' Amanda had said. 'Ugg boots with cheesecloth, army boots with florals and frills. That's fashion for you, Rube. Madonna, Elle McPherson, they're all doing it.'

'We'll *they're* both old enough to know better,' Ruby had replied. 'Madonna – well what can I say? Fashion has always made fools of women if you ask me.'

But it's not just comfort that keeps Ruby from the mail this morning, it's her list, the secret list that might invite rather more affectionate teasing than she would enjoy. Apparently it's called a bucket list, lord knows where that came from, some film, she thinks, but she likes the idea of setting priorities. This morning, woken early by a dream in which she was chasing her mother along a railway line, Ruby had failed to get back to sleep. The dream had left her puzzled and anxious – did it mean she was about to meet up with her mother beyond the grave? Not wanting to dwell on that thought she'd got out of bed, donned the dressing gown and ugg boots and had come downstairs to the warmth of the kitchen. And while she'd waited for the water to boil Ruby had fished the list out from its hiding place in the drawer of the kitchen table. It is not an inspiring document and from time to time she speculates on how much more interesting the bucket lists of some contemporaries whom she admires might be: Vanessa Redgrave, Tariq Ali, Germaine Greer, Tony Benn, Margaret Drabble would doubtless be more inspiring.

The bell rings again.

'All right, Jim, I heard you the first time,' she calls, but now there is a third ring and she gets up and pads irritably to the front door and opens it to discover that it is not Jim but some new postman aged about twelve, his nose and cheeks glowing shiny red from the freezing wind, holding a receipt book and a pen.

'Sorry,' he says. 'Put it through the door and then remembered I need a signature. It's special delivery – overseas.'

'What is?'

He points to a bulky manila package lying on the floor. 'That one. Special delivery for Dame Ruby Medway, can you sign for her?'

Ruby resists the urge to claim her rightful title. Tartan pyjamas and ugg boots could be misleading. He probably thinks dames drift around in lacy negligees and have their mail delivered on a silver tray by a butler.

'I don't suppose she'll mind,' she says instead, and scrawls her name in his book. 'Where's Jim?'

'Jamaica,' the man-boy says, tucking the book into his pocket.

'Jamaica?'

'His kids give 'im and the missus two weeks there for their fortieth anniversary. Lucky bugger.'

'Lucky bugger indeed.'

'On me way then. That's special delivery, mind,' the postman says, pointing to the manila envelope. 'Better give it to Dame what's-her-name soon as possible.' And he is off down the steps into the freezing February morning, where the rain turns to ice on the pavement.

Back in the kitchen Ruby dumps the mail on the table and returns to her list. There's something significant about writing a list of things to do – it seems to constitute some sort of commitment. The list is pretty dog-eared now, littered with cryptic comments and crossings out:

1. Write a history of the Foundation
2. Get the conservatory built (ring Barry re tradesmen etc)
3. Travel on the Orient Express
4. Make amends to anyone I've hurt (too many – not generous enough)
5. Make love to someone twenty years younger than me (pretty unlikely due to lack of opportunity)
6. Visit Cat (do I really mean this?)

The trouble with a bucket list is that it has to be openended; one might have one day left or ten, a year or ten, or maybe even thirty. That would make her ninety-nine, so that's probably overdoing the optimism. And should it be prioritised bearing in mind that certain things need to be done while one is still physically fit or rather on the grounds of passion and enthusiasm? For example – should items 3 and 5 become 1 and 2? The trouble with thinking about it is that it suddenly becomes complicated. Keep it simple is what she would say to anyone else but Ruby's never been good at taking her own advice.

It's another half-hour before she finally starts to shuffle through the mail: an invitation to the opening of an exhibition by an artist with whom she had a brief and torrid affair in the eighties, a message from Readers Digest full of stamps that you peel off and stick in various places on a form for the promise of a prize, a postcard from a friend on holiday in Greece, the latest edition of a quarterly journal, and the special delivery envelope, which has an Australian stamp. Cat? It reminds her that she owes Catherine an email and has done for two – maybe even three months. Pushing aside the other mail Ruby sees that the envelope bears the stamp of a solicitor in Busselton, and she slips a kitchen knife under the flap and draws out the contents with a sense of foreboding.

A small cream envelope with her name scrawled across it in Catherine's characteristically bold hand slips from between the pages of folded documents. Cautiously Ruby puts it to one side and flattens the papers onto the table. The letter regrets to inform, it provides facts followed by instructions. Everything she needs to know and to do, it tells her, is detailed in the attached schedule which is included along with a copy of Mrs Benson's will, and a personal letter from the deceased. It offers condolences and requests a prompt reply.

Ruby reads the letter twice and sits there, staring at the small envelope, realising that although Catherine's writing is still easily recognisable it is also somewhat changed: the letters look wobbly, they have odd tails hanging off them as though the hand that formed them couldn't stop in the required places. It looks, Ruby thinks, like the writing of a very old, frail person, not like that of a robust, outspoken woman only a year older than Ruby herself. It is the writing of someone who is – was – severely diminished, and the thought catches her in the chest and she presses a hand over her mouth, takes a deep breath and opens the letter.

Dearest Ruby, it begins.

By the time you get this I will have gone to God or, more likely, to the other bloke. I know you'll be angry or hurt or both that I didn't tell you what was happening, but what would you have done except worry and feel you should try to get here to see me? Well, selfishly I didn't want that. Oh I wanted you to visit, and

I've been trying to persuade you to do that for years but you kept finding excuses not to. But when I got sick I wanted there to be someone who couldn't see what was happening, someone with whom I could be in denial. So now I have the satisfaction of knowing someone will remember me as I was before I started to look like a bald and withered stranger.

I've left it too late to say all I wanted to say except that you are my oldest and dearest friend, a far better friend than I deserved. It's nearly fifteen years since we met up again and even then the past still haunted us, but the gift of rediscovering you has been one of the greatest joys of getting old. Apologies for the past are useless and self-indulgent; you know I am more than just grateful for your forgiveness.

I have made a will that asks more of you than one would normally ask of a friend. Harry's nephew, Declan, inherits almost half of Benson's Reach but I've left you a controlling interest. Since I got sick I've let things go and someone needs to get it back to its best. I'm not sure Declan can do that alone. He's an odd bod – indecisive, can't hold on to relationships, a bit of a lost soul, but he has a good heart and fine mind when he bothers to use it. Perhaps this is the challenge he needs. In the long term you and he can decide what should happen but please, Ruby, give it a year. Do this for me, for us, for the past and what we once shared.

I wish we had met to say goodbye. Take care, Rube, make the most of what's left, every precious minute of it.

My love, always and ever.

Cat

Ruby stares at the letter and wonders why she isn't crying, why the threat of that first sob has dissipated, why not a single tear is sliding down her cheek. It contains too much, she thinks, too much of the past, too many complex and conflicting emotions; it's an ending which both robs and liberates. Theirs was an old but severely tested friendship that had begun in childhood and was shattered years later leaving them estranged for more than two decades, until the day Catherine turned up here, in London, on Ruby's doorstep, wanting to repair the breach. When she'd left two weeks later to return to Australia, Catherine clearly felt she'd achieved her aim but for Ruby the situation had been more complex. She was prepared to resume contact, but she had been unable, or perhaps unwilling, to give more than that. In the past fifteen years she had disclosed little of her own life, sending just one letter or email for every three or four of Catherine's, which she had read with detachment. Now Cat is gone, and with her that connection made by two terrified children on the crowded dockside more than sixty years ago. Did they ever talk about that moment, Ruby wonders now, about how their eyes locked, each recognising the fear in the other? Two little girls torn from their roots about to be herded like cattle onto a ship that would take them to a country they couldn't even imagine. Ruby had seen a girl a little taller than herself, wearing a double-breasted tweed coat with round leather buttons and a velvet collar, very much like her own. A girl with her hair in two long plaits holding a small brown leather suitcase, and she knew that the girl's whole life was in that suitcase just as her own life was contained in the coarse canvas holdall that hung over her own shoulder.

'Keep calm now. Two at a time,' the man had said, as the lines of children pushed towards the gangplank.

The girl squeezed through the crowd towards Ruby. 'We could go together if you like,' she'd said, holding out a woollen-gloved hand. 'I'm Catherine.' The label on her coat said *Catherine Rogers – London to Fremantle.*

Gripping hands, they were carried along in the throng of children, some crying, some struggling, others, like her and Cat, silent and terrified as they reached the deck.

'Cheer up,' said a man in a dog collar, his nose blue with cold. 'Jesus loves you and you're going to the sunshine.'

And Cat gripped Ruby's hand harder as the ship's hooter fired a triumphant blast into the dank London air.

Ruby reads the letter again and pulls her bucket list across the table towards her. Pen in hand she pauses briefly and then strikes out the last item. 'Too late now,' she murmurs, 'too damn late.' It's more than a year since she compiled it, and almost fifteen since she promised Cat she would visit, a promise which at the time she'd had no intention of keeping.

∽

It's much later that evening when Jessica turns up, sweeping into the house in a cloud of cold evening air, tiny snowflakes melting across the shoulders of the black velvet vintage coat she bought last week in Camden Passage.

'Sorry,' she says, shaking snow from her hair. 'Really sorry, it was one of those days. Are you okay?'

'I'm fine,' Ruby says, hugging her, knowing that she looks anything but – that she looks, in fact, as though someone has punched her in the face. 'Well, as fine as could be expected.'

Jessica hugs her again. 'I'm so sorry, it's very sad. Why didn't she tell you? You'd have gone over, wouldn't you?'

Ruby shrugs. 'She wanted there to be someone who didn't know, someone she could pretend with that it wasn't happening and that was me. So, if it helped . . . well, that's a good thing, isn't it?'

Jessica unwinds the scarf from her neck, and unbuttons her coat. 'I guess. So what have you decided?'

'I've booked a flight for a fortnight today,' Ruby says, urging Jessica into the warmth of the kitchen. 'Drink? I've just opened a bottle of red.' And she pours some into a glass and hands it to her.

'You didn't go all the time she was alive, but you're going now – now that she's dead?' Jessica takes the glass and leans against the front of the Aga. 'I don't—'

Ruby holds up a hand. 'No. I *will* explain, but not now, not yet. It's a very long story and I'm not ready to tell it yet. But I'm going now because it feels right. I need to look at the place, see what's happening, meet Declan. And I need to be there for . . .' she hesitates '. . . emotional reasons as well. You can cope with everything here, can't you? You practically run it all anyway but we can get some help in for you.'

'Of course I can cope. You *must* go, you've been saying for years that you would and now . . .'

'Yes, yes, I should have gone after she came here but it all seemed . . . oh, I don't know . . . too much baggage, I suppose. Anyway I'm going now.'

'Will you be okay?'

'Of course, I'm a tough old bird as you well know.'

'I could come with you if you want. We could get Amy back to run things, or there are other possibilities.'

'Thanks, that's lovely of you, but it's not necessary, I'll be fine. Besides, I think I need to do this alone. So I might be gone for a while, a month, maybe two.'

Jessica nods, and gives her a long look. 'Of course, but you don't need to worry about anything here.'

'You're such a blessing, Jess, and very efficient. The Foundation would have ground to a halt by now without your taking on so much.'

'And twenty years ago I would have ground to a halt without you and the Foundation helping me.'

'I suspect you would have survived without us, one of the few who might, but a lot wouldn't. It's such a fundamental thing, isn't it, providing a safe place to leave a child in a crisis, or even just to go to work?' Ruby crosses to the Aga, lifts the lid on a pot of soup, gives it a stir and turns back to Jessica. 'You know, back in the seventies when it all got going, I honestly believed that twenty-four-hour childcare was just around the corner and every woman would have access to it, but here we are more than thirty years on and we're still only scratching the surface. When you see how desperate women are . . . oh well, you've heard me say this a thousand times, you know it all . . . better than I do, but at least we've made a difference, and you, Jess, are a tower of strength.'

'And you're a handy old dame with a cliché,' Jessica says, raising her glass. 'Anyway, here's to your friend Catherine, and to – what's it called? – Benson's . . . Benson's Reach. After all, it's not every day you inherit fifty-five per cent of a . . . well I'm not sure what it is, really.'

'About thirty hectares of land almost three hundred kilo-metres south of Perth, with eight rammed-earth, self-catering holiday cottages, a lavender and berry farm, gift shop and café. And what used to be a rather lovely old house, all a bit run down by now, I suspect.'

Jessica raises her eyebrows, as well as her glass. 'As I said – to Benson's Reach, and whatever you decide for it. This Declan won't know what's hit him. Have you ever met him?'

'Once – donkey's years ago. He'd have been about seven or eight at the time, I think. Nice kid, reddish hair and freck-les. He was running around, arms outstretched, being an aeroplane. Crop dusting, he said. I thought that was sweet and preferable to wanting to be a fighter pilot. But I've really got no idea what I'm walking into.' She turns to the stove. 'Anyway, I hope you're staying to eat. I've made minestrone and got some of that olive bread from the Italian baker.'

'Of course I'm staying,' Jessica says, pulling out a chair and sitting down at the table. 'If you're buzzing off to Aus-tralia and leaving me in charge there's stuff we need to sort out. Besides, I'm starving, so bring it on.'

Two

Perth, early February 2009

Lesley, sitting on the bed, her open laptop resting on her outstretched legs, leans back against the cushions and listens to the silence. She's never thought much about silence in the past. She's appreciated periods of it, but never considered the nature of it. With Gordon at work and the kids at school there had been peaceful oases of silence during the day, and if she woke in the night it was to the reassuring silence of people sleeping – three kids, the dog, even Simon's goldfish was probably asleep. But it's not night-time, it's midday, mid-week; the kids have long gone – adults now, with homes and silences of their own – and here she is, hiding in the bedroom, and downstairs Gordon is doing whatever it is he does these days – creating this silence which is neither peaceful nor companionable. It pulsates with resentment and disappointment, with confusion and frustration, and it's suffocating her.

What is he *doing* down there? What is the matter with him? It was his choice, after all, it's not as though she pushed him into it. 'Life's too short,' he'd said early last year, just after his sixty-sixth birthday. 'Time to stop, make the most of what's left, do all the things we said we'd do.' And so he stopped. He wound up everything at the office, retired and stayed home. But it's not like other times when he was at home – weekends, holidays. No, this is different, this is something else. Gordon retired is something else: a strange, constant and intrusive presence, expecting things – meals, ideas, attention, answers, company – all of it from her. It is so unfair. Lesley sees her own life disappearing in front of her, day by irritating day.

She had made that life for herself in order to cope with *his* life, *his* obsession with work, the long days, the late nights, the weekend teambuilding, the work-related travel. She learned to accommodate it; he was, after all, a good husband and father, outstandingly good at his job, a generous provider. 'Be thankful,' she'd told herself when the kids were small, 'and be realistic. Get used to it.' She was, she did, and unlike some she could mention she didn't whinge about it, didn't nag or plead for him to change – she got a part time job as receptionist in the local dental surgery, she got on with her life, let Gordon get on with his, and for decades it had been fine. Fine when the house was full of children, then teenagers, then young adults. Fine when the place was littered with footy gear, ballet shoes, dirty washing, homework, smelly socks, scrunchies, boyfriends, girlfriends, appallingly loud music, and hormone charged mood swings. It was exhausting, entertaining, wonderfully reassuring and annoying but it worked well and kept working. Even when the kids had gone it kept working, because Gordon kept working.

It was a good life, and getting better: tennis, lunches, Thai cookery classes, then yoga, occasionally helping out in a friend's boutique. There was time for herself, the house to herself, freedom to come and go as she pleased. No questions, no demands and no expectations – only one other person's needs and timetable to cater for. And then Gordon retired.

They'd talked about it, of course, but a long time ago, years ago when it was far enough away to seem unreal. How nice, they'd told each other, the house to themselves, time to do all the things they couldn't do with the kids around. Travel, take up hobbies, maybe buy a boat, relax, smell the roses. 'Bullshit!' Lesley hisses under her breath. It's like childbirth. No one ever tells you how truly horrendous it is because if they did the human race would die out. And no one ever tells you how crushing it is when your husband retires because, if they did, marital homicides would wipe out the male of the species when they reached sixty-five.

Lesley adjusts her cushions and tilts her head back against the wall, thinking about her parents, about the depressing little house near the railway line where she'd spent her childhood and where her mother still lives. In those days it was always too hot or too cold, too damp or draughty, the outside dunny full of spiders, mice and the occasional stray cat. It's better now, of course. Her mother, Dolly, was always on at her father about it and while he was still working they made some improvements: put on a proper bathroom and an inside toilet, had it rewired, modernised the kitchen. But it was only when Bert retired in '81 that all the other things that her mother wanted finally got done.

'At last,' Lesley remembers Dolly saying. 'Well, there'll be no sitting about all day watching the telly and reading the sports news, I've told your father, I've got plans for him, big plans.'

Well they weren't actually very big plans for a man like Bert Stanhope, who'd no time for sitting around and had been waiting for years for the day he could unleash his inner DIY ambitions. Within the first month of his retirement he had started knocking down old walls and building new ones and then came plastering and painting, some skylights, a covered deck, and the carport was replaced with a brick garage and adjacent shed. And he still managed to fit in bowls, RSL meetings, and delivering meals on wheels.

'He was a good man, your father,' Dolly Stanhope had said to her daughters as they waited for the funeral cars to arrive twenty years later. 'Never idle. Always had something on the go. Made a lovely home for us in the end – a home any woman would be proud of.'

At the time, standing in the duck egg blue room with its frills and chintzes, its dozens of ornaments and framed photographs, and a print of 'The Shearers' over the modernised fireplace where the faux embers of the gas heater flickered in winter, Lesley had rolled her eyes and exchanged knowing looks with Gordon and her sister, Helen. They had listened to this recital more times than they could count in the week since Bert's death.

'He did the garden too, Dolly,' Gordon had said, grinning at Lesley, 'don't forget the garden.'

'I'd never forget the garden,' Dolly had said, drawing herself up to her rather unimpressive full height and crossing to the window. 'Look at that vegetable patch, and the fishpond, built that himself, fountain and everything. A good husband and father, the best.' And she'd allowed Lesley to take her arm and steer her out and down the path.

'What a shame she never told Dad all that while he was alive,' Lesley had whispered to her sister as Gordon helped Dolly into the back seat. 'Most of the time she just nagged him stupid.'

'Oh I don't know,' Helen had said. 'I think she probably did. It was their way of being together – Mum nagging, Dad pretending to be henpecked. But they loved each other, to the last. Some couples don't make it that far.'

Lesley has thought about that in the intervening years, thought about the sort of relationships that hold people together. Some of their friends had broken up after years together and she'd wondered why. What could happen in your fifties or sixties to make you want to change everything after decades together? Surely people knew each other well enough by then to be able to work things out? Her parents had frequently driven Lesley mindless with boredom but she loved them dearly. She admired their restrained affection, their mutual trust, tolerance and tenacity, but she had wanted more for herself, more of everything. More money, more fun, more passion, more choices, more children, more stylish and luxurious surroundings, more satisfying and interesting things to do, more freedom and independence than her mother. Most of all she'd wanted the safety net that money provided. Bert and Dolly had struggled when Lesley and Helen were young. There had been lots of darning, the turning of frayed collars, and of sheets sides to middle. Their school shoes had been resoled and heeled while their friends were getting new ones, there was rarely any money for school outings, and food had been wholesome but plain. It wasn't exactly hardship but Lesley knew that her parents had struggled to make ends meet, and it was only once she and Helen had left home that there was something left over for things Dolly wanted for herself. Her mother's example had instilled prudence; Lesley knew the value of money and she wasn't going to settle for anything less than a solid and secure financial future.

She'd had a few fairly uninspiring boyfriends by the time she met Gordon at a Sunday cricket match where she was helping with the afternoon teas. She was twenty-one, working at the city council, and had just been promoted from the typing pool to secretary to one of the managers. Gordon was twenty-nine, a geologist with a budding career in a mining company. He looked dashing in his cricket whites and racked up a respectable score for the local team. Lesley liked him; he seemed thoughtful, not brash and noisy like some of the other players, a bit serious – maybe even a bit too serious. She plied him with tea and scones, and by the end of the afternoon he'd asked her to go to the cinema with him the following week. More than halfway through *Play Misty For Me* he'd reached out to hold her hand, and soon his warm thigh was pressed against hers and his arm moved along the back of the seat. She'd thought he was a bit slow getting around to kissing her, leaving it until close to the end of the film, but perhaps that was a good thing. He was courteous and cautious and a pretty good kisser. A year later they were married and Lesley got what she wanted – got it in spades, really. Gordon moved rapidly up the corporate ladder as the mining company spread its operations around the country and overseas. And she loved him; she had loved him from the start. He was reliable, uncomplicated and she'd trusted him.

'Straight down the line,' Bert had said in his speech at their wedding. 'A real gentleman. Couldn't ask for a better husband for my girl.'

No one, including Lesley, had doubted that – at least not until recently; but now as she sits here, listening to the silence, mulling over the past, Lesley wonders how it ended up like this. What is she expected to do when, after thirty-five years of marriage, of intimacy and distance, of fights and making up, of shared responsibilities, joys, satisfactions, pleasures and disappointments, she finds she is living with a stranger, an alien space invader who wants to suck her dry, monitor her movements, be part of everything she does. What shall we do today? Where are you going? When will you be back? What time is lunch? What are you reading? Have you seen my glasses? Shall I come with you? Shall we go there together? And her answers are always the same and always wrong. And so there is the silence, this burdensome, highly charged, suffocating silence. Does Gordon honestly think that because *he's* retired from *his* life she's going to do the same to keep him company?

This room, which used to be Sandi's and which Lesley has commandeered as her 'study', is now her refuge. Gordon has always had a study to retreat to, but some flash of insight had inspired her to claim this room once Sandi left home.

There's the bed that she's dressed up with cushions like a sofa, her yoga mat, her books, a CD player, tennis cups, pictures, her laptop. The only place in the house which is hers alone, the only thing that has helped her to retain her sanity over the last year.

'He's driving me to distraction,' Lesley had told her tennis partner when they were sitting on the shady deck of the tennis club a couple of weeks ago (no, Gordon, you can't come to tennis with us, find your own friend to play with). 'It's like he's always there, waiting around every corner, occupying the whole house and wanting something from me.'

'Well of course he's there, it's his home,' Stephanie had said. 'You need to give him time to adjust, retirement is a big thing. Even Pete found it difficult.'

'But Pete wasn't like this,' Lesley had protested. 'He didn't follow you around and want to do stuff with you, and get in the way of everything.'

'Well no, but he was a bit odd, you know – sort of displaced for a while. And anyway, Pete's different, he was never like Gordon about his job. It was always a means to an end and he was raring for the end, dying to get out. You just need to give Gordon time.'

'He's had months,' Lesley had said irritably, sucking warm lemonade through a straw, 'almost a year in fact. Nothing's changed except for the worse.'

'Maybe it's you, you might just need a break, get out of the house, go away somewhere alone for a bit. A little holiday, to think about what's really happening and how to handle it. It's always easier to see things clearly from a distance. And Gordon can have some space to sort *himself* out.'

Lesley leaned forward and looked at her friend. 'Go away on my *own*?'

'Sure, why not? It'll do you the world of good. Him too.'

Lesley had sat there, silently watching the four women

reckless enough to be playing a fast final set in the scorching afternoon sun. 'I've never been away on my own,' she said.

Stephanie turned to her in amazement. 'You're kidding?'

'No – never. Oh well, I've stayed over at my mum's place for a couple of nights when she or Dad were sick.'

'That doesn't count. Surely you must've gone away alone for a weekend or something? What about your sister's place?'

Lesley shook her head. 'My sister lives in Dubai. We went there once with the kids. I'd never go alone, I hated it and Helen and I don't get on all that well anyway.'

Stephanie blinked. 'Hmm. Sounds like you need some time out. Why don't you give yourself a treat? Book a couple of weeks somewhere lovely. Vanuatu, or Fiji. It's not as though you can't afford it. Isn't there somewhere you've always wanted to go?'

'Not really. Certainly not on my own.'

'Well then maybe a holiday *together* would help,' Stephanie had said.

Lesley could tell from her tone that she was becoming bored with the conversation – or was it something else, not boredom, more a sort of bewildered pity? Lesley twitched her shoulders defensively. 'So you really think . . .?' She hesitated.

'I really do,' Stephanie said. 'It's about claiming things for yourself. Gordon's been away on his own heaps of time.'

'That was work.'

'But I bet there was play as well – all those overseas trips.' There was a brief awkward silence. 'Well you don't think he's been keeping himself pure for you all these years, do you?'

Lesley stared at her in shock. 'Yes,' she'd said eventually, 'I do – I really do. Gordon has his faults but he's very loyal, and he always says he's risk averse. Doesn't take chances, doesn't really rock any boats. He's very straight, boringly so sometimes.'

'Well your faith in Gordon's fidelity is touching, but he's an attractive man, you can't honestly believe that he hasn't sat in the odd Shanghai nightclub or some bar in KL playing games and imagining what might happen next. He's a man, Les, get real. At the very least he'll have had some harmless little flirtations.'

Lesley thought about this and dismissed it as unlikely but the conversation had left her feeling as though she had failed some sort of test of independence. Well, not failed exactly, because that would mean she had tried and not succeeded whereas she had simply never considered it, but of course if this was what was needed to graduate into feminist self-sufficiency she could still take the exam. So this morning she has spent some time surfing different holiday destinations on the internet, ending up at a site that caters specifically for women. There are walking holidays, safaris, fashion and shopping holidays and art and culture tours, but she can't imagine doing any of them with a group of strangers, any more than she can imagine lying alone on some tropical beach, or browsing the galleries and cathedrals of a city. Staring now at a picture of a group of women, laughing together as they trawl for souvenirs in a Spanish street market, Lesley recognises that what she's feeling is not simply shyness, not even awkwardness, but actual fear. The realisation disturbs her. She is known for her confidence and assertiveness, but right now, as she considers the possibility of going somewhere alone, she understands that she only knows how to be that confident, assertive person within the boundaries of her present life – within the cocoon of her family and friends. Outside of that she might be someone else entirely – indecisive perhaps, anxious, vulnerable. When did she last – or ever – step outside of her comfort zone, test herself in a broader, different context?

Stephanie is right; the time has come to test the water. Getting away – not just from Gordon but also from the proximity and the expectations of her adult children, her grandchildren, her mother and her circle of friends – might be a good idea. She needs to think about what she wants from this time of her life, and how she might negotiate that with Gordon. But when she looks at the picture of the women in the market she knows that another country is a step too far. If she is really going to try this then it will have to be a cautious sortie closer to home. Somewhere familiar from which she can easily escape if she doesn't like it. Somewhere down south perhaps? Stephanie will probably think that a cop-out but it feels like it could be a start.

'Les, Lesley?' Gordon's voice floats up the stairs and Lesley hears but doesn't really register his footsteps.

Somewhere she could go in the car and know she could get home easily if it turned out to be just too hard. There's that place near Margaret River they went to a few years ago . . .

'Lesley? Are you in the study? I wondered about lunch, it's nearly one o'clock.'

Lesley puts the laptop aside and gets up from the bed with a mixture of annoyance and excitement. That place where they grew lavender and the woman baked her own bread for the café, lovely rammed-earth cottages. If only she could remember what it was called.

Gordon, halfway up the stairs, the remains of yesterday's Turkish bread in one hand, realises too late that this is not a good idea and pauses briefly, leaning back against the bannister. But before he has a chance to retreat the door to Lesley's room opens and she is out, passing him on the stairs at the speed of light, her face locked in that resentful mask that seems to have become her default expression.

'I was just going to say,' Gordon begins as he follows her down to the kitchen, wielding the Turkish bread, 'that if you didn't have plans for lunch I could knock up a sort of mezze for us out on the deck. Pop this under the grill, there's some hommus left and some salami and some of those artichoke hearts, olives . . . you know . . .'

Lesley straightens up, takes the bread from his hand and slaps it under the grill.

'I didn't mean you to do it . . . I was just checking . . .' Gordon continues. 'You could go and sit down and I'll . . .'

Lesley sighs. 'It's okay. You can take these out to the table,' and she hands him tablemats, knives and forks.

'Right,' he says, opening the fridge door and gazing at the bottle rack inside the door. 'What's happened to the chenin blanc? It doesn't seem to be here.'

Lesley joins him at the fridge, leans over, takes out an unopened bottle and hands it to him.

'But I could've sworn there was half a bottle left last night,' Gordon says, dropping to his haunches and moving things on the bottom shelf to see if it's tucked behind something else. 'We didn't drink it all, did we?'

'I might've had a glass or two after you'd gone to bed. You'll have to open the new one.'

Gordon straightens up and looks at her as she turns back to the bench top and picks up a knife to slice a tomato. She's wearing a sleeveless white t-shirt with jeans and from where he's standing she looks much as she did twenty years ago; a little broader around the beam, perhaps, and if he looks hard he can see some grey in her hair and a graininess on the back of her upper arms, but she's still in remarkably good shape. Briefly he is transported back to lunch times with the kids around: Simon groaning about having to lay the table, Karen rolling her eyes in contempt and skulking off with her Walkman, and Sandi charging around crashing into things until someone removed her to safety in the garden. Voices, arguments, awful music, mess, bartering over pocket money and whose turn it was to wash up, one of the kids always needing a lift to somewhere, or extra money for something. There were turf wars and culture wars, times when he and Lesley were the only two people in the house who were speaking to each other, times when they fell into bed at night and lay there, dissecting the day with, he supposes now, a sort of satisfaction at having survived it. Despite the chaos and conflicts they had both got what they had always wanted: three bright, confident children, a family that worked.

Gordon sighs and looks at the unopened bottle of wine, his fingers smudging the perfect film of condensation. It doesn't seem that long ago, really, and yet it's a world away: same kitchen, better equipped; same view from the window but minus the minefield of toys, bikes and skateboards; same deck with much more expensive furniture; and only two of the five people remain. Trouble is, he thinks, you'd hardly know they were the same people; conversations evaporate almost before they've begun, tension hangs in the silence between sighs that shriek of frustration, boredom, resentment. It's as though their shared endeavour, the unspoken understandings, the intimate knowledge that bonded them, began to wither once Sandi, the youngest, left home. The house grew tidier and quieter, they ate out more and talked less, and they bought more wine but he drank less. Lesley, he had thought, was lonely. She wouldn't admit it, wouldn't say outright that she missed the kids, but that's what it must be. And so he'd taken the plunge, retirement.

It wasn't what he'd wanted. He'd been considering negotiating some sort of change that would have allowed him to spend a final few years back in the field again. The price of promotion was that it had taken him away from the part of the job that he loved. He was never really comfortable with life behind a desk, with meetings and boardrooms; it was the science that fascinated him and he missed it. Even so he'd have been glad to have a few more years and the company had worked hard to persuade him to stay. But he felt he owed it to Lesley. 'She's put up with the job long enough,' he'd said. He'd known it would take a while for them to get used to it, to adjust to each other, but a year later things were getting worse rather than better.

'Do you remember,' Lesley asks, tossing the sliced tomato onto a bed of cos lettuce and rocket, 'the name of that place we stayed at once in Margaret River, the place with that big woman who grew lavender?'

Gordon leans against the fridge screwing up his eyes, trying to remember.

'I know the place you mean,' he says. 'The name . . . it was something Reach, wasn't it? Began with a B, Baron's Reach? No . . . it'll come . . .'

He loads a tray with the wine bottle, glasses and cutlery, carries it out to the table, and sets two places. 'Barrett's Reach?'

Lesley, carrying the salad, shakes her head. Gordon sighs, pulls out a chair and drops down into it. It is as though the connections that have held them close over the years have burned out and he has no idea why, or how to reconnect them. He has offered weekends away, overseas holidays, suggested joining her at tennis, or on morning walks. He even suggested that he could join her choir.

'Why don't you find your own thing to do instead of trying to muscle in on mine?' she'd said. 'Get a life, Gordon. For heaven's sake, get a life.'

But he *has* a life; he has golf, a lifelong fascination with science that he now has time to pursue in various ways, he has fishing trips with former colleagues and the tree house he and Simon are building for the twins. He has a life. It's just not a life that he shares with Lesley, and it seems to Gordon that every attempt to forge some connection to bring them closer together is rebuffed.

'I've tried, lord knows I've tried,' Gordon whispers into the silence as Lesley returns to the kitchen for the bread. But he knows that he is dangerously close now to giving up on trying, that he is reaching a point at which he will stop caring about it because it's all too hard, and then what? What does Lesley want? Does she even know the answer to that herself?

'Benson's Reach,' he says, the name sneaking unexpectedly out from its hiding place. 'Benson's Reach, that's it, and she was Catherine Benson, wasn't she? The lavender woman?'

Lesley nods, 'Yes, yes I think that's right.'

Gordon pours the wine and makes a valiant effort. 'Nice place that. We should try it again. How about next week, after the twins' birthday party, a few . . .?'

Lesley looks up and she has a weird expression on her face. 'No,' she says, shaking her head. 'I want to go there but on my own. A week, maybe two.'

'On your own? But you've never . . .'

'No,' she says, 'but there's a first time for everything, isn't there, and this is my first time.'

Three

A lice has waited for this day for years – five years in fact. She has imagined it by day and dreamt of it by night, anticipated it in so many ways, confident of the overwhelming sense of relief and liberation she will feel as she walks out of the gate. Believing in it, visualising it, has kept her going, sustained her when she has feared tipping over the edge into despair. At least that's how it was for the first four years and nine months; it's only recently, in these final three months, that it all began to change.

'It's quite common,' Julie, the Outcare women's officer, had told her. 'It's called exit anxiety. People are longing for release, wanting to get out into the world again, and then when the date gets closer it starts to seem quite frightening.'

What's confusing for Alice is that she didn't feel like this the first time she'd thought she would get out on parole. She'd been in a different prison then, Bandyup, where they'd sent her after sentencing. Five years with two years' parole, so everyone had said she'd be out in three, but when she made the first application to the Prisoners Review Board a new, hardline approach had been adopted and she was knocked back.

'New president of the board, new regime,' her solicitor had told her. 'Doesn't make sense to me, nor a lot of other people.

The judge recommends parole after three years provided you have a good record, and because you aren't considered a risk to the community. And now the board ignores it and keeps you inside at the taxpayers' expense. People are pretty angry about it.'

The same thing had happened the following year, although by that time Alice had been moved here, to the pre-release facility, because her solicitor wasn't alone in thinking she'd get out at the second review. Fortunately they hadn't sent her back to Bandyup when the second application failed, just kept her here and she'd starting watching the calendar obsessively, crossing off days, at least knowing now exactly when she would be out. It was with ninety-one days remaining that she'd felt the first flicker of anxiety and by the time it was down to sixty days she was a nervous wreck.

This place wasn't that bad; it was certainly much better than Bandyup. She shared a unit with two other women. They cooked some of their own food, ate in the canteen sometimes and looked after the unit themselves. There was a shop, and work, and you could train for something. It was all supposed to prepare them for a return to the world and the workforce, although of course it was completely artificial and entirely unlike the life she, or anyone else she knew, had lived in the outside world.

'Cooking,' Alice had said when they'd asked her about retraining – it made her laugh because 'retraining' assumed that, because of her age, she had previously been trained for something. 'Cooking would be good – I mean, I *can* cook, but if I learnt properly then maybe I could get a job when I get out, or do you think I'll be too old?'

The officer smiled, shook her head, wrote 'Hospitality and Catering' on the form and Alice signed it. She'd heard that the chef who was running the course had been trained in one of Perth's Gold Plate restaurants. If she was going to train for something then this was the least frightening prospect.

Not an ambitious choice, perhaps, but a practical one. People always needed cooks, didn't they? Well, now she's about to find out.

So this morning, for the first time in five years, Alice dresses in the clothes she wore that last day in court: a plain black cotton jersey dress with three-quarter sleeves and a flared skirt, and black sandals, the teal jacket because the air conditioning in the courtroom had been really cold, and the pearls – her mother's pearls. Simple things she'd felt good in, things that made her feel confident. It feels good to wear them now although she's so jittery nothing is going to boost her confidence this morning. She rolls the pearls between her fingers. They're not an impressive string but they're small and evenly matched with a lovely mellow tone. Thank goodness her mother never knew; how appalled she would have been to see her daughter go to jail, how devastated by the events that led to it.

Alice fastens the pearls around her neck, straightens her skirt and studies her reflection in the mirror, wishing that she had a photograph of herself on that last day for comparison. But no, that's not what she wants. What she wants is a photograph of herself before it all happened, before that awful night, a photograph of her old self, that's what she wants to see now. The old Alice, or rather the younger, pre-disaster, pre-prison Alice. The Alice who had learned to make it from day to day without cracking up, without having a drink; the loving mother and grandmother, the good friend and neighbour. The woman who had nursed her ex-husband through a long illness towards death, the one to whom others turned in a crisis. She stares at her reflection in the mirror and sighs. It would be good to see what she looked like then, before it all happened. Where are her photographs? What's happened to the rest of her clothes and her books? The contents of the house had been sold and the money put into her bank account. At the time release had seemed distant and she had felt so helpless and defeated that she hadn't asked the right questions. Someone must have them, presumably her daughter, but as none of her family has visited or even written there has been no one to ask.

'You look really nice,' Tracey says, sticking her head around the door. 'Like . . . like you're used to it already. Like you're used to being a normal person again.'

'Illusion,' Alice says, and she picks up the clothes she has discarded. 'I feel as though these were my safety net and now someone cut the ropes.'

'Get off it!' Tracey says. 'You'll be fine once you get out there. And we'll have to put up with someone new. Christ knows who we'll get but she won't be like you, that's for sure. I'm so gonna miss you. I wouldn't have stayed out of trouble if it weren't for you,' and she makes an awkward dash across the room and hugs her.

'You'll be out soon too,' Alice says when Tracey steps back.

Tracey nods, tears running down her face now. 'Yeah, and we'll go out and get rat arsed,' but the words choke her.

'No, we'll go out, get some new clothes and have a nice cup of tea,' Alice says. 'Rat arsed is what got you in here.'

'I know, only kidding,' Tracey says, swallowing hard and stuffing a handful of tissues into her pocket. 'New start, eh? First you, then me. You'd better go or I'll blub again. Thanks, Alice, thanks . . .' and she disappears out through the door and Alice hears the squeak of her work shoes on the vinyl tiles.

Just her handbag now: small, black leather, five dollars in an op shop in Midland a lifetime ago. She strokes the leather, still thinking it was a bargain. The smell of Minties wafts out as she opens it and she retrieves three from the side pocket and dumps them in the bin. There's a handbag size packet of Kleenex, the grey wallet with her bankcard, library ticket, blood donor card, an old bus pass, thirty-five dollars in notes, and a few coins. The keys to the house are useless now so she dumps those in the bin along with the Minties. Her watch needs a battery, her mobile phone is dead but she has the little black notebook with addresses, phone numbers, PIN numbers and other vital stuff. Alice puts her make-up purse and her glasses into the bag, closes it and takes a last look around the room, which now seems so safe, so secure. Then she turns away, out into the passage, where Julie is waiting for her.

'I still think you should take the bus straight to the accommodation,' Julie says as they walk out of the building.

'I'm going right into town,' Alice says, 'shock treatment. It'll blast the fear out of me.'

'I'm not so sure about that,' Julie says. 'But it's up to you. You're free now, you can go where you want when you want.'

Alice nods, turns to Julie and gives her a wobbly smile. 'So much freedom, not sure I know how to use it anymore.'

Julie puts a hand on her arm. 'You'll soon get used to it. A couple of weeks and this will all start to feel like a bad dream. Take care of yourself, Alice. Have a good life.'

And Alice, unable to speak, grips her hand for a second, turns away and without looking back she walks out through the open gate.

By the time she gets off the bus on St George's Terrace it's almost midday, and she stands at the bus stop, marooned in the heart of the business district, wondering why she didn't listen to Julie's advice. She's always found the business district intimidating; the tall buildings block out the sun, plate glass automatic doors, stainless steel railings, marble foyers all make this feel like an alien country, and the strong hot wind is heavy with exhaust fumes. The street is busy with slow-moving mid-morning traffic, bike couriers dart perilously between cars and buses, and pedestrians weave between the cars to cross the street. Around her, on the pavement, young people dressed for success go about their business, Bluetooth headsets clamped to their ears, their progress impeded occasionally by tourists with cameras. Men in suits walking three or four abreast, confident of their own importance, stride on expecting the waters to divide for them, and women with carrier bags from the department stores head towards the bus station.

After years of predictability, structure and confinement all the activity overwhelms her but she's here now and so she just has to try to behave like a normal person. 'Come on,' she tells herself, 'try to look as though you do this every day. Get some money. Have a coffee in a real café.' And she turns left into William Street and then right into the Hay Street mall.

Alice's hand is shaking as she inserts her card into the slot at the ATM. She feels like a criminal, as though she's not entitled to be there. 'It's my card, my account, my money,' she whispers, keying in her PIN. 'My money.'

She takes out three hundred dollars and checks the balance. Just over six thousand; much more than most people have on release, she knows, but it won't last long. She'll need rent and probably a bond. A job, she must get a job, but first she'll have to go shopping, buy some more clothes, underwear, a nightdress. She puts the money, *her* money, into her wallet and cuts through London Court, across Hay Street and through an arcade into Murray Street and the coffee shop in Forrest Chase where she used to have coffee before she caught the train home to Midland. Her legs are weak, trembling, and she's a bit giddy. Is she supposed to order at the counter or is it table service? How will she ever get a job if she hasn't the confidence to order a coffee? She grabs the edge of the counter, steadies herself and takes a deep breath.

'Do I order here?' she asks and the barista gives her a surly nod as the machine hisses steam.

Alice takes her coffee to a table and sits watching the streams of people weaving their way to and from the station, back and forth along the mall. She is calmer now but there's a sense of unreality, as though at any moment someone will order her to move, tell her to do something, tell her what to do next. But there is no one else in charge now, the decisions are all hers, and each time she thinks of that she feels a stab of panic. She's out here, on her own, her children have disowned her, the friends who hadn't known how to handle it have all drifted away. No one visited her inside – actually one person did, even sat in court watching the trial, the last person she'd have expected, visited quite often until he moved too far away.

'Give me a call when you get out,' he'd said. 'I'll help if I can.'

They'd exchanged letters since then but she hadn't told him she was due for release. Maybe she'll call, or maybe not; one final tie to the past, perhaps she should cut that too. Anyway, before she can think about any of that she has to sort out her phone, or get a new one. She sips her coffee, breaks off a piece of croissant and dunks it. She can make croissants now, excellent croissants, chef said, professional standard. Will someone give her the chance to make some, to make anything? Will anyone trust her with that?

The longer she sits the stronger she grows; no one notices her, and even though she feels as though the words 'first day out of jail' are tattooed across her forehead, she knows that there really is nothing about her to indicate that she is anything other than a woman sitting alone with a coffee, just one of many, totally unremarkable. She decides to stay a bit longer, orders a second coffee and plans her next move: the Telstra shop first, and then Myer for knickers, bras, a nightdress, maybe some jeans and a couple of shirts, then the bus to the unit. It all adds up to a daunting prospect: the shops, the people, the choices, the decisions, the bus and then the greatest ordeal of all – the unit and the people she'll have to share with. But if she can do all this today, then tomorrow will be easier, and the day after tomorrow, and the day after

Liz Byrski

that. One day at a time. By this time next week she'll be feeling a whole lot better about everything. At least that's what Alice tells herself as she finally pushes aside her empty cup, picks up her bag and makes her way across the mall to the phone shop.

Four

Margaret River, WA, mid-February 2009

D eclan, alone in the office, surrounded by paperwork in untidy piles, facing a spreadsheet from which he is supposed to calculate staff pay and authorise it, is bordering on panic. Three weeks ago he was parachuted into this place and expected to take over because his aunt was dying, but the end had come within days, sooner than everyone – no, not everyone – sooner that *he* had expected.

'Please, Declan,' Catherine had begged when she had called in late November, 'I don't have long to go, come and stay, come soon, so I can show you the ropes.'

But of course he hadn't. The prospect of being up close and personal with Catherine showing him the ropes of a business that she'd run single-handedly for years was too hard to contemplate. It wasn't that he didn't like his aunt, he liked – even loved – her rather a lot, but she expected so much of him, demanded the same sort of vigorous conversations they used to have when, years earlier, he'd gone down to Benson's Reach in the university breaks. That was twenty-five years or more ago and it had been fun then.

He'd always taken a friend and they'd be planting or cutting back, digging new beds, tying up the fruit canes, sometimes putting up new fences. Then, in the evening, they'd sit with Catherine around the big table, drinking wine and putting the world to rights. But Declan has changed since then. Too much has happened – bad, stupid, embarrassing things that have made him feel vulnerable, fear exposure, keep him from getting up close and personal with anyone. Catherine was too intense, her questions too probing, and although she never passed judgment on him her mere presence made him pass judgment on himself. He'd assumed she was exaggerating when she'd told him she didn't have long and he had stayed away until it was almost too late. Stupid, he thinks now, stupid and selfish. It would have been easy, really. He'd been living in Albany, doing a job that bored him senseless. If he'd come here when she asked, he would by now have known what he was doing.

It had never occurred to Declan that Catherine would leave him a share in Benson's Reach. He'd thought she wanted him to run it until someone else took over or it was sold. So he'd kept putting it off, and then the call came from the hospital. She'd lived just three more days in no state to tell him anything much at all. And he had hovered between here and the hospital, embarrassed, shamefaced, horrified by what he'd done, or rather *not* done. He knew next to nothing about the business and it was too late to learn it from the one person who knew it back to front. The knowledge that he had let down the only member of his family who had ever shown any real interest in him was hauntingly painful.

Declan had run a number of businesses in the past and proved to be not particularly good at it, largely because nothing really grabbed him by the heart or the gut. He'd tried real estate, got to run a small section of a department in the public service, and even been employed to manage a very small non-government agency. He was personable, likeable and very good at *looking* as though he could manage things, but he was never quite up to the task. Things started off well and then began to fall slowly apart. He was actually happiest doing something physical, but he didn't appear that way to others. He looked bookish, more like a friendly teacher. He had soft, pale hands that didn't seem suitable for bricklaying or fencing, no one wanted to employ him to do physical work.

Inheriting just under half of Benson's Reach would have been a dream come true if he could be tending the lavender and the berries, mending the fences, mowing or doing the maintenance on the cottages – anything, in fact, other than actually sitting in this office pretending he knows how to run it and, right now, trying to draft an advertisement for staff.

None of this is made any easier by the fact that his co-beneficiary and therefore business partner could arrive from London at any time. All Declan knows about her is that she and Catherine met when they were sent to Australia as child migrants in 1947. So she'll be about the same age and she'll probably know less about this than he does, which is really saying something. Sadly, the prospect of her grasping the reins and taking charge while sending him off to chop wood and trim the lavender seems unlikely. And she also has the controlling interest. Declan is not keen on the idea of being the one who has the final say, but he's never owned property before, so he's not sure how he'll feel when he has to argue for something he wants or has to defer to someone else. What if she wants to sell it, would that be a good thing or not?

'Ruby's a very smart lady,' Paula had said, 'not that I've met her, but Catherine talked about her a lot. Very smart, she said.' She had been heading for the office with her cleaning trolley at the time, emanating disapproval of his failure to turn up more than a few days before Catherine's death. 'Yes, very smart. Catherine said Ruby was here when you were a kid.'

Paula may be right but Declan can't remember it. Suppose they don't get on or don't agree on what should happen – what then? At this stage Declan doesn't really know what *he* wants, but based on past experience he'll discover what he *doesn't* want if Ruby suggests it. It's always been that way with him.

'I don't know why she even left a share of the place to me,' he'd said to Paula. 'I wasn't a good nephew; in fact I wasn't *her* nephew, just Harry's, and I can hardly remember him. So, why me?'

'She thought a lot of you,' Paula had said. 'Very fond of you, she was. Very sad that you didn't come here for help those times you were in trouble.'

'What? You mean she knew about all that? The, well ... er ...'

'The drink and the drugs – oh yes, she knew all about that.'

'You mean she knew everything?'

''Course she did. Not much got past Catherine.'

'But how – how did she know?'

Paula shrugged, '*Someone* always knows and someone always passes it on. WA may be a huge state but it's a very small community. Catherine knew a lot of people. Shame you couldn't make it here when she needed you.' And she wheeled the trolley into the office, running over Declan's foot and twisting a knife into his already guilt-stricken gut. Paula, he thinks, is both blessing and nightmare. She knows the place well and does a terrific job, but she's too opinionated and nosy for his liking. He watches her now as she zips through the office dusting, wiping, whizzing around with the vacuum cleaner.

'Don't touch anything on the desk,' he calls. Not that it would make much difference, he hasn't a clue what's there or how to deal with it. She's an odd sort of mix, Paula, late thirties, possibly a bit more, very tight jeans and a pink t-shirt with a picture of Kylie Minogue on the front, usually plugged into her iPod, singing along quietly with Kylie while she works. But quite often, when she opens her mouth, she sounds like a 1950s charlady.

He shuffles a few papers on the desk now and, thankful that Paula has vacated the office, finds a pad and starts to draft an ad. It would help if he actually knew what sort of staff he needs but he hasn't been able to work that out yet. What he *feels* he needs is someone who will tell him what to do, how to make the place work. The figures for the summer tourist trade are down considerably on previous years and the whole place is looking seedy. A couple of seasonal garden staff have left, and everything looks sad and neglected. The shop obviously needs restocking, and although the young assistant is still there, Glenda, who had managed it for years, decided that Catherine's death was the signal for her own retirement.

The chef left a couple of months ago and Catherine had apparently run out of the energy required to interview anyone new, so she had closed the café. Declan has no idea what goes on with the lavender products except that for years Catherine made them all herself: the moisturisers and cleansers, the soaps and shampoos and conditioners, the massage oils and refresher sprays and all the rest of it. But some years ago she'd started talking about finding someone to train, and that's when Fleur came along. Fleur, who in so many ways is larger than life – confident, outspoken – makes Declan feel like an awkward child. She's a big woman, younger than him, probably not yet forty, but tall and curvaceous, with lots of wild auburn hair, and big gestures. Something about her conveys the impression that she is the possessor of ancient wisdom and whenever she's around Declan fumbles for words and struggles to remember that he's the one who's supposed to be in charge. But it's easy for him to see why Catherine chose Fleur to be the one to whom she would pass the baton of the lavender products. She oozes competence, believes passionately in the soothing and healing properties of the lavender, and her sense of humour is similar to Catherine's. Fleur plays with irony and takes no prisoners, and if something upsets her she doesn't mince her words. She seems to get on well with the rest of the staff but keeps her distance, spending most of her time in the workroom and production area and not using the staff room. But she's good at managing the volunteers who turn up to collect the dried lavender and bags of fabric to make soft toys and eye and neck pillows.

'Why don't we pay the volunteers?' Declan had asked Fleur as they walked around the gift shop a couple of days after he arrived.

'Because they're volunteers,' Fleur had said, raising her eyebrows and tilting her head to one side as though humouring him. 'All the profits from the cushions and the toys go to charity,' she'd said, showing him the label around the neck of the nearest teddy bear. 'Benson's provides the dried lavender and some of the fabric. The rest of the materials come from local people and businesses who give us offcuts and remnants and also offcuts of the Dacron that goes in with the lavender to make up the filling. Catherine knew various people in Perth so every time she went there she'd come back with bags of leftover fabric and Dacron.'

'But where does the money actually go?' Declan had asked. 'What does it do?'

'The Birthing Kit Project,' Fleur had explained. 'They make up birthing kits for women in developing countries. They're very simple but hugely effective because they reduce the risk of death from infection and bleeding.'

Declan had blushed and swallowed hard; he was not good with discussions about bleeding, especially about women bleeding. 'Really?' he managed to say. 'That sounds . . . um . . . very . . .'

'I can show you a kit if you like,' Fleur had said. 'I've got one in the workroom.'

'No, no need for that,' Declan had said almost too quickly, visualising terrifying sets of forceps and hypodermic needles. 'I'm sure they're . . . they must be . . . um . . . important and obviously we should keep doing it.'

Fleur had eyed him off at the time, and he'd thought she might be having a silent laugh at his expense. Later she'd put some leaflets about the birthing kits on his desk, together with a small plastic package.

'It's very important, you need to read about it,' Paula had said fiercely when she spotted them the following day. 'Catherine thought it was important.'

So he had tucked them away in a drawer and turned his attention to other aspects of the business: the potted lavender plants in fancy gift containers, the berry products – the jams, the sauces and vinegars made up by a couple of women in the town and delivered complete in octagonal glass jars and bottles topped with purple and white checked fabric and ribbon. Then there was the bulk picking (no more now until next summer, thank goodness) and the pick-your-own trade and, of course, the letting of the cottages. Catherine had kept everything in her head and so the history, the daily life and orderly running of the place had died with her. Declan knows he lacks the organisational skill and the sort of passionate energy needed to pull it all together. Each day he comes in here and stares in dismay at the chaos which has not changed since the previous day except to become more overbearing. He is paralysed by anxiety, fearful of messing things up in ways that will destroy the place and with it the jobs of the remaining staff.

The telephone rings and Declan clears his throat and attempts to sound professional and confident as he answers. It's a booking. His first.

'A week certainly,' the woman says, 'but I may want to stay longer. I thought you might be fully booked.'

'Normally we would be,' Declan says in a tone he hopes is genial but businesslike, 'but we've had . . . a few administrative problems, things have slipped a little. We haven't been processing any bookings.'

'Well that's my good luck then,' the woman says. 'It's a lovely place so I'm happy you can take me. In fact, book me in for *two* weeks. I'll pay in advance.'

'I just need to tell you that we've had to close the café for a while,' Declan says. 'It used to cater for breakfast and lunch. But we can provide everything for a continental breakfast delivered to your cottage kitchen, so if you're happy with that . . .'

'That's not a problem . . . Mrs Benson, is she still there?'

Declan takes a deep breath. 'Sadly Mrs Benson died recently. I'm her nephew, Declan Benson.'

There is an awkward silence at the end of the line, then, 'Oh . . . oh my goodness, I'm so sorry, how very sad. Well I don't know what to say now. Your aunt, I only met her the one time we stayed there but she was lovely, so warm and friendly. It must be a great loss.'

The words slip like a dagger into Declan's heart, and for the first time he actually feels that loss. Stunned by the enormity of what he has to take on it is only now that he starts to feel exactly what it is that he has lost. A lump of something hard and painful seems to have gathered in his throat and he tries to swallow it and coughs in the process. 'It is indeed,' he says, thinking his voice sounds as though he's being strangled. 'But it was her wish that we should carry on with the business so—'

'Of course,' the woman cuts in, 'but it's difficult, I'm sure. Well, two weeks then, the name is Craddock, Lesley Craddock – shall I give you my credit card details?'

Declan puts down the phone, enters the booking into the register and leans back in his chair thinking about Catherine, who she really was and what she meant to him. His parents are both long dead, the wider family scattered and unknown to him. His ex-wife despises him for his indecisiveness and his drinking, and hopes never to hear from him again. Years ago, in this situation, Declan would have reached for a drink. He would have opened a bottle of Scotch and poured a liberal amount down his throat, and then some more; or he might have drunk his way steadily through a few bottles of wine until panic and confusion were replaced by the comforting feeling that he was in total control and knew exactly what he was doing. Then he would have passed out, woken up the next morning with a terrible headache and started all over again. There were times, too, when he would have shoved something up his nose or into his arm, but that was a long time ago. It's twelve years since he had a drink and much longer since he's taken anything stronger than a couple of Panadol. These days he attempts to deal with stress through meditation, but times like this are a painful reminder that he was much better at drinking than he seems to be at meditating. He wonders now if he might be better to shelve all this confusing paperwork and go outside and sort out the sprinkler system, or check the raspberry canes. But the raspberries are finished and, anyway, he's done that for the last four days and each time he comes back in here no office fairy has worked magic on any of the problems, a few more of which have landed on the desk.

Declan makes himself a cup of tea, sits down again and steels himself for the task ahead. He opens the diary in which Catherine had thoughtfully put some reminders for various days. On today's date the message in block capitals is SAUSAGE DOGS followed by a phone number.

'Sausage dogs?' he exclaims in frustration, loud enough to make Paula, who is back now and is dragging the vacuum cleaner out of the office, jump almost out of her skin. 'What the dickens are sausage dogs?'

'Bloody hell,' Paula says, 'you frightened the life out of me.'

'How am I supposed to know what this means?' Declan grumbles – it is so much easier to turn the sadness and the guilt into anger. 'Sausage dogs!'

'They're the things you put along the bottom of the door to stop draughts,' Paula says. And she reaches down behind the open door and picks up a long sausage-shaped thing made of purple corduroy. 'Like this. They're very popular with the winter tourists. Catherine would have been thinking about ordering some into the shop for when the weather changes.'

Declan nods. 'Draught excluders,' he says quietly, 'well I'd better get on to Belinda, whoever she—' but he's interrupted by the phone and when he picks it up there is no one there because it's his mobile that's ringing and he slams down the receiver and shuffles more paper to find it buried under a gardening supplies catalogue.

'Declan? Declan, is that you?'

It's a woman's voice. The signal is weak and he gets up and goes outside onto the deck. 'Hello, who's that? I can hardly hear you.' And the line drops out.

'Shit,' he murmurs, 'who *was* that? Oh my god it sounded like—' and it rings again.

'Popular, aren't you?' Paula says dryly, shaking her duster over the edge of the verandah.

'Declan, it's me, Alice.'

'Alice?' Declan is, quite suddenly, short of breath. 'Alice?'

'Yes.' Her voice sounds odd, shaky, or perhaps it's just the line. 'You said to call when . . . well, if . . .'

'Alice?' he says. 'Is it really you, are you getting out?' Goose bumps prickle his skin.

'I'm out,' she says. 'Last week, last Monday.'

'But that's wonderful . . .'

'No, no it's not, it's awful. I thought it would get better, but it's ten days now and it's worse every day. That's why I'm ringing. I'm sorry it's just . . . I don't have anyone else to talk to.'

Declan's spine tingles. Alice!

'Alice,' he says, and he can hear that she's really distressed. 'Alice, listen to me. Everything will be fine, trust me. Where are you now?'

She mumbles something about temporary accommodation, about trying to find a job.

'Listen, Alice,' he cuts in suddenly, uncharacteristically decisive. 'Listen to me. I'm in Margaret River now, my aunt's place, remember? Can you get yourself here? There's a bus you can get from Perth, it takes four or five hours. Do you have enough money for a ticket? Good. Get the first bus you can, it might not be till tomorrow, but ring and tell me what time it arrives. It stops right in the Margaret River High Street and I'll be there to meet you.'

'But I have to get a job, I won't have anywhere to—'

'You can stay here,' he says, 'I've got a job for you, you can have a nice little cottage all to yourself. Lovely place, lots of lavender . . .'

'But I—'

'Do it, Alice,' Declan says, and he hears the pleading in his own voice. 'Do it for you and for me. I need you here and you'll love it. Go and find out about that bus and ring me back. Trust me, Alice, please just trust me.'

Five

Perth, early March 2009

Ruby gasps in shock as she steps outside the airport building and into the heat. She'd forgotten its intensity, the way it grabs you by the throat and leaches moisture from your skin in seconds. And she'd forgotten the sky too – that endless dazzling blue beloved of tourists and cursed by locals in the final days of a painfully long, hot summer. She hesitates, takes a deep breath that seems to burn her nostrils, drags her suitcase towards the taxi rank and waits, sweat creeping down her back, for the next available cab.

It's weird being back here. Nearly forty years since she quit Australia and fifteen years since Cat turned up unexpectedly on her doorstep in Islington.

'Catherine?' Ruby had said, shock fixing her rigidly in the half-open doorway. 'You're here? You didn't . . .'

'No, I didn't,' Cat had said, bluntly. 'I didn't get in touch and I didn't say I was coming because you might have told me not to. But I needed to see you, Rube, needed to talk to you face to face. Are you going to stand there all afternoon or are you going to let me in?'

After shock Ruby's next sensation had been resentment that she had been ambushed. Catherine taking control again, she'd thought, getting what she wants irrespective of anyone else, presenting me with a fait accompli so I've no choice but to open the door and invite her in. 'Stay cool,' she'd told herself aloud while Catherine was in the bathroom and she was making tea in the kitchen. 'Don't blow this because of your pride. Years ago, for a very long time, she was your only friend in the world.'

'It's your turn next,' Catherine had said as they parted at Heathrow three weeks later. 'We've dealt with the past so now you can come to Perth.'

Ruby had hesitated, shaking her head. 'It's not only what happened between us,' she'd said, 'it's the rest of it – being sent away from England, the convent, everything that happened there. I don't know if I can ...'

'You can, you will, I know you will,' Catherine had said. 'I just know it.' Once home again she had continued her urgings and Ruby had hesitated, prevaricated and now it was too late.

'Where to, love?' asks the taxi driver, heaving her suitcase into the boot.

He sounds, she thinks, like a Londoner, but she doesn't ask. The British are no novelty here. She and Catherine had been part of a massive human cargo designed to boost the Australian population with good British stock but there were plenty who came of their own volition as ten-pound-poms, seeking the opportunities of a new life in the sun. People wait years now and have to jump through all sorts of hoops to get in. How times change, she thinks, and how relentlessly that early experience still defines her feelings about the place decades later.

'The Sheraton, please,' Ruby says, and settles back to fasten her seatbelt. Open mind, she tells herself, keep an open mind. Ignore the muddled surge of unsettling emotions that reared as the aircraft began its descent. She didn't have to do this, she could simply have found a local agent to act for her, provide a business assessment, and offer advice. Or she could have sent one of the staff. In fact, she acknowledges now, she could easily have sent Jess, who would probably have jumped at the chance.

They follow the other traffic out of the car park onto a wide and rather boring stretch of road lined with dusty native plants, long-term parking lots and the characteristically bland, crouching buildings that sprout up around airports. Ah well, she's here now and stuck with it. Stuck with Benson's Reach and her co-beneficiary, who, from the couple of telephone conversations she's had with him, seems to be struggling to get to grips with their shared legacy. He'd sounded pleasant, but nervous – as though he knows as little about the place as she does. I'm too old for this, she thinks, it's time for a quieter life, not racing off to Australia to sort out a failing business.

Later, when the worst of the heat is gone, she opens the glass doors of her hotel room and sits on the balcony, watching the sun setting in a spectacular haze of crimson and coral, until her eyelids feel heavy. But the minute she slides between the immaculately laundered sheets she is awake again, her stomach writhing with anxiety, memories clamouring for attention.

'You can still turn around and go home,' she tells herself. 'Pick up the phone, call the airline, get the next possible flight back to London and despatch someone else to do the job.' But as she reaches for the phone a flicker of reluctance stops her and she pauses, equivocating. This is different. Benson's Reach no longer belongs to Catherine and along with some excruciatingly painful memories it also holds some happy ones which are entirely her own. The gut wrenching echoes of childhood in the convent, the cruelty and the shame – well, she may never be able to lay those ghosts, never rid herself of that outrage, but Benson's Reach is different. She is here for Catherine and for herself, for their years of precious but severely disrupted friendship. 'Respect that,' she tells herself, 'make something good from it. Run away from this and you'll regret it later.' And punching her pillows into submission Ruby turns over, pulls the sheet up herself once again and closes her eyes and her mind in the pursuit of sleep.

From the kitchen window Alice can see up the slope to the balcony of the cottage where for the last two days she has sat watching the daily life of the place: Declan heading back and forth to the office, guests arriving and departing, a boy in a black baseball cap sweeping or pruning or riding off home on his bike, staff and tradespeople coming and going, and Paula, the only other person she's met so far, heading up the hill to clean the vacated cottages, or smoking surreptitiously behind the old cow shed. Benson's Reach is supposedly smoke free and Alice wonders if Paula had risked smoking while Catherine was still around.

It's the first time she's been here in the main house, but from the vantage point of her balcony she has studied the outlines of this rambling, single-storey, stone building, with its wide verandahs, which has so suddenly become Declan's property and, for the time being at least, his home. She has imagined what it would be like inside, the arrangement of bedrooms, the place at which the office, added much later, is linked to it by a paved pathway. She has studied the other building too, a large, rammed-earth structure built in the eighties as a café and gift shop. The extent of the place has amazed her, not just the buildings but the sweeping, lavender clad slopes, the serried rows of raspberry canes, and the rest of the holiday cottages, similar in size and style to the one that Declan had taken her to when she arrived three days ago.

'It's lovely,' she'd said then. 'But I don't need a whole cottage to myself.' She was emotionally exhausted by almost two weeks of painful freedom followed by the long bus ride, and was still likely to burst into tears at any moment. Declan's kindness had seemed overwhelming.

'They're just holiday places, but you need some privacy,' Declan had said. 'And Ruby will need to stay in the house; it's partly hers, after all. We're low on holiday bookings now anyway, Catherine dropped the ball in the last few months. I should have been here to help her but . . .'

'But you'll get more bookings,' Alice had said. 'You'll stay here, won't you? Get it going again?'

'It really depends on Ruby,' he'd said, and he'd explained then about the will, about his aunt and Benson's Reach, and the prospect of her old friend's imminent arrival. 'Right now I don't really know *what* I want from it all. But whatever we decide we'll need to get things back on track first. Anyway, you need some time to sort yourself out, get over the trials of freedom.'

The interior of the house is bigger, lighter and more airy than Alice expected. The rooms all open off a wide central passage, and at the heart of it is this kitchen with its quarry tiled floor, the huge old range, a long line of windows and a scrubbed pine table loaded with unfinished paperwork, old newspapers, a bowl of fruit, a jug of dried flowers, and various items of crockery. Alice finishes rinsing the cups she and Declan have used for their coffee and dries her hands on a tea towel that looks as though it needs a good wash.

'I need to know what my job is,' she'd told him earlier this morning. 'I can't sit around in the cottage contemplating my navel; it's no good for me. So tell me what you want me to do. You must have had a role in mind for me when you invited me here.' But as they talked it soon became clear that Declan's invitation had encompassed everything in general and nothing specific.

'I'm a lousy organiser, I needed help,' he said sheepishly, 'someone to talk to and to ... share the load, I suppose. Maybe we could talk about it now?'

It reminded her how diffident he could be, how indecisive.

'All my motivation and decision making abilities disappeared years ago,' he'd told her once. 'It floated off in a cloud of all that dope I smoked in my youth.'

'Then let's make a list of things that absolutely have to be done and done soon,' Alice had said this morning, and they had soon filled a page of Declan's notebook. They were both floundering, she thought, but hopefully they would be able to keep each other afloat. Now, a couple of hours later, Declan has driven off to an appointment at the local council.

'Have a good look around the house, the office, everywhere, while I'm gone,' he'd said. 'Here are the keys for the café and shop. We can talk again when I get back, and if you could make up a room for Ruby that would be good.' He'd handed her another key hanging from a string of small purple beads. 'This is the key to Catherine's room. Apparently she made them lock it when they took her to hospital.' He glanced away, obviously embarrassed. 'I haven't been able to bring myself to go in there yet. And I certainly didn't want Paula nosing around in there. Have a look, would you, see what you think?'

Alice turns the string of beads in her hand and then hangs it back around her neck. She is both curious and cautious and the caution dictates that the impersonal space of the office is the best place to start. Stepping out of the back door she pauses, inhaling the scent of the lavender that lines the path. Closing her eyes she senses, fleetingly, something that has evaded her for so long. Is it calm, perhaps, or hope? Yes, hope. She is free, and despite the awfulness of those first ten days back in the world, she is now somewhere safe and friendly, somewhere with possibilities. She has some control over her future now, but it's still going to be a struggle. A woman only a couple of years off sixty with no one left of her own, no home, no possessions, an ex-con with a terrible scar across her past constantly threatening to overwhelm her – does she actually *have* a future?

When Declan had met her at the bus stop in Margaret River she had been a mess. The freedom she had craved so long hadn't been anything like she'd imagined and as each day passed she had sunk further into despair at her inability to cope without the boundaries to which she'd become accustomed. Stick it out for at least a week, she told herself several times a day. She didn't want to think about what she would do if things didn't improve in that time. And when the week was up the outlook was grim. She'd applied for jobs, turned up for interviews and was knocked back from all of them. They were jobs that she could have got standing on her head back before all this happened.

'When you call for the interview, don't tell them where you've been for the last few years,' the counsellor had told her. 'You don't have to lie, just don't say anything about it. If you get an interview you'll make a really good impression, and that's when you put your cards on the table.'

But Alice, uncomfortable with what seemed like deception, had disclosed the information on the telephone and those first conversations had promptly been terminated. Finally she tried it the other way and landed four interviews in four days. They were jobs in cafés and restaurants that she thought she should easily be able to get. She wasn't aiming high, just hoping for something she knew she could do and that would get her back in the workforce again. One was in a sandwich bar, another waitressing in a city café. The third was on the checkout in a large supermarket. Alice agonised for hours over what to wear – not that she had much to choose from – what to say, and how to appear confident. And then she struggled with the shame that paralysed her when she disclosed where she had spent the last five years. The first three employers cooled immediately at this point. The final interview was for a short order cook in a hotel near the airport. It was a perfect location, walking distance from the place she was staying. The interview went well, and when she told the manager that she had just been released from jail he was warmly supportive. For a moment she thought she'd got the job, but then he shook his head and said he was sorry, he had no problem with her record but he'd tried in the past to employ post-release applicants and the general manager wouldn't agree.

And so she began again, with similar results, until she had hit rock bottom and was drained of energy and unable to muster the confidence to carry on. It was then, desperate for the sound of a familiar and friendly voice, that she had called Declan and the next day she was on the bus to Margaret River. They didn't even know each other very well – at least, not in the way you'd normally know an old friend. They'd met at a particularly difficult time in his life and she'd been able to support him through that. Then, when Alice was the one in trouble he'd been there for her. The first time he had come to see her in prison had been her first connection with her pre-prison life.

'It's a two-way thing,' he'd said, flushing when she told him what it meant to her that he'd visited. 'You were an absolute rock for me when I needed it, so if there's anything I can do now, you only have to say. I'll come again in a few weeks' time.' And he had. In fact he'd come every six weeks or so, until he took a job in Albany, five hours' drive away, so the visits stopped, but he wrote from time to time. They were strange, sometimes melancholy, sometimes light-hearted letters in which he told her more about himself and what he was doing, but spoke mainly of his observations on what was happening in the world. From climate change to celebrity excess, from social networking to the treatment of asylum seekers, Declan had a view – thoughtful, considered and always concisely expressed, and usually remarkably similar to her own. His despatches on the state of the world had grown increasingly important to Alice; they were her only personal contact with life outside the prison and she treasured them. But Declan is still something of a mystery to her as, she supposes, she is to him. What she's sure of is that she trusts him; he has learned from his mistakes, and can acknowledge his weaknesses even if he is slow to acknowledge that he has any strengths.

Alice slips the key into the lock and lets herself into the office. It is a nightmare: the desk buried under a chaotic pile of papers, catalogues and files so large and so messy that they almost seem to have their own monstrous energy. There are days – weeks – of work needed in here but surely that is for Declan and his new partner when she arrives. She skirts the desk, glances through the reservations book and the details of the staff, and retrieves a file that she has knocked from its place on the windowsill. Briefly she pauses to study it, closes it and as she puts it on the desk in a prominent position there's a tap on the office door and a boy, the boy in the baseball cap that she's spotted a few times, pops his head in.

'Sorry, I was looking for Mr Benson,' he says, obviously surprised to see her, shifting his weight awkwardly from one foot to the other.

'He's out, I'm afraid,' Alice says. 'He said he'd be back about lunchtime. Can I help? I'm Alice, by the way, I'm staying here to help out. You work here, don't you?'

'Sort of,' he says. 'Do a few jobs for Cath ... um ... Mrs Benson. I was wondering about my pay.'

'Oh dear. You *will* need to talk to Declan about that. Could you come back later, after lunch? I'm sure he'll sort it out for you then.'

He nods. 'Okay,' he says awkwardly, 'I'll get on with something else.'

'I'll tell him, shall I?' Alice says. 'Tell him you were looking for him and that you'll be back?'

'Okay, thanks.' He turns away from the door.

'Who shall I say . . .?'

'Sorry?'

'Your name? So I can tell him.'

'Todd,' he says, 'thanks, yeah thanks, see ya.'

Alice closes the office door and goes out back along the path to the house thinking that he seems awfully young, and wondering why Declan hadn't mentioned him when he'd told her about the other people who worked here.

There are four bedrooms off the passage and apart from the one Declan has obviously chosen for himself it's clear that the others haven't been used for some time. In the grey and white tiled bathroom the only signs of recent activity are Declan's: his toothbrush and toothpaste in a glass, towels thrown carelessly over the rail and a couple of t-shirts and underpants dropped on the floor.

The dining room has the deserted air of a long-gone dead life that belongs, perhaps, to a time when Catherine and her husband, Declan's Uncle Harry, entertained here. The jarrah table is waxed to a high sheen and not a speck of dust mars the bottles and crystal glasses on the shelves of the cocktail bar. Alice suspects that Paula, with her vacuum cleaner, feather duster and the lavender polish that scents the air, is probably the only life form that this room has seen in a very long time.

Only one door remains and it's locked: Catherine's room. Alice slips the key into the lock, wondering why there is no lounge or sitting room. But when she opens it she can see that this large room, with its pale fabrics and rugs in rich, earthy colours on the polished wood floor, was once the lounge. Bookcases line one wall from floor to ceiling and magazines, newspapers and an open handbag lie abandoned on the sofa. Opposite, below the windows that look out to the lavender beds, a long wooden table is cluttered with cosmetics, an open box of costume jewellery, a hairbrush and dryer, a laptop, papers, books, magazines, a small television and DVD player and a vase of long-dead roses surrounded by their fallen petals. Almost obscuring the beautiful stone fireplace is the carved jarrah headboard of an unmade, king size bed scattered with cast-off clothes, and a night table stacked with packets of tablets, discarded tissues, several dirty mugs and glasses and a half-eaten packet of digestive biscuits.

Alice pauses in the doorway surveying the shockingly intimate story of the last weeks of Catherine's life. The room reeks of neglect, illness and the desperation that must have led her to confine herself here with the things she loved and needed most. The half-open doors of the wardrobe reveal clothes and shoes once organised with precision, but it appears that at some point Catherine had stopped putting things away. Alice senses the shadow of a fading and diminished woman, too sick and exhausted to hang this skirt, this blouse, to pick up these shoes, no longer caring enough to put the beads and earrings into their box, nor roll this scarf and slip it into the drawer alongside the others. Clothes have been dropped on the floor and pushed into a pile in the corner, shoes edged under the bed, underwear tossed close to the linen basket. And the effort of clearing away the old papers, the unwashed cups, the dead flowers, must have been too great. How long, Alice wonders, had Catherine struggled to keep order before giving up? Had she hoped to die here too, planned for it, only to be thwarted by a collapse that meant that her last days were lived out in a hospital bed? The room has a stale, grassy smell but Alice resists the impulse to fling open the windows and let in the fresh air. Suddenly even to step inside seems like an intrusion. Gently she moves back, closes the door, locks it and slips the beads back around her neck and stands again in the passage gripped by the sadness that seems to have leaked out into the rest of the house.

A different room will have to be prepared for Ruby, she thinks. The main bedroom has its own bathroom so that's probably the best bet. She opens the linen press and collects some towels, puzzling as she does so over the picture of loneliness she'd witnessed behind Catherine's locked door. Declan had spoken of his aunt as a warm and generous person and she had lived here for decades; surely there must have been neighbours, local people in the town, friends and of course there were staff, so why was she so obviously alone in her time of greatest need? Had no one seen what was happening? Was there no one she could trust with a glimpse of her vulnerability? Was there no one who cared?

The main bedroom is cool and peaceful, the bed already made, a couple of watercolour landscapes on the walls and a Victorian lavender-patterned porcelain jug on the dresser. Declan had told her that Catherine found Paula difficult to manage and he too seems ill at ease with her, but it's obvious why Catherine kept her on. With the exception of Catherine's lair everything is spotless, and while the kitchen is untidy it's clear it is clean and things that are lying around are undoubtedly Declan's. Paula does an outstanding job; in the cupboard from where she'd taken the towels the linen is immaculately pressed and a muslin bag of dried lavender lies between each set. So why was Paula not allowed in to clean Catherine's room? Alice opens the bedroom windows and the white curtains flutter to life on a warm, lavender-scented breeze. She has a fleeting sense of the days when a very different life was lived here, a passionate life rich with love and laughter, and she wonders how and when it acquired its silent air of despair. She is curious now, more curious than ever about those days, that life, where it went, how it ended and why, because something tells her that this aridity goes back years, decades even, and that the desolation of Catherine's room speaks volumes about her life as well as her death.

Alice looks around the bedroom with satisfaction thinking she'll cut some of the roses in the back garden and put them in the jug on the dresser to make it more welcoming. She closes the door and heads back towards the kitchen, pausing once more outside the locked room. She had recognised something in there, something not only sad but personally disconcerting. It was the desperate and failing effort to retain control and create a sense of safety. She herself had done it in prison, done everything possible to make her space into a haven, a place where she had some measure of control. There had to be some way to compensate for the loss of love and of family, the lack of purpose. There were limits in prison; you could be locked in, but only by others and you couldn't lock those others out, and how often she had longed to do so. Catherine had, apparently, managed to do that, keeping her decline and her despair confined, struggling alone not just with pain and sickness, but with the turbulent emotions of a lifetime that would have crowded in on her.

Alice turns away from the door with a shiver, heads to the kitchen and sits down at the table, resting her head in her hands. Infected with Catherine's sadness, her own fear of the future returns, the earlier tender ray of hope extinguished now. Catherine was seventy when she died, a woman with a beautiful place to live, a thriving business and, apparently, plenty of money, and yet she had in the end been entirely alone with no one to blur the edges of her fear or sadness with some comfort. If this could happen to her what then, Alice wonders, lies in her own future? In three months' time she will be fifty-nine. In ten years' time, what then? Fear surges through her blood making her heart pound, and she does what she has done for more years than she can remember, she gets to her feet and looks frantically around her for something to do, something to distract her, anything to stop the reality of being there, alone with herself in the stillness.

Six

'I still don't understand,' Gordon says, lifting Lesley's bag into the back of the car. 'It's the sort of thing we said we'd do together when I retired – take off for a few days when we felt like it. Go down south, do some wineries, galleries, walks. And now you're doing it and you won't let me come with you.'

'Oh do stop *moaning*,' Lesley says, aware as she does so that he is not actually moaning, he is attempting to understand something that she can't fully understand herself. What can she say? That's she's taking some sort of test of independence? That she actually can't bear to be around him right now? It's not even as though she really wants to go. She doubts it will do anything to solve the real problem, which is Gordon himself in retirement. 'I'm just going away on my own for a few days.'

'For two weeks actually,' Gordon says, and she can hear he's getting tetchy now, irritated, hurt probably, and understandably confused; as confused as she is. Years ago they could have talked about what was happening but the channels of communication have been shut down.

'You'll be fine,' she says, 'I've left you plenty of meals in the freezer.'

Gordon slams down the lid of the boot and turns to her. 'Of course I'll be *fine*,' he says, and his tone is angry now. 'I'm perfectly capable of looking after myself. But this is about *us*. There's more to our marriage than frozen meals, or at least there used to be, but now I'm beginning to wonder.'

Lesley puts her trainers into the back of the car, and straightens up. 'I don't know what you're making such a fuss about. Women do this all the time, get away on their own for a while.'

'You don't.'

'Well I am now.' She turns away and opens the driver's door. 'And it's really not long.'

Gordon grasps the car door to stop her from getting in. 'Why did I do this then?' he asks. 'Why did I retire? I could have stayed on, you know, five years, more probably.'

Lesley tries to push his hand off the door but he's immovable. 'I don't know, why did you?'

Gordon runs his hands through his thinning hair in exasperation. 'I did it for you, for us, for all the things we talked about for years, for our marriage, our future. Doesn't that mean anything to you?'

Lesley opens her mouth to speak, pauses and then looks straight at him. 'I don't know, Gordon,' she says. 'I really don't know anymore.' And as his hand drops away from the door she slips into the driver's seat. She closes the door, starts the engine and accelerates out to the road, leaving him standing there in the middle of the drive, aware that she has wrought terrible damage, but somehow no longer able to care.

———

Lesley's immediate reaction to Benson's Reach is disappointment; the place has lost its edge that's for sure. There is no one in the office and the rather dowdy woman who opens the door to the house seems to know little or nothing about the place.

'I spoke to Mr Benson on the phone,' Lesley explains, 'just a few days ago.'

'I'm sorry, I'm new here and I'm afraid I don't know anything about the business end of things,' the woman says. 'I'm Alice, by the way, and I'm so sorry about this. Let's go over to the office – Declan will be back soon, but meanwhile I can probably find the reservation and then I can take you to your cottage.'

She retrieves a reservations book from the monstrous pile of paperwork on the desk and seems relieved to find details of the booking. 'Declan has a note that you'd be arriving after two o'clock,' she says. 'Not that it matters – your being early, I mean – but it does account for why *he's* not here.'

There is some messing about with a booking form, and eventually the woman says it's best to leave the paperwork until Declan gets back. She opens a glass cabinet filled with keys hanging on hooks, selects one, and gestures to Lesley to follow her out of the office.

The cottage is just as Lesley remembered, light and pleasantly cool, the rammed-earth walls a soft shade of terracotta, the furniture simple but good quality, beds made up with white linen and on each one white towels, folded to make a nest for a sprig of lavender and two foil-wrapped lavender chocolates.

'Did Declan explain that the café is closed?' Alice asks, opening the fridge. 'Fresh bread and croissants will be delivered early each morning.' And she goes on to point out milk, cereals and fruit. 'I know Declan will be up to see you as soon as he gets back,' she says, edging towards the door. 'He can fill you in on anything else.'

'When exactly did Mrs Benson die?' Lesley asks.

'Last month, although I believe she was very sick for a quite a long time prior to that.'

'I'm sorry. I only stayed here once before,' Lesley says, trying to make up for her irritability in the office. 'But I liked her very much.'

Once alone she drags her suitcase into the bedroom, throws herself on the bed and lies there gazing up at the sloping timber beams of the low ceiling. Several times during the three hour drive down here she had been on the point of turning back, trying to unpick the damage before it was too late. She really hadn't set out to hurt Gordon, but of course she has, probably very badly, but she can't go back because she wouldn't know what to say. This morning, after months of irritation and resentment, something weird had happened. As she packed her bag for the trip south she felt confusion, exhaustion and the longing to be gone. Her sharp tone and harsh words were self-defence rather than attack, and then Gordon had asked that question, 'Doesn't that mean anything to you?' and in that instant she realised that she no longer knew the answer, she no longer knew what she felt or what she wanted. The only thing that was clear to her then was that this was the reason she had to go, in order to work it out, to find the answer to a question she had never expected to be asked.

But being here makes no difference, it simply opens her up to the distraction of more practical and comparatively trivial questions. What is she going to do with herself now that she's here? Last time they had visited wineries – well, she won't be doing that alone, although there are some nice little galleries nearby. They'd gone to the beach, but she's really not much of a beach person, especially when it's hot; walking in winter is when she likes it best. They'd gone out for dinner every night, and she won't be doing that – lots of women do, of course, and seem not to mind, but Lesley cringes at the thought of eating dinner alone in a restaurant, being stared at and whispered about by couples and families. She'll put stuff in the fridge and heat food in the microwave. And while Margaret River certainly has some very nice shops it won't take long to check them out. But what about the rest of the time?

The oppressive silence of the cottage wraps itself around her. She can't go home, and she can't call the kids because they'll ask all sorts of questions, and so for that matter will her mother. For the next two weeks she is stuck with herself, in this little cottage in a place where, in spite of its many charms, there is absolutely nothing she wants to do.

—◆—

Todd loves the taste of raspberries more than anything else he's ever tasted. Just thinking about that taste makes his mouth water. It's late in the season, though, and as he wanders slowly between the canes searching for the last of the fruit, he's pretty sure he's going to be out of luck.

'You can eat as many as you want,' Catherine had said to him the first time she'd brought him here and asked him if he'd like to help with the picking. 'And I'll pay you five dollars an hour.'

'It won't seem right to eat them if you're paying me,' he'd said, surprising himself as he did so; usually he'd grab whatever he could get, but he'd liked her. Weird she was, old and maybe a bit crazy. It was only later that he came to realise that she was the sanest person he'd ever met.

'I doubt that even you could devour all my profits, Todd,' she'd said with a laugh, 'tuck in, eat what you want.' So he had, and the funny thing was that he discovered there was a certain amount that you could eat that was enough, and then you were happy to stop. It was cool, once you knew you could have as much as you wanted, you didn't need to pig out. He liked that.

But this year the raspberries have been neglected. A couple of months ago the reticulation for this part of the land packed up. He'd told Catherine about it and so had Fleur, but it was one of those things that just didn't get fixed. Todd kicks at the dusty ground wondering whether the plants will ever recover from a summer without water. Eventually he finds a couple of poor specimens, shrunken and dried up, but they *are* raspberries and he stuffs them in his mouth. They're a disappointment, dry little lumps, and he spits them out, sits down on the ground between the canes, extracts one of the two cigarettes he has in his pocket, and lights it. He's not supposed to smoke out here, fire risk, and he'd never have dreamed of doing it when Catherine was around. But she's not anymore, she's gone, and Todd can't work out what's happening up at the house, and what it all might mean for him. The sun scorches the back of his neck and he turns his baseball cap around so that the peak protects it, and draws slowly on the cigarette, watching the blue smoke curl up and away above the tops of the canes. He wonders why he's smoking because he doesn't really like it much and just does it to look grown up – but what's the point when there's no one around to see?

Nobody's told him what he's supposed to do now. 'Oh that's good,' Mr Benson had said when Todd had mentioned that Catherine paid him to do some jobs around the place. 'Very handy to have someone like you around,' and he'd run off inside the office to answer the phone. But he hasn't said anything about Todd's pay. Perhaps he thinks Todd does all the sweeping and the pruning, washing out the workroom and sorting the rubbish and all the other stuff for free. He might have – if it was for Catherine. He'd have done anything for her, but she always paid him on time, and she'd given him some money just before she died. The last time he went up to see her at the hospital, before Mr Benson even turned up, she'd given him an envelope.

'Did you open that bank account like I told you?' she'd asked, and when Todd said he hadn't she'd said, 'Well, do it today. There's some cash in here. You should pay it straight into the account. It's to help you get organised, get a proper job, and don't tell anyone, especially don't tell your mum – it's not for her to blow on dope or flagons of wine. Just keep it for yourself.'

The envelope contained fifty one hundred dollar notes. He'd never seen so much money and it made him nervous. He'd never been into the bank although his mum had often sent him to the ATM with her card when she wanted some cash. But somehow he couldn't imagine walking into the bank with five thousand dollars in cash. They'd think he'd nicked it, for sure. So he'd kept it with him at the caravan for a few days and then he'd taken it to Fleur and she'd promised to look after it for him at home.

'The cash is to help you get on your feet,' Catherine had said. 'And Declan will pay you as usual. You'll be sixteen in a few months and you can't be doing odd jobs all your life. You're far too bright for that.'

He hadn't spent any of it yet, but he might have to if Mr Benson doesn't pay him soon. Catherine had paid him cash every week, but Mr Benson doesn't seem to notice him and hasn't asked him to do any of the other hundred and one things Catherine might have asked him to do. So he'd just kept doing stuff that needed doing, and this morning he'd gone up to the office and a woman called Alice was there, and she couldn't help him, so now he's killing time, waiting until Mr Benson comes back.

Todd feels helpless, something he never felt when Catherine was there. She'd made him feel safe. Now he doesn't know what's happening, what he should be doing, what's expected of him, but he knows he has to be strong and watch out for himself. Catherine would have stood up for him against anyone – his mother, the police, Paula, who obviously hates him, anyone. But now she's gone. For more than three years she'd listened to him, talked to him, bucked him up, looked out for him and bawled him out when he fucked up.

'Oi!' she'd yelled at him across the pub car park that first night when she'd found him trying to break into her car. 'Get your hands off my car.' And she'd grabbed him by the neck of his hoodie and pushed him up against the nearside door. 'Bit young to be nicking cars, aren't you? Bet you can't even drive.'

He was insulted. 'I did it before,' he'd said. 'Took a Honda and drove it down the beach.'

'And got picked up in the process, I'll bet,' Catherine had said. 'Did they charge you?'

He'd shrugged. 'They just give me a warning.'

She'd slackened her grip then. 'So why're you doing it again?'

'Dunno,' he'd said, attempting to duck away but timing it badly.

She'd grabbed him again and shaken him slightly. 'Maybe you want to spend the night in a cell at the police station.'

Todd said nothing, just shook his head. She was a big woman, tall and broad, and he'd realised then that he'd bitten off more than he could chew.

'So why?' she'd said. 'Just for kicks, is it?'

He shrugged. 'S'pose so . . .'

'Get in the car,' she'd said, dragging him round to the passenger side. 'It's all right, I'm not going to take you to the police. I'm going to take you home and have a chat with your dad.'

'Haven't got one,' he'd said.

'Well presumably you've got a mum, I'll talk to her instead.'

He hadn't known what to say then because the chances of his mum being sober enough to talk to were pretty remote. And it didn't take Catherine long to work that out once they got to the caravan. His mum was totally out of it that night, like always, and she was more interested in watching 'America's Next Top Model' than listening to anything Catherine had to say. 'Yeah, yeah, whatever,' she'd said, without moving or taking her eyes off the screen. She could even pour another drink without taking her eyes off the TV.

'Looks like this is between you and me then, kid,' Catherine had said. She really was pretty old, and very bossy. 'So, here's the deal. D'you know Benson's Reach? Okay, tomorrow after school you come up to see me there and we'll sort this out. Can you do that?'

He'd nodded, kicking at a bit of gravel at the foot of the caravan steps.

'Straight from school then, and you'd better turn up because if you don't I'll be down at the police station reporting you for trying to break into my car. Got it?'

Todd had nodded again, still not looking up.

She'd gripped his shoulder then. 'I said have you got it,' she repeated, looking closely into his face.

'I got it,' he'd said.

'Good.' She let him go. 'Straight after school, remember, Benson's Reach, ask for Catherine.'

And that was how it began, every day after school and often at weekends he went there, loading, unloading, digging, carrying, cleaning gutters, anything. Sometimes she'd just sit with him on the verandah and talk. She'd helped him with his homework, taught him about books and made him read stuff; sometimes she even made him read the newspaper. A couple of months before the end she'd organised to have a great big bed brought in from where it was stored and set up in the sitting room and then he'd gone with her into town to buy a TV and DVD player and he'd managed to set them up for her.

'I'll be like a hermit,' she'd said, and he hadn't a clue what she was talking about. Hermits lived in caves or tumbledown shacks, not great big houses with loads of rooms. 'I'll be living in one room,' she'd said, 'just one room with everything I need. Cosy, less work, less tiring.'

She'd got quite a bit thinner by then but she hadn't lost her sense of humour and she hadn't stopped talking to him about things she thought he should know: politics, climate change, and what would happen if all the grandmothers in the world stopped caring for their grandchildren and their aged parents free of charge. And she'd got him to read to her; it was good for both of them, she'd said.

'Get a decent job,' she told him late last year when he left school. 'You promised you'd stay on at school but you haven't, so for goodness sake start looking for a job. I'll help you.'

She was pretty sick by then, and looked terrible; most of her hair was falling out and she wore a scarf tied around her head, and her hands shook. In December he'd got a job in the supermarket, loading and unloading the trucks, collecting trolleys, washing floors, all that stuff. Three days a week and half a day on Saturdays.

'You're better than that, Todd,' she'd said when he told her. 'You could've got a better job, full time, more money. You're a good worker.'

But of course if he did that he wouldn't be able to help out at Benson's, and there was no way he was going to leave her in the lurch when she was so sick, but now she's left him.

Todd leans forward, peering between the raspberry canes to the office, and sees that Mr Benson's car is back. Might as well get up there now and catch him before someone else does. He grinds his cigarette end into the earth, stands up, unzips his fly, pees on the butt to make sure it's out, and heads towards the office.

———

Declan looks gloomily at the sheaf of papers the woman at the council has given him to complete, then adds them to the pile on the desk. The first thing he has to do is go up and see Mrs Craddock, who arrived about an hour ago. Alice hadn't liked her – 'prickly', she'd said – and she'd encouraged him to go up and have a chat with her.

'And maybe you could walk me through the process for

checking guests in and out, so that I'll know what to do next time,' she'd said.

Declan thinks he'll go and see his new guest first and is about to turn his back on the mess of the desk when he spots Todd heading in his direction from the berry beds. Alice had told him that Todd was looking for him earlier, so he thinks maybe he'll have a quick word with him first. He needs to know exactly who Todd is and what the arrangements are for the work and, presumably, for paying him because he doesn't show up anywhere on the payroll.

'You should get rid of that boy,' Paula had said to him the other day. 'He's trouble. I warned Catherine but she wouldn't listen.'

'What sort of trouble?' Declan had asked.

'Just trouble,' she'd said, and she'd walked off with an armful of linen destined for the cottages. 'Don't say I didn't warn you.'

Declan watches as Todd weaves his way between the loganberries and along the path that leads around the lavender. He seems a nice lad, quiet, works well, but he can't remember Catherine saying anything about him. Declan steps outside the office and calls out to him. 'Hey, Todd, can you come and have a chat with me?'

Todd gives him a thumbs-up and quickens his pace, as if he'd been waiting for the invitation. But as Declan slips into his chair behind the desk there is a clatter of footsteps along the verandah from the opposite direction and Fleur appears in the doorway.

'Got a minute?'

'Well, I . . .' Declan hesitates, feeling his usual sense of inadequacy when confronted with Fleur.

'Good,' she says, moving quickly to the chair opposite him. 'It won't take long.'

He shrugs, 'Okay. Ruby's arriving this afternoon and I know she'll want to meet you.'

'The thing is,' Fleur says, 'I've just come to give in my notice.'

She might as well have punched him hard in the middle of the chest. 'Shit,' he says, 'you're not serious, are you? We'll be stuffed without you – no one else knows how the products are made. What can I—'

Todd's head appears around the door. 'Ah! Sorry,' he says, 'I thought you said to come up to the office.'

'I did,' Declan says, getting up and walking over to him. 'Sorry, mate, can you give me a few minutes, this is urgent.'

'I'll start on cleaning the gutters then, shall I?' Todd asks.

'Thanks, I'll catch you later,' Declan says, giving him what he hopes is a friendly rather than manic smile, and he closes the office door and sinks back into his chair. 'What would persuade you to stay, Fleur?' he asks, trying not to sound desperate. 'I mean, we could talk about money, and I was hoping you might take on managing the gift shop as well. Not working in there – I mean, just a managerial overseeing role.'

Fleur shakes her head. 'I don't think so,' she says, looking away from him out through the window and swallowing hard. 'I think it's time to go. For me this place was really about Catherine and now she's gone . . .'

'But do you have to decide now? I'm sure you and I would get on, and when Catherine's friend arrives you and she . . .' His voice fades away under her unflinching gaze.

'I'll stay till you've had a chance to settle in,' Fleur says. 'A couple of months maybe, but in the meantime perhaps you could be on the lookout for someone to replace me.'

～

Outside the office Todd curses silently. He can hear every word and the prospect of Fleur leaving is a blow. After Catherine she is his favourite of all the people at Benson's. He often sits in the workroom watching or helping her to mix the oils and the lavender and the other stuff, and decanting it into the purple bottles or the little white pots with the purple labels. Fleur is the only person who knows how to have a laugh around this place, and she's got no time for Paula; won't even let her in to clean the workroom.

'Too bloody nosy by half,' she'd said. 'I'd rather clean it myself. Not that I've got any secrets in here, just don't want her snooping around.'

And Catherine had agreed and told Todd she'd pay him extra to clean up in there once a week.

Fleur is like Catherine, a total control freak, but she always does the right thing by people. There's no way she'll leave until they find someone else – she wouldn't leave anyone in the lurch. Todd knows they'll never find anyone like her, and now he's about to lose another friend and the last person he trusts. Straightening up he heads away from the office with a sigh, remembering as he does so the time he'd told Catherine how *she* was a control freak but always did the right thing.

'You've got to be kidding,' she'd said, laughing. 'I've done a lot of horrible things that I'm not at all proud of, let down and hurt people I really cared about.'

'Yeah?' he'd said. 'Well I don't know about that but you're just, like, kind – kind to me, you treat me the same as Fleur or any of the others.' He'd wanted to say that he was talking about respect but he would've felt like a dickhead saying it. That's what it was though, respect. People – adults, teachers, and the like – always talked about respect, about how everyone should have respect for everyone else, but in Todd's experience many of them didn't have any respect at all for him, or for people like him.

'What're you doing hanging around here?' Paula says, appearing around the corner of the house carrying an empty bucket and a bottle of Windex. 'She's not here to look after you now, you know. Nothing for you to do here now, you should just clear off.'

'I'm going for the ladder,' Todd says. 'Got to clean the gutters.'

'Gutters.' Paula almost spits the word. 'Just making work, you are. Well things are going to change around here, I can tell you that. You'd be better looking for a proper job instead of hanging around here sponging off other people. I heard your mother's gone off with some bloke . . . Bali, they said, not coming back.'

Todd turns away without answering. Paula's always had it in for him, but it's been a lot worse since Catherine's gone, she just shoots her mouth off whenever she sees him. No respect for anyone, Paula, he thinks. No respect at all.

'And mind you don't mess up the verandah,' she calls after him as he walks away. 'I've just swept up.'

'Go fuck yourself, you miserable cow,' Todd murmurs under his breath, and he strides up the path to the old cattle shed where all the tools and fertilisers and other stuff are kept and drags out the ladder. Then, lugging it onto his shoulder, he makes his way back to the house, sets it up against the side wall and climbs up in time to see Fleur come out of the office and head back to the workroom. Mr Benson follows her out.

'Todd?' he calls, looking around for him. 'Todd? You here?'

Should've just waited by the office, Todd thinks, could've talked to him after all.

'Up here!' he shouts. 'Doing the gutters like you said.'

Mr Benson gives him a thumbs-up. 'In the office when you're ready,' he says, and disappears back inside.

Meanwhile another car is coming slowly along the rough track from the road and draws to a halt outside the office. Todd shifts his position on the ladder and watches as the driver gets out. She's an old woman, short and sort of squarish, with thick grey hair done up in a bun that makes her look like an old-fashioned school teacher. Some bits of her hair have escaped from the bun and she pushes them behind her ears and looks around as though she'd rather not be here. It must be her, Todd thinks, Ruby, Catherine's friend. He puts one foot onto the slope of the roof and leans forward to get a better look.

'She'll be coming soon,' Catherine had said the last time he saw her. 'Ruby, you'll like her. She'll sort everything out.' And she'd waved to him to look in the drawer in the night table. 'There,' she'd said, 'that picture?' It was a framed photograph of Catherine in one of those long dresses she always wore, standing with a shorter woman who was wearing a suit like she'd just come from the office. They were on the steps of a house – London, Catherine had said – and she had her arm around Ruby and was leaning towards her, but Ruby wasn't leaning. They were standing very close together but Ruby looked as though she was standing there alone: very upright, a bit awkward, straight-faced, as though she didn't really want to be in the photograph at all.

'That's us, when I went to stay with her in Islington,' Catherine said. 'Ruby. You can trust her, Todd. Don't forget that.'

Todd hasn't forgotten, but he's also learned to be cautious and he leans further forward now, straining to see her as Mr Benson comes out of the office to greet her. She looks okay, he thinks, and as he shifts his weight further onto the roof his foot slips, and before he even realises it the space between his legs opens up, the ladder crashes to the ground, and Todd feels himself shoot off the roof behind it.

Seven

Ruby brushes her hair, winds it up into its usual tight bun and fixes it with pins. Bits of it immediately slip free and she sighs and tries to hook them back. Amanda is right, she thinks, staring at herself in the bathroom mirror, she should have it all cut off; a nice short style that's easy to look after.

'And you'd look ten years younger,' Amanda had said when she'd gone in for a trim before she left. 'You won't recognise yourself.'

'Hmm. Well that might be a good thing,' Ruby had replied, but she still hadn't let Amanda cut it short. She had started growing her hair the day that she and Catherine left the convent. Years of having it hacked off first in the orphanage in London and then by the nuns had made her determined to wear her hair long for the rest of her life.

Somewhere in the very distant past she remembers her father: he is lifting her onto his knee; the coarse fabric of his uniform itches against her bare legs but she won't complain because his arm is warm around her waist. He is stroking her hair, winding it around his fingers. 'Just like a princess,' he says tenderly, 'my little princess.' It's all she can remember. After that he was gone, but the war remained. There were nights in the underground, wrapped in rough grey blankets, the stifling air thick with the smells of soot and human bodies. There were streets choked with cement dust, the ruins of bombed buildings, and the sound of sirens. Women queuing for food or hurrying home trundling wheelbarrows heavy with precious coal. And then there was the night when they set out for home after visiting her mother's friend in Lewisham, and they didn't make it to a shelter.

'Come on, Ruby,' her mother had cried, grabbing her hand as they heard the whine of the doodlebug, and they ran, following others who were heading for the safety of the station. 'Can you run a bit faster, darling?' But then her mother had tripped and fallen, and by the time she had struggled back to her feet it was too late. There was just the eerie silence then as they waited, terrified, to see where it would fall.

Later, much later, two men in tin hats pulled her from the rubble. The smoke and dust burned her eyes, and not far away an already half-demolished building collapsed bit by bit as though in slow motion and people fled in all directions. Even now she can remember calling over and over again for her mother as she was lifted into an ambulance. The princess had been transformed into a terrified orphan: homeless, fatherless, motherless, entirely alone, or so they said. The princess hair was matted, black and sticky with blood, ash and dust. That night, as she sat propped up on hard pillows in a hospital bed, a nurse had gently cut it away with surgical scissors. She was four then and it would be twelve more years before she regained control of her hair and could let it grow again.

'I can't let go of it,' she'd explained some years ago in the salon, lowering her voice so that Amanda had to lean closer to hear her over the roar of hair dryers. 'It's about my independence, who I am. A bit like Samson, his strength came from his hair, and when Delilah came along and lopped it off he lost the plot. Can't risk it, I'm afraid.'

She takes a final critical look at herself in the mirror now, and fiddles again with the messy bits of hair. It's the trap of living alone, or one of them, she thinks, this constant self-scrutiny. It was worse in the past, of course, when she was young, when looking beautiful and desirable seemed so important, when it seemed to be all that mattered, when it could mean acceptance or rejection. But even at this age, when no one gives a damn how she looks, when lowered standards could be affectionately regarded as endearing eccentricity, it's still there, this other critical self following her always, feeding back anxiety about how others will see and judge her, and it's always negative. 'Get over it, Ruby,' she tells herself, 'who's looking at you anyway? Who the hell cares what an old woman looks like?' and she strolls out of the bathroom and back into the bedroom.

'I hope this is all right,' Alice had said earlier, leading her in here and setting her suitcase down near the foot of the bed. 'Declan asked me to get a room ready for you. Mrs Benson had moved into the lounge, so I assumed he meant what used to be the main bedroom.'

Alice couldn't have known, of course, nor Declan. Ruby knows she would have done the same thing herself. It was considerate, thoughtful, and the large white porcelain jug filled with lavender and white roses was the obvious sign of a woman's touch. Alice seemed nervous and anxious to please and a request for a different room would have come as a slap in the face.

'It's fine, Alice,' she had said. 'Lovely, in fact, and the flowers are beautiful.'

A look of relief had spread across Alice's face. They have never met before but there is something very familiar about Alice; it's a way of being that Ruby has come to recognise during years of working with women whose sense of themselves has been crushed by circumstance. It's the aftermath of trauma: abuse, incarceration, mental illness, displacement, profound loss. Which, she wonders, is Alice's story? What sort of horror is she emerging from?

'Well I'll get on then,' Alice had said. 'You'll probably be glad of a rest after your drive, and . . . well, everything else. That poor boy, I do hope he's going to be all right. I'm glad Declan went with him to the hospital. It didn't seem right for him to go alone.'

'Absolutely not,' Ruby agreed. 'Catherine mentioned him in her emails. She was very fond of him.'

'Right. Well if you're sure there's nothing else, I'll get on. Shall I make dinner for about seven? Declan's bound to be back by then.'

'Perfect. Is there anything I can do?'

Alice's hasty response that she was best left to her own devices in the kitchen was obviously not mere politeness, and Ruby, still a little jetlagged and somewhat bruised by the reality of being back in Australia, in Perth, and now here in this house, had kicked off her shoes, lain down on the bed and willed herself to lock the memories back into the past where they belonged. It was nearly half past six when she woke, just enough time to unpack a few things and take a shower.

The sun is lower now, washing the skyline pink and gold, softening the outline of the distant tree-clad hills beyond the boundaries of Benson's Reach. Ruby rests her arms on the windowsill. How often had she stood here watching the sun set, the kangaroos hopping cautiously out at first light and again at dusk. It was grassland in those days and there were trees closer to the house; beautiful then, it's even more beautiful now that the purple haze of the lavender beds spreads into the distance. Catherine had changed the place for the better and built a fine business here. Ruby wonders how she managed it alone for all those years after Harry was gone. As young women they had learned the hotel business together, working for Harry's parents in their Perth hotel. Catherine had put that experience to good use but it can't have been easy. Ruby sighs and turns away from the window, wishing she were in any room but this.

There's a tap at the door and Ruby straightens her shoulders and gets ready to face the real world again.

'Sorry,' Declan says, 'sorry about all the drama, sorry that you didn't get a proper welcome. Have you got everything you need?'

'There's nothing to apologise for,' Ruby says, 'and yes, thanks, I have everything I need.'

'Good, that's good,' he says, nodding. 'Alice says dinner's ready when you are.'

'Let's do it,' she says, stepping out and closing the door behind her, sensing that he too seems to need some sort of reassurance from her. 'How's young Todd?'

'He's going to be okay,' Declan says, 'but he presents us with something of a problem. I'll tell you about that over dinner. Alice needs to hear it too.'

❈

Paula is usually long gone by this time of day. Her hours are eight till four but stuff's been going down today and she needs to keep tabs on it. It was different when Catherine was here. Paula knew everything that was going on then – not because Catherine told her but because she was careless. She left paperwork lying around, left doors open when she was on the phone or talking to someone in the office. At first Paula had felt a bit guilty about what some people might think was snooping or eavesdropping, but as time went on she was able to rid herself of that feeling because she recognised that what she was actually doing was keeping an eye on things. Catherine's laxity left both her privacy and her possessions vulnerable; they always had seasonal staff passing through and often they were not the sort of people you could trust. Out drinking every night, hungover and smelling like a parrot's armpit the next morning, they could take off with anything and you'd never see them again. Not that it had ever actually happened, of course, but Paula puts that down to her own vigilance. Besides, Catherine had become forgetful so an occasional nose through the paperwork on the desk enabled Paula to remind her about things. She made sure she did it in a subtle but confident way so that Catherine just assumed she must have told Paula things herself and was grateful for the reminder. Paula was pretty sure this made her indispensable.

It's different now, of course. Things had started going downhill when Catherine, who'd been sick for some time, had taken it into her head to turn the lounge into a sort of makeshift bedsit. The only other places she went to were the kitchen, the bathroom and the office. Of course, Paula understood the logic, and she'd assumed that, apart from Catherine, she alone would have access to the room. At the very least she'd be going in and out to clean it. To Paula's dismay the call to clean the room never came, though others were allowed in. Whatever that bloody Todd had done to be in there with her, Paula had no idea. Sucking up to Catherine, he was, a leech, just like his mother, always working his way in where he wasn't wanted, taking what wasn't rightfully his. The only other person who was occasionally allowed in was Fleur but she wasn't the type to keep a person informed about what might be going on – in fact as far as Paula was concerned Fleur was a snooty cow and not to be trusted.

'You do a fantastic job, Paula,' Catherine had told her more times than she could remember, 'worthy of Her Majesty the Queen, no less.'

Paula didn't have much time for HM the Queen, but she did have a soft spot for Prince William; if she was good enough for Her Maj then why wasn't she allowed to clean the room? Anyway, she needed to get in there now, and on her own. It was in Catherine's best interests, after all: who knows what other people would think if they discovered what she'd been up to in there? And by now the place must be a pigsty. But the bloody door is still locked. This morning, as she passed the window, she'd caught sight of that Alice in there, just standing in the doorway. Then she'd come out again and locked the door and later Paula had seen her still wearing those stupid beads with the key around her neck, just like Catherine used to. As though she owns the place!

'You should get another key cut,' Paula had told Catherine a few times when she first moved her things in there. 'Give me the one you've got and I'll get it cut on my way home and bring it back in the morning.'

But Catherine had said it wasn't necessary.

'Suppose you were locked in at night and got worse, we couldn't get in to help you.'

'I don't lock myself in at night, Paula,' Catherine had said in that withering tone she sometimes used. 'I simply like it locked when I'm not in there myself.'

It wasn't true of course, Paula knew that. Catherine often locked herself in there alone, both day and night, and Paula knew why, but she also knew how to hold her tongue . . . well, sometimes she did, and this was one of them.

But today it's been all action. With Alice snooping in the room and then out in the garden cutting roses while Paula was washing the kitchen floor, it was pretty clear that Catherine's friend was due to arrive. Paula had spun out her work for as long as she could and then found a few other things to do. And then that nice woman in number six had arrived and she'd actually remembered Paula from the last time she was here.

'What a shame about Mrs Benson,' Mrs Craddock had said. 'I really liked her and she had this place running beautifully. But it's good to see you're still here, Pauline.'

'It's Paula, Mrs Craddock,' Paula had corrected her. 'Yes, it's very sad, and Declan didn't turn up to help in the last few months so some things have been let slip. He used to be a big drinker, you see, not a very reliable person.'

'But I guess they'll get it back on track before too long,' Mrs Craddock had said. 'He'll be grateful he's still got you though, your knowledge of the place must be invaluable. And do call me Lesley, by the way.'

Paula had managed to crack a smile of acknowledgement at all this although there was no indication that Declan found her knowledge invaluable. In fact ever since he'd arrived she felt totally excluded. It seemed that as far as he was concerned she was just another member of the staff rather than a trusted insider who had been there longer than anyone, even Madam Fleur, who had been up and down to the office today on some sort of urgent business. And then Catherine's friend had turned up and Todd managed to draw attention to himself by falling off the roof. So Paula has stuck around waiting to see what happens.

Now everything seems to have gone quiet. Even standing as she is, having a quick smoke around the corner from the kitchen, she can't quite hear what's going on. Paula crushes her cigarette end with the toe of her shoe, picks up the butt and stuffs it in her pocket. Well, she thinks, things are probably going to perk up a bit from now on. Ruby Medway seems pleasant enough and if she's anything like Catherine she at least will see Paula's potential and value her long service at Benson's. Meanwhile she'll have to find a way to get into that room and Ruby might be the answer. She, presumably, will have the task of sorting out Catherine's things and she'll need a hand. 'And I,' Paula murmurs, walking to her car, 'am the obvious person to help with that.'

※

She had slept for a solid three hours but as Ruby helps herself to pasta and salad she realises it has done little to restore her energy – rather, it has relaxed the tension in her muscles and allowed the physical and emotional exhaustion to make itself felt. A good thing she had turned down Declan's offer of wine or she would have been incoherent before she even started to tuck in to the food. They're all on water, she notices; perhaps they too feel the need to stay cool and alert. There is something immediately likeable about Declan and it is partly, she thinks, the vestiges of that plump little boy with his reddish blond hair, freckles and intensely blue eyes. He's still a little overweight, and not particularly fit; an anxious man, Ruby suspects, who finds it a struggle to play the role of host and proprietor that has, so recently, been thrust upon him. But she thinks she will both like him and trust him, just as Alice seems to do.

When Declan had introduced Alice that afternoon he'd described her as a good friend whom he'd employed to help them in the collective effort of sorting things out at Benson's Reach. Ruby had assumed that they were lovers, but now it's clear that, although they're friends, they don't know each other very well, and they certainly lack the physical ease conferred by intimacy, or even of people who have spent a lot of time together. There is warmth between them, and respect, affection certainly, but also the tension which speaks of a lack of familiarity. They are feeling their way with each other just as they are with her, and she with them. Like three animals trapped in the same enclosure, Ruby thinks, edging cautiously towards each other, but a change of pace and we will all recoil.

'So,' Declan says as he starts on his pasta, 'is it too soon to talk about what we have to do, Ruby, or would you like to leave it until tomorrow?'

'Not at all,' Ruby says. 'I want to know what you think. At the moment I don't have a clue, but first I'd like to hear about Todd.'

Declan puts down his fork. 'Yes – Todd. Well, the poor kid has broken his ankle in two places but is otherwise okay apart, of course, from the possibility of concussion. The hospital will be keeping an eye on him for the next few days. I feel bad about it because I should have talked to him sooner. Catherine apparently took him under her wing about three years ago. He was living with his mother in a caravan—'

'I knew that,' Ruby cuts in, 'she mentioned him in an email. The mother was drinking and smoking dope.'

'That's right, and Catherine got Todd organised to come up here a few times a week, to do odd jobs, maintenance, pruning, cleaning up, anything that needed doing, really, and she paid him cash.' He pauses, clearing his throat. 'It was quite touching, he was telling me about it while they were strapping up his ankle, and then he suddenly stopped and went quiet. I don't think he'd talked to anyone about it since she died. He seemed to be trying hard not to cry.'

'Cat thought a lot of him,' Ruby says. 'The last I remember her saying was that she hoped he'd stay on at school at the end of last year.'

Declan nods and swallows another mouthful of pasta. 'Mmm, he told me that, but he said he needed to earn a living, and he wanted to keep coming here, so he got a part time casual job at the supermarket in town, which he won't be able to go back to for a while at least. But he apparently only took that because it meant he could also keep working here for Catherine.'

'But you said there was a problem for us?'

'Yes, his mother,' Declan says. 'Apparently she took off to Bali with a man some months ago and all he's heard from her since is the occasional postcard, so he's living on his own in the caravan, going everywhere on foot or on his bike, and when they release him from hospital there's no one to look after him. And I thought that if the hospital knew he was on his own they might get social services involved and send him off somewhere. So . . .' he hesitates, flushing, looking down at his plate, 'I said he could come back here. And I know I should've asked you first, Ruby, but—'

'Of course,' Ruby cuts in, 'of course he should come here. It's what Catherine would have wanted, what she would expect. Besides, he was injured working for us on our property so we have a responsibility to him.'

Declan looks up, relieved. 'Great,' he says, nodding furiously, 'that's excellent, I'm glad we agree about that. Alice?'

Alice, who Ruby is aware has been watching them both closely while appearing to be interested solely in her pasta, jumps at the sound of her name. 'Oh, well it's not for me to say, really, I'm just an employee . . .'

'But you have an opinion?' Ruby says.

'Yes, of course, I think you're right. There's plenty of space. I can get a room ready for him and we can keep an eye on him here. It would be horrible for him to be taken off somewhere else.'

Ruby thinks that they have cleared the first hurdle, established some trust. For a while they talk more generally about the chaos in the office, about the closed café, about how to proceed.

'And the other bombshell that lobbed into my lap this afternoon is Fleur,' Declan says. 'She's given notice. She'll stay until we can find someone else but she doesn't want to hang about for long. She's going to do a stocktake of the products and have a look at the sales figures so we know where we are, but the first thing we have to do is find someone else to take over. Someone new – or maybe one of us – has to get in there and learn how to do it.' He looks pointedly at Alice, who, Ruby notices, deliberately looks away. There is an awkward silence around the table.

'I think what we should do,' Ruby says, 'is start by sorting out what needs to be done in order of priority. We could also make a list of the various things we each think we're good at and what we're willing to have a go at, then we could sort out who does what, and what other staff or maybe subcontractors we need.'

85

Declan does his energetic nodding again, and Ruby thinks it could prove to be a really annoying habit.

'Good plan,' he says. 'Shall we say first thing tomorrow morning, over breakfast maybe, we convene for the first Benson's Reach strategic planning meeting around the kitchen table? The good thing is that we don't have many bookings and it's nearly the end of summer. We can plan to keep the place ticking over during the winter months while we re-organise for next summer.'

Alice clears her throat. 'There is something else,' she says. 'I'm not sure if either of you know about this but I discovered it this morning while I was in the office.' She pauses, looking between the two of them. 'There's a file, I knocked it off the windowsill and had to collect up the papers. It's about the music festival.'

'Huh!' Declan laughs. 'Well that's the last thing we need, a music festival. I think we'll give that one a miss, don't you, Ruby?'

Ruby nods. Her festival days are long gone, although not forgotten: the Isle of Wight and Glastonbury had been part of her new life when she quit Australia and returned to England. But they have more than they can cope with here without getting involved in a music festival.

'The thing is,' Alice says, 'that if I've understood it correctly, you don't have a choice. The festival's in May, and there's a contract . . .'

Declan's head shoots up. 'What sort of contract?'

'Catherine has rented out the five hectares of land on the east boundary,' she says, 'and all the cottages are booked out for that long weekend, and some for a few days either side. There are arrangements for security, a first aid post, coffee carts, sub-contractor electricians and so on. It looks as though Mrs Benson had been working on it for some time, months really, and then she just stopped . . .'

'Phew – well thank goodness for that,' Declan says,

leaning back in his chair. 'I guess she must have given up on it when she realised she was getting sick.'

Ruby nods. 'Yes, she'd have had to cancel,' she says. 'She'd have known for some time that she couldn't take on something like a festival.'

'She didn't,' Alice says. 'There's no indication in there that she cancelled or even tried to and she was still sending emails about it until the week before she went to hospital. You need to read the contract but as far as I can see you're stuck with it. The South West Jazz and Blues Festival is the last weekend in May, and it's here – at Benson's Reach.'

Eight

March 2009

esley knows exactly what she's doing but she just can't stop herself. She's been here for a couple of weeks but somehow on her previous sorties into town she missed this boutique. Perhaps it was the rack of reduced items outside that had made her dismiss it as trashy. Whatever it was, passing it today the yellow linen skirt in the window had caught her eye and when she went inside she found a whole range of her favourite labels, and some really unusual locally made silver jewellery. So here she is, squashed into a fitting room with the yellow skirt, and half a dozen or more other things to try on. There's no need for her to hurry – she is, as she keeps reminding herself, on holiday, her time is her own – but she just can't seem to slow down. Ripping off her own clothes she drops them to the floor and drags the skirt up over her hips without stopping to undo the buttons, consequently pulling one off in the process. It bounces on the floor and rolls out under the fitting room door into the shop, but still she doesn't stop.

She's been like this ever since she got here anxious, restless, combing the shops for things she doesn't need, filling carrier bags with purchases about which she is really only half hearted, and then filled with despair when she tips them onto the bed back at the cottage. She's usually careful with money, both Sandi and Simon have accused her of being a tightwad, although Karen, who is more like Lesley herself, thinks she's just cautious. But now it's as though some spending virus has invaded her bloodstream. And it's not just the spending, it's the restlessness. She wakes several times a night, picks up books by her favourite authors and puts them down again, finding she's gone through half a dozen pages but has no idea what she's read. She can't even lose herself in the television or any of the movies she's borrowed from the supply in the office at Benson's Reach, and she's already drunk her way through much of the wine she'd bought on her visits to the local wineries.

Displacement activity – pointless, destructive, sickening in all sorts of ways – is what she would have told anyone else, but somehow she can't stop, because from the moment she arrived here she has known that she is here for a purpose. There is a lot more at stake than just how she feels about being a confident, independent woman at ease outside her comfort zone. Whether she has propelled herself into a crisis by coming here or she's here because she was already in crisis is immaterial. The walls of her life are crumbling around her and if she slows down, if she stops shopping and drinking and looking for new places to go, then all that's left is herself, alone in a cottage with no one to talk to. The only person who always seems ready for a chat is the cleaner, Pauline . . . no, Paula, she must remember to get that right. Three times the woman has corrected her.

It had started on that first day when Alice left Lesley alone in the cottage. As she watched from her balcony there seemed to be a lot of coming and going. An older woman turned up from somewhere, a younger one was going back and forth between the office and the place where Mrs Benson used to make the lavender products. An ambulance came and went and then, late in the afternoon, it all went quiet – too quiet, and she paced back and forth with nothing to do and nothing to distract her. She would go out, she thought, be brave, have a meal somewhere, a nice café, her first attempt to eat out alone in the evening. She didn't know why it seemed such a hurdle, she frequently had lunch in cafés alone, but dinner . . . anyway, it was early in the evening so if she went straight away she'd probably feel less weird about it.

On the main street she read the menu outside the local branch of a smart Perth restaurant where she and Gordon had been a few times with friends, but the white linen and low lights seemed a bit too formal to manage alone, and she opted for a smaller, more casual place where she could see a couple of families with children sitting close to the window. Walking in was the hardest part but strangely no one, apart from a very young waiter who gave her a menu and directed her to a corner table, even seemed to notice her. As well as the two big families there was a couple in the far corner, holding hands across the table, oblivious to anyone else. Two elderly couples sitting together were just about to start on their food and to Lesley's relief there were two single women. The older one looked up briefly from her book as Lesley walked past; the other, toying with half a glass of white wine, was keeping an eye on the entrance, and glancing frequently at her watch, waiting, Lesley thought, for a date to arrive. Coming in early was a good choice; this wasn't anything like as hard as she'd imagined. She ordered King George whiting with steamed vegetables, and a half-carafe of wine, and sat back feeling quite relaxed as the restaurant started to get busy.

It was eight-thirty when she left and by then the place was humming. Tomorrow, she thought, I'll go a little later, see how it feels. Out in the street, walking back to her car, she felt pleased with herself, as though she had overcome some hurdle. Her more independent friends would probably think it a pathetic effort but it was a big thing for her and she had driven back to Benson's Reach in better spirits. But once back in her cottage her mood faltered under the weight of the silence, a silence more sinister than the tense stand-off silence at home with Gordon roaming around, waiting and wanting. This was the silence of her aloneness in a place where people came with their families, friends or lovers to be together. She opened a bottle of wine, kicked off her shoes and drank two glasses rather quickly as she paced back and forth across the lounge, flicking the remote control to find something on television to keep her company. When nothing caught her attention she poured a third glass and wandered out onto the balcony taking the bottle with her. It was dark by then and where the land dropped away from the front of the cottages she could see the terrace at the back of the main house where Declan, the new owner, was sitting with Alice, and the other woman – the older one with the bun who had arrived earlier.

She could catch only the occasional murmur of their voices but it was clear that they were deep in conversation, leaning forward, helping themselves to food. They were a little clan down there, plotting something, intent on what they were doing, oblivious to anyone else. They must know each other well, she thought, old friends perhaps, family even. Sitting alone in the dark Lesley felt the anxiety rising in her gut. The horrifying significance of the way she had left and the impact of her parting words to Gordon gripped her in a panic and a series of possible outcomes raced through her mind in stark jerky images, as though someone had pressed the fast forward button in her brain. Focusing her attention on the candlelit table, she had watched as Alice cleared the plates and returned with a coffee plunger and cups. Lesley wanted to be down there with them, be part of that conversation, share the coffee and the candlelight, feel the warm lavender-scented air on her skin, anything to take her mind away from what she had done and what might happen next. The longer she watched the more alone she felt, and with another glass of wine she became convinced that they were deliberately excluding her, talking about her behind her back, laughing about her. You're getting paranoid, she warned herself.

But she hated this sense of being shut out – she was, after all, so accustomed to being in her own world – and eventually she convinced herself that it would be fine to walk down there and join them. Getting up she went inside and fetched another bottle of wine from the fridge and was crossing back to the balcony when she saw that they were on their feet now, clearing the table, snuffing out the candles. It felt personal, as though they had sensed her plan and deliberately moved on to avoid her. She flopped down onto the end of the bed, enveloped again by anxiety. Maybe she should just ring Gordon, apologise for what she'd said, but then he might think that everything was okay, and even through the fug of wine Lesley knew that it wasn't okay. She had meant what she said but it had come out as something horrible. She put the wine bottle down on the floor and lay back on the bed, drawing her legs up, pulling a pillow down and clutching it to her chest. She began to cry, softly at first, then more intensely until, eventually, she fell exhausted into a deep and drunken sleep.

The following morning she'd woken with a fearsome headache and parched mouth, and her eyes felt as though they had been sandpapered. It was ridiculous, she told herself, a really irresponsible way to behave; she would have a shower, make some coffee, get her head together and start again. But as she emerged from the bedroom, showered, dressed and ready for her coffee, the anxiety grabbed her again, sucking her into its depths and sending her out time and again in search of something, anything, to stop her thinking about the one thing she should be thinking about – the reason she is here now, and what she is going to do next.

Now as she makes her way back down the slope of the main street to the car park with a carrier bag of clothes she doesn't need and may not even like, she sees him, Declan Benson, sitting alone at a table on the crowded terrace of the pub on the corner, looking as though he might need a distraction just as much as she does, and she crosses the street and hurries up the steps to the terrace.

'It *is* you,' she says, dropping her bag onto one of the spare seats at Declan's table. 'I thought so, I thought I'd come in here for some lunch but there aren't any tables, and then I saw you. You don't mind if I join you, do you?'

He looks up startled, as though he's been lost in some world of his own, and moves to get to his feet.

'Oh please don't get up,' Lesley says. 'It's a bit unfair descending on you like this but there's just nowhere else to sit, and you do look as though you might need a bit of company.'

'Well,' he says, shrugging, 'I was just . . .'

'Let me get you a drink,' she says, indicating his empty glass. 'Wine? We could share a bottle with lunch.'

He holds up a hand, palm outward. 'No, no thanks. Just tonic water with ice and lemon, thanks.'

'And a little gin or vodka with it?'

He shakes his head. 'Just the tonic, thanks.'

Lesley goes to the bar and returns to the table with their drinks and two menus.

'I take it you *are* here for lunch,' she says, handing Declan one of them.

'Well, it was more just a bit of an escape, really,' he says, 'although I suppose I could eat something.'

And so they order lunch and sit facing each other across the table out there on the noisy terrace, and it's clear to Lesley that she's going to have to do all the work.

'It must be a very challenging time,' she says, 'your aunt dying so suddenly, having to pick up the reins and take charge, but it's such a lovely spot. Do you have plans for the place?'

Declan is silent for a moment, looking out across the street and beyond, before he turns back to her. 'The thing is,' he says, 'I didn't come soon enough when Catherine was sick. So I'm feeling very guilty and haven't a clue what I'm doing, or how to get through the next few months.' He pauses, and then, in a great fountain of words, he tells her about his aunt, her death, the legacy of Benson's Reach, his co-beneficiary, the need to get the place running again and the threat of a music festival in May. He tells her that they have made decisions, sorted and actioned the urgent paperwork, written an emergency plan and allocated tasks to each other, and chipped what seems to be a small hole into the mountain of tasks that have to be done. The words pour out so fast that she can barely keep pace with him. And just as she thinks he's finished he starts again.

'We don't know each other, really. Ruby and I are complete strangers. She seems very nice, but I'm cautious. She may want to take over, or she may just want different outcomes from me. And anyway, I don't *know* what I want. That's my problem, really, I never know what I want until someone else tries to impose something on me. I suppose it's lack of imagination on my part.' He looks down at the plate of whitebait and fries that the waiter has just placed in front of him. 'I'm a hopeless case, really, not at all the sort of person who should be left with something like this.'

It's quite reassuring, Lesley thinks, to hear about the mess of someone else's life when your own life is a complete shambles. And there's also something essentially charming about Declan Benson – his apparent naivety is disarming. He seems like someone you could trust. Lesley leans forward, reaches out to rest her hand briefly on his arm.

'It's an awful lot to cope with,' she says, 'especially when you're grieving for your aunt. We always feel guilty when someone dies, thinking about all the things we should have done while they were alive and now it's too late. I think you just need to be a little kinder to yourself, forgive yourself for what you think is your negligence, then you'll be free to get on with what needs to be done. That's what she'd want, after all, that you get the place running again. If you're right and she put her heart and soul into Benson's Reach, then what she's done is to leave you her life's work, her most treasured possession. She'd want you to enjoy it, to make the most of it, rather than dwelling on guilt and what you think is a failure.'

He's embarrassed now, she can see that. Lesley is not used to men like Declan. She is used to the men who work with Gordon: confident, self-assured, accustomed to success. Not that Gordon is like that but he seems to be surrounded by others who are. Declan – awkward, self-deprecating, vulnerable – is a different breed and his presence is rather comforting.

'I'm sorry,' Declan says now, taking his cutlery from the folds of his paper napkin. 'I just dumped all that on you. I've no right to bore you with all this stuff.'

'Don't apologise,' Lesley says, looking up at him. 'To tell you the truth I'm in a bit of a mess myself at the moment, that's why I'm here, so in an odd sort of way it's reassuring to talk to someone else who is flailing around in the dark. The trouble is it's harder for me to put it all into words, but another one of these might help,' and she picks up her glass and sculls the remains of her wine.

'I'll get you a refill,' he says.

'And you'll join me won't you?'

But he shakes his head and when he returns from the bar with her wine and another tonic water, it's clear he's also been to the men's room and splashed his face with cold water. He has washed away some of his vulnerability and looks stronger, more ready for the world. 'Thanks for listening,' he says, picking up two tiny whitebait and popping them into his mouth. 'Just letting it all out to someone else does help. So it's your turn now.'

'Oh I'm not . . .' Lesley picks up her glass, not sure she's ready for this. 'I don't think . . .' and she takes a couple of sips.

'It's always easier to confide in a stranger, in someone unconnected to what's happening,' Declan says, and he blushes slightly and looks away. 'That's what people say, anyway. You can unload the baggage, and if you want you can walk away tomorrow and no one else will ever know.'

Lesley hesitates. She can tell that his outpouring has in some way unburdened him, even restored some authority to his manner.

'The comfort of strangers,' he says. 'It's something I've resorted to in the past.' He even *sounds* different now too, as though he is drawing on some old wisdom. 'Friendship is so terribly complicated, don't you think? Strangers offer some freedom and possibilities.'

'I . . . I don't know . . .' she says, feeling slightly dizzy and as though a part of her might break open at any moment. 'Perhaps you're right . . . I'm so used to being cocooned in the life I've been living for years . . . surrounded by my family . . . the comfort of strangers . . . I don't know.'

'So think of it now,' he says, nodding. 'What have you got to lose? I know I talk a lot but I'm also quite a good listener.'

❦

Alice walks the woman to the door of the café, shakes hands, closes the door behind her and leans back against it with a sigh of relief. It's done, the final step in the process of getting the café ready to reopen in two weeks' time. Interviewing and employing the staff has been the hardest part. She'd felt she lacked authority and still had the 'fresh out of jail' tattoo on her forehead. But it's done and, almost dizzy with satisfaction and relief, she can now justify her decision to ignore

Declan's evident, if unspoken, wish to have her take over from Fleur.

When he'd given her that meaningful look at dinner the night that Ruby arrived Alice knew it was important to him and that he was hoping she'd offer to do it. But she had pretended not to notice and at their meeting the following morning had made a case instead to take responsibility for the café. It was urgent, she'd suggested, to get people coming back to Benson's Reach on a casual basis for coffee, lunches and breakfasts, especially in the cooler weather, and vital to have it all up and running efficiently in time for the music festival. Those two words 'music' and 'festival' had struck terror in all their hearts and it had clinched her argument. The festival was a chance to show local people, music fans and tourists what the place had to offer, and the very least they would expect was a functioning café.

'I believe I can do it and do it well,' she'd said, and it had taken a huge effort to say it, with her confidence at such a low ebb after her failed efforts as a job-seeker. She was about to describe the catering course at the prison when those words died on her lips. Ruby had no idea of her recent past and for the time being, at least, Alice wanted it to stay that way.

'I've recently retrained,' she'd continued, this time with caution, 'and it was with an award winning chef. I could draw up a staffing plan and menus and you could see what you think.'

Alice really did believe that the café was crucial to the future of Benson's Reach but she knew she was equally serving her own interests. This could be the key to her own future. The value of her catering certificate would be considerably enhanced if she could also show that she had reopened the café and turned it into a going concern. Besides, she wanted the challenge: the buzz of the café, the mix of people, and the discipline of getting meals on tables every day.

'Breakfasts, lunches and afternoon teas seven days a week,' she'd said. 'Maybe we might even be able to get back some of the staff who worked in the café before Catherine closed it.' And that is just what she's done.

'Yeah, I know a couple of them,' Todd had said when she'd asked him about the previous staff, and he'd given her a number for the apprentice chef who hadn't yet found a new place, and a young woman who had doubled as waitress and kitchen hand and was keen to come back. With a couple of part timers, and now this older woman, Leonie, who has just moved to the area and has worked in cafés for years, Alice has all the staff she needs, and she is ready to run through her menus with Ruby and Declan. It's a sliver of hope, this chance to prove herself. If Benson's keeps going with Declan and/or Ruby she will probably be able to stay on, and if they decide to sell maybe the new owners would keep her. At the very least she will have a decent start to this precarious post-prison life and some recent experience.

'How'd it go?' Todd asks, hobbling in through the back door of the café on his crutches. 'Was she okay?'

'She was ideal,' Alice says, grinning, and they stand together by the kitchen window watching as Leonie climbs into an ageing Barina, and pulls out of the parking area and onto the drive. 'And she's starting on Monday. So it's all systems go – how are you on the computer?'

He nods cautiously, hoisting himself up onto a stool by the workbench. 'Not bad. Depends what you want, really.'

'Some fliers and some small posters to put up around the town, let people know we're opening again – can you do that sort of thing?'

'I can try – I did some before for the lavender products but they weren't very good. I told Catherine she needed better software, and she wrote down what to get, but I don't know if she did.'

Alice looks at him more closely. He looks so different from the pale and anxious boy whom Declan had collected from the hospital a couple of nights after his fall. He'd clearly been nervous when Declan explained that they thought he should stay at the house for a while. Being alone in the caravan didn't bother him, but he'd said he could also see that for a few weeks at least he wouldn't be able to manage up there alone.

'And the other thing is, Todd,' Declan had said, 'that because you're not sixteen yet, unless I'd said we'd look after you here I think the hospital would have alerted social services. I didn't think you'd want them moving in on you, asking questions about your mum, maybe sending you off somewhere else.'

Todd had looked horrified then and for the first couple of days had spent a lot of time in his room with the television that Declan had moved in there from Catherine's room.

'We need to get him out of there,' Ruby had said eventually, 'get him involved in something.'

And Alice had gone in there the next morning and told him she needed help with the stocktaking. 'I'll go through all the equipment and supplies in the kitchen,' she'd said, 'and call it out, and you enter it into this book, then I can look at what we've got and sort out what we need.'

He'd been reluctant at first but he'd kept at it, and once that was done Fleur took him off to do the stocktake on the lavender products. He was a good worker, and as he grew accustomed to being in the house he'd started to come out of himself more.

'So how's it going then?' Alice asks him now. 'Staying here, I mean? Are you getting used to it?'

He nods. 'It's cool. I never lived anywhere like this before.'

'Was it you who helped Catherine move her stuff into that room?'

'Yeah. Got some help with the bed but I did all the rest of it. We made it nice but it got pretty messed up at the end. She wouldn't let Paula in and she wouldn't let me tidy up. I just used to sit in there with her and talk, and read to her.'

'You read to her?'

He nods. 'When she got sick she was too tired by the evening to read, so she said I should read to her.'

'Really? So what did you read?' Alice asks, intrigued by the idea of a teenage boy spending his evenings reading to a dying woman.

He shrugs. 'Newspapers sometimes, but books mainly.' He leans forward, hands clasped on the bench. 'She said there were books she wanted to read before she died and as she couldn't do it I should read them for her.'

'Like what?'

'Um . . . there was *Bleak House* first, that was brilliant, and then a Russian one . . . *Crime and Punishment*, hard work with all the Russian names, but it's a good story. And then *The Turn of the Screw*.'

'And you didn't mind?'

'Nah! It was cool. Never would've read them if it hadn't been for her.' He pauses, and looks at her awkwardly. 'There were some other books in there that we were going to read but . . .'

'You ran out of time?'

'Yeah,' he says sadly. 'That's it – ran out of time. D'you think I could . . .?'

'Borrow them? I'm sure you could,' Alice says. 'But you'll probably need to go in and get them yourself. No one seems game to take that room on just yet. Shall I ask Declan for you?'

'That'd be cool.'

'Okay. And what about your other job, Todd, at the supermarket? What did they say when you told them you couldn't go in while you're sick?'

Todd flushes and looks away. 'Oh well, they didn't say much, really.'

'But what *did* they say?'

'They said there might not be anything for me when I go back.'

Alice gives a snort of disgust. 'Bastards!' she says. 'What complete bastards.'

Todd laughs, looking at her now. 'It was only casual,' he says, 'they don't have to pay you or take you back or anything if you're sick. Anyway, I hated it there. When I'm okay again . . .' he hesitates, shrugging, 'I'll just have to find something else. How long d'you think they'll let me stay here? They haven't said if they want me to go on working or anything.'

'I don't know,' Alice says. 'But they certainly won't expect you to go home until your ankle is okay and that'll be a few weeks yet. You *can* ask them, you know, Todd, they don't bite.'

He blushes and looks away again. 'Yeah, but . . . they don't have to keep me working here, do they?'

'No, but you've the right to ask.' But she can see that he won't and that his caution is about asking for what seems to him like a favour. 'I could talk to them if you like,' she says.

His face creases into a smile. 'Really?'

'Leave it to me, I'll pick the best time. Meanwhile I'm going over to the house to show Ruby the menus. If you want to hobble along with me we could have a look at the office computer and see if Catherine ever got that software.'

Todd slides off the stool, steadies himself with his crutches, and together they walk slowly towards the office.

'She was my friend, you know,' he says suddenly, looking up at her. 'Not mates like at school – a proper friend, like they write about in books.'

Alice reaches out and puts a hand on his shoulder. 'That's very special,' she says. 'And I'm sure she felt you were that same friend to her.'

He nods and clears his throat. 'No soul is desolate as long as there is a human being for whom it can feel trust and reverence,' he says.

Alice stops and looks at him. 'She said that?'

'Yeah, but she was quoting . . .'

'Quoting who?'

He sighs and screws up his face. 'One of those women who called themselves by men's names – writers, you know.'

'Charlotte Brontë? George Sand?'

He shakes his head. 'No, but George something.'

'Eliot?'

'Yeah! George Eliot, that's it. Catherine said that trust and reverence was what we had to have – her and me. She said it was at the heart of friendship and she hadn't always respected that and so I was her last chance. I think she meant it was her last chance to get that right. She . . .' he pauses again.

'Go on,' Alice says, 'what were you going to say?'

Todd inhales deeply and then lets the air out of his lungs in a rush. 'She saved me from getting into trouble,' he says. 'And then she sort of *made* me be her friend, like she insisted. I didn't have a choice about it. She said she wanted to show me another side of life.'

'And that was in the reading, I suppose?' Alice says.

Todd nods. 'She thought the school was rubbish, because I didn't know stuff she thought I should know.'

'And that was it?' Alice cuts in, seeing now where the conversation is going. 'That was the trust and the reverence, she was educating you and you were accepting it?'

'Yeah,' he says, nodding, 'that's it, I guess. That's cool, isn't it, really cool . . . only then . . .'

'Then she died.'

He nods. 'I didn't know anybody that died, so I didn't know how it would feel.'

'So how *does* it feel?'

He hesitates, trying to find a way of expressing it. 'Like something's been cut out of you and you'll never get it back, and you'll never feel the same again. D'you think it's like that?'

'Just like that,' Alice says quietly after a pause. 'And you won't feel quite the same again, but it won't always feel as bad as it does now.'

'I'm never going to forget her.'

'Of course not, but you *will* find a way of getting along without her, and it won't hurt so much.'

They walk a little further in silence, until they are only a few steps from the office.

'You know,' Todd says, 'she didn't really have friends. She said Mrs Medway was her oldest friend, but they hardly ever saw each other for years.'

Alice stops at the office door and turns to him again. 'Then your friendship would have been especially important to her, Todd,' she says. 'You gave her something very precious when she needed it most.'

uby has taken responsibility for creating order from the chaos of the office, ensuring that the staff and the bills are paid, looking at the ways in which Catherine had organised things and using that as a basis for planning the next few months.

'And the music festival,' Declan had said, 'what about that? I mean, I can sort out parking arrangements, deal with the contractors when they arrive, but the paperwork, well . . . it's not my strong point.'

'I once organised a writers festival,' Ruby had admitted, the words out before she had time to stop them, 'so I guess I can have a go at this.' But she feels she's the last person who should be doing it, too old, too out of touch, but then they don't really have any other options. She is anticipating a minefield of egos and fears an organisational black hole into which emails are sent and not replied to, and the latter is certainly proving to be the case, the chief offender being a saxophonist from North Carolina called Jackson Crow (a made-up name, Ruby suspects) who broadcasts a jazz and blues program on some obscure radio network to what he claims is 'a community of music lovers around the world'. He also has his own band, The Crowbars. 'How ridiculous,'

Ruby had said aloud when she read this. 'The Crowbars indeed! And who's going to tune in twice a week to listen to some obscure musician in the backwoods of North Carolina? Probably about three people. Oh no, Mr Crow,' she went on, grumbling her way around the office, 'you don't fool me. An international audience – I don't think so.' But it seems that Catherine had been taken in by all this, and dealt with him over the previous festival several years ago. In fact from the correspondence they seem to have been quite friendly. So Benson's Reach is stuck with Jackson Crow and the bloody Crowbars have booked four of the cottages. And Jackson Crow, through his network of contacts, is organising the Australian bands and singers and managing the program.

As she set about getting the files up to date Ruby had unearthed more correspondence that fits with what Alice had found, and among it are some printouts from Jackson Crow's website, on which there is an image of a black crow, and the all-black silhouette of a man playing a saxophone. To Ruby this is a sure sign that the man is not keen on being seen. She has him down as a seedy, ageing Elvis look-alike with a toupee, and his failure to reply to her emails has really riled her, although it's only seven days since she sent the first one and three days since the second. But in the black hole of Crow's silence she has also found a box file with all the details of the previous festival, and has now matched that with the paperwork for the coming one. The situation is better than it first appeared. While all of them here at Benson's Reach had been in the dark, several other people have been doing their own bit to get things underway and it's clear that Catherine put most things in place some months ago. The insurance cover is fixed, arrangements for the sound system and the lighting, the stage and canopy are all there, a security service and the portaloos are booked and the various licences have been issued, although these will now have to be transferred into her, or Declan's, name. There is a bank account for the festival, sponsorships and a grant from the South West Regional Cultural Projects funding program. Better get some posters done to advertise it, Ruby thinks, the sponsors will want to see their names prominently displayed. By the time a reply from Jackson Crow arrives in her inbox Ruby is in grumpy mode.

The message is apologetic: he has been in Mexico with The Crowbars, but he has answered her questions and has attached draft of the program for the weekend of the festival and a contact list of the performers. He closes his message with, '*Thank you, ma'am, and please tell Catherine we're all looking forward to seeing her again real soon.*' Better let him know about Catherine, Ruby thinks, and she dashes off a quick email advising him of Catherine's death and that she and Declan are now the proprietors of Benson's Reach.

Glad to have the Crow connection sorted at last, Ruby shuffles her papers into a neat pile on the desk, which now actually *looks* like a desk, and leans back, stretching her arms above her head. Being here is a challenge but it also feels a whole lot better than she had imagined. She'd forgotten what it's like to be far from home and surrounded by people who don't know her, who actually know next to nothing about her. There are no expectations of her based on what she has done in the past. They know nothing of the London Ruby – who she mixes with, how she spends her days nor the sphere of her influence. They take her at face value: she is just Catherine's friend, Declan's business partner, a woman in her late sixties who has a controlling interest in this place. It's surprisingly liberating not to have the baggage of her London life attached to her.

On the morning of their first meeting around the kitchen table Declan had put his hand up to take on the practical side of managing the property, starting with pricing the repairs and then organising sub-contractors, getting the seasonal work done on the grounds, checking all the cottages and getting to grips with the cycle of the lavender crop to make sure Fleur, or rather her successor, will have a regular supply cut and ready for use.

'And I guess I can sort out the day-to-day business of running Benson's and of the festival,' Ruby had told them. It made sense, she thinks now, switching off the computer and getting to her feet. She is a good manager, and it's a crash course in getting to grips with Benson's Reach – its strengths, its shortcomings and even the possibilities for the future. Reading through the files, analysing financial reports and making projections come easily to her. She had thought she'd be here for a month, two at the most, but last night she had called Jess and told her she'd be away for longer.

'Probably three months, maybe a bit more,' she'd said, and she'd explained about the festival. 'I'm thinking that by the end of May we'll have a lot of things sorted, and we'll be in a better position for me to leave.'

'And are you okay, Ruby? Really okay?' Jessica had asked.

'I'm good,' she'd said. 'It's a challenge – you know how I enjoy that.'

It was enough to reassure Jess, who had gone on then to give her a rundown on things at the Foundation. 'You take care, and ring if you need anything,' Jess had said before hanging up.

Ruby knows that she's operating on borrowed time. The past, in its various guises, is lurking around every corner waiting to leap out at her, and this present, intense activity has simply moved it back to a slightly safer distance. 'Lord knows what'll happen when the pressure's off,' she says aloud now, 'but that's not going to be for a while yet.'

She's in the office kitchen rinsing her teacup when the phone rings and she wipes her hands on the tea towel and crosses back to the desk to answer it. As she picks it up the quality of the sound tells her it's an overseas call.

Jackson Crow is, he tells her, 'desolate' at the news of Catherine's passing. So desolate he had to call as soon as he read her message, to ask what happened and to express his sympathy to her and to young Mr Benson. 'She was a great lady,' he says when Ruby has told him about Catherine's illness, and she softens a little because she can hear a crack of emotion in his voice. 'She didn't say nothin' to me about being sick,' he goes on, and it's clear he is genuinely shocked. 'I wish I'd known.'

'She didn't say anything to me either, Mr Crow,' Ruby tells him, 'and we'd known each other since childhood.'

There is a brief silence, slightly longer than the usual delay on the line. 'Of course, you must be her friend from London,' he says then. 'You met on the ship to Australia when you were just little girls.'

'Nineteen-forty-seven, that's right,' Ruby says, 'we'd known each other a very long time.'

'*Dame* Ruby Medway, isn't it?' he says. 'Catherine told me about how Her Majesty Queen Elizabeth made you a dame. I'm honoured to be talking to you, ma'am.'

Ruby feels ridiculous. It's all so over the top but Americans are like that, and she's always embarrassed when people refer to her being what Jessica describes as 'damed'. Accepting the honour had been a difficult decision for her and she has often questioned her own motives for doing so. She fumbles for a response but Jackson Crow cuts across her.

'She admired you very much,' he says. 'I remember she said she was waiting to hear when you'd go back there for a visit.'

'Well sadly I didn't make it in time,' Ruby says briskly.

'That really is sad. Catherine told me how much she was looking forward to that. But I sure don't mean to intrude. Just wanted to give you my sympathy, and learn a little more about Catherine's passing.'

There is an awkward silence and then they both speak at once.

'No,' Ruby says, 'you go ahead. What were you going to say?'

'Just that I thought maybe in your email you were a mite concerned about the festival, about the sort of people who might turn up? So I want you to know we never had any trouble the last time. The jazz and blues crowd down there they're real nice people, older folks. They come along because they love their music. So I want to reassure you that we're not expecting any trouble.'

Ruby is not really reassured by this. She is under no illusions about the collective energy of a few hundred baby boomers seduced by the music into reliving their misspent youth.

'I hope you're right, Mr Crow,' she says. 'This is my first experience of a music festival for a very long time.'

'Well I go back to the old days too, so we're gonna have a whole lot to talk about, you and me,' he says. 'But really, ma'am, you don't need to worry. We had more'n twelve hundred people last time and it was just fine.'

━━━

Todd sits on the edge of the deck swinging his legs back and forth and occasionally knocking his plaster against the verandah post to see if the vibration hurts. It does a bit but not enough to stop him doing it.

'Can't you find something useful to do?' Paula says sharply, coming up behind him with her cleaning trolley.

'I've been helping Ruby and now I'm waiting for Alice.'

'Looks to me like you're bludging. You're just a waste of space, if you ask me.'

'I didn't . . .' Todd begins and then stops, remembering what Fleur had told him. 'Don't get into arguments with Paula, Toddy,' she'd said. 'Whatever she says just smile and walk away. You'll never win, you'll never make her see things your way, so don't waste your energy. And don't tell her anything because it'll come back at you somehow. Didn't

Catherine warn you about that?' She had, of course, told him exactly that, but now that Catherine's gone Todd feels odd, not secure like he used to, as though anything could change from day to day.

'And you'd better keep that bedroom tidy,' Paula says over her shoulder as she walks away. 'I won't be cleaning up after you, don't kid yourself about that!'

Todd sighs and looks off in the other direction, ignoring her. Paula has the ability to puncture a good mood in an instant. Todd swings his legs again and checks his watch. Twenty minutes till he has to go and help Alice. He could go to the café now but he knows she's talking to a bloke who's going to supply vegetables for the café and he doesn't want to get in the way. He sighs again. He likes Alice, and Ruby and Declan too, and it's good staying in the house, having his own room with his own TV, and the food is mega good. Before she got sick Catherine often used to give him a meal in the evenings but her cooking was always a bit hit and miss. She'd remember something she'd meant to do and then just bugger off and do it while the food was cooking, so it was often burned. Better than his mum's cooking though. But Alice is a brilliant cook and Ruby's good too. He keeps thinking about this, about how lucky he is to be here, and how lucky he was not to break anything else or have brain damage or something like that from falling off the roof. But at the same time it all feels so strange, not as if he really belongs here like when Catherine was around. Most of all, though, he worries about what'll happen when his ankle's fixed. So one minute he's cool and happy and enjoying himself and the next he's confused and gets this sinking feeling in his stomach about what might happen. What he does know, though, is that he'd feel a whole lot better if Fleur wasn't planning to leave. He checks his watch again – fifteen minutes. He could go up to the workroom and talk to Fleur now, corner her, see if she's changed her mind about going. And awkwardly he scrambles to his feet and sets off with his crutches up the path to the workroom.

'Ah! Just the man I need,' Fleur shouts over the noise of the stripping machine that is separating the dried lavender heads from the stalks. And she gestures to him to take a seat on the stool at the workbench. Todd hitches himself up and as the machine rattles to a halt, Fleur picks up one of the big sieves, releases the lavender heads into it and puts it on the table in front of him. 'If you've nothing else to do you can check through this lot for foreign bodies – you know what to look for. Why the long face?'

Todd runs his hand through the lavender. 'Paula!' he says.

'Remember what I told you?'

'Yeah, I know. But she's bugging me more than ever since Catherine . . .' He tries to say 'died' but can't manage it. 'And now you're going . . .'

'You'll be fine, mate,' Fleur says, patting him on the shoulder. 'You're sitting pretty, I'd say. Nothing like a workplace injury to make sure you're well looked after.'

He shrugs and says nothing, looking down at the lavender in the sieve.

'C'mon, Todd, you've got a face like a pig's arse. Buck up.'

'I wish you'd stay, Fleur,' he says. 'It's not even like you've got another job or anything.'

'No,' Fleur says. 'But it's time for a change.'

Todd kicks at his crutch leaning against the bench and it clatters to the floor. 'What'll you do?'

'That's my business. Don't be so bloody nosy, you're worse than Paula.'

'But it isn't the same anymore . . . you're the only person who talks to me.'

Fleur thumps the bench with her fist and he jumps in surprise.

'Bullshit,' she says, 'that is complete bullshit, Todd. The three of them, they all talk to you, all the time. What about that conversation with Alice you told me about, with the books and everything? Of course they talk to you.'

'But it's not the same.'

Fleur sighs, pulls out the other stool and sits facing him across the bench. 'No,' she says, more gently now, 'I know what you mean. It's like the soul's gone out of the place. Catherine drove me up the wall a lot of the time but now she's gone . . . well, that's why I have to go, you see, Todd.'

'If you stay you might like them better,' Todd says, anxious to persuade her.

'It's not that, Todd. I don't dislike them. Alice is a very nice woman, and Ruby seems okay, though I haven't really got a handle on her yet. Declan's a bit of a dead loss but he's a decent bloke. But it's a new era and I belong to the old one.'

'That's just what you've decided,' Todd says. 'It doesn't have to be like that.'

Fleur raises her eyebrows and smiles at him. 'Okay, smart-arse, maybe you're right, but that's how it is.'

'They want you to stay. I heard Declan ask you to run the gift shop too.'

Fleur laughs. 'Listening at keyholes, eh? I thought it was only Paula who did that.'

Todd gives a reluctant grin. 'Gotta look after myself now Catherine's gone.'

'And haven't you thought that's just what I might be doing, Todd – looking after myself? Anyway, remember Kermit the Frog?'

'Kermit?'

'Yeah,' and she pulls her face into a huge distorting smile and wobbles her head. 'If you're ever in a jam here I am,' she says in a Kermit voice, 'and don't you forget it, even when I've gone. Now get off outta here and go help Alice check the new stock in.'

'Twelve hundred people the last time,' Ruby tells Alice that evening when she tracks her down in the kitchen. 'I don't know what Declan had in mind but I was thinking it would be a few hundred. Wherever will they stay? Do you know where he is?'

'He's gone out,' Alice says, rinsing salad at the sink. 'Meeting a friend for dinner, he said. I got the distinct impression that he'd got a date.'

'Good for him,' Ruby says, taking a bottle of wine from the fridge. 'I thought *you* were his date when I first got here.'

Alice laughs. 'Me and Declan? No, no we're . . . we're just friends,' and she shakes her head as Ruby offers her a glass. 'No thanks, I don't drink.'

Ruby nods. 'I noticed. Never?'

'Never. One day at a time.' Alice turns from the sink to look her straight in the eye. 'I'm an alcoholic. I haven't had a drink for over five years. Before that I was dry for years, but then . . . there was a crisis and I had one and then another one and several more and ended up having to start all over again.'

'I see.' Ruby hesitates. 'That can't have been easy.'

Alice shrugs. 'As I said, it's one day at a time.'

Ruby takes a sip of her wine. 'And Declan doesn't drink either?'

Alice holds her gaze again. 'No.'

'Catherine told me about Declan being in AA years ago,' Ruby says. 'Is that how you met?'

Alice nods. 'I was his sponsor. It means you take responsibility for—'

'I know how it works,' Ruby says. 'And if it works well it must be a bond, a source of strength for both of you.'

There is a longish silence in which Ruby fears that her curiosity has led her to overstep the mark. 'I'm sorry,' she says quickly. 'It's none of my business.'

'It's okay,' Alice says. 'You're right, it is a bond, and I think Declan and I are still sorting out how it works for us – whether it's a good basis for friendship or something that will always complicate it.'

Ruby pulls out a chair and sits at the table. 'I suppose being here together is one way of finding out.' Alice, she thinks, has more to tell than this, but she's obviously not ready to tell it yet.

'I got the books,' Todd says, appearing in the kitchen doorway with a plastic carrier bag of books looped on to one of his crutches. 'These are what Catherine said I should read next.' He drops the bag of books onto the table and hobbles over to Alice to return the key. 'I locked it again.' He stands watching as she slips the beads around her neck. 'Catherine always carried the key like that,' he says. 'And she always locked it, she never—' he stops suddenly.

'What is it, Todd?' Ruby asks.

He shakes his head and sits at the table, pushing the books towards her. 'We were going to read this one next,' he says.

Ruby raises her eyebrows and takes the book from him. '*Madame Bovary*, really?'

'She said it would teach me something about women.'

'It might well do that,' Ruby says in amusement, looking up at Alice and then back at Todd, who seems to have sunk low in his chair. 'Is everything all right, Todd?'

He is silent for a moment, running his hands over the covers of the books. 'Her room,' he says eventually, not looking up. 'It's just like she left it, everything, her cup, her clothes, the dead flowers, all that. It's a mess.'

Alice joins them at the table. 'No one's had a chance to sort it out yet, Todd.'

'But you *should*,' he says suddenly. 'It's important. Somebody might see it that shouldn't – her clothes in a mess, the bed not made, all her things everywhere. She wouldn't like that, she wouldn't want just anyone to see it.' A tear runs down his cheek and he flicks it away.

Ruby feels his hurt and anger like an ache in her chest. 'You're right, Todd,' she says. 'We should—'

'You're all doing everything for this place,' Todd cuts in, 'the business, the café, the music festival, but that's all you care about. It's like you've all forgotten her already.' He sinks his head down, burying his face on his folded arms.

Ruby looks across at Alice and sees that she too is deeply moved.

'We haven't forgotten her, Todd, but we both . . . Declan and I . . . we haven't really faced up to the fact that she's gone.'

'Well she has, and she isn't coming back,' Todd says. 'She's gone forever and it has to be you or Mr Benson that does it. Not Paula. She wouldn't want that, not Paula.'

Ruby reaches out and puts an arm around his shoulders. 'I know,' she says. 'I know she wouldn't. I promise you it won't be Paula.'

Todd shifts himself around in his chair. 'I miss her,' he says.

And Ruby feels his loss so much more profoundly than she feels her own.

Ten

D espite her recent blitz on the local shops, Lesley can't make up her mind what to wear. Meeting a man other than Gordon for dinner is something she hasn't done for years so how is she supposed to know what to wear or how to behave? Is this a date? Since that first spontaneous lunch with its unexpected sharing of secrets, she and Declan have met for coffee, shared another lunch at a winery south of the town where they'd sat on at the table on the deck by the lake until well into the afternoon. Now he's suggested dinner and as everyone knows – don't they? – dinner is different, so much more intimate than lunch, so does Declan think this is a date or what? As usual they are meeting in town, leaving her car in the pub car park and going in his. He is, she thinks, behaving as though they are having an affair. It's clear he doesn't want anyone at Benson's Reach to know they are meeting, but why not? What's it got to do with them anyway? It's so difficult for women, she thinks, remembering back to the days of being single and wondering how she was supposed to behave, what was expected of her.

She settles, finally, on a sleeveless black linen dress that she'd spotted in the window of a boutique in the main street.

'Very nice that,' Paula had said, appearing alongside her, apparently out of nowhere, while she was contemplating it. 'Suitable for any occasion.'

'Yes, isn't it?' Lesley had said. 'I'm thinking of trying it on.'

Paula is always good for a chat, although she doesn't seem to think much of the new management at Benson's Reach. She's a strange woman, Lesley thinks, opinionated but not very well informed, although she's a useful source of information about the place and the people. Shame about all that pink – the t-shirts, the shoes, the hair scrunchies, even her trainers are pink. And she seems to have an obsessive interest in Kylie Minogue, her 'role model', she says. She even wears a gold chain around her neck with a Kylie name charm on it.

'I reckon Declan's a bit of a loser,' she'd said a couple of days ago when she arrived with clean towels and a basket of provisions from which she replenished the cottage fridge. 'Hasn't got a clue what he's doing. I'm amazed Catherine couldn't see that it would never work with him in charge. I mean, I know she was very fond of him and he was the only relative who had anything to do with her, but that doesn't make him right to run a business like this, does it?'

'Well, he's got that old friend of hers to help him, hasn't he?' Lesley had said, seeing an opportunity to pump Paula for more information. She'd already learned a little about the late Mrs Benson and her friend from Declan, although neither he nor Paula could explain the interesting rupture of their friendship which had lasted for years. Paula had been better informed on the subject of Declan, who apparently has a chequered employment history. 'And what about that woman Alice,' Lesley had asked, 'what's the story there?' Declan had carefully avoided her questions when she'd asked him about Alice.

'No idea,' Paula had said. 'He picked her up from the Perth bus a few days before you arrived. Never seen her before.'

Lesley stares at her reflection in the mirror. One of the things she really likes about herself is her hair. It's thick and straight and when it's well cut it bounces around and needs little attention. She has golden blonde foils put in every couple of months to lift the natural brown and there's some grey in it too. She'd always dreaded going grey but now that it's happening she quite likes it. The dress is good too, suitable, really, for however one wants to view the occasion.

Declan's car is already gone from its usual spot so he is probably waiting in the car park. Lesley steps out of the cottage and closes the door behind her, stopping briefly at the top of the steps. What *am* I doing? she wonders. What do I want from this? Why does it matter? Is this what Stephanie would call a little flirtation, the kind she'd suggested Gordon would have had on his business trips? But there are no answers and she runs down the steps to the car and slips into her seat. She likes Declan, but she has no idea why she is psyching herself up like this about going to dinner with him. No more idea than she has about what she'd really thought being here would solve, why she's still here, or what she wants from it. She is just as confused as the day she arrived. All she does know is that she doesn't want to be at home and she doesn't want to talk to anyone from home, and it all seems a lot more complicated than when she arrived. She's even annoyed that her children keep calling, whereas she usually gets annoyed that they don't call enough. Worse still, they are calling and chastising her for her absence.

It was Sandi who had called first, surprised because Gordon had told her that Lesley was away for a few days. She hadn't asked why or when Lesley would be back, just told her mother about the courses she'd enrolled in for first semester. Since she'd opted for university in Canberra last year, distance had led to a certain detachment. It was, Lesley thought, probably just what Sandi needed. She had always found being the youngest oppressive, and in her final year at home when she was doing her exams and Simon and Karen were both gone, Sandi had seemed strangely displaced and awkward.

'I don't like being the third point in the triangle,' she'd said once when Lesley had asked her if she was okay. 'I don't like having to be on one side or the other, yours or Dad's.'

'But there aren't any sides,' Lesley had said, genuinely confused.

'Well I think—' Gordon had begun, but she had cut across him.

'There isn't a triangle,' she'd insisted. 'How could there be?'

So she and Sandi had talked for a while about the new semester, and Lesley had been about to hang up when Sandi said, 'I guess you'll be home soon then?' And there was tension in her voice. 'Dad must be missing you. I hope you're going back soon.'

It was Simon who called next. 'You've never done this before,' he'd said, and Lesley thought she heard an accusation in his tone. 'Is everything all right? Dad seemed a bit weird.'

Lesley, aware that she sounded unconvincing, had endeavoured to assure him that everything was fine, but added that she might stay on a bit longer than originally planned. And so it was inevitable that the next call was from Karen, the eldest, the one who really needs the status quo to be maintained with no sudden and nasty surprises.

'What's going on?' she'd demanded as soon as Lesley answered her phone. 'What are you doing down there?' Disapproval and anxiety sizzled down the line.

There have been times when Lesley has wondered if her eldest daughter is a changeling. She might look a little like both herself and Gordon but Karen is quite unlike either of them in temperament. She is a total control freak, and although Lesley's mother, Dolly, attributes that same characteristic to Lesley, she herself believes that's unfair.

'You're bossy and you take too much for granted, that's what,' Dolly had said to her recently when she had grumbled about Gordon's presence in the house. 'It comes of having too much money and nothing to worry about. You feel entitled to be in control of everything, but you're not. One day something will happen where you can't get your own way, and then you'll be sorry.' Lesley thinks of this as she drives into town and makes the clucking noise she always makes when she thinks of her mother talking too much about things she doesn't understand. Karen's obsessive desire to control everything is, she's sure, of her daughter's own making. Karen is also cautious, conservative and conventional, and irascible whenever life turns out to be not quite as she planned. She was clearly suspicious when Lesley told her that she'd just needed to get away on her own for a few days.

'But it's not a few days,' she'd said angrily. 'It's two weeks and Dad seems really worried.'

Lesley had realised that her reassurances sounded wobbly, so it's not surprising that Karen has called every day, sometimes twice a day, since then, to chide her and to ask, yet again, when she's coming home. Lesley finds Karen something of a challenge. She can be sulky when she doesn't approve of something or feels slighted, and she has domestic standards higher even than Lesley's own. It's not as though Karen needs her; she and Nick have a perfectly ordered life running their own interior design business and are usually too preoccupied with their own friends and with wooing new clients to spend much time with Lesley and Gordon. But Karen will still be put out when she finds her mother has extended her time away.

Simon and his partner Lucy, on the other hand, are a different sort of challenge. They rent a pretty but rundown weatherboard house with a hugely overgrown garden, have four-year-old twins, Tim and Ben, and are always needing help of some sort – babysitting, short-term loans, the loan of tools or the lawnmower.

For the first time in her life Lesley finds she doesn't want to speak to any of her children. Neither does she want to talk to Stephanie or other friends who have left messages. And she certainly doesn't want to talk to Gordon, although the fact that he hasn't even attempted to call her is unsettling. She could tie herself up for hours speculating on the possibilities of his silence with various levels of anxiety, but as she turns into the car park and pulls up near Declan's car, a frisson of excitement brings her back into the moment.

Declan gets out of his car to greet her and open the passenger door. How nice! She walks towards him, knowing as she does so that she is walking in a way that she hasn't walked for years – with a swagger, with just enough confidence to turn a few heads. Declan has scrubbed up well, she thinks. He's wearing a dark blue linen jacket, a lighter blue shirt and he seems to have had his hair cut. Dinner *is* different, she tells herself, it has possibilities that lunch does not. And as she slips into the passenger seat Lesley feels herself a different sort of woman, a woman she once might have been had she not opted for safety and security. She feels sophisticated, daring; the sort of woman who breaks rules and worries about it later. Dinner is definitely different.

❦

Gordon stops at one of his favourite places along the cycle path, drops the stand on his bike, takes off his helmet and sits down on a seat dedicated to the memory of a former member of the town council. He'd bought the bike about six months ago in the hope that he might persuade Lesley to get one too.

'You're joking!' she'd said irritably when he'd wheeled it proudly around to the back of the house and suggested they might go and choose one for her. 'Ride a bike! Why would I want to ride a bike now when I haven't been near one since I was seventeen?'

'It'd be good,' he'd said. 'Really, you should give it a go, it's a very liberating feeling after years of driving a car. It's something we could do together, and it'll keep us fit.'

'I'm fit already, thank you,' she'd said sharply, and had promptly disappeared inside and up to her room.

Gordon thinks about it now as he sits here looking out over the river to the tall buildings of the city on its opposite bank. Her sharpness had wounded him. When did it all go so wrong? Was it just when he retired? But no, it began before that, during the time before Sandi left home. It had become so different then, the atmosphere often strained and tense – as though the three of them hadn't known how to talk to each other. It wasn't as bad as recently but it was often pretty uncomfortable.

The evening is still and warm and out on the river half a dozen pelicans float calmly as a flurry of gulls scramble for something in the shallow water by the rushes. Gordon sighs, rubbing his hand over his eyes. He has tried to keep the whole thing low key with the children, although yesterday, when he and Simon were fixing the ladder to the tree house, he'd found it hard to maintain that. What he'd felt like doing was to rant and rave and throw himself on his son's sympathy, but that would just generate more anxious calls from Karen and then from Sandi. No point upsetting them when this might all come to nothing, but Gordon knows that *nothing* is what it *has* become. The sexual fire dimmed years ago but that, he thought, was not uncommon. He knew that intensity eventually gives way to something gentler and richer, but not, apparently, for them. It's more as though a slow drip of cold water has extinguished what they once had, leaving the coals dull and smoking in the grate of their life together. Does he still love her? He realises he no longer knows. He feels like a toy that has had all the stuffing ripped from him. His emptiness is frightening.

According to what she'd said when she left, Lesley should have been home two days ago, but this morning she had sent him a text saying that she'd be staying on for a while, but no mention of how long, and no explanation. It drove the final nail into the coffin of Gordon's attempts to get things right. As he sits here now watching the pelicans turning pink and orange in the light of the setting sun, Gordon knows he's had enough. He has, he thinks, two choices. He can get in the car, drive down to Margaret River and confront her, ask her to come home so they can try to make things work again, or he can opt out and do his own thing, just as Lesley is doing hers.

A small dog with a rough white coat, one black ear and a couple of black and tan smudges on his body appears around the end of the seat and stands looking up at him. Gordon leans forward, arms on his knees, and strokes the dog's head, scratching behind its ears. 'Are you a Jack Russell?' he asks, and it moves closer and sits down, leaning against his leg. Gordon looks around for the owner but there is no one in sight. The cycle path and the recreation area beyond it are empty. Everyone, he thinks, has gone home to their families, to a glass of wine and a meal on a beautiful evening. Everyone except him. He strokes the dog again.

'Where did you spring from then, mate?' The dog cocks its head to one side, as if indicating that the other ear needs scratching. Gordon obliges. The dog is wearing a green leather collar with an identity disk and Gordon takes his glasses from the pocket of his shirt to read it. Bruce, it says, and on the other side is a phone number.

'Bruce?' Gordon says, and the dog pricks up his ears and springs suddenly up onto the bench beside him. Gordon looks around again – still no sign of an owner. 'Perhaps I'll give them a call,' he says, reaching into his top pocket for his phone. Bruce looks up and wags his tail ever so slightly. The number has been disconnected.

'Now what?' Gordon asks, and Bruce, in what seems like an extraordinary stroke of emotional manipulation, leans against Gordon's leg and looks up at him, his whole face a question mark. 'Abandoned, are you?' Gordon says. 'Well join the club. I suppose you'd better come home with me and tomorrow I'll try and find your owner.'

Out on the water something disturbs the pelicans and they flap their wings and sweep forward majestically, lifting their ungainly bodies from the water and heading off up river towards the city.

'So it's just you and me then,' Gordon says, and Bruce stands bolt upright and gives a short bark and wags his tail furiously. 'Have you ever ridden a bike before?' Gordon picks him up and dumps him in the canvas saddle bag, and Bruce gives another bark and settles into the bag as though he has lived there all his life.

Gordon kicks away the bike stand, swings his leg over the crossbar and takes off along the path back towards home, and as he does so he's absolutely clear about what he's going to do. There will be no begging dash to Margaret River, no painful discussions about what has gone wrong, because he no longer has the energy or the desire for it. It's gone, Lesley's gone, and his heart has abandoned the fight. He feels nothing. Somehow he has unhooked himself from the central drama of his life and is free, free to do what he's wanted to do for ages and what he has tried to persuade Lesley to do with him. Tomorrow morning he'll find the dog's owner and then he'll get it organised. It shouldn't take long – he might even be on his way before she gets back. It's weird to feel the machinery of more than three decades of his life grinding to a halt, but he's absolutely clear that he's banged his head against the same wall for long enough. Something has died and he can't bring himself to try, yet again, to resuscitate it.

❦

Declan has been wondering if this was such a good idea after all. Having someone to talk to has been good, he'd meant what he said about the value of talking to strangers, but now he feels he might have had enough. It's his pattern, really, he knows that, moving in close and then backing off at a million miles an hour. On the other hand she's a good looking woman, and his ego can do with a bit of a boost.

'Sorry,' Lesley says, slipping into the passenger seat. 'I lost track of the time. Hope you haven't been waiting long.'

'Just a couple of minutes,' he says gallantly, because it's nearer fifteen. 'It's okay, we've got plenty of time, I booked the table for eight.' And he looks across at her. 'Nice perfume.'

'Thanks,' she says, buckling her seatbelt. 'It should be, it cost a fortune.'

Declan smiles and pulls out onto the main street. She is, he thinks, very attractive for a woman of her age – not that he knows how old she is but she's a good bit older than him, ten years perhaps, maybe more. She pulls her skirt down but it's still rising above her knees and he is trying to ignore them.

'I extended your booking, like you said,' he tells her when they are free of the town. 'How did your husband take the news that you weren't heading home?'

'I don't know,' she says, 'I didn't talk to him, just sent him a text.'

'Really?'

'Yes, why not?'

Declan hesitates. 'It's a bit . . . it seems a bit blunt.'

Lesley shrugs and Declan looks across at her, uneasy suddenly. It seems odd to break that kind of news by text, and certainly not the best move if you're trying to sort things out. But what do I know about relationships, he thinks, except how to stuff them up? He gives her a sideways glance. He hasn't had much to do with women like this, older, strong minded and, more significantly, married. Lesley, he thinks, is a challenge; everything she's told him about this current stand-off with her husband has rung warning bells. He can sense the neediness in her as well as the inability to entertain compromise. Everything she has told him about what she sees as her husband's failure to adjust to retirement seems to

Declan to be perfectly reasonable for a man going through such a significant change.

'Retirement must be pretty confronting for him. It just sounds as though he wants to make things work between you,' Declan had ventured. But it hadn't gone down well.

Catherine, he is sure, would have disliked Lesley; they were too similar. And he suspects Lesley's neediness may have a ruthless streak and that is both scary and sexy. Tonight it seems to be more of the latter.

'So how's it all going?' Lesley asks when the waiter has taken their order. 'Are things getting sorted out?'

Declan nods. 'It's starting to look more manageable now we've taken on some promising staff for the café and Alice is almost ready to open it. Ruby is making sense of all the piles of paper in the office. It feels quite good, really.'

'And you've still got that boy staying there?'

'Todd? Yes, he'll be with us for a while yet, I suspect. We'll find a decent job for him. Catherine was very fond of him.'

'Paula says he should go,' Lesley says, indicating to the waiter to pour her wine.

'Paula?'

'Yes, I was chatting to her the other day. She seems to know the place really well, and she says he's nothing but trouble.'

'She told me that,' Declan says, biting into a bread stick, 'but she didn't back it up with any evidence. I suspect that Paula herself is a far greater potential source of trouble than Todd.'

Lesley shrugs and picks up her glass. 'Cheers . . . oh, you're not drinking – *again*?'

'I don't drink – *at all*,' Declan says, knowing that the time has come to make this clear.

'Not ever?' Lesley asks. 'Oh I'm sure we can do something about that.'

Declan shakes his head. 'Not you, not anyone,' he says, and he holds her gaze until she drops her eyes. It feels like a tiny victory, but why does he feel he needs one? Because

127

she's older, perhaps, and he was brought up to defer to and humour older women? But then he's never been out with one before. Perhaps this whole evening was a mistake. Her comment about Todd has annoyed him. He wishes that he was back at Benson's Reach eating dinner with him, and with Alice and Ruby, because right now he feels he's dipping his toes into dangerous waters.

'So what next?' she asks.

'We still need to find someone to take over from Fleur. She makes all the lavender products, the creams and toners, all that stuff. But we've got time for that.'

Lesley leans forward across the table. 'How interesting. I remember your aunt telling me about all that when I was here before. In fact she showed me her workroom. I'd love to see it again.'

'Just ask Fleur,' Declan says. 'Catherine taught her and she's been doing it for a few years now. Letting people see how it's done was always part of the deal. She'll show you around.'

'I'd rather you showed me,' Lesley says.

Declan feels sweat prickle the back of his neck. Dinner is so much more complicated than lunch, he should have known that, but it might be less complicated if he could work out why he set this up and what he wants from it. He has always found it difficult to read the signs that women give out and has frequently erred by reading too much into too little and too little into the obvious. As a result he's been both slapped down and missed out on some tantalising possibilities. He has never thought of himself as an attractive man and is usually surprised to find himself the object of a woman's attention. Is he reading the signs right tonight? Perhaps his hormones have taken over from the rest of his brain? . . . And what would Alice think?

'So tell me about Alice,' Lesley says, pouring herself another glass of wine. 'You were very lucky she could come and help out when you needed her. How did you two meet and what was she doing before this?'

Eleven

or more than five years Alice's sleep has been broken by agonising dreams and attacks of anxiety so intense that her heart pounds in her chest and she has difficulty breathing. They force her out of bed, movement being the only solution for her restless body and mind. In prison she had longed to be able to go outside, gulp down the fresh night air and walk or run until the demons were exhausted. But prison rules didn't accommodate such idiosyncrasies and bellowing with grief and rage and pummelling one's mattress with fists was not an option when sharing a cell. The rules and the accommodation at the pre-release facility were less restrictive but they certainly didn't include the freedom to walk in the grounds at night. Benson's Reach has granted her many freedoms and this, Alice thinks, is a particularly precious one. Now she can let herself out in the dead of night or at dawn to walk off the night terrors. Contained weeping, even roars of anger, are possible now, thanks to Declan's generous decision to let her have a cottage to herself. It's all helping. She can see it in her own face, the colour of her skin and the way the shadows beneath her eyes have lightened. She's fitter too, but the dreams remain – the recurring one, of the night it all happened, replays itself through her sleep time after time and she suspects it always will. It's always the same: the rain driving against the windscreen, the lights ahead of her, the other car and the screech of the tyres as she breaks and spins out of control, the noise and then the silence. That overbearing claustrophobic silence and what it means, what it says about what she has done. Nothing, Alice believes, absolutely nothing will change the dreams, and nothing can ever change what they represent.

Even in this beautiful place, which has soothed and settled her, those dreams still hang like a stone around her neck, sapping her energy and stopping her from feeling fully alive. This is the real punishment and it's what she believes she deserves, a life sentence; prison was just the start. It will always be there, just as there will always be someone who knows hiding ready to blow her cover. She wonders sometimes if Ruby has guessed her secret because occasionally she catches Ruby watching her as though she is looking for clues. Does she look like a woman who has spent years in prison? But if Ruby does know she has said nothing about it. And here at least the days do not begin with locks and keys, with the yelling of orders and crude rejoinders. Here she can have what she has missed for so long, the chance to start the day gently and alone. Often in the evenings or at daybreak she sits, as she does now, here on her balcony, practising meditation, naming the emotions that drive the anxiety – the shame, the guilt and the fear, because naming them for what they are seems to give her some control over them, to minutely reduce their power.

This morning she sits, hands curled around a mug of tea, watching the dawn break, waiting for the kangaroos to emerge cautiously from the cover of the bush and pause, ears pricked, before hopping across the path and between the trees to the field which, before long, will be home to the music festival. She is learning the landscape, spotting tiny changes in the plants, and learning, too, the early morning activity of guests but, more particularly, of the people with whom she now lives. Declan is not an early riser and is rarely seen before seven-thirty while Todd, although not emerging from his room until later, has usually thrown back his curtains before seven. It's unusual for a teenager, Alice thinks; her own children had to be prised from their beds at his age. But the person who interests her most is Ruby, who is not only up at dawn but walks out, circling the lavender beds and the boundaries of the property, often ranging far beyond them. More interesting still is that Ruby also walks outside at night. Her movement lacks the frantic energy of Alice's own sorties, but she is, nonetheless, walking, absorbed in thought. Alice is convinced that, just like herself, Ruby is walking off the burdens of a troubled mind.

What are Ruby's demons, she wonders? Declan told her that Ruby and Catherine met when they were sent to Australia as children and Alice knows enough about the treatment of the child migrants to know that cruelty and neglect were a reality for most. How important that friendship must have been, and yet Ruby left Australia in 1969 – left her oldest friend and has never returned until now. And Todd has told Alice that Catherine and Ruby didn't write or speak to each other for more than twenty-five years, until Catherine turned up on Ruby's doorstep in London. So why did Ruby leave? What caused that rift?

Alice feels drawn to Ruby but can't quite reach her, and she wonders whether Ruby, like her, has the ability to appear approachable, relaxed and open whilst hiding behind an internal defence mechanism toughened by time and circumstance. Ruby is the sort of person you want to run towards while fearing that you might make a complete ass of yourself if you do. And who is she anyway? Alice's curiosity is eating away at her. She is not usually a nosy person but in this case a little information would help. This morning, she thinks, she'll risk it. Ruby and Declan have an appointment in town with Catherine's solicitor; it's her chance to pop over to the office and see what she can find out. Just a Google search will do it, nothing more intrusive than that. People do it all the time.

The kangaroos have completed their morning trek across the path and are disappearing through the trees. It's almost five-thirty and Alice is contemplating the ethics, or rather the lack of them, in this plan, when something very surprising happens. Another creature breaks cover, this time a human one. A door opens and Declan appears on the balcony of cottage six. He is wearing the clothes he was wearing when he went out last night, his shoes are in his hand, and he looks around just as the kangaroos had done, only rather more furtively. Then he sits on the top step, slips on his shoes, creeps quietly down the stairs and sets off at a brisk walk towards the back door of the house.

Alice grimaces and sips her tea. So she was right, he did have a date, but Lesley Craddock is the last person she would have expected. Is this why she has extended her stay? Alice is not keen on Lesley Craddock, who she thinks is imperious and condescending. Indeed, the more she thinks about it the more surprised she is that Declan – usually so cautious, diffident and lacking in confidence – has fallen so quickly into this . . . this . . . whatever it is, with such an unlikely person.

Declan disappears through the kitchen door and closes it behind him, and Alice finds that she is suddenly uneasy. Declan has an awful lot to cope with right now, the last thing he needs is someone like Lesley Craddock complicating things. 'But it's none of your business,' she tells herself, and then remembers that it actually is. She might be working for Declan but she was once and still is his sponsor. The worst thing for Declan, and indeed for Alice herself, now is complications. One of the most valuable lessons she learned in AA was the importance of navigating stressful periods in her life by avoiding extremes and complications. For some people, getting sober involves a commitment to stay out of relationships until a period of sobriety is established. Declan had fallen foul of that rule in his first year and had hit a crisis that set him back months. Admittedly that was a long time ago, but Alice's unease niggles. On the other hand, perhaps this *is* Declan's way of looking after himself – uncomplicated sex works for some. The trouble begins when one party takes it more seriously than the other. So what about Lesley Craddock, is she looking for a way to sort out some crisis in her life? Alice knows she can't confront Declan as she might otherwise have done. They are friends and colleagues but Declan is also her employer now. Their lives have become linked in a different way. All she can do, she thinks, is try to keep an eye on things and hope that Lesley Craddock will soon disappear back to wherever she came from.

<hr>

'Jackson Crow!' Declan says, practically choking on a flake of croissant. 'Jackson Crow is coming here?'

Ruby nods. 'Yes. He's some obscure saxophonist from North Carolina, and he seems to have struck up a working relationship with Catherine. He sounds like a bit of a poseur to me. Anyway, he's the person who's mustering the local bands through some sort of jazz and blues online network. Why, what's wrong?'

Declan bursts out laughing. 'There's absolutely nothing wrong. It's just that Jackson Crow is not some obscure saxophonist, Ruby. He may not be as famous as John Coltrane or Charlie Parker, but for serious blues fans he's a musical legend. You must've heard of him.'

Ruby shakes her head. 'Never. I just assumed he was some weirdo that Catherine latched on to. If he did all that why is he bothering to come here to the wilds of south west Western Australia for some little music festival?'

'He dropped out of the big time years ago because he was sick of it. Disappeared off the scene for quite a while and then, about twelve years ago, he turned up as a lecturer in the music school at Duke University in North Carolina, teaching saxophone in the jazz and blues program. They also set up a radio program for him on the university radio station, but it goes out all over the world. You know how people love the Garrison Keillor radio show? Well it's like that – unique. He's got a really dedicated audience, of which I am one.' Declan stops to finish the remains of his croissant.

'I see I've done him a disservice,' Ruby says, although not entirely convinced. 'He seems to have been fond of Catherine.'

'She was always going on about Jackson Crow,' Todd says through a mouthful of cereal.

'There, you see,' Declan says triumphantly.

'But this must be a tiny event to him.'

'These days he and The Crowbars just get together a couple of times a year to go to small festivals. It's a fun thing for them. I bet you Catherine hassled him for years to get him to come here the first time. I don't know why she didn't tell me about it.'

'He's pretty old.' Todd says. 'I've seen a picture of him.'

'Well then he and I will have something in common,' Ruby says. Declan is looking as though he won the lottery and it seems unkind not to show an interest. 'Have you seen any of the publicity from last time, Todd?' she asks, turning to him. 'Maybe we should have a look at it and get some ideas for this time.'

Todd nods. 'There are some posters and stuff in a big plastic box on the top shelf in the office. She asked me to get the ladder and put it up there one day when she was tidying up.'

'Well I think we'll keep you off ladders for a while,' Ruby says, looking at Declan. 'Maybe you . . .?'

'Oh absolutely,' Declan says. 'I'll get it down today. I'll look after all that, Ruby, the posters and so on, just try and stop me.'

'Excellent,' she says. 'I'm a musical fossil and it needs to be done by someone with a feel for it.'

'If he'd agree to do something big in Perth, maybe at the Burswood, I bet they'd fill the place,' Declan says, spreading marmalade on another croissant. 'But he won't go that way, I think he prefers teaching and the radio program these days. I'd better rethink the parking arrangements. Good thing there's plenty of space.'

'But where will they stay?' Ruby asks.

'We'll be able to fit some of them in here, but there's going to be a hell of a lot of caravans and tents. Come on, Ruby, you remember what it's like. And I bet quite a few will make for the caravan park and campsite on the other side of town. I'd better warn them. And I might just talk to the people who own that vacant land opposite, see if they'll let people park and camp there. But we'll need some volunteers to direct the traffic and we might not have enough toilets – maybe have to order a second block of portaloos. I'll talk to those guys that play at the pub. They may have been involved last time, they should be able to tell us what it was like.'

Declan gets up to make more coffee and mimes playing the saxophone as he waits for the kettle. 'Jackson Crow,' he says again, 'at Benson's Reach. Good thing Alice is ready to go with the café. We'll need a whole lot more than that though. We've already got Rotary doing the hot dog stand. I wonder if the fish and chip shop would bring that caravan along, the one that they take on the road sometimes. It'll be huge.'

He looks incredibly young, Ruby thinks, fooling around over there by the sink, making saxophone noises and dancing. So often he seems burdened but this is another side of him, playful, energetic, that she's not seen before. This is the young crop duster, running wide circles, arms outstretched, emitting a low buzz to simulate the aircraft engines. Something about him touches her deeply and she realises how fond she has grown of him in just a few weeks. He looks only remotely like Harry, so is it the link to Catherine, or just Declan himself, that endearing mix of indecisiveness and competence, and now the boyishness? But he's not a boy anymore. This morning, as she set out for her early walk, she had turned the corner at the end of the house just in time to see him putting on his shoes outside Lesley Craddock's cottage and then skulking back to the house. At the time she'd laughed to herself. 'Oh really, Declan, if you're going to bonk the guests don't be so furtive,' she'd murmured, but as she walked on amusement evaporated to be replaced by concern. Declan, she suspects, is vulnerable. He hates confrontations and would probably go a long way to avoid an argument. Lesley Craddock, on the other hand, is a very different sort of person, Ruby thinks; one determined to get what she wants in the way she wants it. Of course, she reminds herself as she watches Declan, it's none of her business. All being well Lesley will be gone soon, and Declan will have more than enough on his plate with the festival.

Alice, in the café kitchen testing some of her recipes, watches from the window as Ruby and Declan pile into his car and head off down the drive. She stops what she's doing, rinses her hands under the tap, dries them on a tea towel, and stands there for a moment contemplating her next move. It still doesn't seem quite right but she knows she's going to do it anyway so it might as well be now. Closing the café door quietly behind her she walks quickly to the office. It's a pity Todd hasn't gone with them but a few minutes ago she saw him hobbling up the slope to the workroom. He likes Fleur and Alice knows that he often gives her a hand in there so he's unlikely to appear in the office in the next ten minutes or so.

There are no restrictions on her use of the computer so, feeling very shifty, Alice slips into the chair, types Ruby's name into Google and hesitates briefly, her hand on the mouse. It's probably a waste of time. People think you can find anyone on the internet but it's not true – hundreds of thousands of people slip through the nets of cyberspace because they are just ordinary law-abiding people who live quiet lives and don't attract attention; others are invisible behind aliases. Alice takes a deep breath, clicks the mouse and leans forward in amazement. There are 91,207 results.

'No,' Alice murmurs, 'surely not? There must be someone else with that name.' So where will she start? Wikipedia seems a good bet; she should at least be able to see if she's got the right Ruby Medway. The picture makes it clear that she has. It was obviously taken some years ago – a black and white portrait of an unmistakable Ruby, the unflattering bun, the characteristically fierce expression and she's wearing some sort of insignia, because she is – 'Oh my God!' Alice clasps a hand over her mouth – she is not Miss, Mrs or Ms but *Dame Ruby Medway, born (Eleanor) Ruby Medway 23 January 1940 in Lewisham, London. In 1947 Medway was transported to Western Australia under the British Government's Child Migration Scheme and returned to England as an adult in 1969.*

Alice stops, leans back and studies the photograph again. Declan has said nothing of this – maybe he doesn't even know? When Ruby's arrival was imminent he had speculated on what sort of person she might be and it was nothing like this.

Alice scrolls down past the index and reads on.

In 1971 Medway campaigned tirelessly against the decision by then Secretary of State for Education, Margaret Thatcher, to withdraw school milk from children over the age of seven. She was twice arrested for disturbing the peace and for damage to property for which she served a five-day sentence in Holloway Women's Prison. In 1978 she started a 'day home' where single or deserted mothers could leave their babies, night or day, in times of crisis.

'Free, twenty-four-hour childcare,' Alice says aloud, exhaling slowly. 'Brilliant.'

Medway went on to open four more centres in the Greater London Area, and established the Child Rights Foundation. She also advised on the establishment of other centres throughout the country. During the years of the Thatcher Government (1979–1990) and the subsequent conservative Government under John Major (1990–1997) Medway continued her advocacy for underprivileged women and their children leading the fight for safe, reliable and affordable childcare, and for subsidised childcare for women on benefits, or low incomes.

In 1998, she was appointed by the Blair Labour Government to head the controversial committee to determine the rights of children in Britain which resulted in the establishment of the Office of Children's Rights. In 2000 she was made a Dame of the British Empire for services to women and children.

There's more, lots of it, but Alice is so gobsmacked by what she's read so far that she stops, sitting back to think. She wants to print it out to read back at the cottage, but she doesn't want to be caught in the act – not, of course, that they will be back anytime soon. Glancing up she sees Todd outside the workroom, laughing with Fleur, who is standing in the doorway. And as Alice watches he does a sort of hopping turn on his crutch and sets off down the slope towards the office. Alice feels a bolt of panic, clicks back to the home page, remembering as she does so that something in the computer stores the history of searches or websites visited – where is it? Her skin is prickling with tension. The last thing she wants is for Ruby to discover that someone has been doing a search on her. She'd be pretty sure to guess that it was her rather than Declan. 'History', she murmurs, 'search history, how do I find it? Can I delete it?' And she starts hitting various keys in panic. Todd adores the computer and has a habit of walking into the office and around the desk to look at the screen. A drop-down list of searches appears at the top of the screen, but she can't get rid of it. And as she stares at it in dismay she sees something else, something far worse, a name, Alice Fletcher, her name, and below that the web link to the Prisoners Review Board of Western Australia and, worse still, the link to 'Decisions of the Board'. She knows that website, it lists all the prisoners who have been granted or refused parole, the details of their sentences, reasons why parole was refused or granted.

There is a knock at the door and she doesn't answer. Someone has been searching for her and has found her. Not Declan, obviously he knows everything, but Ruby – it must be, *can only* be, Ruby. Alice closes her eyes, dizzy with panic.

'Hi,' Todd says, opening the office door and popping his head around it. 'You said to come to the café this morning, but I was on my way and I saw you in here . . .'

'Yes! Yes of course,' Alice says in what seems to be a very loud voice which bears no resemblance to her own. 'I . . . er . . . I wanted a hand in the kitchen. I'll just close this . . .' and she quickly closes everything that is open and then clicks 'shut down' just as Todd hops over behind the desk.

'Oh,' he says, 'you logged off. I was just going to—'

'Not now,' Alice says, getting to her feet. 'There's stuff to do in the kitchen. And, Todd, you really shouldn't do that, you know.'

'Do what?'

'Walk behind someone's desk and look at the screen they're working on. I know you don't mean any harm, but it might be private. It's a bit . . . well . . . intrusive.'

He shrugs. 'Sorry. Catherine always said to come around and help her. She was pretty hopeless with the computer. I didn't mean . . .'

'I know,' Alice says, putting her hand on his arm in an attempt to calm herself as much as to reassure him. 'But some people might not like it. It's about privacy, confidentiality, you know . . . we have to respect that.' And as she says it she feels herself to be both duplicitous and dishonest.

'Come on,' she says, 'let's get back to the café. I want you to taste test my chocolate and raspberry ice cream.'

He pulls a face. 'Oh well, if I really have to . . .' then bursts into laughter. And Alice steers him out of the office and back towards the safety of the café kitchen.

Twelve

April

Something really weird has happened. Lesley's phone hasn't rung for several days. She barely noticed at first because she was so shocked by what she'd done, what it meant, and what would happen next that she could think of nothing else. But now she realises that the constant calls that had been so irritating have stopped. *Why* haven't they called? What does it mean? Could they somehow know what she's done? No, that's ridiculous, there's no way they could know, so has there been some sort of disaster at home? But no, if that were the case someone else would know and would have called. But of course some other people *have* called and she didn't answer and hasn't listened to the messages. Shocked by her ability to forget everything else in the heat of her anxiety about the night she spent with Declan, Lesley sits down on the steps of the balcony to listen to the messages.

There are two from Stephanie about partnering her in a tennis tournament, three from other friends about various social events. And the final message is from her mother.

'Well I've no idea what you're doing down there, Lesley,' Dolly says, a familiar tone of disapproval in her voice, 'but

141

Gordon says you won't be back for a while. It doesn't seem right to me, but I suppose you know best. Anyway, I still need you to take me out to find a new washing machine like you promised. You've obviously forgotten all about it and in the meantime I'm doing it all by hand. So please let me know when you'll be back or I'll just have to ask Karen to take me.'

Lesley *had* completely forgotten, and while she knows there is no way Dolly would ask Karen to help her buy a washing machine the inference is clear – you are a failure as a daughter so I'll have to ask my granddaughter. Dolly is great at generating guilt and it certainly works on Lesley now, but she is also relieved because the message was left earlier today and if there was anything wrong Dolly would have known about it. Even so the silence really is very odd and Lesley decides that the time has come for her to make a call and that Simon will probably be the easiest person to talk to.

'Just checking to make sure everything's okay up there,' she says when he answers his mobile.

'Yeah, fine,' he says. 'No dramas. How are you?'

'Fine, yes,' she says. Can he tell from the sound of her voice that she has been unfaithful to his father? 'So everyone's okay?'

'Yeah. Lucy's good, and the boys are great. Dad and I finished the tree house so they're really over the moon about that.'

'Lovely – they must be so excited. Have you heard from Sandi?'

'Only on Facebook, she seems to be having a good time.'

'And Karen? It's just that I haven't heard from anyone for a few days, so I got a bit worried.'

'Oh well, Dad told us we should respect your space. He said you'd gone away for a complete break and it wasn't fair for everyone to keep hassling you.'

So now Lesley is relieved but guiltier than ever. 'Oh, I see . . . that's nice of him. All right then. Even Karen hasn't rung.'

'Of course not. You know Kaz, Dad's word is law. She just keeps ringing me instead. Anyway, we should get together, all of us, when you get back. Well not Sandi obviously, but the rest of us. Lunch, a barbecue at our place.'

'That would be lovely.'

'I guess you'll be back at the weekend, so let's say Sunday.'

Lesley hesitates, unable to come up with a reason why she won't be back by then. 'It's a date,' she says, and hangs up feeling trapped. But it's not over yet, there are still calls to make to her mother and Karen, and she takes a deep breath and steels herself. There is no doubt now that she will have to go back as promised, but what will she do when she gets there? She hasn't resolved anything by being here, all she has done is divert herself with shopping for things she doesn't want or need, often driving great distances to small galleries to find somewhere else to spend money. And now there is Declan, who is clearly much more than a diversion, and has the potential to change everything.

It had been an odd sort of evening and at first he'd seemed a bit distant, defensive even – especially when she'd teased him about not drinking. Everybody drank, surely? But he'd made it clear that it was a no-go area. And he hadn't liked it when she told him what Paula had said about Todd, nor when she had asked him about Alice. She'd been starting to feel quite uncomfortable but by the time they got to dessert he'd warmed up a bit.

'It really helped talking to you that first day in the pub,' he'd said. 'Strangers don't bring any baggage to what you say, and they can be dispassionate about a situation.'

'I suppose so,' she'd said, 'although I guess we all take our own baggage with us wherever we go. I certainly brought mine with me to Benson's Reach, as you now know. But I hope I'm more than just a stranger now.'

'Yes, but you're detached,' he said. 'Detached from me and from my situation, and you barely know the other people

143

involved. You're a detached observer. It doesn't matter to you how things work out for me in all this.'

She hadn't actually liked all that detachment stuff because after three glasses of shiraz she was feeling quite attached. 'Well it *does* matter to me,' she'd said then, 'because already I feel we're like close friends.'

He'd hesitated then, poured some mineral water into a tumbler. Loosen up and have a drink, for God's sake, Lesley had thought then, and she had attempted to tip some wine into an empty wine glass for him but he'd covered it with his hand.

'Well that's a nice thought,' he'd said, and he sounded a bit nervous, 'but I think it takes more than a couple of conversations to become close friends.'

It had felt like a rebuff, but she was determined not to let it upset her, and to simply press on until he seemed more at ease. 'Well then, we'll have to get to know each other even better, won't we?' she'd said.

As she replays this conversation to herself Lesley feels deeply embarrassed. It sounds like the biggest come-on of all time, and at that moment she really wasn't thinking of anything like that. She'd always been clumsy about flirting. What she had wanted was the comfort of being understood in what was really quite an intimate way but she had no idea how to convey that, so there she was, stuffing it up with almost everything she said. But she had blundered on, had another glass of wine and then a brandy, so that by the time they got up from the table she was feeling quite woozy.

It was a beautiful night and they'd eaten on a glorious deck built out over a lake and around the trunk of a huge tree at the lake's edge. Tiny white lights were draped through the tree's branches and tea lights flickered in shaded glasses on the tables.

'Do you want to have a walk around the lake before we go back?' Declan had asked as they left the restaurant. She slipped her hand through his arm and they strolled in companionable silence towards a bridge that crossed the lake some distance away.

She was relishing it all, the place, the atmosphere and the unusual experience of being out alone with a younger man. She could see herself as she hoped others might see her, as an attractive, even desirable, woman for whom anything might be possible. Were people looking at her? She has no idea now but at the time it felt that way. She was starring in her own movie in which the situation and the location and her own need had set the scene for what was to come. Home and all its problems had faded conveniently into the background.

It was as they walked onto the bridge that it happened: she tripped, not deliberately, although she wonders now whether he might have thought so. He grasped her around the waist and stopped her from falling, but he didn't let go immediately, and that's when she did it. She leaned in closer and kissed him. It was, she thinks now, a Jane Austen moment, except that Jane would have had Declan kiss *her*, whereas what happened was that he'd pulled back in surprise. But then he'd tightened his grip and kissed her – quite nicely really. It was so long since she and Gordon had kissed other than in a light and friendly way that it felt just like the first kiss of her youth.

Intoxicated by the situation, the kiss and, more significantly, too much alcohol, Lesley is vague about what happened next – how they got home, how they ended up in her cottage. But she *does* remember being glad that she'd worn the new underwear she'd bought in Busselton. It's strange, she thinks, how dinner and the walking bit and the kiss are so clear but it goes a bit fuzzy after that. The effect of the brandy kicking in, she supposes. But she *can* also remember a blinding reality check about her body – at least ten years older than Declan's, but it passed in a flash with the recognition that she was considerably fitter than him. And Declan's body, heavy and pale, was so much younger than Gordon's lean, muscular frame; comforting, like hugging a big soft toy.

Later he'd told her that he hadn't been with a woman for about four years, and she'd told him that she and Gordon hadn't made love for at least two years, possibly more. It was only the next morning, when she woke – nauseous and with a pounding headache – that the reality of what she had done hit her. What was she thinking? But of course she hadn't been thinking at all. How did she get through all the embarrassment of taking her clothes off with a comparative stranger? Well, she had the alcohol to thank for that. She had never been sexually adventurous, and it was the first time in the whole of their marriage she had been unfaithful to Gordon. It seems both a momentous event and a monstrous betrayal. She can't begin to think what the consequences might be, but after three and a half decades of marriage betrayal must mean something significant.

That first day in the pub, Declan had talked about the freedom of talking to strangers but Lesley sees now that it was far more than that. They had been drawn to each other in a very powerful way, so powerful that she had done something completely uncharacteristic. This is not just a one night stand; clearly she and Declan have feelings for each other. Guilt, fear, erotic memory and the thrill of new possibilities battle for her attention, leaving her drained and anxious. Since the morning, four days ago, when she woke to find Declan had gone she has been doing her utmost to pin him down to a time to meet, but so far he has eluded her, racing off to talk with contractors, or to sort things out with staff. Even when she has called him on the office phone he's been too busy to talk. 'Call me back then,' she's said, 'you've got my mobile number, and text me yours.' But he hasn't called or texted and now her time is running out, she's promised to be home for lunch with the family on Sunday. Failing to turn up will be pushing her luck too far.

But home looms ominously as a place of reckoning. Gordon's silence, the shared bed, his disapproval. And yet she really doesn't want to hurt him, although of course she already has. He would be devastated if he knew about Declan. Will he know? Will he be able to tell immediately she looks him in the eye? Lesley buries her face in her hands, trying to make sense of what is happening. She feels sure now that she and Declan have been drawn together for a reason – to provide each other with the love and reassurance they both need. They reached out to each other and found something precious. Declan had felt it too or why would he have suggested the second lunch or dinner? What had seemed like distance in the early part of the evening was simply his effort to conceal his feelings, and his elusive behaviour now confirms that. The relief is enormous, the implications terrifying, the logistics impossible. What will they do?

Lesley's panic is rising, her head spins, her face burns. She lies back on the bed reliving the evening time and time again, reliving their earlier meetings, searching for phrases, gestures, smiles, casual touching, and she finds them, plenty of them, which simply prove what she now believes. She'd thought that her decision to come to Benson's Reach was random but she knows now that it was some sort of predestination. She came here because she was supposed to meet Declan. She wraps her arms around herself remembering the warmth and soft weight of his body, how cosy, how comfortable, how reassuring it was. She's desperate now to see him, to talk to him, to tell him she feels just as he does, and that, she decides, is what she's going to do and she's going to do it right now.

❦

Todd is sitting at the bench in Fleur's workroom reading some of the stuff that she has written for him about making the lavender products.

147

'Seriously, Todd,' Fleur says, bringing a tray of small purple glass pots and some taller plastic containers from the steriliser across to the bench. 'You should ask them, ask Declan or Ruby. I'm not going to be here much longer and you can't expect them to read your mind.'

'They'd never let me,' Todd says, watching as she begins to fill the pots with the lavender moisturiser. 'They'd say it's a job for a woman, not for a boy.'

'Why isn't it? What is there about this job that makes it only a woman's job? Stop thinking about what your stupid mates would say and use your brain, which is pretty good if you give it a chance. Anyway, they couldn't say that because it would be illegal. You can't make jobs gender specific except in certain, very particular, situations, of which this is not one.'

Todd grins, picking at the plaster on his ankle. It's one of the things he likes best about Fleur, that she's so fierce, and she does all that posh talk – 'gender specific', 'of which this is not one'. No one else he knows talks like that.

'If you stayed they might let me be, like, your assistant. You told Catherine you needed someone and she said she'd fix it.'

'But Catherine's gone, hasn't she, and I'm going too.'

'But if . . .'

'Enough! You're like a bloody Jack Russell nipping at my heels all the time. I've given my notice – remember? I'll be forty next year and this is a good time to make a change. All I'm thinking is that young Kim can't manage on her own in the shop so if they're going to replace Glenda and get someone in to manage it, that person could manage the bookkeeping and the ordering and so on for the lavender products, and you could do the production.'

Of course he wants the job, but there is no way they'll give it to him. And there's no way he will ask. Alice has said she'll talk to Declan for him and he has to leave it at that. Besides, he's feeling a bit more sure of himself now. They're really nice to him and keep telling him he's useful. Alice has been teaching him to cook. Right now he doesn't want to do anything to rock the boat.

'Heard from your mum recently?' Fleur asks.

Todd nods. 'Got another card last week. She's still in Kuta, I think.'

'That'd be right,' Fleur says with a grin. 'Bit of a party girl, your mum. Is she still with that Stanley bloke? What's he like?'

'A wanker,' Todd says. 'He wears a lot of gold chains and carries a man bag. He thinks he's so cool but he's a real dickhead. You'd hate him.'

'Probably would,' Fleur says, and she pushes the tray of plastic containers towards him. 'These have been sterilised too so can you wash your hands and start filling them with hand cream, please? But your mum must see something in him.'

'He's got loads of money,' Todd says, washing his hands at the sink. 'He's always flashing it around. He buys Mum lots of stuff, clothes and that.' He hesitates, looking up at her, grinning. 'She always says she's like that woman on *Kath and Kim* – "high maintenance".'

Fleur nods slowly, watching as he dries his hands and sets up the hand cream dispenser. 'Wouldn't suit me, all that drinking and clubbing and being dependent on a man. But I suppose as long as she's happy . . . and you're getting on all right now, aren't you? Here, I mean.'

Todd nods. He wants to tell her that he's worried about what'll happen to him when the plaster comes off his ankle. He'll be sixteen soon so he could go back to the caravan and social services wouldn't bother about him. The doctor says he'll have to take it easy on his ankle for a while when the plaster comes off but after that . . .

'Well, if you're not going to say anything to them then I will,' Fleur says. 'You know more about this than anyone else, all the times you've sat in here with me, all the stuff you've helped me with. I'm not going to stay around here forever waiting for them to find the right person for the job when the right person is here already.'

'But they're letting me stay here, I can't ask them for something else.'

'Well you don't have to ask, do you? I'll do it, that's what I've just said.'

'I dunno,' he says, shaking his head. 'I dunno.'

'Bloody hell, Todd, you're irritating,' Fleur says, stopping what she's doing and turning to him, hands on her hips. 'You're pissing me off so much over this I could cheerfully break your other ankle.'

Todd laughs and stretches out his good leg. 'Yeah! Go on,' he says, 'then they'll have to keep me on longer. Do it now. Be my guest.'

'Gone?' Lesley says. 'Gone to Perth? But I saw him early this morning out there talking to that man who plays guitar in the pub.'

'That's right,' Alice said, 'and then he left to drive up to Perth.'

'But why? Why has he gone there?'

Alice opens her mouth, falters and shuts it. It's really none of Lesley's business why Declan has gone to Perth.

'He . . . er . . . well he had some business to attend to.'

'What sort of business? He didn't say anything to me about it.'

Alice blinks and tries to hide her annoyance. Maybe Lesley and Declan have unfinished business from the other night. But he does seem to have been avoiding her since then and Alice can't assume that he would want her to know where he's gone or why.

'I don't think it's my place to—' she begins.

'Oh, don't be so ridiculous,' Lesley cuts in. 'Just tell me where he is and when he'll be back.' Her face is flushed and her eyes very bright, she's clearly quite hyped up.

'Look, Mrs Craddock, I'm sure you can understand that I can't discuss Mr Benson's business with a guest.'

'You have no right to tell me what I can understand or not,' Lesley shouts into her face. 'How dare you—'

'Is there a problem?' Ruby cuts in from the doorway.

'I just want to know where Declan is,' Lesley says.

The shock of seeing Ruby has snapped her out of something, although she eyes Alice with disapproval before giving Ruby her best smile.

'Well I think that's his business, don't you?' Ruby says with a remarkable chill in her voice. 'Had Declan thought you needed to know that he was going away I'm sure he'd have told you.'

Alice is gobsmacked by the authority that Ruby brings to the situation. It's not just what she says but how she says it, slow, cool, dignified.

'How rude,' Lesley says, 'how dare you speak to me like that!'

'Mrs Craddock,' Ruby says, 'Declan and I are the proprietors here and you are a guest. Declan's business in Perth is nothing to do with you, or, as I said, he would have told you about it. We'll certainly let him know you'd like to speak to him. I'm sure we have your number in the file. Now, is there anything else we can do for you this morning?'

Alice is holding her breath, eyes flicking back and forth from one to the other.

'You can tell me where he is and when he'll be back.'

'I will not tell you where he is but we do expect him back in a few days' time. And I must ask that in future you do not harass members of the staff. If you have any other problems please come and see me personally.' Ruby stands there,

Liz Byrski

all five-foot three of her looking six-foot plus, unsmiling, immovable, implacable. Just waiting.

'Well really!' Lesley says, grabbing her bag from the desk where she'd put it when she came in. 'I shall have something to say to Declan when he gets back.' And swinging around she storms out of the office and slams the door behind her.

Alice exhales and sinks down into the desk chair. 'Wow! Thanks for rescuing me.'

'My pleasure,' Ruby says. 'But don't let anyone speak to you like that, Alice. Not ever, and most definitely not here.'

Alice closes her eyes briefly. For a moment she thinks she might burst into tears. It's so long since anyone actually stuck up for her she had forgotten how it feels. 'Thanks anyway,' she manages to say. 'It means a lot.'

Ruby nods and smiles. She is about to walk away but then stops. 'I don't think she's a bad person, you know, just a very unhappy one.'

'Probably, yes,' Alice says, getting back to her feet. 'But it might be a bit more complicated than you think.'

Ruby turns back into the room. 'Ah,' she says, 'so you saw it too. Declan doing his morning-after-the-night-before skulk. I wondered if you had. I know you're often up and about early.'

'Yes, I did see. Poor old Declan, he's not really made for this sort of thing, is he?'

Ruby laughs. 'I suspect not. But men, they never learn, do they? Not where sex is concerned. He's a very sweet man. Let's just hope she's calmed down a bit by the time he gets back.'

Alice nods. This is the time to tell her, she thinks, all I have to do is tell her that I poked my nose into the internet to find out about her. Then she can tell me she did it too and we're square. 'Ruby,' she says and Ruby, now heading out of the office, turns back.

'Yes?'

152

'There's something I need to . . .' But she just can't make herself say it. She needs more time, time to think about how to say it.

'What is it, Alice?'

'Nothing,' she says, 'just thanks for sticking up for me.'

Ruby nods. 'I'm off to get into the tough stuff in Catherine's room. See you later.'

In Catherine's room Ruby's heart sinks at the prospect of what needs to be done. A few days earlier she had surveyed the mess: no curtains of cobwebs yet, no rats or bats, but the clock has stopped, dust has settled and the room reeks of Catherine's attempts to hold on to the threads of a disintegrating life. Todd had been right, the overall mess was very personal: dirty clothes, old newspapers, unwashed crockery, dead flowers, the unmade bed. For a woman brought up as both she and Catherine had been Ruby recognised the effect of this. She understood how Catherine must have hated knowing that someone would have to deal with what she no longer had the time or energy to manage herself. Ruby had sunk down into the big chair and studied the painful evidence of those last weeks. 'I wish you'd told me, Cat,' she'd said aloud. 'I could have come.' But as soon as the words were out she wondered if it was true; she *might* have come but she would have resisted it, fought it. The last thing she ever wanted had been to be here, in this house with Catherine, either healthy or dying.

She had got to her feet rapidly, gone to the shed and returned with boxes and plastic sacks and had cleared away the embarrassing surface of the mess. The scattered, unwashed clothes, the newspapers, empty envelopes, dead flowers and other rubbish she bagged and put into the outside bins. Then she stripped the linen from the bed and took it, along with the towels and a couple of crumpled tea towels, to the laundry and loaded the lot into one of the washing machines in which Paula did the laundry for the cottages and the house. She stacked the crockery and vases into the kitchen dishwasher, and carried a couple of almost dead plants out to the deck, soaked them with water and left them to recover in the sheltered sunlight. It didn't take her long and she was rewarded by the dramatic improvement in the appearance of the room. But the bed still had to go.

She remembered this bed all too clearly; a Benson family heirloom, a wooden frame with a slatted base and carved head and footboards. It was always an ugly bed and Ruby wondered why Catherine had chosen to use it at the end. Memories, perhaps. The mattress looked almost new. She had been on the point of going outside to find Declan to ask him if he had feelings about what should be done with it when she stopped. Declan was having trouble keeping up with everything, particularly with his feelings about Catherine. The last thing he needed now was to have to make a decision about the bed. Instead she asked the two young men he'd taken on to help with some repairs to the barn to dismantle it and carry it out to the storeroom. Its fate was something to be decided another day. She dusted, vacuumed and sat back and admired her own handiwork. The room was respectable now although the odd smell was still there.

'Come with me, Todd,' she had said later that day, 'there's something I want you to do for me.'

Relief shone like sunlight across his face when he saw what she'd done but he was clearly too choked up with emotion to speak at first.

'This is better, isn't it, but there's still a lot to do in here in terms of sorting out Catherine's things. Would you feel okay helping me with some of it?' Ruby asked.

Todd nodded, getting himself back together. 'Yeah, course, if you think she'd think it was all right.'

Ruby turned to face him. 'I think that you're absolutely the best person for this. And the first thing I'd like you to do is to take this thumb drive and download all the files from her laptop onto it, and then delete them from the machine.'

'Cool,' he'd said. 'That's easy,' and within minutes he was working silently at the long table under the window.

Ruby perches now on the edge of that table, looking out of the window to where she can see Lesley Craddock heading up the path to the cottages where Paula is just about to emerge from number four, from which the guests checked out this morning. So now Lesley will start pumping Paula for information, but that too will be a wasted effort. Paula has no information to pass on. Late yesterday Declan had got a call telling him that a cancellation meant that the minor surgery he'd been waiting for could be scheduled for tomorrow if he could get to the hospital by four o'clock today. It was nothing too serious, but being Declan and embarrassed, he'd mumbled something which she couldn't quite hear, but she did catch 'pretty routine' and he obviously wasn't worried about it. Right now he is probably checking into his ward and if there is a delay, or if, as he suggested, he decides to take an extra day or two in Perth, Lesley will have left before he gets back. Ruby feels a touch of sympathy for her; the cloud of anger, frustration and general unhappiness that travels with her is almost tangible. Whether it's mid-life angst, relationship problems or something else entirely, Ruby doesn't know, but she can see that Lesley is battling with something, and it makes her a difficult person to like. She slips off the edge of the table as Lesley nabs Paula and starts to interrogate her.

The boxes are her next task. Catherine's personal things – private papers, letters, journals, photographs, news clippings, email printouts, certificates going back to childhood, jewellery, and mementoes. What else? And where to begin? The task seems enormous and Ruby knows that each box she opens has the potential to strip bare her own emotions, and start the unravelling of her own past. A process that's certain to open up old wounds and splash acid into them.

Once Todd had cleared the files from the laptop she had told him to disconnect it and gather all the leads together and put the whole thing away in its case. That was several days ago, and since then she and Declan have done some serious talking – about Benson's Reach, about Todd and Alice, and about themselves. This business partnership that has been thrust upon them is working amicably, better than either of them had expected, but it's still early days. Some things, though, need to be sorted out now.

Through the window Ruby sees Todd heading back from the café towards the house. Leaning forward she throws open the window.

'Have you got a minute, please, Todd?' she calls, and he nods and changes direction slightly to come in through the kitchen door. Declan had planned to talk to Todd today but as he hurried to pack his bag she had volunteered to do it. Todd taps on the half-open door and comes in, perching on the arm of the sofa.

'Good,' Ruby says, walking over to close to the door. 'We need to have a chat.' And she sees a flash of fear cross his face. Surely he can't think he's in trouble?

'Don't look so worried,' she says. 'There's nothing wrong. Have you heard from your mum recently?'

He shrugs. 'When Declan took me up to the caravan the last time there were a couple more postcards. She's still in Kuta . . .'

'We can try to find her if you like, but if she's okay there and you're okay here – well, we can leave things as they are for the time being.'

'Yeah,' he says. 'That'll be good, no need to get her back.'

'Okay.' She takes the laptop and hands it to him. 'So, Todd, this is yours now. Declan and I think you should have it. You'll use it, won't you? I know it's not the latest version but it's pretty good and all the software's there.'

It's clear that he's over the moon but before he can start fumbling for words she begins again, handing him a roll of red dot labels. 'We'd also like you to go through the bookshelves and stick a red dot on all the books you'd like to have for yourself. When Declan gets back he's going to get the books down from the top shelves so you can go through them too, on the table. He was going to do it today but of course he had to go to the hospital. So *don't* get up onto the steps, okay? You can take as many as you like but the one rule is that you don't try getting onto the ladder with that plaster.'

'Wow,' Todd says, his face flushing. 'Really? The laptop and books . . . that's so . . . that's so totally cool, thanks, Ruby.'

'Thank Catherine, it's what she would have wanted.'

He nods again. 'Thing is though, I won't have anywhere to keep them.'

'There's plenty of shelves and cupboards in your room,' she says.

'But . . . well . . . after that, when I have to go . . .'

'You mean to the caravan?'

He nods.

'Do you want to go back? I don't think you can manage yet.'

'No, 'course not, I want to stay. I told Fleur just now, break my other ankle so I don't have to go back.' He laughs nervously.

'Well you don't need to go to those lengths,' Ruby says, sitting down beside him now. 'We should have sorted this out with you earlier. I guess you've been worrying about it, and we've been busy so we didn't notice. This whole thing came as a surprise to both Declan and me, you know, and we haven't decided yet what will happen to this place – it's too soon for that. It'll take a few months, maybe more, but one thing we are both clear about is that we will look after you.

I don't mean "look after", like you look after a little kid – we will look after your interests. You can stay here with us until that decision's made, if you want to. You're earning your keep in all sorts of ways and when you're back on both feet again there will be more for you to do. When we do make a decision we'll talk to you about what that means, for you, for all of us. By that time you'll be sixteen and you may have had enough of Benson's Reach – who knows? Meanwhile, you can line up your books on the shelves and your laptop on the desk, and I'll drive you up to the caravan so you can collect anything else you want from there and we can get the mail redirected so you'll get your mum's cards here instead of having to collect them. Is that okay?'

A few minutes later she watches as he heads out towards the workroom. What a delight it had been to see the relief on his face, the sparkle in his eyes. Unable to find words he had lurched forward to hug her and she had hung on to him. He was a slight boy at the gangly age, long bony arms and legs, his feet seeming too large for his body. It was his eyes that revealed that he was so much wiser than his years. 'He's just as you described him, Cat,' Ruby murmurs, 'and I know just what you were trying to do and why.'

Thirteen

There is a plate of sandwiches, tiny triangles of white bread with the crusts removed, lined up in three neat rows, four in each row and each with a little paper flag: egg and mayonnaise, cheese and tomato, ham and lettuce. Declan tries to multiply three by four but it seems awfully difficult, the numbers keep slipping away. He hopes it's just the anaesthetic from which he is still quite dopey.

'Now, you should eat something,' says the nurse who has just taken his pulse, 'and there's a nice cup of tea as well. You'll feel a lot better when you've got something inside you.'

Declan hauls himself up in the bed and she props him up with more pillows and smooths the sheet. He thinks he would like to stay here for about four weeks, being fussed over and having someone cut the crusts off his bread. How long is it since he had sandwiches like these? Decades. They remind him of birthday parties when he was a child: tiny sandwiches, tinned mandarins trapped and glistening in orange jelly, cupcakes scattered with hundreds and thousands, homemade lamingtons and birthday cake – round and white with jam in the middle, or later, when he was a little older, a possum shaped mound covered in chocolate butter icing roughed up with a fork to look like fur, Smarties for eyes and a line of candles in a ridge down the middle of its back.

His tongue feels sludgy and swollen; he flexes it, and tries speaking. 'Was everything okay?' he asks the nurse.

She pats his arm. 'You're fine, Mr Benson. Mr Tran will be along in about half an hour to tell you all about it.'

He knows that this is the procedure – that the nurse can't tell him anything, and there's not likely to be a problem, but still it makes him anxious. It was only a small prostate problem but he'd like to know if they fixed it, and he'd like to know now because he is, he thinks, too young to have a prostate problem. He nods and leans back and the nurse takes one of each of the sandwiches, puts them on a smaller plate and hands it to him with a paper serviette.

'See what you can do with these,' she says. 'I'll be back shortly.'

Cheese and tomato is delicious, he thinks. Why would anyone ever eat anything other than cheese and tomato? It's the best flavour in the world. But then the first thing you eat after an anaesthetic always tastes wonderful, probably because of the dead feeling in your mouth, plus the relief of recovering from being rendered unconscious. His mother had made sandwiches like these, and organised a birthday party every year until he was twelve, but by his thirteenth birthday she had been dead for seven months and his father, who hadn't a clue about birthdays, had taken him to Benson's Reach for the weekend. Catherine was there with his Uncle Harry and she had made a square cake with green icing marked out with white lines like a football pitch and scattered with tiny plastic footballers. It was totally amazing and he'd felt horribly disloyal to his mum when he'd told Catherine that it was the best birthday cake he'd ever had. Recently Ruby had reminded him that he had also spent his eighth birthday at Benson's Reach, she was there then, and for some reason Catherine wasn't, but it was when he'd made up his mind to be a pilot and he had been practising. He thinks he remembers it but that might be just because he wants to please Ruby.

Declan likes Ruby – his concern about how they would get on in this strange alliance which Catherine has set up had dissipated within a few days of her arrival. She is, he thinks, very straightforward and fair, and she says exactly what she thinks. Similar in some ways to Catherine, but Catherine could be manipulative and, as an adult, her intensity wore him down. She needed attention of a sort he could not give. Sometimes he felt she kept him on the edge of a sort of emotional black hole into which he could be sucked at any moment. He liked her, loved her, was frequently very grateful to and appreciative of her, but he struggled to escape from her need to know everything about him, and to control him. He knew it had been hard for her when Harry left, and died soon after that. She was still in her thirties then and he thinks back now, trying to remember whether there had been anyone else of significance in her life since then. Not another partner, certainly, and her aloneness strikes him now in a way it has never done before. Catherine seemed always to know everyone but be close to no one. How little he really knew about her. He feels shamed now by his own lack of curiosity, of even considerate enquiry. So caught up in personal disasters of his own making, he had never paused to look at her life, to wonder what she might need or want from him.

Declan shakes his head, sighing, and studies the remaining sandwiches. Ruby is, he thinks, less complicated than Catherine and not dependent on anyone else to affirm her. He knows little of their friendship except for their childhood as migrants, the hellish treatment they endured in the convent, and that when they left they were both sent as domestic helps to the Perth Bensons, who owned the hotel. Those were

Harry's parents, of course, while Declan's father Robert, Harry's cousin, was from the less well-heeled side of the family. What could it have been like, he wonders now, for those two girls leaving the convent and moving into the hotel? His Aunt Freda was lovely but she would have been tough with the staff, and then there were the guests. Had they escaped the tyranny of the nuns for the tyranny of demanding and inconsiderate hotel guests?

He's not thought about this before, but sitting here now, peacefully filling himself with delicious little sandwiches and tea, it does all seem rather intriguing and strange. Ruby had told him the other day that she had left Australia in 1969 and had gone back to England, to try to find her family. She, like so many of the child migrants, had been told that her parents were dead, but she had never allowed herself to believe it. And if she and Catherine were such great friends, why hadn't they been in touch again for more than twenty-five years?

'So why didn't you and Catherine see each other for so long?' he'd heard Paula ask recently.

Ruby, unsurprisingly, had turned to her, given her a very long look and said. 'I don't think that's any of your business, Paula.'

But what she did tell him and Alice one evening was that early in '69, back in England, she had shared a flat in Earls Court and later that year she'd gone with her flatmates to see Bob Dylan at the Isle of Wight festival. The following year they'd gone there again and to Glastonbury, where she'd met the man she later married. It's hard for Declan to imagine this plump, grey-haired, serious looking woman sleeping under canvas, smoking dope and going crazy for Dylan, Marc Bolan and Leonard Cohen. The thought of it actually made him want to chuckle.

'Jackson Crow would've been there that year, I'll bet,' Declan had said when she'd told them that. 'He probably played there. You two might have more in common that you imagine, Ruby.'

He wants to know more, but Ruby will talk about the past only when it suits her, and if he's ever to find out what happened between the two women it will be because she wants to tell him. For the time being, however, Declan is very happy with the way things are going at Benson's Reach. Alice, by her mere presence, makes him feel safe in a way he hasn't felt with anyone since his mother died. It wouldn't matter to him if Alice sat up there in her cottage on the hill and didn't do any work, just being there would be enough. As it was she had been determined to set up a proper business arrangement between them and that was probably a good thing for both of them. Alice, he thinks, is tough as steel and tender as a small child. Declan knows he would not have got sober without her.

When she had been in crisis he had done what he could. In court on that last day he had been incandescent with rage when the sentence was handed down. Couldn't the judge see what sort of person she was? Couldn't she see that the consequences were already a more devastating punishment than prison could ever be? Alice had been hard to talk to in prison – guarded, always on the edge, but obviously pleased to see him. The letters they'd eventually exchanged were better, and he felt they'd grown to know each other through those letters in a way they might never have done through occasional conversations on visiting days.

Declan eats his third small sandwich and sips his tea – delicious – so simple. Who needs anything more complicated than crustless sandwiches and tea and the sense of childhood they invoke? Is there a part of him that has never grown up? Catherine used to say men never really grew up, and he'd resented it because it was said, he'd felt, with bitterness. Surely there was a child in both men and women that never really gave way to adulthood and that, he thinks, is not necessarily a bad thing. When he reflects now on the boyish comfort he draws from the presence of Alice and Ruby, the pleasure of their company, he knows that he has found something precious and unexpected. And Todd, what a bloody excellent kid he is despite his hellish background. There is a marvellous sort of chemistry when the four of them, although each very private, each to some extent holding back, are together. It's almost like having a family, Declan imagines, although family is not something he's ever known much of. He feels he would be quite happy for things to go on as they are forever – except, of course, for the spanner that he himself has thrown into the works.

He shifts restlessly in the bed and puts his plate down on the tray as he thinks about Lesley Craddock. Why did he do it? It would be nice to be able to say that the drink was to blame; in the past it had frequently been both excuse and reason. But he couldn't blame it on that this time, he hadn't succumbed to her attempts to get him to drink, but of course she hadn't held back. She'd had a skinful by the time they'd left the restaurant, which was all the more reason why he shouldn't have responded when she kissed him. He should have steered her back to the car, dropped her at her cottage and made a swift exit. But no, he was a cliché – the man who couldn't say no when sex was a possibility. But there he was creeping out next morning with her car keys and his own, waiting for one of the maintenance guys to arrive to drive him into town, pick up her car and drive it back for her and so avoid having to make that journey with her later in the day. The car was back and parked outside her cottage by eight in the morning, and Declan had studiously managed to avoid her ever since. He had, however, felt her. He'd felt her reaching out for him, her clinginess, he thinks now, like Catherine's – greedy as quicksand. He should have spotted it that day when she bowled up to his table at the pub, should have backed off, not agreed to coffee nor organised a second lunch, and as for dinner – well how stupid was that? But he hadn't realised she'd get so full on. If he let her get close again he would be up to his neck in an instant.

It wasn't all her fault, of course, he'd always been attracted to slightly domineering women – but attraction was different from compatibility. What a stroke of luck the hospital called at just the right time. All being well they will discharge him the day after tomorrow and he's promised himself a day, perhaps two, in Perth before driving back. As he drives south Lesley will already be home, hopefully making up with her husband and kissing her grandchildren. And the disastrous, although certainly not unpleasant, incident will be history.

—◆—

Alice has tried many times to write this letter, but almost six months ago she gave up. Why torture yourself with it, she had asked herself, when they don't want to hear from you, they will never forgive you and you shouldn't expect it? All you're doing is setting yourself up for disappointment. They never answered the earlier letters, why would this one be different? But since she's been at Benson's Reach some of her self-esteem has returned. Guilt and shame, for so long inextricably linked, are starting to separate out. She can see herself and what happened rather more clearly, even a little more dispassionately, than she has in the past. While she still feels the overbearing burden of guilt she can now claim her own grief and loss, as well as the rightness of having served her sentence. And so she has decided to try again, just one more time.

My Dear Jacinta, she begins, and then stops immediately. Should she drop the 'my'? Is this just a red rag? Will the 'my' only further alienate a daughter who hates her and cannot forgive her? But 'Dear Jacinta' sounds almost impersonal for a daughter whom she loves as she has loved her since the day she first held her in her arms. Be yourself, Alice murmurs, what have you got to lose? This will not run aground on the strength of a blasted pronoun – it's already aground. What you have to do now is haul it off the rocks.

My Dear Jacinta
It is more than a year since I last wrote to you, and perhaps you have been glad of my silence since then. Believe me I do understand how you must feel. I know you can't forgive me, and that you and I will never be able to recapture what we had before that terrible night . . .

She stops again. It's a glorious still evening and she is sitting at the table on her balcony writing by the light of two candle lamps. It's April now, and soon the weather will start to change; the mornings will grow cooler, the evenings are already closing in. On Wednesday she will open the café for the first time and test her newly acquired cookery skills as well as her ability to manage the staff and mix with customers. Perhaps it's this that has given her the courage to try again. She doesn't expect to be forgiven or accepted but she needs to reclaim the few things from the past that matter to her.

Alice leans back for a moment, taking in the stillness. Down at the main house the lights are low; Declan is in Perth and Ruby has driven Todd to a friend's house where he will stay overnight. He's been getting out a bit recently, since Johno and Bundy, two of his old school mates, turned up to volunteer to help at the festival. It's good for him, Alice thinks, he needs to be spending more time with people his own age. Most of the guests are probably eating out in town. The lights are on in cottage six but there is no sign of the occupant on the balcony outside. Out on the road she sees the lights of a car, which slows and turns into the drive. Ruby probably. Ruby – she must, she absolutely must, find the right time to come clean about the Google search. Alice reads through what she has written and thinks it trite. It is so unnatural, so careful, so reasonable, and so unlike how she feels.

Ruby pulls up outside the house, turns off the lights, locks the car door and instead of going inside she walks around it to the back and up the path towards Alice's cottage.

'Is it okay to come up, Alice?' she calls from the bottom of the steps. 'I'm sorry to disturb you but I need to talk to you.'

'Of course,' Alice says. 'I was about to make a cup of tea. Will you have some?' There is a copy of the local paper on the table and Alice pulls it across to cover her writing pad.

'Thanks, that would be lovely,' Ruby says as she joins her on the balcony and follows her into the cottage. 'These cottages are rather cosy, aren't they? I hope you don't feel excluded up here, though. You're welcome to stay in the house, you know.'

Alice switches on the kettle and turns to her with a smile. 'Thanks but I really love having this space to myself, after . . . well, for the last few years . . . um . . . green tea or English Breakfast?'

'Oh green, please,' Ruby says, and when the tea is made they take the pot and two cups and saucers out onto the balcony.

'Look, there's something I really want to discuss with you,' Ruby says as she settles into her chair.

The knot of anxiety in Alice's stomach rises through her chest to her throat where it seems to choke her.

'I'd quite like to say something first,' she cuts in, and continues without waiting for a response. 'I feel very bad about this, Ruby, but I need to come clean and tell you that I used the office computer to Google you.' Saying it is a relief that brings its own new terror. The doors are open now, and Ruby will, Alice is sure, admit to also having Googled her and will want to talk about what she discovered. It had to happen sometime but despite the fact that she's been thinking of little else for days, speaking it out loud seems sudden and shocking.

Ruby's eyebrows shoot up and a smile crosses her face. 'Oh dear, my cover is blown. One of the joys of being here has been being able to be myself with no one else's expectations or assumptions attached.'

Alice smiles. 'Well that doesn't have to change, but of course what I learned is pretty impressive and there is so much I want to ask you.' She is dizzy, shaking with anxiety, her head spinning with questions. Has Ruby come to tell her she must leave? Is she concerned that guests might recognise her and it will be bad for business? Does she think her unworthy of trust? She closes her eyes and takes a deep breath.

'Alice? Are you all right?' Ruby asks. 'You've gone awfully pale.'

'I'm fine,' she lies. 'I know you Googled me too. I know you found my record with the Prisoners Review Board. I should have told you . . .'

Ruby's forehead creases into a frown and she leans across the table. 'Hang on, Alice,' she says. 'I haven't done anything of the sort. I know nothing about you except what you and Declan have told me, which is really very little.'

The silence seems endless and Alice is blinded by confusion. 'Well someone Googled me because I saw it in the search history,' she says.

'Well, not me. Declan perhaps?'

Alice shakes her head. 'Declan has known everything from the start,' she says. 'He was in court the day I was sentenced. He wouldn't need to look for anything on the internet.'

'Well then I don't know,' Ruby says, 'but it certainly wasn't me.'

Alice stares at her in confusion. 'But who . . .'

'Alice, I've said, I don't know,' Ruby says, firmly now. 'But I can see you're very upset about it – do you want to tell me why?'

The air seems heavy with threat and the light of the lamps, which only minutes ago were barely sufficient for her to see her own writing, now seem to glare in her face. She can duck and hide but what's the point? 'Yes,' she says, taking a deep breath, 'I do have something I need to tell you.'

So now there is no going back, only forward to the truth and wherever that might take her. 'I arrived here a few days before you, Ruby, and ten days before that I was released from prison where I'd served a five year sentence for dangerous driving causing death.' The words seem to fall out and circle her, tightening in an iron grip around her chest as she waits for the look on Ruby's face to change. But Ruby's expression remains impassive.

'I see,' she says eventually. 'And is that it? Do you want to tell me more? You don't have to, it's entirely up to you.'

Alice is confused. Where is the shock, the dismay, the disapproval, the anger? 'Well first I should apologise,' she says cautiously. 'You're my employer, or half of my employer. I should have told you sooner. I could have told you any time since you got here but I didn't, despite your kindness to me, despite your trust and the fact that you have treated me more like a friend than an employee.'

'I'm sure you talked this through with Declan before I arrived,' Ruby says, 'so if I had a problem about it, it would be with him, as my business partner. But it's not a problem. I'm going on what I see, and what I see is an intelligent, responsible woman who's working hard to get her life together.'

Alice hesitates. What is supposed to happen now? she wonders. What will change? Will this always stand between them to her disadvantage? 'It's hard to believe we're having this conversation,' she says eventually.

Ruby picks up the teapot and pours them both some tea. 'Here,' she says, pushing a cup towards Alice. 'Drink some.'

Alice picks up the cup and inhales the sweet jasmine tones of the tea but doesn't drink, just puts it down on the table so sharply that it spills onto the newspaper and soaks through to the writing pad beneath it. She both wants and doesn't want to tell Ruby what happened. It would be the first time she's told anyone outside the prison.

'You don't have to tell me,' Ruby says again, sipping her own tea. 'But you might find it helps.'

Alice nods. 'I think so too,' she says. She turns the teacup around in her hand, staring down into the green gold tea. 'I'm an alcoholic,' she says, 'just like my father. He was a beautiful man when he was sober and a monster drunk. It was like living with two different people. He died of liver cancer when I was thirteen. My mother was a shy, quiet woman, always worried about what the neighbours might think. Her life was a battle for safety and respectability, and the need to protect both of us from the effects of his drinking.' She pauses. 'This is a very long, confused and self-indulgent story when I tell it to myself. I'll try to keep it free of excuses and justifications, but I think that to understand it you do need a bit of background.'

'Of course,' Ruby says. 'Take your time.'

'You'll have heard stories like this a million times in the years you've been working with women. I don't suppose mine is so different. I got pregnant when I was seventeen. My mother was devastated. She thought it was her fault for not bringing me up properly. Anyway, I wanted to keep the baby and I moved in with Mike, the baby's father. He was nearly ten years older than me and he'd been working in the north west – Wittenoom – but the mine had closed in '66, the previous year, because the workers were found to be inhaling dangerous levels of asbestos fibres. It was a big issue here . . .'

'I remember it,' Ruby says. 'I was still here in those days.'

Alice nods. 'Okay.' She takes a first sip of tea and then gulps it. 'Mike had moved back to Perth to look for work. His father was an alcoholic too. I suppose we thought we could look after each other and for a while we did. He was a very sweet natured man. Our son, Gary, was born early the next year, and we had a daughter, Jacinta. Several years later it slowly became clear that Mike was sick. He couldn't work, he had no energy, there were problems with his lungs, and he was diagnosed with mesothelioma. I was working full time, to keep us all, and he started drinking, and I began drinking with him. I suppose we'd both thought that because of our backgrounds we could drink quite a bit but we would know when to stop. Only of course we didn't.

'Mike went down that track faster than I did. The prescription drugs he was on made it worse. He became very moody and was always angry. It was a big change from how he'd been when we first got together. He was angry with the company, with the government and he couldn't seem to see or hear anything else. I was scared for him, but particularly for the kids, and it was that which drove me to AA. I had to stop drinking and I hoped that Mike would eventually come along. He was drinking every day. He wasn't well but he would wear himself out going on protests, and meeting with other former asbestos workers and come home incandescent with rage and incapable of doing anything.

'In the end I couldn't bear it any longer. I told him he must either go to AA or get out. He chose to get out. He was still around, he saw the kids from time to time, and that was usually okay. In the mid-eighties we got a divorce. He'd met a woman and they wanted to get married and move to Queensland. The kids had a few holidays up there with them. He'd cut back the drinking, and we were in touch from time to time when it was necessary.

'Well, to cut a long story short, Gary took off for a job in New Zealand when he was twenty-five, and Jacinta married Alan, and then she got pregnant. They had a girl, Jodie, and then, a couple of years later, they had Ella. I was so thrilled – two beautiful granddaughters. I had a decent job managing a bookshop and was just about keeping my head above water financially, and then one day, right out of the blue,

Mike turned up. His wife had left him some months earlier. I hadn't seen him for years and I couldn't believe the change in him. He was very sick – in fact he was dying and that's why his wife had left. She was much younger than him and she just couldn't cope.'

Alice stops and finishes her tea. 'You see I am making it very long after all,' she says, looking at Ruby. 'Sorry, but it all seems so important. It matters to me that you understand how it all happened. Of course this is just my version. I'm sure others would tell it differently . . .'

'I'm sure I'd be doing the same thing,' Ruby says.

'I haven't told it before, not like this. Just dribs and drabs to people when I was in prison. But it's always in my head, of course, always back and forth, trying to explain it to myself, trying to reduce my own guilt, trying to make it different, but of course none of that works. In the end I always come back to what I did. Nothing changes that.' She's silent for a while.

Ruby gets to her feet. 'I'm going to get more water for the tea,' she says.

Alice nods. She sits alone on the balcony, listening to the strangely comforting sounds of Ruby in the kitchen.

'I was thinking,' she says, when Ruby comes back, 'that all the time I was in prison, all the time I was telling this story to myself over and over again, I never imagined that when I eventually told the whole thing to someone else it would be in a place like this, that I would actually feel safe to tell it.'

Ruby puts the teapot back on the table and sits down. 'Well that's good, isn't it? Perhaps this place has something to do with it. I didn't want to come here, Alice, for all sorts of reasons that I'll explain to you some other time, but now I'm here I know it was the right thing to do. There's something so peaceful and nurturing about the landscape, I'd forgotten that. I only remembered how much everything hurt. Once I got here I felt it again. Old man Benson knew what he was doing when he put his stake in this stretch of land. You know, people told him he was overreaching himself at the time. That's how the place got its name, Benson's Reach.'

They sit in silence for a moment and there is a sudden change in the light as the door of cottage six opens and Lesley Craddock walks out onto her balcony. She leans on the rail, apparently straining to see down to the stretch of ground where Declan usually parks his car. Then she turns and goes back inside and closes the door. The two women look at each other and smile.

'She's out of luck again,' Ruby says. 'I fear he won't be back before she has to leave. Did you tell him she wanted to speak to him?'

'I did,' Alice nods. 'He didn't seem too keen on the idea.'

'Poor Lesley, but I think she's probably her own worst enemy. Anyway, are you going to tell me the rest of your story or have you had enough for one night?'

'No, no, I need to tell you now,' Alice says. 'I need to get through to the end.' She takes a deep breath and begins again. 'Well, to cut it as short as I can, Mike moved in with me. He wasn't drinking, he was too sick for that, and he was more like the man I'd married. I'd never wanted him back but once he was there I was glad of it. I nursed him for more than three years. He was very weak, and towards the end he was on oxygen most of the time, fading day by day. Jacinta and Alan helped when they could and the girls were beautiful with him. But eventually he died, at home, which was what we'd all wanted, especially him.

'At first I just had a sense of relief that the awfulness of watching him die was over and, frankly, that I was free from the burden of caring for him. I'd had to keep working part time as well and I was worn out. Anyway, after the funeral everyone came back to the house – you know, food, wine, reminiscences, tears, laughter, and then suddenly everyone had gone and I was alone with the mess of the wake, and still with the mess of his dying: the hospital bed, the oxygen cylinders, all that stuff. That night I walked around the house and all I could feel was despair. I was totally exhausted, as though everything had been sucked out of me. I felt incapable of getting out from under all the mess – not just the physical mess around me and the work of winding up his affairs, but the emotional mess inside. And all I could smell was the wine. I started to clear up the glasses, carry them out to the kitchen, pour away the dregs, load the dishwasher. But the smell was driving me insane. It was like a live presence demanding that I pay attention to it and eventually I did. I picked up a glass with a little wine left in it and sipped it. It was my first taste of alcohol in more than twenty years and it made me heave, but then I tried a bit more, and then a whole glass. I felt really nauseous and giddy, but that soon faded and I worked my way through the leftovers. The next morning I went to the bottle shop and bought more wine.

'I was drinking again. I wasn't thinking about it: no regrets, no self-flagellation and no worries about what it meant. No thought of going to AA, where I had been going once a month for years. I was anaesthetising myself, keeping my feelings at bay. I kept going to work and no one seemed to notice, or if they did they didn't say so. I kept it up for four weeks and then Jacinta and Alan wanted to go away for a weekend. Jodie was going to stay with a school friend, and they asked me if I would have Ella, who was six by then. I thought Ella was just what I needed. And I do remember thinking, "I mustn't drink this weekend because I'm responsible for a child." But of course I did.

'It was a terrible weekend, wet and windy, lashing storms. Ella was a bit snuffly when Jacinta dropped her off on Friday, and by late on Saturday she'd got a temperature and I had nothing to give her. So I wrapped her up well and put her in the car. I thought I would go to the pharmacy and come back via the drive-through bottle shop. I'd been drinking slowly all day and I was sure I was fine, but of course I wasn't. We never made it to the bottle shop. I overshot an intersection on a red light and a car coming from my left hit the tail of my car and I swung and skidded across the intersection and rolled the car on the opposite island.'

Ruby smothers a gasp.

Alice looks down at the table, at the wet patch on the newspaper and writing pad, and the letter that will never be written.

'And the other driver . . .?'

'A young man,' Alice says, 'in his thirties.'

'I can't begin to imagine how you must have felt, how you still feel . . .'

'Ruby,' Alice says, lifting her eyes to face her now. 'Ruby, the man, he survived. A cut on his head, severe bruising and some damage to his shoulder that had to be rebuilt . . .'

'Then who . . .' Ruby begins, before realisation crosses her face. 'Oh my God . . . no, surely not, not . . .?'

Alice nods. 'Yes, it was Ella. I killed her, Ruby. I killed my granddaughter that night. It would have been terrible enough if it had been that young man and it so easily could have been. How crazy was I? How arrogant! But it wasn't him, it was Ella, six years old, wearing red woollen tights and a check dress that I'd bought for her in Target and wrapped up in a blanket with a little red beanie pulled down over her ears. Is it any wonder that I was twice refused parole? Is it any wonder that no one in my family wants anything to do with me? I killed a child, Ruby, an innocent little girl with her whole life in front of her. And I killed a part of my daughter, my other granddaughter and my son-in-law at the same time. There is no forgiveness for this, not from anyone, most of all not from myself. In AA we say 'one day at a time', just get through one day at a time, and it works. To look further ahead is too hard; the future is too huge, too scary.'

She stops suddenly, relieved that she has told it at last, but exhausted by the emotion of reliving it all. 'And so that's what I've been doing for the past five ... nearly six years. Getting through one day at a time. But then I came here and I began to glimpse bits of the future: a home, a job, what it's like to have friends, to be trusted again. And then I close my eyes and that vision disappears because I can really only have one day at a time and even that is more than I deserve.'

Fourteen

Lesley, driving home on Sunday, has trouble keeping her eyes open. She's been up since dawn, outside on the balcony searching for a sign that Declan might have returned during the night, but there was none, and she knew she had to leave this morning. For one thing there was a long-standing booking for her cottage as from today, but more importantly she had said she'd be at Simon and Lucy's for lunch with the family and she could tell they were all getting edgy with her. She'd intended to go home on Friday but had waited as long as she could in the hope of seeing Declan.

'Can't you give me his mobile number?' she'd asked Paula on Friday. 'You must know it.'

'I *don't*,' Paula had said. 'I told him when he first came I'd need to have it for emergencies, and he simply said, "What sort of emergencies do you have in mind?" and I couldn't think of anything so that was that.'

'Well you must be able to get it, find it in the office or something?'

Paula had shaken her head. 'No way, not with that nosy Alice hanging around all the time and Madam Ruby, the Grand Inquisitor, asking questions about what I'm doing.

The other day I'd just slipped round the back for a cigarette and suddenly she's there, right in my face. "Benson's Reach is smoke free, Paula," she says. "That applies to the staff as well as the guests."'

Lesley had hesitated. She had already noticed Paula's furtive lighting up when she thought no one was looking. But now, more than ever, she needs an ally here. 'So did you smoke when Mrs Benson was here?' she'd asked.

''Course not,' Paula had said, 'but the Grand Inquisitor isn't Catherine, is she? And it's not really her place – she'll be gone soon. Strutting about as though she owns it – who does she think she is?'

'Well she does own it, or most of it, doesn't she?'

'Not for long. She'll be out of here with the money as soon as she can and back to London. She's that type, you can tell.'

Clearly the chances of getting the number were nil and all that Lesley could do was wait. And wait she did, to no avail. But Declan will certainly be back there next week – before they open the café. She'll call the main number, many times if she has to, until she gets to speak to him. Now she just has to get home and face the first dreaded conversation with Gordon. Maybe she'll go straight to Simon and Lucy's place. It'll be easier to see him the first time with the rest of the family around. She has to try to keep it in her head that although she's done something very wrong Gordon doesn't know that, and what he doesn't know can't hurt him. The main thing is to behave exactly as normal. And, she reminds herself, it's partly his fault anyway – after all, if he hadn't tried to take over her life she'd never have gone away.

The road is wide and straight, lined on either side with dense bush, and there is not much traffic about. Lesley yawns and rubs her eyes. She's been going for an hour and a half, just under halfway there, and ahead a sign points to petrol and a café in 500 metres. Coffee is just what she needs and she slows down and pulls off the road into the car park. The café is decidedly seedy and smells of meat pies and sweat. Lesley buys a coffee and a rather sad looking chocolate muffin, takes them outside and heads towards a seat in the sun. The muffin is considerably better than the coffee but as she eats it she realises that the horrible emptiness in her gut has nothing to do with food or the lack of it; it's a deeper sense of emptiness about herself and the fact that these weeks away from home haven't provided any answers, just simply added to her confusion. There were moments at Benson's Reach when she'd tried to concentrate on how Gordon could organise his life so that he didn't intrude on hers, or on what she really wanted as a plan for the future. But the future now, she believes, includes Declan and that thought occupies her mind most of the time. Fleetingly it occurs to her that some people might think her recent behaviour obsessive. Maybe she should have talked to someone, a therapist, perhaps, but it's too late for that, all she can do is get through today, and tomorrow she'll call Declan, get things sorted out with him. After that who knows? Just try to concentrate on today, she tells herself. Best to get back on the road as soon as possible.

The coffee is hot but lacking in everything except bitterness and she gets up to walk to the car thinking she'll finish it as she drives. The bleak open space of the car park is drenched with blinding morning sunlight and she blinks against it. She is fumbling in her pocket for the car keys when she stumbles and suddenly the ground rears up and hits her in the face, and she is flat on the tarmac, splattered with scalding coffee and with the distinct feeling that her face has been smashed to pieces.

Lesley lies there for a moment, eyes closed, groaning softly, fighting back tears, then rolls onto her side in an attempt to get up, but everything hurts too much.

'Don't,' says a voice just behind her, 'don't try to get up yet. Just take your time.'

Lesley rocks back slightly and lies down again, on her back this time, squinting up at several anxious faces looking down at her against the background of the brilliant blue sky.

A woman stoops down beside her and takes her hand. 'Wait until you're ready, dear,' she says. 'It's such a shock, falling, when you get to our age.'

Lesley's first reaction is dismay that this woman with the lined face, untidy beige hair and a dull beige dress thinks that they are the same age. She is about to protest that she is only fifty-eight when the woman gestures to a man standing behind her.

'The pillow, Ted, give me the pillow,' she says. And the man silently hands it over and she gently lifts Lesley's shoulder and slips the pillow under her head and neck. Lesley thanks her, rubs a hand across her face and finds it streaked with blood. The woman tugs a wad of tissues from a box and passes them to her. It's clear that her nose is bleeding, and when she lifts her head she sees that her top is soaked in coffee, and she has ripped the knees of her cotton trousers. Everything is spinning and she closes her eyes and drops her head back onto the pillow, waiting for it to stop. Eventually the world seems to right itself again and after various suggestions from the onlookers she is able to sit up. Most fade away now, just the beige woman, Ted, and a young girl from the café remain.

'You can come inside and get cleaned up if you like,' the girl says.

But the smell of meat pies is not something Lesley thinks she can revisit right now.

'Thanks,' she says, 'I'll just get cleaned up in the toilet, but a drink of water would be nice.' The girl hurries away and returns with a bottle of water.

'It's this tarmac,' the man says to the girl, kicking at a rough ridge in the surface. 'Bloody dangerous, the lady probably tripped on it. You should get it fixed.'

'I'll tell the boss,' the girl says, and heads off back to the café.

'You could sue them, you know,' he says, leaning down towards Lesley and peering at her. 'Made a shocking mess of your face.'

'Shut up, Ted,' says the beige woman, 'that's the last thing she wants to hear right now.'

Lesley struggles to sit up.

'Let me help you,' the woman says. 'My name's Marion, by the way. I'll come with you to the toilets. You'll probably be a bit unsteady.' And she takes Lesley's arm, helps her to her feet and steers her towards the toilets, talking comfortingly about there being a lot of blood but probably no real damage.

Lesley cups her hands under the cold tap and plunges her face into the water several times before burying it in the towel that Marion has ordered Ted to bring from the car. Does this woman travel with a complete set of linen? she wonders.

'Just a bit of luck I have things with me,' Marion says, watching Lesley as she examines her face in the flyblown mirror. 'We're on holiday, on our way to Margaret River, but I like to have my own pillows and towels. You never know what the place will be like, do you? I don't take chances with pillows. See, it's not too bad, is it, a bit of gravel rash, and I think you're going to have a nasty bruise across that cheekbone, but the nosebleed has stopped now.'

Lesley wants to point out that her face looks like a war zone. Her nose is crimson – rapidly turning blue – and in addition to the cheekbone her chin is red raw and there is already a purplish mark on her forehead. Her knees are bleeding and she has ripped a shirt she bought only last week. But she manages to restrain herself.

'You've been very kind,' she says, 'but I don't want to hold you up. I think I can manage now. I'll get back on the road – be home before too long.'

Marion is aghast. 'But you can't *drive*! What about concussion? You might just pass out and veer across the road, who knows . . .?'

'I'll be fine,' Lesley says firmly. 'I'm not dizzy or anything now.' She hands Marion back the towel. 'Sorry about the blood on the towel. Thank you so much for your help.' She turns towards the door.

'You really shouldn't, you know,' Marion, says, pale blue eyes fierce with anxiety. 'It's not very responsible of you—'

'I said I'll be fine – thank you,' Lesley says firmly, and walks away as quickly as she dares in the direction of her car.

'Well really . . .' Marion says.

And as Lesley slips into the driving seat she can hear Marion reciting the details of her ingratitude to Ted. She grasps the steering wheel with both hands and rests her forehead on them. The fall has totally disarmed her, wrecked the veneer of confidence she had tried to establish in order to face Gordon and the children. Now all she feels is guilt and loneliness – something she has never felt before. She is alone with her secret, lacking even a conversation with Declan to help her make sense of it all, unable to confide in anyone. It seems to her now that in going away she cracked open the cocoon of security in which she had for so long reigned supreme. That could have been a good thing had she used the experience wisely; instead she wasted it in diversions, and then capped it off by sleeping with Declan.

Lesley is not used to being in the wrong. She has thrived for years on being right, on being a good wife to Gordon, a good mother to her children, a good daughter, and as far as possible a good sister, albeit at a distance. Her sense of rightness has defined her. She is the one to whom people come for advice, for help and solutions. And through it all she has greeted any hint that she might be wrong about something or someone with a dismissive smile. But even as she reminds herself that this all began with Gordon being so selfish, she knows that to be in the right over this would look very different indeed.

Lifting her head she stares at her face in the driving mirror. She looks appalling. She can't go straight to Simon and Lucy's place now, she'll have to go home first and get cleaned up, make an effort to look more like her old self. But she fears that her guilt will cut through her attempts to appear normal. In the mirror she can see Marion standing with Ted near their car, staring at the back of hers, and as she watches she sees a look of concern cross Marion's face and she begins to walk in her direction. Lesley switches on the engine, releases the handbrake, slips into gear and moves out of the forecourt towards the road just in time. Back on the road again, she turns on the radio and fills the car with the sounds of an orchestra playing *The Blue Danube*. Strauss she thinks, good tunes, this will help. Anything, anything to drown out how she feels. But not even Strauss can do that because as the music swells and fades and swells again, it all comes surging back and the tears begin to flow, burning her sore face as she drives.

— ❦ —

'Crikey! You look terrible,' Simon says, opening the door to her. 'What's happened to your face?'

'I fell over. In a petrol station on the way home,' Lesley says, stepping inside with the big canvas bag into which she has packed some gifts she bought for the children, along with honey, wine, cheese and pâté.

There is a clatter of feet along the passage and the twins hurl themselves at her.

'Nana, Nana, Nana's back,' Tim croons, butting her hip with his head. 'Did you bring us something?'

Ben, the quiet one, gives her a huge grin and grabs her hand to lead her through to the kitchen where Lucy and Karen are making salads.

'Oh your poor face, Lesley,' Lucy gasps, wiping her hands on a tea towel and coming across the room to kiss her.

Karen, her lips pursed into a familiar disapproving pussy's bum, stares at her from a distance, hand on her hip, 'What did you do, Mum?'

Lesley, hoping that sympathy might banish disapproval, sighs, shrugs, explains once more, unloads the twins' gifts from her bag and starts to unpack the rest of the contents onto the kitchen table. 'No Nick?' she asks.

'Gone to the bottle shop,' Karen says, 'he'll be back shortly.'

Lesley looks around again. When she had got back to the house the place was locked up and Gordon's four-wheel-drive was in the garage. She'd assumed that he was already at Simon and Lucy's place but there is no sign of him here.

'Glass of wine?' Simon asks, holding up a bottle of chilled semillon.

'Please, yes,' Lesley nods. 'Where's your father?'

'Oh he's gone,' Simon says, pouring wine into her glass. 'Left on Thursday.'

'Left?'

'Early Thursday morning. He should be there by now.'

Lesley takes the glass from him. 'Where?' she asks. 'Where's he gone?'

'Up north,' Simon says, looking at her in surprise. 'He emailed you. That work he's been wanting to do with the Land Council. He's gone to the Kimberley.'

'He emailed?' Lesley asks, confused by what this new development might mean.

'Early in the week,' Karen says, irritably.

'But he should've called.'

'Ha! Well a lot of good that would have done seeing you haven't been answering your phone or returning messages. I expect he got fed up with having to speculate about what exactly you were doing and when you were coming home,'

Karen says, ripping the leaves from a lettuce she has just pulled from the fridge.

Lesley's initial shock turns to relief – a couple of weeks, maybe, before he'll be back, time to get herself together, talk to Declan, work out what to do. 'I said I'd be here for lunch today, I said so to Simon . . .'

'You didn't answer your phone or call back when I rang on Friday evening or yesterday,' Karen snaps. 'But perhaps I should be used to that by now.'

'Look, Karen—' Lesley begins, knowing she is on shaky ground.

'Stop!' Simon says, holding up his hand as if he's controlling traffic. 'We don't need an argument, Kaz, Mum's back now.'

'Well how gracious of her,' Karen says, continuing to torture the lettuce. 'Pardon me if I don't join in the applause.'

For a terrible moment Lesley can hear herself in Karen's voice: her sarcasm when things don't go her way, the sharp tongue that often gets away from her when she's hurt or angry.

'Loosen up,' Simon says, 'that's not going to help.'

'No,' Lesley says, feeling her face flush. 'No, she's right. I'm sorry, Karen, I'm sorry, everyone. I've been going through a bit of a bad time and I haven't been very thoughtful. I owe you all an apology.'

'Accepted,' Nick says, swinging in through the back door with a dozen beers, and doing a double-take at the sight of her face. 'Hmm. What's the other bloke look like?'

Lesley smiles at him, thankful for the interruption. The tension seems to be broken. Lucy starts to examine the cheeses and pate, and the boys, having opened their presents, sprawl across the floor throwing wrapping paper at each other. Karen gives her a long look, nods and turns her attention back to what's left of the lettuce.

'So when's Dad coming back?' Lesley asks, trying to keep her tone as light as possible. 'This week, next?'

Simon, who has just opened one of Nick's beers, takes a swig from the bottle and looks awkwardly across at his sister. 'Ah well, quite a while, I think. Look, you need to check the email, Mum, but it could be three months or more?'

'Or more,' Karen says without looking up. 'He'll be checking email at least once a week but a lot of the time he'll be out of mobile range.'

'Three months . . . but that's . . .'

'Ages, yes,' Karen says, 'but then you've been gone more than a month yourself.'

Lesley ignores the jibe. 'Is he on his own?'

'He's working with people up there.'

'But he went alone?'

'Of course,' Karen says. 'Who else would he go with? You'd already said you wouldn't go.'

The tension is back now and with a vengeance.

'He took Bruce, though,' Lucy says in an apparent attempt to break it once again. 'He said he'd keep him company on cold nights,' and she gives an awkward little laugh.

'Bruce?'

'He's got a dog,' Simon explains, 'an abandoned Jack Russell that adopted him when he was out cycling. Cute, really, got a face that looks as though he understands every word you say. Anyway, the barbecue's doing well now so you and I can get cooking, Nick,' and the two men saunter off out of the kitchen, with Tim and Ben close behind them.

'Three months,' Lesley says again.

'It might be less,' Lucy says.

'But he can't just—'

'Why not?' Karen cuts in. 'Why can't he? Why shouldn't he? He's wanted to do this for ages and now he's doing it. At least he told us, which is more than you did.'

Fifteen

he café is half full – not bad for breakfast on the first day of trading. Alice had decided to open on a Wednesday to allow time for them all to get into the swing of it before the first weekend, but it's busier than they had expected or even hoped.

'It's a really good start,' Ruby says, 'and Alice has done a terrific job.'

Declan, tucking into a potato cake with crispy bacon and a poached egg, nods energetically. 'I knew she would,' he says. 'Alice has very high standards.'

Ruby watches him for a moment, wondering whether or not to broach the subject and deciding eventually that she will. 'We talked while you were away, Alice and I,' she says. 'I know what happened, the drinking, the accident, prison, all of it.'

He looks up from his plate, sits up straighter and pats his lips with his serviette. 'I see.'

'You could have told me, you know. It's not a problem.'

'But I didn't know that at the start,' he says. 'I wanted to protect her, and I suppose myself as well. I needed an ally.'

'In case *I* turned out to be a problem?'

'Exactly.'

187

She smiles. 'Fair enough. But just for the record I think bringing her here was a fine decision, generous, thoughtful and sound judgment.'

He smiles and blushes slightly. 'Thanks, but I really should have told you earlier. Once I realised that . . . well, that it wouldn't be a problem.'

Ruby shrugs. 'We've made a good start,' she says, 'that's what matters. It could have been very different . . .' She hesitates, glancing across to the counter where Leonie, whom Alice has employed to help manage the orders and the table service, seems involved in some sort of altercation with Paula. 'Oh dear, I think we've got a problem now, but hopefully Alice will sort it out.'

They watch as Paula, not satisfied with whatever Leonie has told her, demands to speak to Alice, who is summoned from the kitchen. There is a short, apparently hostile conversation and Paula, obviously affronted, tosses her head in annoyance, slaps some coins down on the counter and, picking up the order number Leonie has given her, heads straight for their table.

'The hide of that woman,' she says, pulling out a chair next to Ruby. 'You need to do something about that Alice and her helper. They charged me for my coffee, like I was just some customer, bloody cheek. I told them both I was going to take it up with you.'

Ruby and Declan exchange a glance.

'Well you *are* just a customer in here, Paula,' Declan says firmly. 'We all are. Did you read the notice I put up in the staff room?'

'Yeah, but I thought that was for the new people and the casuals,' Paula says, fiddling with the scrunchie that is holding her ponytail in place.

'It applies to all of us,' Ruby says. 'Even you.'

'You're kidding. Well I bet it doesn't apply to you.'

'Actually it does,' Ruby says, 'although that's really none of your business. Benson's Café has to become self-supporting, a viable business in its own right. It can't do that if everyone who works here gets their coffee and meals for free.'

'Bloody hell,' Paula says, her face flushing. 'What sort of place is this? In Catherine's day I always got free coffee or tea whenever I wanted it.'

'You get that now,' Declan says, 'same as you always did. There's always tea and coffee in the staff room, and you, Paula, have the added freedom to make yourself something in the house kitchen whenever you want. That hasn't changed.'

Paula, visibly annoyed, sits back in her chair, folds her arms and glares at him across the table. 'Can't see the difference myself.'

Ruby turns towards her, her own annoyance mounting. 'Well whether you see it or not, Paula, is immaterial. *We* know the difference and *we* get to decide.' She doesn't like her own tone as she says it. She has had a number of difficult staff in her time, many of whom were far less efficient and more awkward to deal with than Paula, but right now she can't recall anyone whom she has found so damned annoying.

They sit in silence for a moment and Paula flashes a killer look at Leonie when she brings her take-away coffee and doughnut to the table. Then she straightens up, takes the lid off the beaker, empties two sachets of sugar into the coffee and stirs it with unnecessary vigour.

'Anyway,' she says, 'I really came in here to talk to you about my job. I've been thinking I'd like a bit of a change.'

Ruby holds her breath. Is Paula going to leave? It would be a great relief if she did. On the other hand it will be hard to find a replacement who measures up to Paula's standards.

'What sort of change?' Declan asks. 'Are you planning to leave us?'

''Course not,' Paula says, twisting the gold chain with the Kylie charm that she wears around her neck. 'No, I was thinking I'd like to take over from Fleur. Nice job that, and quite a bit more money I should think?'

Declan looks like a deer caught in the headlights, and Ruby holds his gaze and shakes her head, hoping the movement is imperceptible to Paula alongside her.

'Well . . . that's difficult . . .' Declan begins.

Ruby thinks she has never seen anyone so obviously fishing around in desperation for something to say. She clears her throat. 'Actually, Paula,' she says, 'we're rethinking the management of the gift shop and the production of the lavender products right now and we haven't come to a decision yet. But it's good that you've told us you're interested. Just leave it with us and we'll come back to you when we've decided what we want to do.'

Paula looks affronted. 'No one told me you were going to change things,' she says.

'No one else knows yet,' Ruby says. 'And until we decide how we want to run things it's not appropriate to discuss it, but we need to work out a plan for the gift shop and with Fleur moving on, it's a good time to rethink things.'

'Well I'd've thought I'd been here long enough to be told about things that are likely to happen,' Paula says. 'Catherine used to tell me everything.'

'Did she really?' Ruby says, holding Paula's eyes in a fierce, unblinking gaze.

Paula looks away and fidgets in her chair. 'I did a lot of confidential work for her,' she says.

Ruby does not relax. 'What did that involve exactly?' she asks.

Paula hesitates, flushing, not making eye contact with either of them now. 'It's difficult,' she says, eventually. 'Some of it was, well . . . personal.'

'And you can't give us an example?'

'It was between Catherine and me,' she says, clearly aware that she's trapped herself. 'I don't like to talk about it.'

'Well if it was personal that's not really our business,' Ruby says. 'But as far as operations at Benson's Reach are concerned, we have been looking at everyone's pay and conditions. We plan to make some adjustments, draw up proper job descriptions and provide you all with new contracts before too long. I'm sure you'll be glad to see some improvements there.'

Paula is apparently unsure what to make of this, which was of course Ruby's intention; it will, she hopes, deliver a warning shot.

Paula shrugs. 'I suppose so, but I've been here a long time and I think I have certain rights because of that.'

Declan opens his mouth and shuts it again on a signal from Ruby. Any sort of response to Paula's last remark could take them into choppy waters. They sit in silence until Paula, with a huge artificial sigh, picks up her coffee and doughnut and stands up.

'Well, I'd better be getting on, I suppose,' she says, and she is about to walk away when she stops and turns back. 'By the way, Declan, Mrs Craddock rang earlier when I was doing the office floor. She wanted to speak to you. She said it was important so I looked up your mobile number in Catherine's old teledex and gave it to her. She was chasing you all last week.' And she gives them both a disapproving nod and weaves her way between the tables and out of the café.

Declan sinks his head into his hands and Ruby lets out a hiss of irritation. 'Since when has Paula been answering the office phone?'

He shakes his head. 'I don't think she's done it before, but recently she seems to think her duties extend beyond the cleaning, the laundry and provisioning the cottages.'

'Well we'll have to stop her doing it in future. I'll talk to her about it, if you like, but you need to speak to her about giving out your number. She really is a pain in the bum.'

'And Fleur's job?'

Ruby pulls a face. 'There's no way we could give Paula that job. I'm sure she could manage the production but there's all the rest of it, the bookkeeping, the ordering – I'm not sure about that, but I do know she couldn't do all the PR and the demonstrations that Fleur does with the visitors. Perhaps we can find a way to reshape her job so it makes her feel a bit more important, and I'm working on the contracts so that all the staff will get the full award rate. Hopefully that will satisfy her.'

'Staff,' Declan says, 'I hate this part of it. It would be so easy if we didn't have staff.'

'And easier still if we didn't have guests or customers,' Ruby says with a grin. 'Let's drown our troubles in another cup of coffee. I'll go and order.' And she gets up and heads for the counter just as Declan's mobile phone begins to ring.

❧

On nights like this it's the stillness that Gordon loves. You can be with other people but still feel completely and blissfully alone. Lying flat on his back gazing up at the vast inky blackness of the sky scattered with more stars than you can ever see in town, he tries to remember when he last did this – twenty years ago, at least. When he was younger it had been part of the job – checking out various sites, with a surveyor, sometimes a couple of others. He remembers one time – he'd have been in his thirties – the company had taken on a new surveyor, a woman, a really attractive woman in her mid-forties. There had been plenty of blokey joshing and jockeying about her before the first field trip but when it came to it he and the other three men had just felt awkward and stupid. In the truck on the first day they'd been unable to think of anything else except that she was a woman, and to manage their own awkwardness they'd focused the entire conversation on her – how weird it must be for her out there in the bush with three randy blokes. How did she cope with sleeping in the open? Was she okay with snakes and spiders? – on and on and on and on until she . . . Vivienne, her name was . . . Vivienne finally called their bluff.

'Look, guys,' she'd said in a tone that combined total self-confidence with mild boredom, 'I think we should get one thing clear. This isn't awkward for me. I've done trips like this dozens of times with blokes who make you guys look like school kids. But it's obviously awkward for you, so why don't you just pull over, hop out into the trees and have a nice little jerkoff about it together, and then we can get back on the road and behave like adults.'

There'd been a long painful silence after that until one of the others had mumbled something under his breath.

'What?' Vivienne had barked, 'What did you say?'

'Sorry, I said sorry,' the guy said, clearly this time. 'Sorry, I . . . we behaved like dickheads. Sorry.'

Gordon and the others had mumbled their apologies, and the tension had subsided. An hour or so later they were talking about the place they were heading for, laughing and later even singing.

Now as he lies here – his bedroll outside his tent so he can feel the night air on his face, hear the sounds of the bush – Gordon remembers the third night of that trip, in a place not unlike this one. They had cooked sausages over the fire, heated up baked beans and sat around with beers and as the evening wore on the conversation slowed and they drifted off to their tents. It was a still, cold night and he had slipped into his sleeping bag and lay there wide awake, wondering about Vivienne, wondering whether he had misread the looks she'd given him in the light of the fading fire. Not that it mattered anyway, he was far too cautious to risk anything. And suddenly a shadow fell across the opening of his tent and she was there, crawling in, swift and silent as a bush creature, unzipping his sleeping bag, sliding her long, cool legs alongside his. 'What the . . .?' he had started to say, but she had put her hand over his mouth, shaking her head, her hair, no longer tied neatly back, brushing his face in the darkness as she slid one leg across his and shifted her weight onto him and tugged to free his penis from the pants from which it was eager to escape.

'Shh,' was all she said, taking her hand from his mouth and holding a finger to his lips as she raised her hips and slipped him inside her.

It was probably every man's fantasy, Gordon thinks now, the sexy older woman, experienced, confident, silent and so unexpected. Sometime later she'd left as swiftly as she had arrived and he was alone again, wondering what next, what about tomorrow night, why me? They hadn't exchanged a word and that had disturbed him, but in the light of day he knew it was right. Words were what they exchanged as colleagues, but this was different. Silence quarantined day from night, it was a boundary that neither of them crossed. The next night he'd lain awake waiting but she didn't come, nor any of the following four nights. But then, on the last night, she came back just as before, and the following day they sat beside each other as colleagues on the flight back to Perth, talking about the possibilities of the site for future exploration.

He had been married to Lesley for seven years then, Karen was a particularly fractious three-year-old and Lesley was five months pregnant with Simon. On his first night at home he broke out in a cold sweat, wondering what Lesley would do if she ever found out, terrified by what he stood to lose. But there were other nights over the years when he had longed, not for Vivienne, but for what she represented: freedom, the unfettered life, the silence that brought a kind of anonymity, the intense uncomplicated intimacy of strangers.

Well one thing's for sure, Gordon tells himself now, gazing up at the grandeur of the night sky – it's not going to happen tonight, out here with Fred from the Land Council and Ray the tracker. Bruce, with his damp, cold nose, is the only one who has aspirations to share his sleeping bag tonight, but what if . . .? Well, of course he wouldn't fight off any present day Vivienne who wanted to unzip him. He is shocked suddenly to realise that as she was about ten years older than him at the time, she must now be in her mid-seventies. He wonders if she ever thinks about him, if she even remembers him. He'd like to think she does, that he was special, but he thinks it more likely that he was just one of many.

Sixteen

By the end of her first weekend of trading Alice is feeling cautiously confident that she has the right mix of staff and the right menu for the café. The figures have been surprisingly good all week and over the weekend the place was packed and they were rushed off their feet. By the time they closed at five o'clock on Sunday everyone was exhausted and when Declan turned up with champagne they had locked the doors and sat down with their feet up on chairs, chewing over everything that had happened. As the staff finally trailed off home Ruby, Declan and Todd were ready for their evening meal but Alice wanted nothing more than a cup of tea in the stillness of her cottage. Having made it up the hill she flopped down onto her bed thankful that tomorrow the café would be closed and she need do nothing at all. Flat on her back, arms outstretched and still wearing her shoes, she fell into a deep and comforting sleep in which she dreamed she had grown huge, white, angel-like wings and was flying in large leisurely circles looking down on Benson's Reach, the town and surrounding countryside, observing people scurrying about below. It was a rather better dream than usual.

It was morning when she woke, amazed to find that she

had slept for almost ten hours, barely stirring and still wearing her shoes. She wandered into the shower, groggy with sleep, and stood under the stream of hot water waiting for it to bring her fully awake, thinking only of the indecent amount of water she was using. Now, as she takes her mug of coffee out onto the balcony, she feels almost restored to normal. She is too late for the kangaroos this morning but not too late to enjoy watching the other early signs of life: Ruby returning from her walk, Declan and Todd eating toast on the back verandah, and two lots of guests loading their bags into their cars with the reluctance of people about to head home after a holiday. A white van and a small flatbed pick-up make their way slowly up the drive – Phil and Ray, the contract workers whom Declan has taken on to deal with maintenance, lay a couple of new paths, and prepare for the music festival. They are followed, minutes later, by Paula, who parks her car alongside Declan's and heads for the staff room.

Alice is curious about Paula: the obsession with everything pink, her assumptions about her role here at Benson's, her efficiency and her unerring ability to alienate people. It's a strange combination of traits. The night that Ruby had come to the cottage it had been to ask Alice to work with her on the job descriptions and contracts for the staff. When they sat down to it a few days later Paula's was the first.

'I want to formalise the arrangements with her as for everyone else,' Ruby had said. 'Despite the fact that she can be so frustrating to deal with she's a valuable member of the staff and she's currently being paid below the award rate. We need to fix that and create a clear job description which, by definition, should also make it clear what's off limits. I'm sure that like everyone else here, Paula's been affected by Catherine's death, but I wonder if she hasn't also used it to redefine her job. You see, I think that Paula sees herself as the keeper of the flame, Catherine's flame, as though it's up to her to keep that burning. She just has this intrusive way of going about it.'

It hadn't been easy. They had spent an inordinate amount of time trying to shape a job description that would enable Paula to feel that her work was valued, and define specific areas in which she had some authority, at the same time creating boundaries that would give them a benchmark for managing her in future. Alice had never worked through a process like that before and felt she learned a lot from it, but her level of tolerance for Paula seems to be lower than Ruby's; perhaps, she thinks, because she herself feels she lacks the authority to deal with her. She suspects that while undoubtedly being affected by Catherine's death, Paula has probably always been just the way she is now. In a lifetime of work in shops, and then years in prison, Alice had come face-to-face with people she had never expected to encounter, but she had never come across anyone quite like Paula. The outstanding work performance combined with the unerring ability to get under everyone's skin seems to Alice to be unique. And she's cautious too, because she's now convinced that Paula was behind the Google search, and she fears what she might do with that information.

But, since talking to Ruby and with the success of her first week's trading, Alice also feels she is grasping at a new sense of herself as a stronger person weathered by years of grief and incarceration.

'You've paid your debt,' Ruby had said, 'and of course you'll go on paying it for the rest of your life, but it doesn't mean that you've lost your rights as a citizen, nor the right to want things for yourself.'

Outside the office Alice sees Declan waving off the couple who have just vacated cottage two, and Todd, whose plaster was removed a week ago, taking the paperwork from the driver of a delivery truck. 'I'm part of this,' she tells herself, 'a really useful part. I've been given a chance so maybe what I need to do now is to give myself a chance.'

Later, towards midday, she fetches her pad of notepaper, returns to the balcony table and reads the first lines of the letter she had started to Jacinta the night that Ruby came to see her. The ink is smudged, the paper stained and crumpled from the spilled tea, and the words she has written infuriate her. Angrily she rips this and then the other damaged pages from the pad and tears them into shreds. Then she picks up her pen, writes the address of Benson's Reach at the top of the page and begins again.

Dear Jacinta

I was recently released and am now living and working at the above address. I doubt you will want to have any contact and I respect that, however I would like to have my personal possessions which I assume you still have: my books and clothes, my jewellery, and particularly my mother's things, which were packed in the leather suitcase with her initials on it.

Please let me know what sort of arrangements you would like me to make to collect these. I can arrange for them to be collected if you could let me know when and where would be convenient for you. I am not going to turn up on your doorstep but will ask a friend to pick them up for me.

As always I send my love to you, Jodie and Alan. My thoughts are with you always.

Mum

She puts down her pen, takes a deep breath and reads through it again, surprised by the cool assertiveness of it compared to the grief-stricken pleas for forgiveness that she has sent in the past. She has asked for nothing that is not hers, she hasn't begged or pleaded or thrown herself on her daughter's mercy. It is painful to be writing like this but it's also powerful: she is taking back something for herself. But she knows she must send it now, in case she caves in later. Inside the cottage she addresses an envelope, finds a stamp, and goes out to the top of the balcony steps. It's just after midday, and most days around this time Declan, Ruby or one of the staff drives into town to collect the mail. Alice runs down the steps and walks briskly to the back door of the house and into the kitchen where Todd is studying a recipe book and writing a list of ingredients.

'Has anyone been for the mail yet?' Alice asks.

Todd looks up, shaking his head. 'I'm going with Declan in a minute. We're getting the mail and stuff for me to cook pizza tonight.'

'Sounds good,' she says, 'am I invited?'

'You're guest of honour,' he says, getting up and stuffing the list into his pocket. 'You taught me how to do it.'

'Are you going to make the dough yourself or buy some bases?'

Todd looks shocked. 'Make it, of course,' he says. 'That bought stuff tastes like old thongs.'

'Good on you,' she says, and holds the letter out to him. 'Can you be sure and post this for me when you're in town? Don't forget it, please. It's really important that it goes today.'

He takes the envelope and gives her a mock salute. 'Done,' he says. 'Pizza, seven o'clock. Don't forget.' And he limps out of the kitchen and along the verandah to where Declan is waiting for him in the car.

Declan watches as Todd hops down the steps and begins his lopsided walk towards him. What a difference, he thinks, remembering the anxious boy who had appeared at the office door wanting to talk to him a few weeks earlier. Todd now seems confident and at home in the house with him, Ruby and Alice. Declan struggles to remember what he was like at that age; surly, he thinks, awkward, resentful, and lacking Todd's willingness to attempt whatever is put in front of him. He remembers the anger and, more than anything, the vulnerability of being alone with no one of his own to turn to. Shortly after his mother's death, Robert, his father, had withdrawn into a deep depression from which he had never really emerged. It had been his Uncle Harry who had stepped in then, and organised Declan's move to boarding school in Perth. At thirteen, still mourning his mother and confused by his father's retreat into the depths of his own darkness, Declan had resented it bitterly. He had always been a loner, happy in his own room listening to his cassettes, reading books. He would take off on long bike rides, sometimes meeting up with other boys but more often alone. The prospect of living at school with organised sports, team games, dormitories, crowded showers, and having to do almost everything with other boys appalled him.

For the first two years he'd been thoroughly miserable and had learned that loneliness when surrounded by others is more painful than being alone. But by his fifteenth birthday he'd grown accustomed to the place and worked out where he fitted in the hierarchy. At eighteen, exams finished and on the verge of leaving, he'd realised he had developed affection for the school, the masters and some of the friends he had made there. But at eighteen he was far less prepared for the world outside the school than Todd is now as he approaches his sixteenth birthday. Neither of them has been equipped for family life but Todd seems to possess an inner fortitude that Declan envies. It's why he's brought Todd with him into town when he could easily have driven in alone for the mail and ingredients for tonight's pizza. He'd wanted Todd there, not just for his company, which he always enjoys, but to insulate him against the possibility of an awkward chance encounter.

'Come with me to get the mail and we'll go to the bike shop too,' he'd said, 'have a look for a new helmet for you.'

'But I can't ride it yet,' Todd had said, 'it might be a few more weeks.'

'By which time the festival will be on and I'll be too busy,' Declan had said. 'And we can pick up anything else you need for the pizza.'

Now, as they turn into the main street and he swings into a parking space, Declan looks across at Todd. 'Look, mate,' he says, 'do me a favour, will you? Stick with me. Don't wander off on your own, and if we meet anyone the story is we're in a bit of a rush. No time to stand around talking.'

'What – like Scooter and Will from the pub?' Todd asks. 'I thought they were your mates, helping with the music festival and stuff.'

'No,' Declan says, switching off the engine. 'No, not them. Anyone else, you know, like – well, like a woman, for example.'

Todd laughs. 'Oh, you mean that Mrs Craddock. I heard she was coming back.'

Declan turns to him sharply. 'Who told you that?'

'No one told me, I just heard Paula talking to her on the phone. She was telling her the names of places to stay.'

'What places?'

'Dunno really . . . well, the guest house, and the pub, and that place out on the road to Busselton.'

'Bugger,' Declan says. 'Trust Paula to get involved.'

'She fancy you then?' Todd asks.

Declan feels his face flush. 'Oh . . . um . . . I don't know exactly . . .'

'She was hanging around looking for you when you went to the hospital.'

'Was she?'

'Yeah, asking everybody where you were and if they could give her your number.'

'Did she ask you?'

'Yep, coupla times, said she needed to talk to you urgently.'

'So what did you say?'

'I said she should tell Ruby or Alice and they'd ring you and ask you to ring her.'

203

Declan smiles. 'Well done.'

'So I'm like . . . protection today, am I?'

'Spot on,' Declan says getting out of the car.

Todd slides awkwardly down from the high seat of the four-wheel-drive and does a few swift karate chops accompanied by appropriate whooshing noises. 'Todd the Terminator, personal bodyguard to Declan Benson,' he says, grinning. 'No task too dangerous, no one gets past these hands.'

Declan shakes his head, laughing, 'You're wasted here, Todd,' he says, 'you should be in the movies.'

'I'm counting on it,' Todd says, looking around as though guarding the president from potential assassins. 'Meanwhile you can count on my services in keeping you safe from dangerous women.'

'Just the one woman will be fine,' Declan says, 'you can let the others through. You got a girlfriend, Todd?'

Todd shakes his head. 'I did last year but it sort of fizzled out. I've got other things to think about right now.'

'You and me both,' Declan says, and as he locks the car and they head off to the post office he has the distinct feeling that there are eyes everywhere watching him. It's all in his head, of course; Lesley can't possibly have arrived yet. She would have called to say she was on her way – after all, she has called him every day, sometimes twice a day, since she got his number. Even so he can't shake off the feeling that she might suddenly step out of the newsagent's or screech to a halt alongside him in the car. He will eventually have to face her and he's dreading it, but he's also sure that it will be better if that meeting is planned, if it takes place in controlled circumstances, although he has no idea what those circumstances might be. It's difficult for him to understand quite what's happening but she's obviously under the illusion that something emotionally profound has developed between them.

Her husband, she'd told him, once he'd caved in and taken a call from her, has taken himself off to the Kimberley and isn't coming back for a while. She was relieved but also offended that he had let her know by email instead of waiting to see her. Declan found this entirely understandable – she, after all, had taken off from home with little explanation, failed to answer her phone for days on end and then delayed her return with a text message. Sauce for the goose, he thought, but he kept that thought to himself. It is the rest of it that bothers him.

'I have to see you and talk to you,' she has said several times in her phone and text messages. 'We need to talk about us, about you and me and what we're going to do.' And Declan, who fears misunderstanding on both their parts, has been trying to say as little as possible in the hope that she will eventually see that what happened between them as just what it was: a pleasant but fairly superficial encounter that is best forgotten. As far as he's concerned there is no 'us'. He liked her and it had helped to talk to someone detached from Benson's, but taking it further had been a big mistake. At the same time he thinks he has done nothing worse than most men would have done in the circumstances, and others prob-ably would have cut her off quite brutally by now.

Declan can see that he has made things worse by avoiding her, but how is he supposed to respond when she tells him that it is the first time she has been unfaithful to her husband in more than thirty-five years? Is she attempting to assuage her guilt by confusing sex with something more like – oh shit – like love?

'I'm coming back to Margaret River as soon as I can,' she'd said. 'We need to spend some time together and work out what to do.'

'I've got a lot on at the moment,' Declan had said. 'The music festival's coming up, other stuff – I don't have a lot of time.'

'Never mind,' Lesley said, 'you won't be busy *all* the time – after all, you have to eat and to . . . to sleep, of course.'

Declan had opened his mouth to say something but nothing came out, which, he thinks now, was probably a good thing.

'But I can't come yet. Just the day after I got back my daughter-in-law collapsed with a ruptured appendix. She's going to be okay, but I need to stay on here and help with the twins for a while. Maybe book one of the cottages for me from . . . now let me see, I think the . . .'

'We're fully booked for some time now,' Declan had cut in. 'Easter, you see, and then the jazz and blues festival.'

She'd gone very quiet then. 'Well I suppose I'll just have to find somewhere else to stay . . .' she'd said, her voice trailing away as though expecting him to take responsibility for this, or at the very least to suggest something.

Lesley, he thinks now, as he and Todd empty the post box and take the mail back to the car, is in a very fragile state, almost a loose cannon, and his own stupidity has added to that. If, as he suspects, she thinks that they are at the start of a relationship he is going to have to set her straight about it and the prospect brings him out in a cold sweat.

'Freeze!' Todd hisses as they are about to cross the road. 'Check out, target approaching from the right.'

Declan's heart pounds in his chest and he drops the mail as Todd doubles up with laughter.

'Gotcha! You're too jumpy, gotta stay cool, man.'

'Wanker!' Declan says, hitting him over the head with a large envelope. 'Some bodyguard you are. You nearly gave me a heart attack.' He sinks down onto a nearby seat laughing, and as Todd hops around doing karate chops he wonders what he has missed. Is this what it's like to have a son, growing up and becoming a mate? Someone who accepts you for who you are, who will laugh with you and at you, forgive you and be there for you even when you've totally pissed them off or let them down? And for a brief moment he is overcome with longing, and with a sort of melancholy for what might have been if things had been different, if *he* had been different – if he'd been brave enough, sober enough, mature enough to risk love.

'Come on, Todd,' Declan says, getting to his feet. 'Let's get this stuff back to the car and then we can go to the supermarket. What sort of pizza are you making?'

'It's my own recipe,' Todd says, 'thin crust with chorizo, mushrooms, green capsicum and buffalo mozzarella.'

'Onions?'

'No onions.'

'And no pineapple, I hope. Can't stand pineapple on pizza.'

'Yuk, no way. No pineapple.'

'Plenty of chorizo then?'

'Heaps.'

'Good,' Declan says. 'That sounds like a pizza for real men.'

'Sure is,' Todd says. 'But you can have some anyway,' and despite his dodgy ankle he manages to duck out of reach as Declan wields the envelope again.

Seventeen

May

Ruby has reached the end of the line. No more distractions, no more excuses, time to face up to the past – at least the part of it contained in Catherine's room. Outside in the grounds teams of people are doing things with temporary fencing, and bales of straw are being stacked under tarpaulins in case the threatened rain reduces the car park to mud. She has been thinking of London – she's been away longer than she anticipated. Jessica is more than able to run things in her absence but Ruby feels it unfair to expect her to manage everything for much longer.

'How do you know I'm not enjoying it?' Jessica had joked on the phone. 'With you out of the way I can do things my way. I'm drunk with power. But really, Ruby, just stay as long as you want, it's fine, really it is.'

The prospect of her London life holds little appeal for Ruby right now. Years ago Benson's Reach had helped to heal the wounds of childhood, but then her life here had soured suddenly and dramatically and she had left vowing never to return. But she *is* back, nothing terrible has happened and once again the place has worked its magic on her. Even so the past waits and she is still avoiding it. Cleaning up Catherine's room was one thing, but what remains is the task of sorting the contents of the boxes in which Catherine had stored her personal possessions. This seems like the final rite, after which the room can be returned to its original purpose as the heart of the house. Ruby unlocks the door and crosses immediately to the window to fling it open. Despite her many attempts to air it the same musty smell remains. Turning away from the window she surveys Catherine's boxes and, determined to put an end to her procrastination, picks one at random. It's quite heavy but she lugs it onto the table, puts on her glasses and opens it.

It's full of papers, most of them recent, in no sort of order and most of them of no particular significance: some receipts, guarantees and instruction books for small household items – an iron, a hair dryer, the kitchen toaster, other bits and pieces. There are letters or printouts of emails from acquaintances. Ruby retrieves those from people who have not yet been advised of Catherine's death, her guilt growing with each new discovery. She really should have done this weeks ago. She makes a small pile of the essentials and tosses the rest into a larger box – Todd will be spending some time with the shredder if the rest of the boxes are like this. But of course they're not, most of them will be nothing like this, and that's what she's dreading.

The next box is packed with trinkets, souvenirs, some small gifts. There are china ornaments concealed in bubble wrap, a collection of framed photographs of the lavender fields and other shots of Benson's Reach, some with Catherine standing awkwardly alongside smiling strangers, mementoes probably from satisfied visitors who have scrawled messages on them: 'A wonderful holiday, so lovely to have met you.' 'We'll be back again and that's a promise.' 'We love Benson's Reach, thanks for everything.' 'Another splendid visit, thanks Catherine.' All followed with illegible signatures and some adorned with kisses.

There are other gifts too, obviously from people who didn't know Catherine well: a box of lace trimmed handkerchiefs embroidered with the initial C. A couple of printed silk scarves, one decorated with riding crops and stirrups, another with exotic plants accompanied by their Latin names. There are several strands of ugly and unmatched beads that look homemade, some purple leg warmers, a pair of Christmas reindeer horns on a black velvet headband, and some green earrings in the shape of Christmas trees. There is a hip flask, an imitation leather writing case and more, all packed carefully away with their original gift wrapping folded loosely around them. Ruby dumps the wrappings, removes the photographs from their frames keeping them in a pile, returns the frames and everything else to the box and scrawls 'Op Shop' across the lid in black felt pen. There – two boxes done already, not so bad after all. Maybe Catherine didn't keep much from the past, their past, maybe she, like Ruby herself, disposed of it all years ago.

She leans back, putting her feet up on the op shop box, reliving her own ritual burning of the past, now such a long time ago; the early seventies when she and Owen had just moved into the Islington house that he'd inherited, along with a healthy share portfolio, from an aunt. It was a glorious June day, a day for fresh starts. From the window of what would become their bedroom when he'd finished the decorating, Owen, wearing an old green viyella shirt spattered with paint, looked down to where she was standing in the garden, feeding the remains of her Australian life into a bonfire.

'Hey, Rube, what are you burning?'

'The past,' she'd said, looking up at him, shading her eyes against the sun with one hand and poking a stick at the embers with the other. 'My past. Start of a new life, clean slate, all that.'

'You'll regret it,' he'd said, waving his paintbrush. 'One day you'll wish you'd kept it. I can put all that stuff up in the roof. We're not exactly short of space.'

She shook her head. 'I'll never regret it, there's nothing here I want to remember.'

He was down the stairs in seconds, running up behind her, wrapping his arms around her. 'Stop, please, darling. It's history, your history. It'll be part of our family's history. What about our children and grandchildren? They'll want to know about you.'

But she had kept on burning. 'Not this part,' she'd said, 'no one would want to know this. The things worth keeping are happening now. I'll keep our stories, tell them the stories that began here in London.'

Ruby sighs now, remembering how he had turned away in frustration and walked back to the decorating. The house and Owen himself had seemed unusually quiet that evening, as though something really quite important had been consumed by the flames.

'You weren't there,' she'd said. 'You can't know what it was like. If you did you wouldn't want me to preserve it.'

Owen had shaken his head. 'But that's the point,' he'd said. 'I *can't* know and neither will our children. Even if you can't face looking into it now you should still preserve it, write it down. Stories are important. Sometime in the future you'll find out more about what happened to that shipload of children, and why you were sent to such an awful situation, in fact why you were sent away at all. You'll wish you'd never lit that bonfire. I just can't help feeling that what happened to you is part of something much bigger. I wish you'd hung on to that stuff. And I wish you'd try to find out more—'

'No,' she'd cut in then, 'I just want to be free of it. All I want from the past is to find my mother. I still don't believe she died that night. It's just a gut feeling, that's all. Everything else is . . . well, it's ashes now, in every sense, and that's how I want it to stay.'

And she hadn't regretted it, at least not then, not even when she had been searching for her mother, nor even when in the fourth month of pregnancy she lost the baby and was told she would never be able to carry a baby to term. She threw herself into a demanding and rewarding life in the present, into the work and activism that would sustain her then and has continued to demand her attention and her energy ever since. It was only in the early nineties when the stories of children who had been shipped out of the country to different outposts of the Empire began to trickle through in the press that she allowed herself some regret. Owen had been right: stories are important, far more important than she had realised the day she had set fire to her own and willed herself to forget. But painful memories, she knows now, always remain, however many bonfires you light.

'Owen,' Ruby murmurs softly. 'I still miss you. I really do.' She had promised to bring him here one day, but when she'd made that promise she hadn't really meant it.

'We can go together and you can make your peace with the place,' he'd said, and so she'd promised, crossing her fingers behind her back, hoping she would never have to keep the promise, and she hadn't, but for all the wrong reasons.

They were going to grow old together, surrounded by children and grandchildren. They would restore the house to its original Edwardian charm, and fill it with old furniture, books and paintings, mementoes from places they would travel to. It would be a place of memories and imagination where family and friends would find a welcome and a bed whenever they needed it. It would be everything that Ruby believed she had been robbed of and it would house the story of their lives together. But that story was cut short by Owen's death.

'I haven't been very good at hanging on to the people I love,' Ruby says aloud, 'and now it's too late. But you know all about that, don't you, Cat? That's why you've brought me back here.' And pushing the op shop box aside she reaches out and picks another at random.

Confident now, with two boxes under her belt, Ruby opens it quickly, gasps in shock and closes it again. It's only now that she notices that this box is actually marked: a note in felt pen on the side reads '1947–1969 Me and Ruby.' She jumps up from the chair, takes several steps backwards and stares at the box as though it might explode at any minute. Then, very slowly, she walks around it, viewing it from every angle, trying to calm herself.

There is a tap on the door and it is opened immediately.

'I thought you might be here,' Paula says, stepping inside. 'It's months since I've been in here. Catherine kept it locked, very mysterious about it, she was. Anyway, I spotted you through the window so I thought I'd come and give it a clean.' And as she walks past Ruby towards the long table and the boxes, her eyes flick back and forth, apparently registering everything from the pictures on the wall to the pile of discarded wrappings on the floor.

'Not now, thanks, Paula,' Ruby says, pointedly walking briskly to the door and holding it open. 'I've got some work to do in here,' and she gestures to her to leave.

'It's months since it was cleaned,' Paula protests, running her fingers along the edge of the table and then examining them for dust. 'I've got a bit of time this morning if you want to leave me to it. It won't take me long.'

'Well as you can probably see I've cleaned and reorganised it myself quite recently,' Ruby says, 'now if you don't mind . . .'

Paula tosses her head. 'Okay, well it's up to you,' she says, looking around again, this time as though searching for something. 'But there might be some things of mine in here. I'd like to come in sometime when you're not busy and have a look for them.'

'What sort of things?' Ruby asks, still holding the door.

'Things I lent to Catherine. I can't remember exactly, but you know how it is, you lend someone something and then you forget until they give it back. Only now, of course, she won't be able to give anything back.'

Ruby grits her teeth. 'Well I suggest you think hard and try to make a list of things you might have lent her, and I'll look out for them. In fact,' she says, in a moment of inspiration, walking over to pick up the op shop box, 'they might be in here. Why don't you take this box off to the staff room now. You can check whether there's anything of yours, and if there is anything you or any of the staff would like. You're welcome to help yourselves. There may be more for you to go through when I've finished. Anything that's left can go to the op shop in town.' And she thrusts the box into Paula's arms and urges her to the door.

'All right, all right,' Paula says, awkwardly clutching the heavy box, 'I know when I'm not wanted,' and she makes her way out of the door and down the hall.

Ruby closes the door, locks it and returns to the box. Tentatively she lifts the double layer of tissue paper that covers the contents. The nightdresses are a shock: small, wafer thin white cotton yellowed with age, their initials, CR and RM, still readable among the other faded laundry marks inside the back of the collar – Catherine Rogers, and the smaller one, Ruby's own, Ruby Medway. Ruby lifts hers from the box and shakes out the folds. It was already well worn when it was issued to her on arrival at the convent. There is a very neat darn under one armhole and she puts on her glasses to study it closely, remembering the nun's metal ruler rapping her knuckles until they bled when she got the stitching wrong.

She holds it up in front of her, picturing her own skinny arms in those flimsy sleeves, clutching the folds of the fabric around her body, feeling the brush of the fabric against her thighs. How long did she wear this? How many times did she wet the bed in it, peeing herself with fear, knowing she would get a beating? But how did Catherine manage to keep these, to get them out of the convent? Did she hide them somewhere? Steal them from other younger girls to whom they had been passed on? The fabric is so fragile it seems as though it might fall apart any moment. Ruby inhales the scent of it – lavender, of course, Catherine had it everywhere, but another smell too, the smell of the past, of sadness. It brings back the terror of dark nights on a thin mattress that barely protected her from the coarse steel springs of the iron bedstead. Her heart pounds at the memory of lying there listening for the sound of footsteps in the passage, the swish of a nun's habit, the rattle of rosary beads, the creak of the door. She holds her breath now, just as she did then lying rigid with fear as the nun's hand felt under the coarse grey blanket searching for a damp patch on the mattress. She shivers with the terror of being dragged from the bed, stripped of her nightdress, the leather belt slashing indiscriminately at her back and buttocks. And now – sixty years on – she bites her lip again as she did then to stop herself from crying.

'Filthy child. You girls are scum, that's what you are,' the nun would shout. 'All of you, filthy, lazy scum.'

Closing her eyes now, Ruby can hear the hiss of contempt, smell the fear in the dormitory as the girls lay in silent terror waiting to see who would be next. There were always three or four, sometimes more, ordered to gather their sheets and carry them down three flights of stairs to the laundry, returning to spend the rest of the night naked and shivering on damp mattresses, their blankets confiscated, listening to muffled sobs, and greeting the dawn in shame.

Ruby sets the nightdresses on the table and turns back to the open box. There, wrapped in tissue paper, are their rosaries: Catherine's made of small black beads, her own a pale amber colour, the only things – other than ragged second-hand clothes, well-worn shoes and combs with broken teeth – that they were ever given in the convent. Alongside the rosaries are the two prayer books they had stolen from the chapel on their last day, just to see if they could get away with it. There are more clothes next, a cotton dress with a faded floral pattern that Catherine had worn that last day, socks, vests and knickers, a threadbare cardigan with darns at the elbows; the things that would have been in her bag when they left. Ruby can barely remember what had been in her own bag – very little, she thinks, maybe just one change of clothes and shoes. What else? Now she wishes she could remember what she might have found if this were her own box, if she had listened to Owen that day and stopped feeding the fire.

Beneath the clothes are some papers. The map of Perth with the location of Benson's Hotel marked on it that Freda Benson had given them, a faded Benson's Hotel brochure offering 'a warm welcome and outstanding facilities, for the whole family or business travellers'. Next a small brown envelope with Catherine's name and the date written on it – her first pay packet – a newspaper clipping from some years later about the Bensons selling the hotel, and a plastic envelope full of black and white photographs. Ruby peers at it through the plastic. The top photograph is of herself arm in arm with Catherine, both in their bathers, knee deep in the water on Scarborough beach, the wind whipping their hair back from their faces. She can almost feel the chill of the water and the salty sting of the wind; a spring day, a Monday, their day off from the hotel, and Harry with his camera, urging them to smile.

'Come on, girls, this one'll make the front cover of a magazine – Australian beach belles,' waving his hand to describe a banner headline. He always had delusions of grandeur when it came to his photographs.

Ruby bites her lip and puts the package of photographs on the table. Later, she thinks, not now, can't cope with it now, and as she turns back to the box her heart seems to stop.

A book, an exercise book with a familiar but previously for-gotten cover. One of Catherine's journals. Ruby can see her now, sitting up in bed in the room they shared when they worked at Benson's Hotel. She is wearing a red and white spotted nightdress with thin red shoulder straps that she'd bought with her first week's pay, and scribbling away in the dim glow of the bedside lamp.

'I'm writing it all down, Rube, our adventures, everything that happens to us from now on.'

'Whatever for?' Ruby had asked. 'Who's going to want to read about that?'

'We will, you and me. One day when we're old we'll be sitting in our rocking chairs on a verandah, with crocheted rugs over our knees, and we'll read it together and remem-ber. Best friends, we'll still be best friends then, and we'll laugh and cry together.'

A lump swells in Ruby's throat – a lump of grief. Not grief over Catherine's death, but the older grief for what they had lost, the dislocation of everything that these journals repre-sent. Ruby tries to focus once again on the present, not daring to drift back into the morass of hurt and anger that she has stored for so long. Breathing deeply she steadies herself and begins to flick cautiously through the pages. The notebook covers several months and on the inside of the back cover Catherine has written 'More follows . . . watch this space.' Leaning back over the box Ruby sees that there are several similar notebooks, their dates scrawled across the front cov-ers. Catherine's post-convent life and her own are contained in these books. Ruby toys briefly with the tempting idea of destroying them, unread. Who's to know? And who would care? But the painful answer is that she herself would care. She will read this journal and all the others, line by line, however painful. For too long she has walked wide circles around the past, savouring only the hurt, allowing the good times to fade into oblivion.

A tap at the door jolts her out of her reflections. Paula again? Shaking her head, Ruby puts the journal down on the table, straightens her shoulders and walks briskly to the door.

'Yes, Paula,' she calls, 'what is it now?'

'It's not Paula, it's me,' Alice says, popping her head inside. 'Should I come back later?'

'Only if your name is Paula,' Ruby says, opening the door wider, 'in which case it would be best not to come back at all.'

'That bad, eh?'

Ruby nods. 'Come on in. Are you okay? You look as white as a sheet.'

Alice steps inside and closes the door behind her. 'You look a bit pale yourself. I'm sorry to disturb you, but I had to talk to someone.'

'You came at the right time,' Ruby says. 'I was just about to start wallowing in grief and maybe some self-flagellation. What's happened?'

'It's this,' Alice says, holding out a sealed envelope. 'It came in today's mail – I can't bring myself to open it alone. It's a letter from my daughter.'

In the last few weeks she seems to have got into a habit of doing everything very quickly, probably because of the pressure of getting the café up and running, but now as she walks back to the café from the house Alice slows her pace, and then stops. She can't go back in there yet, she just has to read the letter again and this time she needs to be alone. It's a glorious day and Benson's is busy with visitors. She hesitates. She could go up to the cottage, or find somewhere quiet outside, and looking around she remembers the bench in a shady curve of the path that leads from the office to Fleur's workroom. No visitors there. Once there she is about to settle on the bench but opts instead for the huge camphor laurel on the other side of the path and flops down on the ground, leaning back against its broad trunk, well out of sight. The last thing she needs right now is someone coming over to talk to her.

Reaching into the pocket of her jeans she pulls out the envelope that, until it was posted yesterday, was in Jacinta's hands. It seems like a physical connection. Did Jacinta post it herself or perhaps ask Jodie to post it for her? Alice strokes the envelope, trying to feel her daughter, feel that intimate connection. Then she takes out the letter and unfolds it again.

'How rude,' Ruby had said when she had done as Alice asked and read it with her. 'Rude and unkind; honestly, Alice, not even a polite greeting. I know she's your daughter but I really want to shake her. Of course it's terrible for her but you're her mother, and it's terrible for you too. Doesn't she have an ounce of generosity?'

'She used to,' Alice had said, staring at the letter, unable to take her eyes off it. 'Perhaps I killed that when I killed Ella.'

Ruby was right, it isn't much of a letter, no salutation, no real sign-off, certainly no affection. 'Like a note to the milkman,' Ruby had said. And Alice can see that it is, but it is also more than that. It's a communication and that surely is better than no communication at all. And there is something else quite remarkable about it although Ruby, practically incandescent with anger at Jacinta's two curt sentences typed in the centre of the page, had failed to see its possibilities: *'I have your things. We're going away today until the end of the month so tell your friend to get in touch after that to arrange a time to collect them.'*

'But look,' Alice had said, her hand shaking as she took the letter from Ruby. 'Look at this.'

'What?'

'The phone number,' Alice said, 'she's put her phone number. Remember they'd moved and I didn't have the new address, and I had such a job finding where they'd gone?

It felt as though they'd deliberately hidden themselves so I couldn't find them. But I *did* find the address and now Jacinta's included the phone number. Don't you think that's good? Don't you think it means something?'

Ruby hesitated. 'I think it means she's being practical,' she said. 'Don't try to read something else into it, Alice, I don't think you can handle having your heart broken a second time.'

Ruby had pulled Alice towards her then, hugging her, hanging on tightly as though trying to compensate for the chill of Jacinta's message, and Alice had absorbed every second and every nuance of that hug. In prison she had lived, night and day, shoulder to shoulder with other women, but affectionate physical contact, while not forbidden, was looked upon with suspicion. When she had arrived at the bus stop in Margaret River, Declan, apparently rendered speechless by her arrival, had hugged her as though both their lives depended on it. But Ruby's hug was different; it was empathy and affection and Alice had longed to collapse into it.

Now, in peaceful seclusion under the tree, she believes more than ever that the telephone number is significant. It is, she thinks, a sign of trust. Jacinta has provided the number for, as Ruby rightly says, practical reasons, but in doing so she has trusted Alice not to use it for any other purpose. That has to be a good sign – trust and perhaps a test? And if she passes . . . what then? Ruby's scepticism hasn't dulled the sense of possibility that Alice had felt when she saw that number at the top of the page. Perhaps Declan will see in it what she sees, but she wants more time to think before she shows it to him, this evening perhaps, or later in the week.

The end of the month, Jacinta said – it's not really very long and Alice rests her head against the tree trunk, closes her eyes and for the first time in years of not allowing herself to believe in the possibility of reconciliation she pictures herself and Jacinta facing each other. She imagines the smallest of cautious smiles playing around her daughter's lips as she reaches out her hand.

It's the sound of a voice and footsteps that drags Alice back to reality and she folds the letter, tucks it into her pocket and is about to get to her feet when she recognises the voice as Paula's, and she's talking on the phone. Alice decides to stay put and let her pass.

'Bloody Todd,' Paula says. 'Nothing's too good for him, living in the house and that, but what about me?' And then there's a scuffling sound as she drops down onto the seat on the other side of the path.

Alice is not given to eavesdropping but she's stuck now, and while Paula is silent listening to the person on the other end of the line, Alice can also hear her attempting to light a cigarette. Well hopefully she won't be there long. Alice sits tight and Paula, never one to modulate her tone, continues her conversation.

'Yes, but I've told them I want to take over the lavender products. I could do that job standing on my head, I said, and Ruby said they might combine it with the job in the shop . . .'

Alice freezes. It's the first she's heard of the possibility that Paula might take over from Fleur and her immediate reaction is dismay. Paula must be making this up. Ruby hasn't finished the new job descriptions yet, so either Paula has got the wrong idea from somewhere, or it's pure fantasy. Just the same, it's disturbing that Paula might believe that this is what's going to happen.

'Well I don't know : . .' Paula is saying now, 'she just said they're restructuring things. They'll let me know. I told them it makes sense. I mean, I know this place as well as anyone, better than either of them, and they're always saying what a good job I do.'

There's a pause, presumably while the person she's talking to asks a question. 'Yes, that's right,' Paula replies, and

Alice can hear her inhaling on her cigarette, 'a few days after Catherine died Glenda resigned, and then Fleur said she was leaving too. There's just that Kim in the shop now. She's about as much use as tits on a bull. It needs a mature person, a proper manager. Madam Ruby and her handmaiden Alice are keeping an eye on it in the meantime. Keeping their bloody hawks' eyes on everything, if you ask me. Anyway, Lesley, did you find somewhere to stay?'

Alice holds her breath. So is that Lesley Craddock she's talking to? Paula had seemed to be getting quite thick with her before she left. There is a scuffling and it sounds like Paula is getting to her feet.

'Okay,' she says, 'well let me know. Better get on now, bit behind today . . .' and her voice fades as she starts to walk away.

Alice slips out from behind the tree and watches as Paula walks back down the track towards the house, the phone still clapped to her ear. Distracted now by what she's heard, she takes a deep breath and begins to make her way back to the café.

'There you are!' Fleur says as soon as Alice walks in the door. She is standing at the counter with a menu in her hand. 'I popped over for some lunch, hoped we might eat together?'

Alice hesitates. She ought to get back into the kitchen, but Fleur so rarely comes to the café and Alice would like to know her better. Fleur is, she thinks, a person she could confide in. She's younger, more like Jacinta's age, and Alice likes her forthright manner and her sense of humour. She glances around the kitchen to see if the staff can manage without her a bit longer.

'Sure,' she says, 'that'd be lovely. Give me your order and grab a table, and I'll be with you in a minute.'

It's more like five minutes before she gets to the table and flops into her chair.

'Sorry – there's always something.'

'No worries,' Fleur says. 'I thought you might not be free at all, it's just that we've all been so busy since . . . well, for the last few weeks. I just thought it'd be nice to get to know each other a bit better.'

'Absolutely,' Alice says. 'It's a shame you're going, though. Ruby and Declan will really miss you . . . we'll all miss you. What are you going to do?'

Fleur shrugs. 'Who knows? When Catherine died I felt it couldn't be the same for me. It seemed like time for a change.' They sit in silence as Leonie puts their meals on the table.

Alice bites into her sandwich and chews on it for a moment. 'Mmm,' she says, 'I can see that you'd feel like that. But you never know, it might be better. I don't mean that to be critical of Catherine, she obviously did a fantastic job. But with other people here it might be different, possibly even better.'

Fleur looks down into her soup and stirs it slowly. 'That's more or less what Todd says.' She laughs, looking up. 'He's trying to talk me into staying, mostly for his own sake, I think. He reckons I'm his safety net, probably because I've told Paula to wind her neck in a few times when she's been having a go at him.'

'Well you *could* think about it a bit longer,' Alice says, 'stay on a bit and see how you feel – unless Declan and Ruby have found someone else.'

Fleur shrugs. 'Not that I know of. They've asked me to stay and I said no, but since then I've been wondering whether it was the right decision.'

Alice opens her mouth to say something and then hesitates. Gossiping is dangerous, particularly in a small community like this one, but she's still concerned about Paula. 'Between you and me,' she says, 'Paula's got her eye on the job.'

'Paula!' Fleur almost chokes on her soup and holds the paper napkin up to her mouth. 'Don't make me laugh. That'd be like Mother Teresa hosting *What Not to Wear* – instant ratings disaster. You're not serious, are you? I mean, did Ruby or Declan tell you that?'

Alice shakes her head. 'No way, and please don't mention it to them. I heard it . . . look, to be honest I accidently overhead Paula on the phone, but then that's Paula. Probably just wishful thinking.'

'Well I bloody well hope so,' Fleur says. 'I've put a lot of work into the lavender business and there's no way I'm going to hand it over to just anybody and particularly not to Paula. Catherine would turn in her grave. She was fond of Paula, she made a lot of allowances for her because she thought she was a bit of a lost soul, but she was very clear about her limitations.'

'She must have had the patience of a saint then.'

'She did with Paula, more than with most others.'

'So did she start the business with her husband?' Alice asks.

Fleur shakes her head. 'They were living here, and he'd been talking for years about turning it into a winery, but then he took off out of the country somewhere with some other woman. I think Catherine must have got Benson's as a divorce settlement, or maybe inherited it because he died a few years later. Anyway, it all came to her – the house, the land, everything.'

Alice smiles, raising her eyebrows. 'Lucky Catherine!'

'Indeed. From what she told me it seems that Catherine could either have sold and got out or turned it into a business. Everyone else was planting vines so she thought she'd do something different.'

'That must have been a bit of a risk at the time,' Alice says.

'Yes, but she was like that. She'd make up her mind she wanted something and then go for it and she'd read how in the Middle East lavender was used for healing and calming. People were really getting interested in natural products then, so she thought it was worth a try.'

'But did she know anything about it? I mean, how did she start it all on her own?'

'Apparently there was a woman who lived in an old bus on the outskirts of the town,' Fleur says. 'Local people went to her for herbal ointments and so on. She called herself Cassandra and no one knew much about her but she seemed to know what she was doing. So Catherine went to see her and it turned out that Cassandra not only knew a whole lot about lavender, but years earlier she'd worked for Elizabeth Arden in New York and was a fount of information on skin products and their constituents.' Fleur takes a final spoonful of soup, pushes the plate away and leans her elbows on the table. 'What Catherine learned from Cassandra enabled her to make the first Benson's lavender products. She started out buying in the lavender, and it worked out well, so she had the fields planted and before long she had her own crop. Over the years she tweaked the formulas that Cassandra had given her, experimented with different components, and developed new products, but that's how it all began. She was selling the lavender products through shops in the town and in Bunbury and Busselton, and then she was sending them up to Perth. But the tourist trade down here was growing and I think she may have inherited some money, enough to enable her to take a risk, so she borrowed more money and built the cottages, and then the café and shop.'

'So when did you come along?'

'Six – almost seven – years ago. She couldn't manage it all on her own and the lavender side of things was really important to her so she wanted someone that wouldn't just make the products but would take over running the whole thing.'

They sit for a moment, silent amid the noise and bustle of the café.

'She was pretty amazing really,' Fleur says eventually. 'She put her heart and soul into this place to the exclusion of everything else. And she looked after Cassandra, who hadn't got two pennies to rub together. Had her living here at the end, looked after her for about a year before she died. Catherine didn't make friends easily but she was a good person to work for – and with. I was very fond of her.'

'But she seems to have been very much alone at the end,' Alice says. 'I mean, locking herself away in that room . . .'

'It was her choice,' Fleur says. 'I think she couldn't bear people to see her as less than she had been. She just withdrew and became quite prickly and difficult. It was heart-breaking, really.' Fleur is silent again now and Alice can see that she is struggling with her emotions.

'You must miss her . . .'

'I do. She was a bloody good woman, and she worked her guts out here. The lavender business was Catherine's starting point and it meant a lot to her. That's why it needs to be run by someone who cares about it and believes in it, someone who cares about the history and wants to preserve it. That's why I hope this is just Paula's fantasy, because I don't believe that Paula could or would do that.'

Lesley is listening, once again, to the silence, but it's a different sort of silence this time, as though the house, on which she has lavished care and attention for more than twenty years, has turned against her and is emanating its disapproval. Gordon's absence, for which she had at first been thankful, has now become a burden. There is a sense of finality about this silence, as though something is coming to an end but is taking a very long time about it. A few days after her return home she had started to compose an email to Gordon. It had taken ages, days, to get the tone right, conciliatory but not submissive, apologising for her sharpness and extended absence but at the same time not apologetic (did that even make sense?). Time apart, she had added, was probably the best thing for both of them right now. She had ended it by wishing him a good trip and asked him to let her know how it was going. So far he hasn't replied, although this is just as likely to be due to his location as anything else. She imagines him up there, somewhere in the north west, probably sleeping rough and loving it, doing the sort of work in the same sort of conditions he had enjoyed so much when he was younger, and for which he had since, so often, longed.

She feels a sliver of envy that he has so much passion and purpose. It was something she had loved about him when they were younger and, she realises now, something she had forgotten in the strange dislocated months that followed his retirement. Her passion had always been the family, the whole edifice with herself at its heart, and for so long it had been all that she wanted. But now it seems as though everyone has moved on, stretching out the ties of love, of blood and duty to the furthest possible distance, connected still but in absence rather than presence.

This morning she had taken her grandsons to the little park by the river for a picnic. Lucy is home now and much better after the wretched drama of the burst appendix, but she tires easily and the boys can be exhausting. Lesley had piled them into the car and unpacked them again at the park where they had raced around discovering a few brown ducks on the riverside beach, several snails, and a ladybird. When the wonders of the park began to pall the three of them had walked together barefoot along the beach where the shallow water lapped towards a spidery line of foam littered with tiny stones and fragments of shells.

The exuberance and boundless energy of the children nourished something in her, but more precious was the feeling that they loved her and approved of her. She might have stuffed up as a wife and mother but as a grandparent she seemed to be doing fine. It was a relief to feel she was getting something right. She had thrived for so long on the knowledge that she was essential to and loved by Gordon

and the children. For decades she had taken the decisions
about what they would eat each day, what they wore, where
they would or wouldn't be allowed to go, and what Gordon
needed or didn't need to know. Slowly, as if by stealth, all
that power, because that's what it was, had slipped away as
first Karen, then Simon and finally Sandi left home. Lesley
thought she had managed the 'empty nest' thing rather well.
She had even felt somewhat superior to acquaintances who
were struggling to come to terms with the fact that their cen-
trality was diminishing, their opinions, advice and presence
not always required. But perhaps she hadn't managed it at
all. What if the yoga, the tennis, the little helping out job in
the boutique and everything else was all just cover for the
underlying fear of her own irrelevance?

Watching her grandsons splashing through the shallows,
greeting passing dogs and assessing other small people
who might possibly be worthy of their interest reminds
her of walking here with her own children when they were
small. She was busy then, someone always wanting something – food, clean clothes, a lift, help with homework, a
friend to stay. It was endless but purposeful. It was leading
somewhere – to the time when they would be self-sufficient
adults, when they would have homes and children of their
own and she and Gordon would stand back, taking pride
in what they had created, enjoying each other's company.
She had thought that Gordon himself was the problem but
the events of the last few weeks have made her question
just how much of what has happened between them is due
to her.

She had left the house this morning with the distinct feeling that she was falling apart, and that she was the least
suitable person to be looking after two small children. But
the twins, with their sunny enthusiasm for the small things,
and their delight in the very simple picnic, had gone some
way to reassembling her. After the picnic she had taken

them to Target to buy new t-shirts and hoodies and when, just after four o'clock, she had finally delivered them back to Lucy, they were pleasantly tired and ready to flop down in front of the television.

'You're a lifesaver, Lesley,' Lucy had said as she filled the kettle. 'I slept for four hours and feel like a new woman.'

'Good,' Lesley said, slipping into a chair at the kitchen table, 'but you still need to take it easy.'

'I know. I'm so grateful you're here to help out. I don't know how I'd have managed without you. You're not going back to Margaret River again just yet, are you?'

'Not until you're really back on your feet,' Lesley said, hoping she didn't sound as fed up about it as she felt.

Lucy put a cup of tea down in front of Lesley and joined her at the table. 'Are *you* okay? You haven't seemed yourself for ages.'

For a brief moment Lesley had thought she might burst into tears there and then, simply because Lucy was asking her about herself. Her approval rating with her own children is at an all-time low. Karen has not called once since their tense exchange on the day Lesley got back, and while Simon is fine with her and is grateful for her help with the children, she senses that he has taken a backward step, not knowing where to position himself in this awkward gap between his parents. As for Sandi, she's far too busy with her new life in Canberra to do more than send an occasional text or email, sometimes accompanied by a picture of herself pulling a weird face for the camera.

'It's just a very difficult time,' Lesley had said. 'Gordon and me, you know . . .'

'You'll work it out,' Lucy had said, resting her hand lightly on Lesley's arm. 'We're all thinking of you – you and Gordon. You'll sort it out, I know you will.'

Lesley is touched by Lucy's affection, and her hostility towards Gordon has dissipated, but this evening, sitting alone on the verandah, she has no idea how this might be sorted out. Everything is different since Declan walked into her life. She's made a fool of herself, no wonder he stopped answering her calls. She would have scared off the most confident and ardent of men, let alone such a cautious one. But he has given her a glimpse of something different – an adventure at a time in her life when she had thought adventures were over. She's always been conscious of her appearance and with Declan she had felt younger, attractive, sexy, and as though age didn't really matter at all. She wants that sense of herself, wants it so much that she can't really focus on anything else and she can no longer sit still. Getting up from her chair she gathers the empty wine bottle and her glass. Not long now and she'll be back there and they can see each other again, talk about it. She stares at her silent phone lying on the table. Could she try calling him again? 'No,' she murmurs, 'no, I won't call until I can tell him I'm on my way,' and sighing she puts the phone in her pocket and goes back into the house.

Eighteen

Declan is totally into the mood of the festival. All the anxiety and the pressure of the last few weeks have floated away in a cloud of anticipation and excitement. He knows he ought still to be anxious, to be scurrying around checking his notes, doing all sorts of stuff, but all he can think of right now is how brilliant it all is. For a short while, at least, this feels like his place, his thing, his festival and as though he is recapturing a part of his youth – the good part, while he was at university and before he started on the long and painful downward slope into drink and drugs. It starts tomorrow and all day people have been arriving, cars, campervans and people movers have formed a continuous slow stream of traffic along the track that's been railed off for them. The fields are scattered with small tents, and caravans and the campers are pumping up their oil stoves and spreading their sleeping bags. Not far from where he's standing near the café an elderly couple wearing Jackson Crow t-shirts are draping a set of fairy lights around the entrance to their tent and connecting them to their car battery. Further up a young woman strums a guitar, while others unfold camping chairs and tables, and pull stubbies from ice-packed Eskys.

Declan has happy if somewhat hazy memories of music festivals in Australia and Europe from the year he spent travelling with a couple of uni mates when they'd graduated. He knows a good atmosphere when he sees one and while this festival may be small it feels really special.

'Hey, man!' Todd says, appearing beside him. He's wearing a baseball cap that one of the musicians had given him earlier in the day, and proudly fingering the festival lanyard with his official pass that says he's the runner for the musicians. His eyes are bright with excitement.

'Hey man, yourself,' Declan says, grinning back. 'How's it going?'

'It is totally mega cool. I got to help with testing the sound equipment, and I unloaded a set of drums, and I've been doing all sorts of stuff for the guys.'

'Good man,' Declan says. 'How's the ankle holding out?'

Todd picks up his foot and flexes his ankle. 'It's okay, bit achy. Good job I got rid of the crutches before all this started.'

Declan nods. 'It is, but don't go mad. We don't want you ending up in plaster again. I was just going to get something to eat and then take a walk around. Want to join me?'

Todd nods. 'I'm starving. Are we going back to the house?'

'I thought we'd get something in the café. Burgers maybe?'

The café is packed. Alice's decision to take on some extra casual staff and stay open in the evenings for the weekend is paying off. It's almost seven-thirty and they're flat out. Todd and Declan join the queue and as they wait Declan watches the action in the kitchen, Alice, he thinks, has done an amazing job, beyond what even he had hoped. In fact, if he's honest, he hadn't had any idea of what he'd hoped for when he asked her to come here. He'd just known that with Alice here, he'd feel better, more confident, that he might actually be capable of behaving like an adult with a business to run rather than a hopeless case floundering about in chaos.

'Gentlemen! What can I get you?' Alice says with a big grin as they reach the counter.

'This is amazing,' Declan says, looking around. 'I can hardly believe that just a few weeks ago this place was closed and silent as the grave. Todd and I are off on a walk around the boundaries, marking out our territory. Want to join us?'

Alice laughs, indicating the packed tables and the frantic activity in the kitchen. 'You're kidding! There's no way I can leave now.'

He nods. 'Thought you might say that. So, any chance of us getting two man-size burgers to take with us?'

'Huge ones,' Todd says, grinning at Alice.

'Double with cheese?' she asks, tugging at the peak of his cap.

They stand together, watching as she gathers the buns, takes the burgers from the grill, adds the cheese, tomato, pickles and salad and wraps them in thick paper serviettes.

'Your order, gentlemen,' she says as she hands them their food. 'Enjoy your meal.'

Declan gives her a twenty dollar note and she takes it from him, rings up the charge and drops the change into his open hand, but before she can move away he grasps her wrist and draws her towards him across the counter.

'Alice,' he says, his voice low but still audible, 'thank you. I feel like you've saved my life.'

She leans forward further now, putting her other hand on top of his, and stretches across the counter to kiss him on the cheek. 'It's mutual,' she says. 'It really is, just like it's always been.' And then she turns away, back to the kitchen where one of the casual staff is panicking about an overcooked quiche.

Todd bites into his burger and feels the delicious meaty juice trickle down his chin. He's had the best ever day and it looks

235

like tomorrow will be better still. The musicians are treating him like one of them, but a special one who belongs to this place and knows how to find what they need. Some of them have come in their own small coaches or mini buses and are planning to sleep in them. And later this evening Jackson Crow himself, along with The Crowbars, will be here and Declan has given Todd specific instructions about looking after them. He can hardly believe how his life has changed in the last few months. He's even stopped feeling guilty about not wanting his mum to come back and while he still wishes that Fleur would stay, he knows now that he'll be okay if she does go because he's got a place of his own here now, at least for the time being.

It's still and warm as they perch for a moment on the low wall to concentrate on eating. Beyond them people sit on rugs, or in collapsible chairs, talking and occasionally singing, and the light from the oil lamps seems to grow stronger as the final vestiges of daylight fade away. Sitting on a big Esky a man with long straggly hair and a bandana tied around his head is strumming a guitar and singing something vaguely familiar.

'Look at that,' Declan says, nudging him, 'a Willie Nelson look-alike. He's even singing "On the Road Again". In your dreams, brother.'

Todd has never heard of Willie Nelson, but he laughs because he likes this, likes being here with Declan. He's never felt close to a man before. His dad had done the disappearing trick before he was even born, and he'd grown up with his mother in the caravan, very much alone. He had grandparents whom they'd visited a few times in Perth, but Pop was mostly drunk and Nan was always shouting at him, or at Todd and his mum. So it hadn't bothered him when they'd stopped going there. Todd thinks about his mum quite a lot. He likes getting the cards because it means she's okay, but he doesn't really miss her because she's so hard to be around.

They toss their rubbish in a nearby bin and stroll around the field, stopping from time to time to chat to the campers, listening to the music from various tents. Sometimes, like now, Todd pretends Declan is his dad, that they have some sort of shared history that links them not just now but into the future, a future in which they will always be there for each other. Declan treats him like an equal but Todd senses that he's also looking out for him, and that's a really good feeling. It's as good, no – it's better – than being with Catherine, although he feels a bit guilty thinking that, as though he's being disloyal. But that's how it is. He tries hard not to think that he's living a charmed life which could soon come to an end: Benson's Reach sold, and the people who now seem like a family to him dispersed, Ruby back to London, Alice and Fleur to who knows where. And Declan, where will he go? And, Todd wonders, is it remotely possible that wherever it is there might also be a place for him?

'Looks good, doesn't it?' Declan says, smiling with satisfaction as they reach the newly erected stage. Close up it seems huge, high and wide with a flight of steps at the side and an imposing canopy. 'Let's go up there and take a look around.'

As they mount the steps Todd imagines himself running up here and out onto the stage into the glaring white cone of light from a super trouper. He hears the roar of applause and the adoring fans chanting his name as he grasps the mike and launches into his first song.

'It must be awesome being up here,' he says as Declan joins him in the centre of the empty stage. And they stand together in the darkness, looking down the slope where, for the next few days, there will be a solid mass of people. 'Imagine it, all those faces, all those people waiting to hear you, clapping and yelling your name. Awesome.'

'Right on,' Declan says. 'We should've been rock stars, Todd. Fame and fortune, women screaming and throwing their knickers at us.'

'Gross,' Todd says. 'I'd have a stretch limo standing by, with pizza and a huge flat-screen TV.'

'You still may,' Declan says, 'who knows what's ahead for you, Todd? Sometimes I think you could do anything you set your mind to.'

Todd is not sure if this is a compliment or whether Declan is just being nice. 'Mrs Craddock's back,' he says. 'She was in the café just now. Did you see her?'

'Our café?' Declan says, turning to him in surprise. 'No I didn't see her, but she sent me a text saying she was coming back today.' He sighs. 'I stuffed up there well and truly, Todd, and I'm going to have to meet up with her and sort it out. Word of advice . . .' He stops suddenly and Todd looks up at him. 'No,' Declan shakes his head, 'you don't need advice from me. I'm a total loser when it comes to women.'

'Well then, you could tell me what *not* to do,' Todd says, trying to sound encouraging. 'You must've worked that out by now.'

'Not sure if I have, mate, not sure at all. But I will tell you one thing – short-term gratification has its rewards but in the end it's just that, short term, essentially unsatisfying, and usually comes with messy complications.'

Todd is not sure he knows what gratification is, but he does grasp Declan's overall meaning. 'When Alice came I thought you and she were . . . like . . . a couple,' he says.

'Me and Alice?' Declan pauses, looking down across the wide open space to the soft lights of the oil lamps and the shadowy shapes of the campers and their tents. 'Me and Alice,' he says again. 'No, man, she's way out of my league. Besides, she's got a few other things on her mind right now.'

'What, about the prison and that?' Todd asks.

Declan swings round towards him so fast he almost trips over. 'Prison?' he says, grabbing Todd by the shoulder. 'What d'you know about that?'

Todd twists away from his grip. 'Get off,' he says, rubbing his shoulder. 'Nothing, I just know she was in prison, that's all.'

'Who told you that?'

'No one *told* me, I heard Paula talking to Mrs Craddock on the phone, she was telling her about Alice then. I overheard it, that's all.'

'Have you told anyone else?'

''Course not, not my business, is it? I only said something then because of what you said, about her having other things on her mind. Sorry.'

Declan relaxes his grip. 'No, no, *I'm* sorry,' he says. 'I should've known you wouldn't . . . but look, Todd, Alice isn't a criminal, you know. She was driving, she had too much to drink and there was an accident, and someone . . . well someone died. It could have happened to anyone. There were many times in the past when it could have happened to me.'

'But Alice doesn't drink.'

'Not anymore, but she used to. We both did. That's how we met, at Alcoholics Anonymous. Have you heard of that?'

Todd nods. 'Mum went there once. I think she went because Paula was always nagging her to, but she came back pretty quick and never went again.'

'Paula told her to go?'

Todd nods. 'Yeah, she went on and on about it.'

'So Paula knows your mum?'

Todd laughs. 'Knows her? Yeah, 'course she does, they're sisters.'

'You never told me that.'

Todd shrugs. 'I thought you knew. Catherine knew. Paula told her when I first came to work here. She told her she shouldn't let me come because I'd only be trouble.'

'That's interesting,' Declan says quietly, 'very interesting. She told me that too. So what's Paula got against you?'

'Dunno,' Todd says, bored now with the conversation. 'She's always been like that. Mum just said they had a big fight a long time ago and never made it up. So Paula hates Mum and I s'pose that's why she hates me too.'

———

Lesley has been trying to find Declan in the crowded field. It really is like looking for the proverbial needle in a haystack because the place is swarming with people who all seem to be in a party mood, although the festival doesn't start until tomorrow. Lesley has never been to a music festival. In her youth Perth had not had much to offer in terms of the counter-culture and in any case her parents would have been horrified by the mere idea. Music festivals were for hippies, hotbeds of illicit sex and drugs, something from which daughters should be protected. Indeed, Bert and Dolly had very little interest in music at all and their record collection could be counted on the fingers of two hands: some Vera Lynn, the soundtracks of *The Student Prince*, *The King and I* and some Mario Lanza LPs are all Lesley can remember. By the time her own children were heading for the Big Day Out she knew there was no stopping them but that didn't prevent Lesley from worrying about their being captured by the forces of darkness. Now, as she picks her way through the growing maze of campers cooking meals by the light of oil lamps, dancing to the music from a guitar or the blue notes of an amateur saxophonist, or kissing in the shadows, she wonders what she may have missed. This world has passed her by. While others were hanging out at festivals enjoying all the things her parents had feared, she was a girl guide leader making scones, teaching Sunday school and, later, proudly collecting items for her bottom drawer. Has Gordon ever been to a music festival, she wonders, and would he enjoy this? When they married he had a large record collection, most of it jazz, and she remembers an argument about where they would fit in the little flat that was to be their first home. Where are those records now, she wonders, packed up in the garage, given to a jumble sale?

Lesley sits down on a low wall looking around her, screwing up her eyes to peer into the semi-darkness. It's hopeless – she's never going to find Declan among all these people. She should have grabbed the opportunity when she saw him earlier in the café, but he had the boy with him, Todd, the one Paula was always complaining about. The obvious thing is to ring his mobile but he has consistently ignored her calls. Besides, a call won't solve anything. She wants to see him, to have a conversation like they had in the first few days, face to face, honest, companionable.

She takes out her phone to check whether by any remote chance he has responded to the text she sent this morning telling him she was driving down today, but the record of calls shows three and a text, all of them from Paula. Paula had called much earlier just as Lesley was collecting the keys to the house she had rented.

'You wanna get together later?' Paula had asked. 'We could drive out to Benson's – see what's going on. Maybe get something to eat in the snotty café.'

Lesley had prevaricated. 'Not sure yet,' she'd said. 'I'll call you back later. I might just have a quiet night in. I had a near-miss on the road on the way down and it seems to have knocked the stuffing out of me.'

'Those bastards in four-wheel-drives,' Paula had said. 'Think they own the road. If I had my way I'd have them banned. You'll probably feel better if you have a bit of a lie-down. Ring me later.'

Lesley had agreed but had hung up with no intention of calling back. Going out on the town with Paula was never going to happen. She had been helpful over Declan's phone number and with other bits of information but they have nothing in common and it's not as though they're friends, or ever likely to be. Except for a couple of times when she'd been in a strangely dark mood Paula was far too full on for Lesley's liking. Besides, what she'd said was true, the near-miss on the road had been a horrible shock and its impact is far more complicated than Lesley had made it sound.

She'd been travelling fast on a wide straight road lined with tall trees and dense bush. A couple of patchy showers had left the road itself and the surrounding trees glisten-ing as the sunlight flickered through the branches. It was the first rain for months and she wondered if it had rained at Benson's Reach. What would they do if it rained on the festival, rained really hard? She drove on singing along to a compilation album of sixties hits which she only ever plays when she's alone in the car because Gordon and her children think it's tacky. She was doing a splendid accompaniment to Gary Puckett and the Union Gap with 'Young Girl' when she realised that a song she had always thought of as being about love was actually about a man's desire for sex with an under-age girl. In fact, the more she thought about it, a lot of the songs on the album were like that. Suddenly the innocence of romantic first love was obviously something quite differ-ent. And as Gary gave way to Billy Fury and her favourite, 'Halfway to Paradise', she heard for the first time that Billy was not singing about unrequited love but frustrated lust. Abruptly she stopped singing and flicked the button to go back to the start of the track and make sure, but as she did so she missed the moment that the dog darted out of the bush and into the road and she had hit it before she knew it was there. Braking sharply she skidded into a wide semicircle across the wet surface of the road into the opposite lane and ended up in the red gravel of the hard shoulder, facing back in the direction from which she had come. A four-wheel-drive whose trajectory she had crossed with terrifying proximity roared on past, the driver furiously blasting his horn while a passenger gave her two fingers from the nearside window.

'Well thanks for stopping, guys,' Lesley yelled as she switched off the engine. The dog was dead, the seriously flattened sort of dead, she could see that from where she was sitting. Should she remove it from the road? But as she considered what to do a panel van flattened it further and was soon followed by half a dozen other cars. She sat there wondering: there might be something in the boot she could use to move it, although by that time a few more vehicles had passed over the poor thing and it looked more as though it would take a scrubbing brush and a bucket of soapy water to get it off the road. Lesley stopped thinking about the dog and began to think about herself.

Billy had wound up now and Mark Wynter had launched into 'Go Away Little Girl'. Lesley switched off the CD player, leaned back in her seat and closed her eyes, thinking back to her youth, to the other songs on the album, 'Sweet Sixteen', 'Little Sister'. Alone in the car she blushes at her own naivety, and it reminds her that it wasn't only the music that was not all it seemed. She remembered the occasions before she met Gordon when she herself had confused desire with love. Dolly's attempts at sex education had been of the 'save it for the one you love' variety. For Lesley and probably for many other girls, this instruction translated to doing it and then convincing yourself that you'd done it because you were in love, which would somehow make it all right. Lesley had not done it much – she was too frightened of getting pregnant – but whenever she had 'gone all the way' there had been a brief period of romantic self-delusion to justify what she had done, and to enjoy the feeling of being sexually attractive, desirable. It usually didn't take long before the boy concerned either dumped her, or the scales would fall from her own eyes and she would dump him.

Sitting there, facing in the wrong direction, her heart only just slowing to normal rate after her near-miss, Lesley saw that she had done it again. She had conned herself at almost

243

sixty just as she had at sixteen, only this time there is much more at stake, and very much more to be embarrassed about. She had embarked on an adventure which, like the shopping, had been a distraction from the fact that her marriage, in fact her whole life, seemed to be falling apart. And then the combination of guilt and that same old longing to be loved and wanted had come to her rescue. Only of course it was no sort of rescue at all, it was a potential disaster. And now her skin crawled with shame as she remembered how she had behaved, not simply that night, but more importantly since then.

For some time Lesley had sat there in the car by the side of the road thinking over everything that had happened. What if this had been Karen? Well, she would have told her daughter that she was being ridiculous, would have sent her away to sort out whatever it was that had happened with Nick and told her to grow up. Not that Lesley thought it was immature to fall in love, just foolish to pretend that a one night stand with a comparative stranger was the answer to the complex problems of mid-life and a marriage in crisis. In that moment she considered heading back home. She was, after all, facing in the right direction. Perhaps the incident with the poor dead dog was a message from the universe. Maybe even her fall on the way home last time was part of it, a message that she was not supposed to be on this road at all.

But she couldn't stand the thought of the house; the house, which had become unbearable with Gordon in it, was even more unbearable in his absence. She would carry on, sort things out with Declan with as much humility and dignity as possible, and then pay some attention to her future. She unscrewed her water bottle, drank the remains and, once the road was clear, pulled out, swung the car back to face south and drove on, rather more slowly and without music, in the direction in which she had been travelling. And as she did so she had contemplated how she could talk to Declan about this in the least embarrassing way, if she could get him to talk to her at all.

And so, earlier this evening, she had driven down to Benson's Reach, parked the car and wandered around among the tents and up the hill, looking for him. There was no sign of him but as she passed the office window she could see Ruby sitting at the desk reading intently. Lesley knew that she should apologise to her and also to Alice. In the past both Sandi and Gordon had chided her for her brusque, sometimes imperious manner in shops and restaurants, but on this occasion she needed no chiding – she knew she had been downright rude. If she was to clear up the mess of her own making she had more than one apology to make. So she had headed for the café thinking she might catch Alice, apologise, and find out where Declan was likely to be. It was very busy in the café and there was no sign of Alice when Lesley ordered her coffee and toasted sandwich at the counter, so she sat down at a table which was partly obscured by one of the old telegraph poles which were both structural elements and design features of the building, and from where she could see both the entrance and the counter. Even so she had somehow missed the moment at which Declan came in with Todd, because when she looked up there they were at the counter, apparently waiting for take-away food.

It had seemed like the perfect opportunity; she would catch him on his way out. She saw Alice emerge from the kitchen and hand two hamburgers across the counter, the first to Todd and then to Declan. He took it from her and smiled, reached out to take her hand, said something to her, and Alice, smiling in return, leaned across the counter and kissed him on the cheek. There was something tender and quite moving in the whole exchange and it brought a lump to Lesley's throat. Even with her new and more realistic understanding of what happened between her and Declan she still felt a stab of jealousy and as Declan left the café with Todd she made no attempt to speak to, or follow, him. She just stayed there remembering the expression on his face and the respect and affection that was so obvious whenever he spoke of Alice.

She had stayed on at her table for almost half an hour and when eventually she left the bright warmth of the café for the shadowy buzz of the outdoors there was no sign of him and she wandered around once more, finally coming to rest here on this low wall in the half-light. Her phone rings suddenly, jolting her out of her stillness. It's Paula again, and Lesley switches it off and gets to her feet. Ruby is still alone in the office poring over a book. Maybe she knows where Declan is, and anyway, Lesley thinks, it's time for her first act of humility and she takes a deep breath and sets off along the path to the office.

uby is hiding. Officially she's on duty in the office, a responsibility that Declan had felt was his but for which she has volunteered. He was clearly longing to be out among the crowd and this was a legitimate way for her to stay away from it. The prospect of the festival is daunting and she would have loved an excuse to disappear completely and return only when it was all over, but her conscience got the better of her. She feels she has a responsibility to Declan and Alice, and indeed the rest of the staff, who have all worked so hard on the preparations and will be putting in long hours over the next four days, so she has decided to grit her teeth and survive it.

'I'll take the early part of the evening in the office if you like. It'll give you a chance to meet people, and you can come and take over for the last couple of hours.'

Jackson Crow had called to say that they were running late and would arrive around ten, by which time Ruby planned to be tucked up in bed with a book.

Even though she hadn't been looking forward to it Ruby hadn't anticipated her own reaction to the visitors who had been arriving since early this morning. She knew it was unreasonable but as the first few tents were erected it seemed

247

as though Benson's was being taken over and as the numbers grew so did her resentment. She wanted to march out onto the track that had been railed off for the cars and shout at them to turn back and go away. Even when Benson's was fully booked it was usually peaceful; it attracted guests looking for quiet and relaxation rather than a party atmosphere. But now the place has been transformed into something frighteningly unmanageable where anything could happen. It's just your age, she'd told herself several times, but when, towards the end of the afternoon, she had ventured out to see what was happening, she realised that many of the festival goers weren't all that young – most of them were older baby boomers, some even as old as she was.

As she stood watching from the verandah she was briefly back in 1969 on a crowded ferry heading for the Isle of Wight to see Bob Dylan. She was with Rowena, whose flat she had shared since she arrived in London a few months earlier. Rowena was a party animal and festivals were her favourite parties. The following year they were back again for Joni Mitchell, Jimi Hendrix and Leonard Cohen and a month later to Glastonbury, a festival Ruby remembers more for being the place she met Owen, and the collective grief that overtook the crowd as word got around that Jimi Hendrix had died. And although festivals today hold no attraction, they do draw her back into nostalgia.

In the almost thirty years since Owen's death she has lived alone, at first with difficulty, but later with increasing satisfaction and undeniably enjoyable freedom. She had been devastated when he died suddenly and dramatically of kidney failure caused by an infection contracted on a trip to Venezuela. In medical school he had specialised in tropical diseases and had soon made a name for himself in the field. When he was invited to visit a research project in the Amazon he had jumped at the chance and had laughed off Ruby's concern. Three months later she was a widow. Since then there have been other short-term relationships that have fizzled out mainly due to her own lack of enthusiasm and commitment. Friendships grew stronger and more important as she battled through layers of grief over the losses in her life: her childhood, her friendship with Catherine, her first marriage, her inability to have children and finally the loss of Owen. These days she lives a pretty quiet life, declining most invitations to openings, launches and parties, finding pleasure and satisfaction in her work, a few close friends, her books, and the constant battle with the garden. Relationships – the hunt for them and the difficulties of being in them – are a thing of the past and that is both a relief and a regret. The excitement charged atmosphere of a music festival is alien to her now and burying her head in the sand seems infinitely preferable.

Sitting in the office, her feet up on a chair, leaning sideways against the desk with one of Catherine's journals in her hands, she's expecting a quiet evening. Festival goers have no real need of the office but they'd decided to keep it open in case of unforeseen problems. Struggling with Catherine's erratic writing she barely notices the sound of footsteps along the verandah. It is the shadow in the doorway that makes her glance up.

Lesley Craddock looks the same but different, very different; vulnerability is apparent in both her posture and the expression on her face.

'Hi,' she says, hesitating in the doorway, as though going inside might be a step too far. 'Sorry to disturb you.'

Ruby puts down the journal. 'You're not,' she says. 'We're open for business, so come on in. What can I do for you? If you're looking for accommodation I'm afraid we're fully booked,' and she gestures to the chair on the other side of the desk.

'I know,' Lesley says, and she steps inside and perches stiffly on the edge of the chair. 'Declan told me you were booked out for the festival. And in any case I'm planning on being around for a while, so I've rented a place in town.' She pauses and the silence is awkward. 'But I wanted to see you and just spotted you through the window . . . I've come to apologise. I was very rude to you and of course to Alice when I was last here. I can't think what got into me. It's been a difficult time and I suppose I let that get the better of me. When I thought about it later . . . well I'm sorry, very sorry.'

Ruby nods. 'Thank you. I appreciate that and I know Alice will too.' The apology seems genuine, but there is clearly something else on Lesley's mind and Ruby senses that humility does not come easily to her. 'I hope things are settling down for you now.'

'Sort of . . .' Lesley says, 'it's messy.'

'So you're back here for a while – is your accommodation all right?'

'It is, thanks. Very comfortable. It's pretty busy out there, isn't it?'

Ruby pulls a face. 'It certainly is – which is good, of course, but it's all a bit much for me. These days I tend to panic at the prospect of large groups of people.'

Lesley nods, and gives a nervous laugh. 'Me too . . . do you think it's a sign we're getting old?'

'You may be *getting*, I've *gotten*,' Ruby says, grinning. 'But I think you're right.'

The silence is less awkward this time. 'I've been looking for Declan,' Lesley says. 'I caught sight of him earlier in the café, but by the time I'd squeezed out through the crowd he seemed to have disappeared.'

'He's pretty busy,' Ruby says. 'It's been a chaotic day and I suspect tomorrow will be the same, or worse. All I can tell you is that he'll be somewhere on the property if you want to wander around and see if you can find him.'

She nods. 'I've tried that but I might give it another go.' She gets up, hovering awkwardly in front of the desk. 'If you see him could you tell him I was looking for him, please?

And thanks again.' And with a nervous smile she heads out of the door and back towards the café.

Eight o'clock. Ruby sighs, longing for the delicious seclusion of her own room. She gets up from the desk, fills the kettle and stands waiting for it to boil, wondering what has happened to create this change in Lesley. She makes her tea, turns off the harsh central light, switches on the standard lamp and, picking up Catherine's journal from the desk, she settles herself on the small two-seater sofa with her feet up.

Catherine's style is erratic: part catalogue of events, part poignant reflection on their time in the convent, and all of it woven through with dreams for the future. It's a future in which the two of them are always together, travelling together, working together, side by side, like twins – inseparably linked by the shared traumas of their childhood. For Ruby it is a powerful reminder of the years when Catherine was her anchor, her protector and the only person she could trust. Even when they had left the convent for jobs at the hotel in Perth they had continued to cling together, but as Ruby's confidence grew their closeness seemed suffocating.

The words weave sentences that prise open memories of enmeshment and mutual dependence, and she feels her chest tighten now, as it did then, when she struggled to break free from what had been her life support, but which had become a barrier to independence. They'd had their first arguments then, the first painful and challenging silences, the first hurts and small jealousies, the inevitable intrusion of others into what had for so long been exclusive. It is all there, all in the journal, raw, honest, and it makes for painful reading. Is it just tiredness, she wonders, or the desire to escape from this vivid evocation of the past that makes it so hard to keep her eyes open? The exercise book slips from her hands and she shifts further down on the sofa. Muddled images of the steep flights of the hotel stairs, the deep red flocked wallpaper of the restaurant, the harsh bright lights and clatter of the kitchens, whirl and blur through her head, drawing her down into memories fraught with tension.

'Excuse me.' A tap on the already open door. 'Excuse me, ma'am.'

Ruby's eyes snap open, the journal thumps down onto the floor and she stumbles to her feet, heart pounding with the shock of waking.

'Goodness me,' she says, flustered. 'Goodness me, I'm so sorry. I'm supposed to be on duty but I must have fallen asleep.' Her glasses slip down from the top of her head, skimming her forehead and settling conveniently on the bridge of her nose. And, smoothing down her hair, she looks up and sees him – a dark skinned man with crisp silver grey hair that curls around his neck and ears, and deep, disturbingly familiar eyes. A stranger, yet a man she feels she knows like she knows herself, and her heart seems to lurch, stop beating, then struggle to start again. 'Ah!' she says as their eyes meet, and for an instant she thinks she hears his heart hesitate too. But that, of course is just too fanciful for words. 'You must be Mr Crow. You're rather earlier than we expected.'

— ◆ —

Paula can count on one hand the things that make her feel peaceful; watering and talking to her plants is usually one of them. They don't need watering every day but she still goes down to see them, to chat to them. But this evening they don't seem to be having the required effect. It's been a hard day, new guests arriving, cars everywhere, people asking questions and putting up tents, noise, all messing with her head. She's feeling really spacey tonight. Maybe she shouldn't have stopped taking the medication. It's a while now, and she's done it before, but always gone back on it again. But right now she can't be doing with that dozy feeling the drugs give her, the awful thirst and the constant need to pee. It's unfair, Paula thinks, because it's other people who need her to take them – they find her easier to get on with when she's on the drugs – but what she wants is to feel okay without them, to be just like everyone else – and how will she know if she can be like that if she doesn't even try?

'What do you think?' she asks, leaning in closely to the last plant in the line and taking a leaf between her fingers. 'Pills or no pills? To take or not to take?' The plant moves slightly in the breeze and she takes it as a sign that she should stay off the drugs – keep trying to manage without them. 'I agree,' Paula says to the plant, setting down the empty watering can. 'Thanks for the advice.'

Tonight she feels as though she is made of very thin, brittle ice that could shatter at any moment, each little shard melting away to nothing while she watches herself disintegrate. It's better than the dozy feeling but it makes her seem unreal and so she talks more and louder to try to make herself seem real again. She might even say or do a few things that aren't quite right. She'd be very clear about what should happen, and then other people would argue with her and she'd know they were wrong but she'd be the one who'd come out of it looking bad.

'You don't seem to understand about boundaries, Paula,' Catherine had said to her once. 'You can be really intrusive, even overbearing. You only seem able to see things your way and you don't listen. It's like you're disconnected from everyone else, only focused on yourself. I know it's hard for you, and I understand you don't want to keep taking the drugs, but you're difficult to get along with without them.'

Paula had trusted Catherine, but twice in the time she's worked there she's come off the drugs and twice Catherine had told her that she had to get back on them or leave Benson's. But Catherine's gone now and, anyway, she didn't know everything. Maybe, Paula thinks, I'll be okay this time.

She walks along the little path of irregular shaped, broken slabs back to the kitchen. It's deadly quiet in the house and the 100 watt bulb in the kitchen makes her feel she's about to be interrogated by the thought police. She wishes there was someone to call, to talk to. All day, every day she is surrounded by people who are ringing other people on their posh little phones. Paula has a phone, nice, Samsung, in a shiny pink plastic cover, but nobody ever rings it – well, not for a conversation; work stuff or someone telling her she's forgotten to make a payment on her credit card, or trying to sell her something, that's all.

'You can always ring me if you need to talk to someone,' Catherine had said. And quite often Paula had done that and it had worked, but most of the time just knowing she could call was enough. It was odd because Paula had never felt that Catherine actually liked her, it was more like she tolerated her, perhaps she felt sorry for her, but she also needed her because Paula is the best cleaner for miles around. Anywhere else she'd be paid more and would be called an executive housekeeper or a domestic manager, but nobody at Benson's sees her potential, she's just Paula the Cleaner. She imagines her card in the Benson's deck of Happy Families: Paula the Cleaner, Ruby the Inquisitor, Declan the Loser, Alice the Intruder, Fleur the Outsider and Todd, of course, the Spoiler. But she can't quite get herself together to go and look for a different job because the whole idea of it just does her head in. If they don't sort things out soon, or end up giving Fleur's job to someone else she's definitely going to go. Sod 'em, no point staying on where you're not appreciated. Not that she's ever really been appreciated. If she had been, if someone had only really appreciated her, she wouldn't be here now, living in this little matchbox, which she keeps as spotless as she keeps the rooms at Benson's Reach. She wouldn't be stuck here all on her own with no one to talk to and no one to call.

'People always seem to slip away,' she says aloud to the empty kitchen. 'Just when you think you've made a friend they're gone. They need you, use you, then leave you when they've got what they want.'

Lesley Craddock, for example, inviting her in to chat in her cottage, making her cups of tea and pumping her for information, and just when she'd thought they were friends it all stops. Just like that. 'Too busy to talk now, Paula.' 'Must dash.' 'Must get on.' 'No, don't call tomorrow, I have to look after the twins.' 'No, I don't want to go out, had a near-miss in the car.' Typical, Paula thinks, you put yourself out for people and they just make use of you. Catherine had understood that. Paula thought she and Catherine probably had quite a lot in common. That's why she's keen to get into that room now, make sure Catherine's little secret is not going to come sneaking out to damage her reputation.

Eating something seems like a good idea right now, and she opens the cupboard above the bench top, takes out a tin of baked beans, opens it and eats the cold beans with a spoon, just as she did when she was a kid. Knowing she is doing something that would send her mother right off her trolley has always been extremely satisfying. When she's had enough she puts the tin, with the teaspoon still in it, into the fridge, pulls out a bottle of juice, takes a swig and wanders across to look at herself in the kitchen mirror. She doesn't look bad for her age, though not as good as Kylie.

When Paula was younger people used to say she looked like Kylie – or Charlene, as she was then. She'd had the same hair, but she was a bit taller. Paula turns side on to the mirror and does a few Kylie moves that she's spent a lot of time perfecting. Years ago when she and Gary used to go to karaoke nights she would always do a Kylie number, and back then, when Kylie started singing, Paula had reckoned she looked and sounded just like her. '*I should be so lucky,*' she sings. Kylie, well *she's* really lucky. You'd think she was a goddess the way some people go on about her; there's even a statue of her in Melbourne. Of course she had the cancer but she even made that into a hit. '*I should be so lucky.*'

Paula reaches up, pulls the scrunchie off her ponytail,

fluffs out her hair and swings her shoulders from side to side. It's all luck, she thinks. She could have been just as good as Kylie, she could have been a goddess, an icon, all she needed was the luck, but there hadn't been much of that around when she was growing up. While Kylie was starring in soap operas and cuddling up to Jason Donovan, Paula was doing night cleaning at the supermarket and screwing spotty losers in the car park.

She'd been lucky once, though, only once and not for long, lucky with Gary, lucky in love. Until she was unlucky, until her bloody slut of a sister cut her right out of the picture. Paula has another big swig of juice. What she'd really like is to be up on that stage at Benson's, singing 'Dancing Queen', wearing sequins and silver tassels and a big headdress thing with ostrich feathers, like Kylie wore at the Olympics. She'd driven up there earlier this evening and pushed her way through the people and gone up onto the darkened stage and stood there looking down, imagining herself strutting her stuff, microphone in hand. That'd give them all something to think about.

Paula closes her eyes, wishing she felt more like normal. Perhaps she just needs to sleep. If only they could see what she can do. Tomorrow, maybe, she'll get all dressed up and get up there on the stage and sing, she'll make them listen to her and see her. Nobody ever sees her, and they don't listen when she tells them interesting stuff or gives advice. She slips a CD into the ghetto blaster, and she's singing along with Kylie to 'Dancing Queen', strutting back and forth across the spotlessly clean vinyl tiles, swinging her hips, pouting at the audience, one arm raised above her head. And she sings and dances and swings and pouts and twists and sways and struts until her feet hurt and her arms ache and the music stops, and in the silence of the empty kitchen she sinks into a chair and bursts into tears.

Declan keys Lesley's number into the phone and waits – one ring, two rings. It's late, he thinks, maybe he should leave it and call in the morning. But then she answers and his stomach clenches. Had he made this call weeks ago things might by now be sorted. Faced with the emotional and practical consequences of his procrastination in the weeks before Catherine's death, he had promised himself that in future he would face up to the next emotional challenge as soon as it reared its head. But here it is – his first crisis and again he tried to solve it by pretending to ignore it. He's only calling Lesley now because Ruby passed on Lesley's message so he feels he has no choice.

'Er . . . hi,' he says, 'it's me, Declan.' He knows he sounds pathetic, so he clears his throat and tries again. 'Sorry, it's Declan here, Lesley, Ruby said you were looking for me.'

'I was,' she says, 'but I couldn't find you so I left. I really need to talk to you . . .'

'Sure,' he says, 'sure, absolutely, but it's difficult now. The festival . . . you've seen the crowds here . . . it's going to be pretty frantic—'

'Declan,' Lesley interrupts, 'I need to talk to you, it won't take long. I know I've made a fool of myself and I'm sorry. I just want to put things right.'

'Ah . . . I see, that's good,' he says, not at all sure what putting things right might involve. 'We must get together sometime soon . . .'

'Yes, tomorrow morning,' she says. 'Can you meet me for breakfast?'

He hesitates, again.

'Look, I've been really stupid but you were pretty stupid too,' she says, 'sneaking off at dawn, fetching my car and leaving it outside so you wouldn't have to face me, and then ignoring my calls. Let's just get this painful bit over and done with, then we can start behaving normally again.'

Over and done with is just what he wants. 'Okay,' he says,

'but I really do have a lot on tomorrow. Could you come down to the café at, say, eight o'clock?'

'I'll see you then,' she says.

And she hangs up, leaving him standing there in the darkness feeling as though the conversation is not quite finished. He pockets his phone with a sigh as a light goes out behind him and he turns to see Alice locking the back door of the café.

'There you are,' she says, strolling over to him. 'How were the hamburgers?'

'To die for. Todd says he could have eaten four more.'

'Only four? Everything go okay today?'

'Pretty good,' he says, 'no major dramas, and Jackson Crow and his merry men arrived about an hour ago so everyone's here now. Cup of tea or are you too tired?'

'I'm tired but also too wide awake to go to bed so, yes, tea would be good. Strange, isn't it,' she says as they walk towards the house, 'all those tents, the cars, all those people just moving in and setting up camp and waiting – you can actually feel them waiting.'

They let themselves in through the back door and Declan fills the kettle.

'No Ruby?' Alice asks.

'She's gone to bed,' he says. 'Her first meeting with Jackson Crow seemed to be something of a shock, and of course it's been a very long day. Look, Alice,' he crosses to the table and sits down to face her, 'there's something I need to tell you. It's about that business with the computer search. It's . . . well, it's just as we suspected – it was Paula, it must have been.'

Alice nods. 'I was pretty sure it had to be but how do you know?'

'Todd,' Declan says, 'he knows you were in prison. He overheard Paula on the phone when she was talking to Lesley.' He sees her face, white in the bright fluorescent light of the kitchen. 'Now, I know this is a shock, but you really don't need to worry about Todd. I talked to him, he hasn't told anyone and he won't, I trust him, he thinks the world of you—'

'I'm not worried about Todd,' Alice cuts in, 'and I'll talk to him myself. But Lesley, and Paula . . .'

'I'll talk to Lesley when I see her tomorrow.'

'She was really friendly tonight, she came to see me to apologise.'

'Apologise for what?'

'Oh, of course, you didn't know. Well, when you were up in Perth she wanted to know where you were and was asking for your number and she was really rude when I wouldn't give it to her. But tonight she just said she was sorry, she'd been in a bit of a crisis and knew she'd behaved badly.'

Declan leaned back in his chair. 'And that was all?'

Alice nods. 'Yes – well, we talked about other things, the festival, whether it might rain . . . She seemed different, I think she meant it.'

He nods. 'She's a nice woman having a really difficult time, and I made it more difficult.' He's about to elaborate but stops himself just in time. 'I think it will be fine with Lesley, honestly. It's Paula I'm concerned about, not just her talking to people but the fact that she went into the office and logged onto the computer. I'm going to set a password tomorrow and only you and Ruby and I will have it, but we're also going to have to do something about this, we can't just ignore it.'

Alice sighs. 'I suppose we can't, but Paula will never admit it. And, really, there's not much we can do about it.'

Declan gets up to make the tea. 'I think there is. If we – by which I mean if *Ruby* – carpets her she might just take offence and leave. She thinks I'm a wanker but she's a bit scared of Ruby.'

'If she does leave she'll tell everyone, all the staff, everyone.' Alice pauses. 'And there's another thing. Paula's one of the most irritating people I've ever met but she's really good at her job, and sometimes I think it's all she's got. Sometimes I think the brashness that we find so abrasive is just a cover. She's quite fragile, really.'

Declan carries the teapot and mugs to the table and fetches the milk from the fridge. 'You're being very generous. I think you'd be well within your rights to ask us to sack her.'

Alice shakes her head. 'When Ruby found out about me she could've asked – or told you – that I had to go, but she didn't. I don't like Paula, and I'm furious that she's done this, but I sort of think it's more about the power of having the information than about malice.'

'Frankly, to me she is just a pain in the arse and I'd be glad to see the back of her,' Declan says.

'Declan, you and I know all about stuffing things up, we've both been experts at that. Maybe what Paula needs is someone to take an interest in her.'

He shrugs. 'Maybe, but there's something else too. I found out tonight that Paula is Todd's aunt, his mother's sister. Apparently Catherine knew this although she didn't tell me. But then I didn't get here in time for her to tell me half the things I needed to know. It seems there was some big bust-up years ago and they've never spoken to each other since.'

'How odd,' Alice says, 'I wonder what that's all about. Not that it makes any difference to this situation. I do think we need to know a bit more about her, but it might be best to wait until after the festival. We'll all have more than enough to cope with over the next few days.' She sips her tea and, putting her hand into her pocket, brings out a folded piece of paper. 'Look at this,' she says, handing it to him, 'it came a while ago.'

'What is it?' he asks.

'Just read it.'

Declan unfolds the letter, reads the curt message once and then a second time and looks up at her. 'She put her phone number,' he says. 'She actually gave you her number.'

Alice nods and he sees that there are tears in her eyes.

'You haven't used it, have you? You haven't called her?'

'No,' she says, 'of course not.'

'Good.' He nods slowly and reads it again. 'It's a test, isn't it? I think it's a test.'

'That's what I thought – a test. And if I pass it . . . well, who knows . . .?'

'You'll pass it,' Declan says. 'You'll pass it, I know you will. You're not alone now, I can help. You can pass all her tests, one at a time. Alice, I know how much you want your family back, but promise me one thing – don't sacrifice yourself in the process. You've come so far in the past few months, nothing is worth sacrificing that for.'

Twenty

I t's after midnight and Ruby is wide awake, sitting up in bed surrounded by Catherine's journals. She's trying to find a specific entry from some time during their first year at Benson's Hotel but before Harry had arrived back from London. The faster she flicks through the pages the more agitated she becomes. There are long entries for almost every day: stuff about their work, what Mrs Benson said to the chef, what the chef said about Mrs Benson once she'd left the kitchen. And there are earlier reminiscences that Catherine has woven into her journal often for no apparent reason. Ruby stops at one which she'd almost forgotten. It was that moment on the dock when they had just set foot in Australia, when she was seven and Catherine eight, just a year between them.

'We'll pretend we're the same age,' Catherine had whispered as they were lined up on the dock in Fremantle. 'Then we won't be separated. Say you're eight. Don't forget when they ask you, Ruby, say you're eight years old.'

Ruby wonders now how Catherine had known to do this. She'd been right, though. Quite soon after that the girls had been separated from the boys, and then the man in charge began asking each one how old they were. Catherine had given Ruby a nudge and she had promptly announced her age as eight and the two of them had been moved in with the other eight-year-olds. She was always such a knowing child, and so authoritative, at least that was what Ruby used to think. Later she changed from authoritative to controlling, but back then it was different. Changing her age had meant that they were together in the convent and that they were able to leave the convent together. It was pure luck that Mrs Benson had approached the nuns about finding two girls for the hotel.

'You'll be cleaning the rooms, changing linen and so on, and there'll be work in the kitchen and the restaurant too. You'll get all your meals, and you'll share a room. One day off a week, no mixing with the guests,' she'd said, looking them up and down with an obviously critical eye. But then she'd smiled and Ruby can still remember that smile, not just how it looked but the sudden intense joy of a smile from someone in authority.

'So what do you think?'

They were in Mother Superior's office at the time and they hardly knew what to think. She was actually *asking* them if they wanted the job, as if they had some sort of choice, as if their opinions were worth something. They had no choice, of course, the alternative would have meant being separated. In the years since then Ruby has often thought of this as one of her 'what if?' moments: what if someone else had arrived at the convent instead of Mrs Benson? What if they'd been separated then? What if their lives had gone in totally different directions? But there they were, Mother Superior glaring at them, willing them to go, Freda Benson waiting for an answer. All they had to do was to say yes to freedom.

But what Ruby's looking for now in the journals is something she had forgotten but which had returned to her the moment she looked up and saw Jackson Crow – a conversation and then an entry in the journal from the night of Catherine's first date. They had been at the hotel for some time by then because at first Mrs Benson was very strict about what they could and couldn't do and dates were not on the agenda. She was kind but firm and although the work was hard it was nothing like as hard as the convent. The nuns had treated them with dislike and disgust but Mrs Benson seemed to like them, and she hadn't forgotten how it felt to be young.

'I feel I'm responsible for you,' she'd said. 'You're not only young, you're very naive. I don't think they taught you much at all in the convent so someone has to look out for you.' She had taken that responsibility very seriously, behaving at first more like a guardian than an employer. On this particular night Catherine, who had been told to be home by ten-thirty, had scraped in with about thirty seconds to spare, and Ruby was sitting bolt upright in bed, breathless for details.

'So, how was it? Did he try to kiss you? You have to tell me everything, absolutely everything.'

Catherine had pulled off her clothes and climbed into bed. 'He was so boring,' she said. 'Don't you think that's the worst sin a man could commit, Ruby, being boring?' And Ruby, in her ignorance, had agreed. Now she knows that there are far greater possible sins, although being boring still rates fairly highly.

Catherine groaned. 'I swear he told me his whole life story, and then everything about his football team, and probably every other team in the whole world. He never stopped talking and he didn't even *try* to kiss me in the cinema, just held my hand. You really can't tell, can you?' she went on. 'I mean, how would you know if you'd met the right man? We know nothing about this, Ruby, we just don't have a clue. I bet other girls know much more than we do.'

And she was right. Even a few months of Freda Benson's guidance hadn't prepared them for the shark infested waters of the dating game. Men hadn't figured much in the life of the convent, apart from the two local priests, but they were remote, almost godlike figures around whom the nuns, normally hatchet faced, vicious tongued and prone to physical violence bordering on torture, turned into fawning, simpering creatures hungry for a word or nod of approval. Other men came and went: the maintenance man, a local builder, delivery men, the man who serviced the nuns' ancient car, but they too were creatures apart – alien beings with whom the girls were not even supposed to exchange a greeting. There was no television, no magazines, not even newspapers, and although there were books the ones the girls were allowed to read were not the stuff of romance, nor did they contain even the elements of human biology. It was only in their final year that the subject of boys somehow became the topic of whispered conversations and speculation, all of which was firmly rooted in ignorance.

Once freed from the convent, however, their knowledge increased exponentially. In that little attic bedroom at the hotel they dived into Mrs Benson's copies of *New Idea* and *Australian Women's Weekly*, and lay with the lights out far into the night, listening to Harry's LPs on his old record player that Mrs Benson had loaned them in his absence. On days when there were few guests and the hotel lounge was empty, they discovered the wonders of black and white television, or escaped to the cinema on their afternoons off. But it was when they joined the library that they really started to learn about life, love and the opposite sex as they worked their way through the novels on a list Mrs Benson had drawn up for them.

'So how will we know?' Catherine had asked again. 'How will we know when we meet the right man?'

'We'll know,' Ruby had said, and even now she can remember the conviction with which she had said it. 'I'll know, I'm sure I will. It's like that song, you know in the movie, in *South Pacific.*' She had struggled for the words then. 'About some magical evening when you see a stranger across a room, and you know that he's the one. It'll be like electricity, like being struck by lightning.'

Catherine had rolled her eyes. 'You mean "Some Enchanted Evening", when you went all dopey about Rossano Brazzi? But he's *so old*. Oh well, I'll write it down anyway, you never know when we might need it.'

'You can't, a journal is to write down what you're doing, what happens to you, not stuff about men we haven't met yet.'

'Now *you're* being boring, Rube. Like I said before, when we're old we'll want to read this. We'll want to see what we thought and how we felt – how we feel right now. And we'll be able to see if we ended up with the right man.'

'And what if we haven't?'

'Well, that'll be just too bad, won't it?' Catherine said, sighing with exasperation. 'But at least we'll know.'

Not that knowing after the event is a lot of use, Ruby thinks now, finally finding the page she was searching for. She reads it through twice, leans back against her pillows and closes her eyes, remembering Rossano Brazzi's face, his voice. In that moment in the cinema, she had felt herself softening and opening, felt her senses spring overwhelmingly into life in a way that was as thrilling as it was unnerving.

'You are totally ridiculous,' Ruby tells herself now, opening her eyes, sitting up straighter. 'You were a teenager then and now you're sixty-nine – pull yourself together.' But somehow she can't. Somehow from the moment she looked up and saw Jackson Crow standing in front of her she might as well have been back in that dark little cinema, the music soaring in the background, naive, impressionable, totally disarmed but utterly certain. She has butterflies in her stomach now, her heart races, slows and races again, and until she got off them her legs had been trembling. Could he tell the effect he had on her? Was it written all over her face? Could Declan see it when he came into the office?

Her restless imagination is now unbearable and Ruby throws off the bedclothes, gets up again and begins to pace the room as though the exercise might burn off the heat of her body. 'Ridiculous,' she says again. 'You are a ridiculous old woman, overcome with ... well what? Lust? Desire?' But alongside her dismay is the conviction that something powerful had happened and not just to her – as though a connection had sparked and crackled into life. She had gasped for breath at the power of it, and through the conversation that followed, through the pleasantries, through the condolences about the loss of Catherine, and the process of checking Jackson and his band into their cottages, it continued to burn.

And what is she supposed to do with this? Ruby is a realist – or so she has always believed. Scorched by the disaster of her first marriage she had been cautious when she met Owen. She had taken time to trust him and then to risk loving him. There had been no lightning bolt at Glastonbury, no swooning, no aching, just a sense of something special and safe, something to nurture and tease into life; together they had grown into love. But that was decades ago. Love and desire is everywhere – on screens, on billboards, in magazines, advertisements and song lyrics – but all its images, its enactments, its literature and music are about youth, young love, first love. Even mature lovers are beautiful, firm, and either surgically or photographically enhanced. It is all about beautiful bodies and fierce sexual passion, not about old people gripped with desire and bodies soft, slack and wrinkled with age. It is about a particular sort of look, a look Ruby knows she never had even when young. She had always been uncomfortably aware of how little she resembled the images of female beauty all around her.

'I should've been around in Rubens' day,' she had once said to Owen. 'I'd have been a hit with him. He had an eye for generous proportions like mine, for dimples and pale skin.'

'Well you may have come along too late for Rubens,' Owen had said, wrapping his arms around her, 'but fortunately you *are* here now, and you're a big hit with me.'

Ruby drags her nightdress over her head and stands naked in front of the long mirror, staring at her reflection. Her blood is racing through her veins with the heat and power of youth, but what she sees is the body of an old woman. What was she expecting? That the lightning bolt would have made her young again, lifted and firmed her breasts, flattened her stomach, dissolved several rolls of fat, smoothed and tightened her skin and bleached the age spots? She looks away, pained, then back again, remembering the other times she has studied her body in a mirror trying to imagine how a man might see her. In her twenties, at thirty and forty, and terrifyingly at fifty, even then she had gazed at herself in fascination, at the curve of a shoulder, the soft pale flesh of her inner thighs, the outline of a breast. She has looked at herself through the decades and always, despite her misgivings, seen herself as a lover. She has seen swells and curves, smooth lines, tenderness, a willingness to melt into another's flesh. She has imagined how she would look lying beneath a man, considered her breasts as they might appear when she was above him, how they might feel against his face.

A lover, always a lover. Was this how other women experienced themselves, the way they measured themselves as women in the silence of their rooms with just a mirror for company? 'In the end,' she thinks, 'we are all the same, old women, fat or thin, loved or unloved, past the bloom, decaying fruit ready to drop from the branch.' How long has it been since she made love to a man? Ten – no, more like fifteen years, so long it seems unreal, unrelated to her and who she now is.

Had she thought then that it would be the last time? Why would you? You don't ever think that it might be the last time you will make love, the last time you will feel the stroke

269

of a hand on your thigh, the brush of lips on your breast, the weight and warmth of another body. Slowly, Ruby picks up her nightdress from the bedroom floor, pulls it back over her head and, crawling slowly into bed, puts out the light and lies there in the darkness, struggling with the reality that part of her is suddenly young again, hungry, yearning, ready to take risks, flushed with desire. Twisting and turning she drags a pillow to her chest, rolling onto her side to hug it, and as she eventually begins to relax and sink towards sleep she is still waiting: waiting and wondering whether, not so far away in his cottage, Jackson Crow feels this restless, longing, waiting energy and, if he does, whether he or she will have the imagination and the courage to do anything about it. I'm too old for this, Ruby thinks, too cynical, too sensible. But of course she's not, in her heart she knows that one is never too old for this, never too old to be yearning in the darkness for the word or the touch of a stranger who has glimpsed your soul.

— ⊷ —

'And . . . that's it, really,' Lesley says, her eyes fixed on the paper napkin that she has folded into a long strip and is now weaving nervously between her fingers. 'I guess you have Billy Fury to thank for bringing me back to my senses.' And she gives a nervous laugh and looks up at him again.

'"Halfway to Paradise", we used to sing that at school,' Declan says, but he doesn't add that it had been the boarding school version that one of the boys had learned from his father. The whole conversation has been awkward and embarrassing and he's hugely relieved it's over. The woman he had talked to that first day seems to have returned, and he likes her much better than the one with whom he had dinner, and who has haunted his conscience in the last few weeks.

'So back to square one, or at least back to where we were before we—'

'Yes,' he cuts in, 'before that. And what about your husband?'

Lesley inhales deeply. 'I don't know, really I don't. I thought it was all his fault, that he was trying to take over my life. But now I'm not so sure. We had so many plans, you see, we always talked about the things we'd do when the kids had left home and he'd retired. I think now that perhaps he was just trying to make that happen. The trouble is that he wants that but I've changed, I don't want it anymore.'

'So what *do* you want?'

She shrugs. 'I'm not sure but what I do know is that I want something that I can feel passionate about, something that gives me a sense of purpose, makes me feel useful again, but I haven't found it and I don't know where to start looking.'

'Mmm. Well maybe Gordon actually wants something different too,' Declan says, and he sees the shock register in her face.

'You mean another woman?'

'No, of course not. I mean like the thing he's doing up north. Maybe he was just trying to do what he thought you wanted – all those plans – but perhaps he's really moved on from those too. Have you talked to him about it?'

Lesley looks at him, not speaking, just staring hard for a moment. 'You mean . . . no . . . actually no, of course I didn't ask him.'

'So maybe you should,' Declan says. 'I mean, maybe you both just need to talk about it.' He leans back slightly in his chair as Alice brings their breakfasts to the table.

'I take it yours is the full English?' she says.

''Fraid so,' Declan says, grinning up at her. 'Heart attack on a plate for me.'

'And scrambled eggs for you, Lesley. Coffee will be along in a minute. Sorry for the delay, we had a problem with the machine but it's okay now.' And she puts Lesley's breakfast in front of her and heads back towards the kitchen.

Declan looks down at his plate. They eat in silence, Declan devouring his eggs and a sausage in a few mouthfuls. His discomfort is not only about the earlier conversation with Lesley. He's not sure why it seemed okay last night to walk in here with Todd and wait while Alice prepared their burgers, and yet it feels all wrong to be sitting here with Lesley this morning while Alice cooks their breakfast. He pushes his bacon around the plate, needing to deal with something else before he can give it his attention. 'Look, I need to tell you about Alice, although I think Paula may already have . . .?'

'Ah yes, Paula, she did mention something . . . well, she actually said that Alice had been in prison.'

Declan clears his throat. His face burns with anxiety, his knife and fork are trembling in his hands. He had thought that he would have to tell Ruby about Alice, but in the event it had all been dealt with in his absence. He'd certainly never given any thought to the fact that he might have to explain to someone else. And it's suddenly so important that he gets the right response, that Lesley doesn't say anything judgmental or negative. But what if she does? He can hardly get up and walk out. He'll just have to set her straight, but that might be . . .

'Were you going to tell me something?' Lesley asks.

He clears his throat again. 'Well, it's like this . . .' he begins, and falters.

Lesley swallows a mouthful of scrambled egg threaded through with smoked salmon. 'It's okay, Declan,' she says. 'I do know what happened. Paula didn't tell me the details, but yesterday when I had that near-miss on the way here I was thinking about it and I remembered Alice's case. It was her granddaughter who was killed, wasn't it? I thought that could have been me, driving, not thinking. It happens in a split second. I was lucky it was just a stray dog, not myself or, worse still, someone else, especially a child. It's terrible for Alice. I don't know how you ever get over something like that.'

Declan nods. Is it really going to be as easy as this? He wants to leap up and tell Alice, wants to race into the kitchen and hug her. He wants to tell her that it's another sign, another hurdle out of the way, first Ruby, now Lesley. 'You see,' he wants to say, 'you *can* have a normal life, you don't always have to be looking over your shoulder.' But instead he returns to his toast and the remaining bacon – crispy, just as he likes it.

'Ah, there you are, Declan,' Ruby says, appearing suddenly alongside him. 'Good morning, Lesley. Sorry to interrupt but I need to talk to Declan about Plan B,' and she slips into a chair and leans forward, elbows on the table.

'Do we have a Plan B for something?' Declan says around a mouthful of bacon, and he feels the anxiety building in the pit of his stomach.

'Unfortunately not, and that's the problem. We should have had a Plan B for staffing this weekend. Kim rang. She's got another job in town and she's starting today. She's known for two weeks but didn't know how to give in her notice. She was so nervous I hadn't the heart to insist she work another two weeks.'

'Shit!' Declan says, pushing his plate aside. 'So we've no one to run the shop?'

'No. I just told Alice.'

Alice comes out from behind the counter and joins them at the table. 'Do you think Todd could manage it?' she asks.

Declan shakes his head. 'Todd's the runner for the musicians and he'll never forgive me if I take him away from that. It just wouldn't be fair and, anyway, someone's got to do that job.'

Alice looks nervously across to the counter where several people are now waiting to place their orders. 'Well who? Because it can't be anyone from here, we were flat out yesterday and it's building up again right now.'

Declan rubs his hands over his face. 'I suppose we could ask Paula.'

'No,' Alice says quickly. 'Please don't do that. You can't, not after . . . well, not after what we talked about last night. You can't ask her to help today and then reprimand her for . . . for the computer thing.'

'Definitely not,' Ruby says. 'And also, Paula would take it as a sign that we were going to give her the job. We have a responsibility to manage Paula's situation properly.'

Declan shrugs. 'Then maybe we just have to close the shop.'

'But we can't,' Ruby says. 'It'll be a terrific trading day, and it would look pretty silly for the shop to be closed.'

'Well Fleur can't do it, she'll be flat out too,' Alice says. 'She was doing demos in the workroom and chatting to visitors all day yesterday.'

'Well then . . .' Declan begins.

'I could help if you like,' Lesley cuts in. 'I mean, I don't want to interfere, and I don't know much about your shop, but I've helped out at a friend's shop from time to time so I know how to do all the EFTPOS and credit card stuff.' She looks from one to the other. 'I assume everything is priced, and I could always yell for help if I needed it. It might be better than closing it.'

There is silence around the table. Declan sees that Alice is looking at Lesley, probably remembering the incident she'd told him about last night, but also perhaps the apology. And now both Ruby and Alice are looking at him, waiting for *him* to make a decision. His stomach turns to water and he feels the sweat breaking out on his neck. How he hates decisions. In view of everything that's happened this one is particularly sensitive. He looks back at Alice and she gives him a tiny, almost imperceptible, nod. Women, he thinks, they do this subtle messaging stuff, stuff he's been misreading all his life. Ruby had warned him off with just a glance when they had been talking to Paula. He simply must get better at it.

'Are you really serious?' he asks, turning to Lesley.

'Of course.'

'Could you start soon?' He glances at his watch. 'Like right now?'

She nods. 'Why not?'

Declan looks back to the other two women. 'Then I think it's a good idea,' he says.

'Thank goodness,' Ruby says, getting to her feet. 'And thank *you*, Lesley. You'll really be getting us out of trouble. I need to get back to the office but just ring across if you need anything and I'll lock the office and come straight over. Alice, would you be able to show Lesley—'

'Of course,' Alice cuts in.

And Ruby heads for the door, patting Declan on the shoulder as she passes his chair.

'If you're okay to start now,' Alice says to Lesley, 'I could talk you through it, before it gets too busy in here. The shop doesn't open until ten so you've got time to feel your way around.'

'Let's do it,' Lesley says, grabbing her bag. 'See you later, Declan, and thanks for the lovely breakfast.'

Declan watches as Alice takes out her keys, unlocks the door to the gift shop, and she and Lesley disappear inside. So that's it then, he thinks, fixed, panic over. Did I do that? But he knows he didn't – the women did it. Somehow they had decided what would happen, the three of them knew it, they even knew what was in his head, but they let him think he was making the decision. Women! He doubts he'll ever understand them. He shakes his head, gets to his feet and walks over to the counter to pay for breakfast.

Twenty-one

It's two o'clock when the music begins and Ruby, hearing the roar of the crowd, leaves the office to see what's happening. On the stage the Watermelons, a local band that was a big hit at last year's Bridgetown Blues Festival, have launched into the first set and the audience is ecstatic. The sooner it starts the sooner it'll be over, she thinks, her own impatience and anxiety now expressed as hostility. So this is how it will be, today and most of tomorrow – music, the swaying joyful crowd, hundreds more cans of beer and casks of wine turning some people feral as the afternoon and then the night wear on. But as she stands there, determinedly grumpy, something in the music lightens her mood and she leans forward, resting her arms on the verandah rail, and allows herself to listen through an unfamiliar song. She's about to turn back to the office when the singer, a slight young woman who looks not much more than a teenager, launches into 'I Am a Single Woman'. The depth and resonance of her voice seem to belong to an older, larger body and she sings with such passion and intensity that Ruby is lifted briefly out of herself and into the music.

'Pretty good, isn't she?' says a voice behind her, and for the second time in less than twenty-four hours Ruby jumps out of her skin. 'Whoa! Sorry, not again,' Jackson Crow says, grasping her arm as she sways perilously near the top of the verandah steps.

In the hours since they first met Ruby has agonised over her dishevelled state at the time, and she has hated herself for caring again, after so long, about what a man might think of the way she looks. Today she is wearing her best jeans and a white linen shirt, but the surprise has made her blush, and she feels her hair slipping around, messy as ever.

'Do you make a habit of this?' she asks, unsure whether she has struck the right note of amusement.

'Creeping up on women, you mean?' he asks. 'Sure do, at every possible opportunity. I thought I might grow out of it when I got past sixty but that was some years ago and nothin's changed. She's the real business, this one, don't you think?' he asks, indicating the singer.

'She certainly is, what an amazing voice.' She pauses, trying to get herself together, to stop feeling like a teenager, to behave as a calm and rational woman of her age should behave. 'Have you settled in all right? Is there anything else you need for your cottage?'

'Not a thing, but Declan said it would be fine to walk on down to the house when I felt like some peace and quiet. And I was feeling kinda nostalgic for my last visit here. Catherine and I had some great conversations. It's hard to believe she's gone.'

There is a roar from the audience as the last notes of the song fade away and the singer responds, bowing first, then waving, before focusing once again on the microphone and her next number.

'Would you like to come across to the house for a coffee?' Ruby asks. 'I can close the office for half an hour. It's quieter than I expected – everyone's out there enjoying themselves.'

'Well that'd be great,' Jackson says. 'I was trying to avoid the café. It's a real nice place but I nearly got mobbed in there this morning, and it's kinda hard to escape. The boys, my boys, they're cool with all that stuff but I'm so over it.'

'Come on then,' Ruby says. She collects her keys from the desk, closes the door and hangs up the sign that directs callers to the house, and together they walk along the lavender lined pathway to the back door.

'I suppose this is all familiar then?' she says, leading the way into the kitchen.

'Sure is,' Jackson says, hesitating briefly in the doorway, looking around. 'Such a beautiful place, and it looks much the same, just like Catherine had it.'

'We haven't really had time to think about doing anything to the house,' Ruby says, hearing the nervousness in her own voice. 'Declan and I came to this as total amateurs. We were both taken by surprise, not only by Catherine's death but by finding out we were suddenly joint owners and business partners. Catherine had been very sick for some time and the place was really neglected. We've been struggling to get it up and running again and keep our heads above water.'

Jackson pulls out a chair and leans on the back of it. 'Well, it looks like you're doing a fine job. That little café is a winner and getting this show on the road can't have been easy. You know, I loved this house the first time I saw it. It's gracious and real homely too, a fine mix. Catherine and I spent several evenings in that lovely old room with the big fireplace. "Come on down to the house when you need some privacy," she told me, and we sat in there and talked like we'd known each other a long time. That happens sometimes, don't you think?'

He looks at her intently, searching her face as if seeking an equally intense response, and Ruby, caught unawares by his intensity, flushes and struggles to respond.

'It does,' she says finally and, unable to hold his gaze, continues spooning coffee into the plunger. Catherine would have taken you into the lounge,' she continues, pouring water onto the coffee, and she turns towards him, leaning back against the bench top. 'It was Catherine's favourite room and . . . it's quite sad, really, but sometime before she died she moved everything, including her bed, in there and packed all her personal things into boxes. It became her den.' She stops suddenly as grief rises in her throat and she feels her eyes filling with tears. 'Sorry,' she says, shaking her head and pressing the tears away with the back of her hand. 'Sorry, I didn't expect that.' She gives him a sheepish smile of embarrassment and notices that he too seems moved.

'Me neither,' he says, clearing his throat, pausing before he goes on. 'I can only imagine how you must feel, being her oldest friend. I only knew her over a few days but we got on real well. I don't mind getting old, Ruby, but I mind losing people. She was a real special lady and I have some fine memories of my short time here.'

'Would you like to go in there?' Ruby asks. It seems right – what point is there in keeping it locked now? Declan, Alice, Todd – they should all get to use the room. She'll ask Todd to help her move the boxes when the festival's over. Catherine's memory can be equally well served by sharing the place with people who felt connected to her. 'We've been keeping it locked,' she explains as they head down the passage. 'Todd and I cleaned it up and I've just been going through some of her personal things.'

'Todd's a fine young man,' Jackson says. 'Smart and got a real nice manner with him. He's gonna be an asset to you here.'

'He certainly is.' Ruby unlocks the door. 'Todd and I are the only people who've been in here since Catherine died,' she says. 'I'll open the windows for a while. I just can't get rid of this smell. Each time I come in here I open the windows and spray it with air freshener but it won't go away. I can't work out what it is and where it's coming from. Come on in.'

Turning back from the windows she watches as Jackson, hesitating still in the doorway, steps inside looking around, sniffs the air and walks slowly through the room, running his hand along the edge of the table, and then crossing to the fireplace, resting his palm flat against the beautiful old stone for a moment before leaning down to look at the pine cones stacked in the grate. He puts a hand out to steady himself and gets down on one knee, tilting his head up towards the chimney, sniffing again. When he straightens up there is a broad grin on his face.

'It's in the chimney,' he says, pointing. 'A nice little stash right up there.'

Ruby looks at him and then at the fireplace. 'Really? That's where it's coming from? But what is it, d'you think?'

Jackson throws back his head and laughs out loud. 'Hey now, Ruby, you're sure as hell not gonna tell me you don't know what that smell is. You and I are the same generation, and I don't know about you but I was smoking weed before I even tried tobacco.'

Ruby stares at him, 'No . . . is it? Oh my God, it is, of course it is. It's so long ago I'd forgotten what it smells like . . . it was just familiar but I couldn't . . .' She sticks her hand up the chimney.

'Here, let me do that,' Jackson says, 'you don't want to get dirty.' And he edges her aside, thrusts his arm up the chimney and pulls out a plastic bag stuffed with marijuana. 'That's some stash,' he says, laughing as he brushes soot from his sleeve. 'Do you think it was Catherine's?'

'I suppose it must have been,' Ruby says, looking in amazement at the bag. 'It's not closed properly, that's why I could smell it. But if it was Catherine's, where would she have got it and why? She never really took to it when we were young. Neither of us did, but especially Catherine. And she'd banned smoking here, so I don't see . . .'

'And no one else was using this room?'

She shakes her head, turning the bag over in her hands. 'Well, only Todd, he was coming in here to keep her company and read to her. She wouldn't even let the cleaner in apparently.'

'So could it have been Todd?'

'No, no. Certainly not with Catherine's knowledge, anyway. Besides, he told me she'd told him that if she ever caught him smoking dope she'd ban him from Benson's. Todd adored Catherine, he wouldn't have taken any risks with her friendship.'

Jackson slides down off the edge of the hearth to sit beside her on the floor.

'Well then someone else got it for her,' he says. 'Medicinal purposes, maybe, that's my bet. There's a whole lot of people swear by it. If Catherine was in pain—'

'Of course,' Ruby cuts in. 'That's what it must be. When I cleared up in here I found an ashtray with some cigarette ends, hand rolled. I just assumed she had a visitor who smoked. It did seem odd . . .' Her voice trails away at the sound of approaching footsteps.

'I thought it must be you in here,' Paula says, popping her head around the half-open door. She stops suddenly, clearly taken aback by the sight of Ruby and Jackson sitting side by side on the floor in front of the fireplace, surrounded by traces of soot. 'Oh, I . . . er . . . I didn't realise you had company.' She is wearing a t-shirt with Princess Kylie written on it in pink sequins, white jeans and a pink baseball cap with 'Kylie' in more pink sequins on the peak.

'Some sort of blockage in the chimney,' Ruby says, getting to her feet. 'You're looking very festive today, Paula.'

Paula's eyes dart back and forth around the room as though searching for something and eventually end up on Jackson, who is still sitting crossed legged on the floor. 'I'm really getting into the festival,' she says, smiling at him and apparently registering who he is. 'You aren't . . . yes you are, you're Jackson Crow, aren't you?' she says, stepping forward, but Ruby, on her feet now, blocks her path and steers her back to the open door.

'Mr Crow's looking for some peace and quiet, Paula,' she says. 'I've just made some coffee. Why don't you go into the kitchen and pour it for us and one for yourself, if you like. We'll join you in a minute or two.'

'Right-oh,' Paula says, craning her neck past Ruby to get another look at Jackson. 'I'm on my way, coffee coming up. See you shortly,' and with a flirtatious little wave to Jackson, she turns and heads off to the kitchen.

Ruby breathes a deep sigh of relief, closes the door and leans back against it as Jackson gets to his feet and picks up the bag which he'd hidden behind him.

'Wow,' he says, 'Princess Kylie? Who was that?'

'Paula. Our cleaner,' Ruby says. 'Probably the best cleaner in the south west but not the easiest person to have around. Lord knows what she thought you and I were doing sitting on the floor all sooty. But it's a bit of a worry. If this *is* Catherine's and she used it there's no way she could have got it herself. We need to find out who got it for her and make sure they don't bring drugs in here again.'

Jackson bends down to brush some soot back from the edge of the fireplace with his hand. 'Well I don't know any of your staff,' he says, 'except for Todd, and you're pretty sure it's not him. But I reckon Princess Kylie there could be a candidate.'

'My thoughts exactly,' Ruby says, tucking the stash inside one of Catherine's boxes. 'She's been trying to get in here to have a look around, probably to retrieve it. But don't say anything about it. We're going to need to be very careful how we handle this. So could you turn your famous charm on Paula for me while you drink your coffee, so she doesn't smell a rat?'

'Sure can,' Jackson says with a smile, opening the door for her. 'And, Ruby, thanks for bringing me in here.

I think we're partners in crime now, but I also feel like we're friends already.' And as Ruby locks the door and turns back to face him, he drapes an arm casually over her shoulders. 'So let's go have coffee and charm the sequins off Princess Kylie.'

⸻

Paula is over the moon. She is so chuffed as she heads out of the house kitchen that she simply has to tell someone. Jackson Crow really likes her, she can tell. He kept calling her Princess Kylie, in that sort of knowing way, like he knew there was more to her than just being a cleaner. Actually she thinks he probably fancied her – not that he could do any-thing about that with Ruby hovering around all the time, but you can always tell when someone fancies you, it's like elec-tricity, really. And best of all he'd really wanted to hear her sing.

'Love to,' he'd said. And she'd jumped up from her seat at the table to do 'Santa Baby'. She's watched Kylie do it on YouTube so many times that she has all the moves down pat.

'Love to, Princess, but not right now. I have to get back to The Crowbars, something we have to run through, they'll be waiting for me.'

'Later then?' she'd said, and she'd done that thing Kylie does, like she tilts her head sideways and backwards with a little toss and lifts her shoulder and looks up from under her eyelids. 'Much later!'

'Sure thing, kiddo,' he'd said, and off he went.

He'd given Ruby a bit of a hug on the way out but Paula could tell he really wanted to stay and watch her 'Santa Baby'. What Paula thinks now is that she might shoot off home and do a quick run through with Kylie on YouTube, and then she can come back with her red reindeer horns, and the red mini Santa dress so she can do it for him properly. But first she has to tell someone all about it.

Lesley, she thinks, she might just give Lesley another chance. After that near-miss in the car she probably did feel a bit rough and needed a quiet evening. Paula pulls her phone out of her pocket and dials Lesley's number, but the phone goes straight to voicemail. She looks around her – who can she tell? Most people seem to be watching the band that's on now, which, in Paula's opinion, is rubbish, but there you go, some people have no discrimination. She could go over to the café but it's not as though there'd be much point telling Alice nor that weird Leonie woman. And then she remembers Kim. Kim will be creaming herself when she hears about Jackson Crow, and Paula tugs the peak of her baseball cap down a little further like Kylie does, at a really cute angle, and heads towards the gift shop. She's so excited the more she thinks about it that it's almost doing her head in. She can see herself up there on the stage tonight, singing with Jackson and The Crowbars. She can hear the applause, see that great mass of people in front of the stage, cheering and begging for more. The images swirl in front of Paula's eyes so she can hardly see where she's going but as she passes the shop window she spots Lesley in the shop, talking to some woman who's holding a vase. Brilliant! Kim and Lesley, two people to tell, and she hurries inside.

There's no sign of Kim and although Lesley looks up and smiles at her she's still listening to the old woman with the vase, so Paula slips behind the counter and out through to the stock room. No Kim; odd that. She opens the door that links the shop to the café – no Kim there either. Despite the distraction of her forthcoming appearance on stage tonight, Paula is clear that this is not right. It's a good thing she's popped in because Ruby would have something to say about no one looking after the shop. Anyone could just walk in and help themselves – there's all the jewellery, the pottery, the glassware, cards, books, anything. They could even get their hands in the till. Paula closes the door, slips back into the shop and stations herself behind the counter, just as Lesley and the other woman walk towards it.

'Can I help you?' Paula says, giving the customer the same dazzling smile she will turn on the audience. But to her amazement Lesley walks round to the back of the counter, moves a big glass paperweight out of the way and sets the vase down onto the stack of tissue paper.

'That's all right, thank you, Paula,' she says. 'I'll look after this lady.' And she turns to the customer: 'That's thirty-five fifty, please,' she says, peeling the price tag off the vase. 'Would you like me to gift wrap it for you?'

'Oh yes please,' the customer says, handing over her credit card, and as Paula reaches out to take it from her Lesley is there first.

'Which account is it?'

'Savings, please,' the woman says, and Lesley is keying numbers into the machine as though she owns the place.

'*Excuse me!*' Paula says. 'I don't know what you think you're doing but—'

Lesley turns to her and smiles. 'Not now, Paula,' she says, sounding like she's a school mistress talking to a naughty child. And off she goes chatting away, wrapping up the vase in purple tissue and tying it with a white bow, as though she does it every day.

Paula blinks a lot, struggles to get her head back from the stage and into the shop. The images are mixing up now. Lesley on the stage? No, that's not right. But she's here in the shop like she's taking it over.

'So what the fuck do you think you're doing, Lesley?' she asks, almost before the customer is out of the door. 'You can't just barge in here and start serving people. Good thing I came in when I did. Ruby would have a fit if she knew.'

'Everything's fine here, Paula,' Lesley says quietly, straightening things on the counter. 'Kim is sick and I'm running the shop until she gets back.'

Paula is appalled. She's so horrified that she feels giddy. She just has to hang on to herself because she'd really like to punch Lesley in her posh, self-satisfied face.

'Since when?'

'Since this morning. I was here when they got the news about Kim so I volunteered to fill in.'

Paula's head is spinning now and her face is burning.

'There are some boxes in the storeroom that need to be unpacked if you want to give me a hand,' Lesley continues. 'And the glass cabinet could do with dusting.'

A big steel band grips Paula's head. 'Liar,' she yells, 'this is *my* job, I'm taking over so if they'd wanted someone in the shop they would've got me. You've got no chance, and don't you even fucking dream of getting up on that stage. Just get out of here right now before—'

'Something wrong?' Alice asks, appearing in the connecting doorway.

'*Something wrong?*' Paula says. All she can see now is this red mist before her eyes and a great wave of fury and hurt is welling up inside her. 'Yes, if you must know, you nosy cow.' She sees Alice exchange a glance with Lesley, like they're in some sort of conspiracy.

'Take it easy, Paula,' Alice says, standing by the big glass cabinet, all sort of soft and calm like she's talking to a kid, and Paula's head starts to explode and she wants to smash them both, smash the stupid anxious expressions on their faces, smash everything, and she grabs the big paperweight with the orange bubbles and hurls it at Alice.

Twenty-two

'**M**an, you've sure done good with this place,' Jackson says, appearing in the cottage doorway. 'I don't know how I managed to make such a mess of it. Just trying to keep up with things, I suppose. It doesn't stop just because we're away from home.'

Todd grins – he hasn't grown up with praise. Catherine was good at it, though, as is everyone around here, with the exception of Paula, of course, but praise from Jackson Crow is something else, even if it's just for cleaning his cottage. 'Thanks, Mr Crow,' he says, rinsing out his cloth in the cottage sink. 'It wasn't too bad. You should see the way people leave these places sometimes.'

'Can you cut the Mr Crow, please, Todd. I'm Jackson to my friends, and you're one of them. You know, you've been looking after us so well I reckon you've got the makings of a first rate roadie. Ever fancy a job like that?'

'You bet!' Todd says. 'That'd be totally awesome . . .' he hesitates, 'but I don't think I'm old enough. I mean, I'd have to do a whole lot of stuff, like managing things, driving, telling people what to do.'

'Sure you're too young right now, but in a coupla years' time you'll be ready to work with a band as assistant to

289

the roadie and you go on from there.'

'Really?' Todd asks. Being on the road with a band is high on his list of desirable futures. 'What would I need to do to get a job like that?'

Jackson drops down heavily onto the bed that Todd has just made and leans back against the pillows, hands clasped behind his head. 'Get your licence as soon as you can and . . . how old are you anyway?'

'I'm sixteen today,' Todd says, a huge grin splitting his face. 'And Ruby's making me a birthday dinner tonight.'

Jackson nods, narrowing his eyes and looking him up and down. 'Well, happy birthday, man. I'd thought you were older – you're pretty mature for your age. Anyway, get your licence and as soon as you can after that get a licence for a bigger vehicle. You know the sort of thing, bands travel in buses mostly, and everyone has to take a turn at the driving. How are you with figures?'

Todd shrugs. 'Pretty good. I did all right in maths at school. Didn't like it much, though.'

Jackson laughs. 'Who does? You gotta be a special sort of person to really like math, I guess. But you'd need to learn the music production business, know the equipment. Y'know if you could get to some college and learn sound engineering it'd give you more options. And work out what's your music – you can't be working in heavy metal if what you love is jazz or country. And another thing –' he leans forward now, looking straight at Todd, 'when you're ready you let me know. You email and tell me, I'll talk to some guys and we'll fix you up. You remember that now, Todd, I mean it. Music is like any other business, you gotta have friends, so now you got me and I've got friends in all sorts'a places.'

'Awesome!' Todd says. 'That's so cool, thanks, Mr . . . er . . . Jackson, that's brilliant. Sound engineer . . . awesome.' He can see himself now, working the panel, sliding the mixers up and down until he has the sound just right.

'Okay, and don't you forget it.'

'I won't,' Todd says, thinking it's the thing he's least likely to forget in his whole life.

'And do I get an invite to your birthday dinner?'

Todd wonders if he's dreaming. 'You want to come?'

'Sure do. And why is it you're cleaning the cottage? I thought Princess Kylie did the cleaning around here.'

Todd begins to gather up his cleaning gear. 'Yeah, Paula, she's the cleaner, but she hasn't turned up this morning so everyone's helping out and I said I'd do your cottage.'

Jackson nods slowly. 'Didn't turn up, eh? Well, she didn't show last night either. She'd threatened me with a rendition of a Kylie Minogue number. Can she sing?'

Todd looks away. 'Not really,' he says. 'She just thinks she can.'

Later, as he heads back down the hill towards the house, the cleaning stuff in a bucket and the mop over his shoulder, Todd wonders if he could really do what Jackson had said. Where would he have to go to learn that stuff? Maybe Declan will know, but he might just check it out on the internet first. And as he looks up he sees Declan waving to him from the kitchen doorway, beckoning him down to the house.

'Well done, mate,' Declan says as Todd puts down the bucket and leans the mop against the wall. 'Thanks for mucking in. Jackson okay up there?'

Todd nods. 'He's fine,' he says. He thinks he might ask about a course right now but Declan looks a bit worried. 'I invited him to my birthday dinner. D'you think Ruby'll be okay about that?'

'She'll be fine,' Declan says, 'just make sure you let her know. Look, come on inside a minute, will you, Todd?' And he leads the way through into the kitchen. 'Want a Coke? There's something I need to talk to you about.' He opens the fridge, takes out two bottles of Coke, hands one to Todd, unscrews his own and takes a swig. 'It's like this . . .' he begins.

Todd hates it when people say 'it's like this' or 'the thing is', because they only say it when it's something bad; either it's a bit bad or seriously bad, but it's always bad. He knows he's been doing okay with the bands, it's not only Jackson but all the other guys seem pleased with him, so whatever this is he hasn't a clue.

'The thing is,' Declan continues, clearing his throat in that nervous way he does, 'well, Todd, the thing is . . . I have to ask you a couple of questions and I need you to be honest with me. I trust you, so you have to trust me when I tell you that whatever you say it's not going to get you into trouble – not with me or Ruby, or anyone else – so I don't want you to worry about that.'

So now Todd is *really* worried because a build-up like this means it's seriously bad. He nods slowly as he unscrews his Coke, and wishes Declan would get on with it, stop huffing and puffing and just get it out. All he can think is that five minutes ago he was on top of the world and right now his own safe little world here is about to fall apart and, worse still, on his birthday.

'I want you to think back to when Catherine was living in that one room and you used to go and read to her in there . . .' Declan looks up, obviously making sure he has Todd's attention. 'Did you ever see her smoking anything?'

Todd feels his face colouring and looks down at his drink. 'Catherine didn't smoke,' he says quickly. 'She hated it, she made this place smoke free, you know she did.'

'Yes,' Declan says, 'she did. But I didn't actually mean tobacco, what I meant was do you think Catherine could've been smoking a bit of dope?'

Todd sits absolutely still but inside his head all hell has been let loose. He'd been expecting this weeks ago – after all, the room reeked of weed, still does. He thought Ruby would've noticed when they were cleaning it but although she kept saying the room smelled musty it was like she never cottoned on. It was so strong he'd kept thinking they'd find some stashed away but they never did. But why hasn't Declan done something about it before now? He takes a deep breath.

'She never smoked when I was there,' he says, looking Declan straight in the eye.

'But you knew, or thought, she was smoking it? It's okay if she was, Todd,' he says quickly. 'Catherine's dead, it can't hurt her and it won't damage her memory if you tell me what you know.'

Todd looks away and nods. 'I knew she was smoking.'

'So she smoked a bit for medicinal purposes?'

Todd takes a deep breath. 'Yep. She was smoking, more than a bit, quite a lot, I'd say.'

'Did she say anything to you about it?'

'Yeah, she said, "Don't do as I do, do as I tell you, Todd. Stay off it, it's no good and if I ever catch you using it or carrying it you're out of here."'

He sees the corners of Declan's mouth twitch into a half-smile.

'That sounds just like Catherine,' he says, and he pauses for a moment, looking quite sad, and then he sort of gathers himself together again. 'Okay, Todd, next question – do you know where she got it? I mean, did she go to meet someone in town, or did someone bring it here for her?'

And now Todd freezes. Whatever he says, whether he tells a lie or tells the truth, he's in trouble.

'I realise this is really hard for you, Todd, so let me help you,' Declan says. 'Catherine was really sick for the last few months and she wouldn't have been able to get out to pick it up. So I think someone brought it here for her. They either grew it or picked it up for her. What do you think about that?'

'It wasn't me,' Todd says quickly. 'She never would have asked me to do that and she never smoked when I was with her.'

'Okay, mate, I know it wasn't you, I never thought it was. But here's the thing, Todd, and I'll be straight with you, we've found a bag of dope in Catherine's room, and we need to know how she got it. We need to find out if that person is bringing it to Benson's on a regular basis, selling it to the staff or the visitors, because if they are that's very serious for us, for Benson's, very serious because—'

'It wasn't like that,' Todd cuts in. 'Not selling it, no, never.'

'I see, but you *do* know who was bringing it in for Catherine, so would you be willing to tell me who that was?'

Todd sits silently, twisting the Coke bottle round and round between his hands, saying nothing, not knowing what to say.

'Okay, you don't want to dob anyone in,' Declan says. 'Fair enough, I can understand that, so how about if I tell you who I think it was and you can tell me if I'm right?'

Todd knows there is no way out of this, he's stuck. After everything Declan's done for him he can't lie to him, he can't refuse to cooperate. He nods.

'Well, I think Paula was probably growing the stuff and bringing it in and either selling it to Catherine or giving it to her to help her out.'

Todd's head shoots up and he looks at Declan in disbelief. In fact he's so amazed that he can't stop this weird snort of laughter that bursts out of him at the mere idea of it.

'Paula!' he says, laughing properly now, shaking his head. 'Paula! Are you kidding? No way. D'you really think Catherine would've let Paula in on a secret like that? Paula's a nutter about drugs.' And he holds his two forefingers up in front of him like a cross and in a voice that bears a remarkable resemblance to an angry Paula he shakes them at Declan. 'Zero tolerance, Todd, zero tolerance.'

Declan's mouth twitches into a smile.

Todd drops his hands. 'Catherine looked after Paula, like the times when she went off her rocker, but she'd never have let on to Paula about what she was doing. That's why she kept her room locked all the time and never let Paula in to clean it.' He looks up at Declan. 'You didn't really know Catherine. I mean, you knew her for a long time but I don't think you sort of *got* to know her.' Declan's face is changing now, it's really weird, and Todd studies his Coke bottle so he doesn't have to look at him.

'You hadn't been here for yonks. You hardly came to see her. She told me about you, about when you used to come with your friends and you'd all stay here. She said it was one of the best times of her life, and then you stopped or just came only once or twice a year. If you'd come more often you'd know that she . . .'

Todd looks up and sees to his dismay that Declan is crying. His elbows are resting on the table and his head is in his hands and although he's not making any noise he's crying so much that his shoulders are shaking. Todd stares at Declan, not knowing what to do, and then he gets up and does what Catherine used to do when he'd cried. He walks around the table, sits down beside Declan and puts an arm around his shoulders.

'It's all right, mate,' he says softly, stroking Declan's arm with his other hand. 'Catherine loved you, she loved you better than anyone.' But the awful thing is that instead of making Declan feel better it just seems to make him more upset.

⚬

'I got it,' Fleur says, putting a small carrier bag on the table and looking over her shoulder to make sure Todd isn't around. 'He's been going on about an iPod for ages, I think he's going to love it.' And she reaches into the bag and takes out a rectangular box with the design of a silver apple on the top. 'Isn't the packaging great? Everything Apple is so well designed.'

Alice smiles, picks up the box and runs a hand over it. 'I always think about those rows and rows of women with their hair in white caps and masks on their faces sitting for hours in factories doing all the minute detailed work on these.'

'Oh don't,' Fleur says. 'I'm sure it's perfectly awful but I don't want to even think about it right now. I'm just thinking about Todd's birthday. Thanks for coming in on it with me. It'll be nice to give it to him together at dinner tonight.'

'Thanks for asking me,' Alice says. 'I'd no idea what to get him until you suggested this. Here's my share,' and she pushes the money across the table. 'I told Ruby what we were getting him and she drove into town yesterday and got him an iTunes voucher, so he can start loading music.'

'We won't be able to get a word out of the little bugger once he's set this up,' Fleur says.

'That'll be a change,' Alice laughs. 'Hang on, Leonie's done our coffee, I'll go and get it.'

The café is quiet this morning, the breakfast rush is over and the day's program kicked off at ten-thirty and is well underway, leaving only a trickle of people coming in and out for drinks and snacks. Alice carries their coffee back to the table, looking around with satisfaction, enjoying this lull in the hectic push of the last few days. It's mid-morning on Sunday, just the rest of today to go and another big session with Jackson and The Crowbars late this afternoon, then tomorrow back to normal.

'I think our Todd has fallen in love with Jackson Crow,' Fleur says, scooping the froth off her cappuccino and licking it from the spoon. 'He was goggle-eyed earlier, telling me about becoming a roadie with a band, or maybe a sound engineer. Apparently Jackson said he'd help him when the time comes.'

'Well Todd may have to fight Ruby for him,' Alice says with a grin. 'I think she may have fallen for Jackson too.'

'Ruby? Never!' Fleur says. 'You're kidding. What makes you think that?'

Alice laughs. 'She's all flustered when he's around. I think it's rather sweet. I just never thought of her actually being interested in a man.'

'You think she's gay? I doubt it, I'd have picked it up on my gaydar by now – takes one to know one.'

'No, no I didn't think that,' Alice says. 'It's just that I assumed she was past being interested, just sort of left it all behind.'

'What? Moved to a higher plane, you mean?' Fleur says with a noisy laugh. 'I doubt it. I don't think people give up on finding love just because they're knocking on. None of us is beyond falling in love or lust, even though we might like to think we are. And you've got to admit that Jackson's awfully cute for seventy plus.'

'He sure is. I think Paula had the hots for him too.'

'Which reminds me,' Fleur says, leaning forward across the table, 'what actually happened with Paula yesterday? I heard you only just escaped being hit in the face with a paperweight.'

Alice stirs her coffee and grimaces. 'It was awful. And it all happened so quickly. One minute she was in here, pretty hyper, in one of those awful Kylie t-shirts, looking for Kim. And the next thing I knew she was in the gift shop shouting and screaming, so I went in to see what was happening and she slung that great big paperweight at me. Fortunately she missed me and hit the cabinet with the jewellery in it and everything went flying. None of us was hurt but it took Lesley and me and Ruby ages to get rid of all the glass.'

Fleur grimaces. 'What set her off?'

'Apparently she didn't know Lesley was helping out in there and when she found out she wasn't too pleased about it. It was like we were talking about before – she'd decided that Ruby and Declan were going to give her your job and the one in the shop, and she just snapped and threw a wobbly. She hasn't turned up for work today, no phone call, nothing, which is very unlike her.'

'Mmm. Well . . . yes and no,' Fleur says. 'I mean, things like this have happened before. Paula gets really hyper and then if something upsets her she gets in a strop and blows a fuse. Then she sort of drops off the planet for a couple of days. Catherine was very good at dealing with her. Mind you, I don't think she's actually chucked stuff around before – in the past it was more like stamping around, waving her arms and yelling abuse. This sounds really dangerous. Poor old Paula, she's hard work but she's a bit of a sad case in some ways. Was Lesley okay?'

'Fine, very calm. She actually grabbed Paula and physically stopped her because Paula was screaming her head off and she'd picked up another paperweight. Yes, Lesley was great, really. She was pretty shaken though, we both were. Thank goodness there were no customers in there at the time. Paula was totally out of control and then she took off and none of us have heard from her since. I've seen people lose it like that – in prison, you know, you get . . .' She stops suddenly, horrified by what she's just said. Heat floods through her body, prickling her skin, and she covers her face with her hands.

'It's okay, Alice,' Fleur says. 'Really, I knew you were in prison, and I know why, please don't get upset.' She reaches across the table and grips Alice's wrist. 'Please don't feel bad.'

Alice rubs her hands over her face and tries to muster a more normal expression.

'Sorry,' she says, 'sorry. Paula told you, I suppose.'

'Well yes, she did,' Fleur says, 'but not really in a nasty way. She was just . . . she was just being Paula. She likes to be the one who knows things. This might sound silly but it wasn't about you, it was about her knowing something and being able to pass it on. Anyway, she didn't get much satisfaction from me because I knew already.'

Alice looks up. 'You knew?'

Fleur nods. 'I knew your name when you first came here

but I couldn't think how, and I kept looking at you and then I remembered it all from the papers.'

'Well I hope not everyone has such a good memory,' Alice says. 'I thought it was pretty safe here until Paula found out.'

'Most people won't remember,' Fleur says, 'they won't put two and two together, and even if they do they won't really care.'

They sit for a moment in silence, Alice, shaken, wondering how to move on from here. 'Are you still planning on leaving?' she asks.

'I don't know, ' Fleur says. 'I was so sure and now I'm not. I should've left straight away but I knew it was difficult for Declan and Ruby so I hung on. It's nearly three months now and the longer I stay the more confused I get. It's good having you around, and I'm really getting to like Ruby. Even Declan's starting to grow on me. Some days I just want them to hurry up and find someone so I can bugger off and have a new life, and others it feels really good, as though Benson's might have a future. It'd been running down slowly for a long time and now it feels like it's turning around. I must sound like a complete moron but I don't know what I want anymore.'

'I think it feels good too,' Alice says. 'It was very sad and flat when I got here, but there's energy now. It could be quite exciting, you know, Fleur.'

Fleur nods. 'Yes, that's what I'm starting to feel. I'd better get a grip on it and make up my mind, I suppose, or I may be too late. Alice, can I say something personal?'

Alice looks up, shrugging. 'Of course.'

'Tell me to mind my own business, but I don't think you've set foot outside this place since you got here. I know it must be tough but if you don't bite the bullet and get out into the world soon it'll just get harder.'

There's something about being alone in the shop that gets Lesley itching to move things around. It's like staying in someone's house when they're out or away, she thinks, you want to try the ornaments in different places, mix the cushions or shift a chair. She had done that once in a friend's house. She was babysitting the friend's sick mother who was fast asleep upstairs while the daughter went to a funeral. Lesley had forgotten to bring a book and there was nothing in her friend's small collection that interested her, so she started experimenting. She'd done the cushions, moved a large exotic vase and was standing back to admire the chair in its new position when the door opened. Her friend was not amused. It could be different here, though, Lesley thinks – after all, no one is actually managing the place and she can see now, towards the end of her second day, that Kim has only been doing the essentials. There is a lot of unpacked, unpriced new stock in the back room, and quite a few things were on the shelves but not priced, so she's been sorting those out today. It's as though no one really has a sense of ownership, and it's probably been like that for several months. She doubts that anyone would mind if she changed things around and put out some more stock. It's pretty quiet now; a very popular band has just started playing and ten minutes ago people who had been wandering around aimlessly suddenly headed like lemmings into the field.

Lesley has a quick look around and gets to work. She unloads a display stand with scarves, aprons and tea towels, and moves it across to the opposite corner. Then she moves the cookery, gardening and wine books and the meditation CDs to the same shelves as the other books. And from the back room she pulls out a rather nice tiered stand which looks as though it hasn't been used for a while, dusts it, and sets up a very different display of Benson's lavender skin care products. Then, thinking that this is enough for a while at least, she perches on the stool to survey the changes. It looks good.

What she'd really like, though, is to redo the whole place, and she gets a sheet of paper and begins to draw up a plan.

She's well aware that this, yet again, is a distraction. It's designed to take her mind off the email she needs to write to Gordon. Her conversation with Declan yesterday morning had cleared the air between them, but what he said about Gordon had really started Lesley thinking. Could Declan be right? Could it be that Gordon, while he was giving out all the signs of wanting to embark on their long-planned future, really wanted to do something entirely different? After all, he had gone off to do his own thing pretty quickly once she was out of the way. Had he always wanted to keep working, not in the same job but back in the field again, on projects like the current one, which is so similar to what he was doing when they first met: gathering soil samples, testing things, bagging up bits of rock, drawing up plans and calculations? She realises now that she has very little idea what Gordon did on those trips, which means that she's never taken enough interest in his work, but thinking back she knows he seemed happier, or at least more at peace with himself, in those days. Each time he left on a field trip it was as though he was setting out on an adventure. But of course a series of promotions brought him the daily non-adventure of hopping on the train from Claremont into Perth and strolling along St George's Terrace to the office. And he'd never seemed as delighted to be heading off to KL or China as he had in the days when he left for the bush.

Lesley runs her fingertips idly along the shelf near the counter and inspects them. They are covered in dust. Pulling the duster out from under the counter she gets to her feet and unloads the shelf. She's going to email him, that's what she's decided, tell him they have to talk, and soon. It has to be soon because she's confused now, confused and stuck. She'll ask when he's coming home and if it's not for a long time maybe he can come back sooner or, she thinks, she might just fly up there to the Kimberley for a couple of days. But only if there's a proper hotel with clean linen and hot water; camping has never been Lesley's style.

'Oh, this looks different,' Ruby says, taking her by surprise.

'Goodness, I didn't hear you come in,' Lesley says, blushing. She hadn't expected to be caught out changing things quite so soon.

'That stand with the lavender things on it is lovely.' Ruby stops in front of it, looking closely at the labels.

'I hope you don't mind me moving things around,' Lesley says, 'but the shop was looking a bit jaded, especially with the gap where the glass cabinet used to be.'

'Not at all,' Ruby says, 'I'm delighted. It's desperately in need of revival. We've all been so busy with other things that the shop has been neglected.' She moves on around the shop, inspecting the local pottery, picking up one of the scarves and examining the fabric. 'Lovely,' she says again, and turns back to Lesley, smiling. 'I haven't come to interfere, I've come to make sure you're okay after yesterday's drama, and to thank you for stepping in like this, and for calming Paula down. I hope it didn't upset you too much.'

'No, no, I'm fine,' Lesley says. 'And I don't think I did calm her down much. I just managed to get her in an arm lock so she couldn't throw anything else. Have you heard from her at all?'

Ruby shakes her head. 'Not a word. Todd tells me she's blown up like this before and then she usually lays low for a couple of days. Good thing probably, but it leaves us without a cleaner just when we need her most. I've arranged for the agency to send us a couple of people – I suspect it'll be another day or two before she shows up.'

'Well if you need anything done I'm happy to help out,' Lesley says. 'I mean, it may take you a while to find someone to replace Kim so I can stay until then if you like.'

'Could you? We'd pay you the proper rate, of course.'

'Okay – well, I can stay as long as you want,' Lesley says. 'I'm really enjoying it. Can I change a few other things too while I'm here?' She blushes. 'Actually, when you came in I was drawing up a plan to reorganise it. There's so much that you could do to make it more inviting. And you could get some new lines in – jewellery, novelty items . . . sorry, I'm being too pushy.'

'Not at all, I'd love to see the plan. But aren't you going back to Perth soon? You have family there, don't you?'

Lesley shrugs. 'Yes, but my children are adults with lives of their own, and my husband's working on a project up in the Kimberley. We're . . . well, we're going through a bit of a difficult time, I'm not sure what's going to happen in the long run. In the meantime I'm planning to stay down here for a while.'

'So would you be interested in doing more than just filling in for a couple of weeks?'

'I'd love it, but I don't know what Declan would say, you see—'

Ruby holds up a hand. 'You don't need to tell me anything about that. Look, I'll talk to Declan. Would you leave it with me? I may not get a chance to talk to him properly until tomorrow morning, but I'll pop over then and we can talk some more.' She reaches up behind her head and tries to gather the strands of hair that have slipped out of the combs. 'My hair is driving me madder than usual,' she says, trying to twist the delinquent hair back into her tight little bun. 'It's always a mess. I haven't had it trimmed since I've been here. I'm terrified of everyone except my own hairdresser in London.'

'You could have it really short,' Lesley says. 'It would be easier to manage and it would suit you. You'd look like Judi Dench – you are rather like her, you know.'

'Other people have said that too,' Ruby says, still fiddling with it. 'I'm not sure Dame Judi would see it as a compliment.

I can't have it cut. It's my phobia. A nurse cut my hair off after we were bombed, and then for years the nuns hacked it off with kitchen scissors, sometimes even with secateurs. A couple of times they cut it so close with the secateurs that I had little cuts all over my head. It was punishment for something. So I grew it as soon as I escaped from the convent and keeping it long is about . . .' she hesitates. 'This probably sounds silly, but it's about who I am.'

Lesley smiles. 'It must be an awfully long time ago,' she says, keen to know more but aware that this is not the time to ask. 'And I don't think anyone would be confused about who you are if you cut it, not even you.'

Ruby opens her mouth to say something, but Lesley goes on: 'If you do want to keep it long you could do something else with it that would keep it tidier.'

'Really?'

Lesley comes out from behind the counter and goes over to the glass topped display case of interesting pieces by local craftspeople. Opening the lid she takes out a large double comb clip, in purple perspex shot through with turquoise.

'May I?' she asks, indicating Ruby's hair. And she unwinds the bun and draws the thick silver hair into a ponytail, then twists it like a rope up the back of Ruby's head and clips it into place. 'There you go,' she says, turning Ruby's shoulders so that she can see herself in one of the mirrors. 'What do you think?'

Ruby studies herself, twisting her head from side to side, and Lesley unhooks another mirror and holds it up so she can see the back. 'That's nice,' she says, 'very nice. That clip thing is really lovely. But of course my hair won't stay, bits will keep slipping out, they always do.'

'I think you'll find it's pretty secure – the clip is really well made. Shake your head around a bit and we'll see.'

Ruby shakes her head, side to side, up and down, several times. Nothing moves.

'Goodness, you're right,' she says. 'Well that's amazing, but would I be able to do it myself?'

'Of course you would,' Lesley says, and she takes the clip out and shows her again. 'Now you try.'

'I see,' Ruby says, and she pulls her hair together and starts twisting and then secures the clip. 'It's quite easy, and it does feel secure.' She pats her hair a couple of times. 'Thanks, Lesley, I think this might work for me. I'll certainly give it a try,' and she takes one last look in the mirror before heading for the door. 'And we'll talk again tomorrow.'

'Fine,' Lesley says. 'Look forward to it, and Ruby . . .?'

'Yes?'

'You haven't paid me for the clip.'

———

Even the twin distractions of Paula's blow-up and subsequent disappearance and the discovery of the marijuana haven't dulled Ruby's senses nor her conviction that something has been set in motion and is moving inexorably to some sort of climax. Indeed, the discovery of Catherine's stash yesterday morning had, she felt, simply brought her and Jackson closer, albeit in the most unlikely circumstances. Last night she had sat with Alice among the ecstatic crowd and discovered for the first time the Jackson that people around the world had known for decades: the professional musician, the artist, the consummate performer who brought his own unique magic to the instrument and the music. Watching him play gave her the chance to study him closely. He was totally unlike any other man she'd been attracted to. For a start, Jackson was mixed race, his mother from Ethiopia, his father, he'd told her, from North Carolina. Todd was fascinated by his curly silver hair – 'mega cool', he'd said – and Ruby silently agreed. And when he put the saxophone aside, took the mike from its stand and launched into 'I Just Want To Make Love to You' she was just as weak with longing as she had been when she had ached for Rossano Brazzi to claim her across a crowded room.

Today she has grasped at her efficient, practical self and held on to it long enough to do what she had to do to without making a fool of herself. In the mirror, thanks to Lesley's attention, she can see that she looks different – softer, more modern, not so messy or dated. But what she wants is not just to look, but to *feel* different – to feel like a woman who is still in the game of life rather than merely kicking around on the sidelines.

This evening, now that the final performance is over, the party atmosphere is winding down. Out in the field some campers are getting quietly drunk, setting the world to rights while they cook sausages on their picnic stoves, and others grasp the last hours of the weekend, singing to guitars or strolling among the tents reliving the performances, swapping phone numbers, relating memories revived by the music itself or the mere fact of being once again at a festival. But in the house kitchen Ruby has her hands full. Todd's birthday dinner feels like the sort of ritual meal that in the early years of both her marriages she had believed would be a regular feature of her family life: a heaped table surrounded by children and later their girlfriends and boyfriends, spouses, and then grandchildren. Ruby switches off the heat and pushes the curry and dhal to one side of the stove then fetches Todd's birthday cake from the pantry and counts out the sixteen candles, pressing them into holders and then spearing them into the cake. Todd, Declan and Alice, of course. 'And Fleur,' Todd had insisted, 'and can I ask Bundy and Johno?'

And this morning he had invited Jackson, which she would have done if he hadn't beaten her to it, and since then Lesley has been added to the guest list. Ruby stands back surveying the cake, and then she takes off her apron, bundles it away and walks down the passage to change her clothes for dinner.

Twenty-three

It's the sort of occasion that makes Declan realise how glad he is that he stopped drinking. Since Todd had unknowingly given him such an emotional kick up the arse this morning, he has been feeling exceptionally fragile and wobbly, but if this were a dozen years ago he would by now have been blind drunk, argumentative, rambling and abusive. Ruby has done them proud this evening: several curries, rice, salads and naan bread, followed by a lemon tart and Todd's magnificent birthday cake. Todd's face when he saw the cake had almost reduced Declan to tears again.

'It's awesome,' he'd said, and he did indeed seem awestruck. 'I never had a birthday cake – just once I had a cupcake with a candle in it but never a proper cake, a big cake for me.'

Declan thought that Ruby seemed moved almost to tears by this, and looking carefully at her now he thinks she looks different this evening. By the light of the lamps out here on the deck she is a little flushed, her eyes rather brighter than usual, and she's done something different with her hair, which is a big improvement. It's odd, he thinks, watching as she helps Todd to cut slices of cake and hand them around, that he knows so little about her past, particularly about her friendship with Catherine. Everything Catherine had told him about their childhood had been harrowing. It had taken years for the full story of the child migrants to be extracted from reluctant government departments and the defensive organisations to which the children had been sent, and when those stories were finally told they had been met with horror, disbelief, even threats. Now, watching Ruby, Declan wonders how much of what he had found difficult about Catherine was the result of the trauma of her childhood. He curses the self-centredness that has so often dulled his curiosity and blinded him to the reality of other people's lives. Why had he never asked Catherine more about her life? His mind is filled with questions for which it is now too late. But it's not too late for Ruby, not too late to find out what led to all those years of hostile silence to which they never seemed to fully recover.

Todd and the other boys have left the table now. Fleur and Lesley left half an hour ago, just Alice, Ruby and Jackson remain. Alice gets up to make coffee, brings it back to the table and begins to pour it. Jackson yawns, stretching his arms above his head and putting his feet up on one of the chairs that the boys have vacated.

'I was thinking about the birthday cake Catherine made for me years ago, Ruby,' Declan says, adding cream to his coffee. 'I would have been thirteen then and it was all iced in green like a football pitch. You weren't here then, were you?'

She shakes her head. 'No, you were much younger when we met. You were eight, I think, when you were being the crop duster.'

He nods slowly. 'Yes. And the more I think about it the more it seems that you were living here then, is that right?'

'Such a strange career choice at that age,' Alice says, smiling at him.

'I thought it rather sweet,' Ruby says. 'I thought then, and I still do, that small boys whose aerial ambition is crop dusting are unlikely to grow into the sort of men who start wars.'

'Sounds about right,' Jackson says. 'What would you say about a boy who at seven wanted to be in charge of the ghost train at the funfair?'

'I'd say that boy would turn out to be a lot of trouble,' she says, smiling at him. And briefly Declan has the sense that something subtle is passing between them, something more than pleasant conversation.

'And you'd be dead right,' Jackson says, holding her gaze for just a bit longer than one might expect.

'So were you?' Declan intervenes, frustrated by the interruption of his attempt to grasp a shadowy memory. 'Were you living here then?'

'I was, for a while,' Ruby says. 'Would you like some more cake?'

He shakes his head. 'No thanks. But you weren't living here later, not at the time of the football cake? It was soon after Mum died and it was just Catherine and Uncle Harry then.'

Ruby shrugs and looks away as she starts to draw the plates across the table towards her to stack them. 'I guess so, but I certainly wasn't living here then.'

'So what happened?' Declan asks, leaning towards her across the table. 'Why were you living here before that, because wasn't Uncle Harry here then too?' Something has changed, Declan can feel it but doesn't know what it is. It's as though some sort of chill has descended and in the light of the tall candles in the lanterns the colour seems to have drained from Ruby's face. Even so he goes on, intrigued now by the prospect of what he doesn't know, by the huge gaps in their related histories, gaps that have always been there but which are now, suddenly, so fascinating.

'So, where was Catherine then?' he asks. 'Was she away or something? I've never really known much about what happened before that time, when Mum died and I started coming here more regularly. Did you live here with Catherine and Uncle Harry then?'

Silence descends like the safety curtain in a theatre, hiding the turmoil happening backstage. Ruby has stopped stacking. Jackson swings his legs off the chair and leans forward too.

'But that time that Declan's talking about,' he says, 'when he was a little kid, that would have been when you were still married to Harry, wouldn't it? Before Catherine cut in and stole him from you.'

Ruby fires him a look that could slash tyres at fifty metres, and Jackson actually tilts backward in his chair as if to dodge its power.

'Well, that's how Catherine put it,' he says. 'That's what she told me. She and Harry had an affair. It broke your heart, she said, and that's when you left and went to England, and you didn't talk to each other for years, until she went to find you in London . . .' He stops suddenly. 'What?' he asks, looking at Ruby, who appears to have turned to stone. 'What did I say?'

Declan gulps for breath, his heart lurching around in his chest. 'No,' he says, narrowing his eyes to focus on Ruby's face in the candlelight. 'You were never married to Harry, were you, Ruby? Catherine didn't—'

'Excuse me,' Ruby says, getting to her feet. She leans towards Declan and rests a hand briefly on his shoulder. 'You and I will talk about this another time.' And she turns away from the table and disappears into the house.

—

Alice takes a deep breath and knocks lightly on Ruby's door. Half an hour has passed and it's clear that she's not coming back to the table. Jackson had wanted to follow her, to explain and apologise, but Alice had stopped him.

'I really think it would be better if you didn't,' she'd said. 'Ruby's a very private person, give her a bit of time.'

'But what did I do?' he asked. 'I mean, you guys, you're

family, and her close friends, it's not as though you didn't know.'

'We *didn't* know,' Alice said, looking across at Declan, who still seemed speechless. 'I've only known her a couple of months and Declan only met her that one time as a child before she arrived here after Catherine died.'

'Jesus, what have I done?' Jackson had said, burying his face in his hands. 'Catherine told me the whole thing, all about her life. I only met her that weekend but we talked, shared a couple of bottles of wine, exchanged our stories, so I thought . . . I thought . . .'

'You thought it was common knowledge.'

'Sure, Alice, that's it exactly,' he says. 'Declan, man, I'm so sorry.'

Declan shakes his head. 'It's not your fault, Jackson. I guess I'd have found out eventually anyway, but it doesn't really matter now. It's all so long ago.'

'It still matters to Ruby, though,' Alice says softly. 'However long ago it was it's obviously very painful for her.'

'I thought – well, I guess I *didn't* think,' Jackson says, 'I assumed that because Catherine told me . . .'

'It's just unfortunate,' Declan said then. 'My family – it's a strange jumble of people, most of them quite disconnected and with almost no sense of a collective history. Ruby would have known Harry's mother, my Aunt Freda, really well. She and Catherine worked at their hotel for years when they left the convent. She probably knows more about my family than I do. But for now, what are we going to do about Ruby?'

Cautiously Alice taps again on Ruby's door. 'It's me, Alice,' she says. 'May I come in? I've brought you a cup of tea.'

There are footsteps and the key is turned in the lock. Unsure whether this means it is now locked or unlocked, Alice tries the handle and it opens. Ruby, still fully dressed, is crawling back onto the still made bed, which is scattered with hardback notebooks. Her face has a crushed expression; she looks used up, bereft.

'I came to see if you're okay,' Alice says, setting the tea on the bedside table and then sitting uncomfortably on the foot of the bed. 'We, all of us, we were worried about you.'

'I'm okay,' Ruby says. 'Actually no, I'm not okay, obviously. I'm sorry, I . . .'

'There's nothing to apologise for,' Alice says. 'Jackson wanted to come, but I thought you might prefer . . .'

'No . . . not tonight,' Ruby says, bundling some tissues in her hands. 'I can't talk to him tonight, tell him that will you, Alice? Tell him it's not his fault. And Declan too. I must explain it all to him, and I will but not tonight.'

They sit there for a while in silence.

'It's all a very long time ago . . .' Alice ventures.

'Yes, and you must think I'm overreacting. These things happen, after all, husbands defect, they have affairs, marriages survive or they don't – mine didn't. Harry was a charming philanderer. His mother warned me of that many times but I chose not to listen. Catherine wasn't the first but until then I had managed to look away. He was good to me in every other way, and I have to admit that I had married him as much to become part of the family as for himself – more, perhaps. But then it was different, it was Catherine's deception that really mattered.' Ruby heaves a sigh and moves her legs so that Alice has more room on the bed.

'She must have been very important to you,' Alice says.

'Hugely. You see, back in 1944 after the bombing, I was taken to a hospital. No one seemed to know anything about my mother. They just kept saying she'd probably turn up soon. But a few days later they packed me off to an orphanage. I was four years old and frantic because I thought she wouldn't know where to find me. Anyway, she never turned up and soon after that I was told she was dead, my father too. I never believed it. Then one day a man came to the orphanage and told us we were going to a place where the sun always shone and we would live by the beach. I was still frightened that Mum wouldn't find me but they told me, over and over again, "She's dead, she's dead, the bomb killed her." Catherine and I met on the dock and I don't know what would have happened to me if I'd had to get on that ship alone. They kept telling us how wonderful it would be and how much Jesus must love us to have picked us to go to Australia.

'So we made that terrible journey together, and then the convent – I don't know how I'd have survived all that without Catherine. I can't begin to describe what that was like. The nuns seemed to thrive on humiliating and hurting us. Our clothes were little more than rags, the soles of our shoes were full of holes. Everything we did was wrong – they seemed to hate us and went out of their way to grind us into the ground. Nine years we were there, nine years, and all that time Catherine kept me going. She was a year older but she always seemed more than that, she was such a knowing person. An old head on young shoulders, Freda Benson said once.'

Ruby pauses to take a small sip of her tea.

'She and her husband Maurice ran Benson's Hotel and Catherine and I were sent there together. Things got difficult sometimes then. I had relied on Catherine for so much, but once we were let loose on the world I began to resent that. We had this little power struggle going on for a while but we got through it, and we kept looking out for each other, doing everything together.'

'Was the hotel okay – I mean, were they kind to you there?' Alice asks.

Ruby nods. 'Yes, yes it was good. Freda Benson was a lovely woman. She expected us to work hard but she mothered us and that was something we both needed. She gave us everything we'd been deprived of till then – a nice place to live, people who seemed to care about us. We had nice uniforms and we were earning money, so we could actually go shopping for new clothes. Neither of us had ever done that before, we couldn't remember ever having new clothes. We were so nervous when we first went shopping that Freda had to come with us.

'Harry, Freda and Maurice's son, was working in England and we'd heard a lot about him, but we'd been there a couple of years before he came home. That's when things started to change. He was handsome and good fun and he really took to both of us. We were always together, the three of us, going to the movies, eating fish and chips by the harbour. On our days off we went to the beach or sailing with Harry's friends, or to the races. We were doing things we'd only dreamed of until then. And then Catherine fell for this friend of Harry's – Jack, his name was – and she was gone. I mean, we were still living together at the hotel, still working together, but her head wasn't there anymore. He was rather dashing, very handsome and extremely rich, and Harry said that Jack had just turned her head and there was no way it would last.

'So then there were just the two of us, and Harry and I ended up spending a lot of time together. We were really good friends, and then one day he told me he loved me, and asked me to marry him. I don't know if he ever really loved me, but he was lazy, really, he wanted a wife who'd look after him, make things easy for him. And we got on well.'

'Were you in love with him?' Alice asks.

Ruby shakes her head. 'No, to be honest I wasn't. I did love him, but not in that incredibly romantic, falling in love way. I felt safe with him, and I loved the Bensons and the idea of this big sprawling family. I wanted to be a part of that and I was sure I would spend all my life with them. I felt I had found something that could never be snatched away from me.

'Freda and Maurice owned this place as well as the hotel. They'd inherited the properties from Maurice's father, who'd inherited them from his father. Harry wanted to move down here and plant vines. It was a time when people were exploring the possibilities of the wine industry and he wanted to turn Benson's Reach into a vineyard. He always had big ideas but he wasn't very good at following through. So we moved down here. Catherine was still in Perth, still working at the hotel, still seeing Jack, but then it all crashed. He left her for someone else and she was devastated. She stayed on there for a while and the Bensons made her assistant manager . . .' Ruby hesitates, taking several deep breaths, pressing tissues against her eyes.

'You don't have to go on,' Alice says, 'you don't have to tell me this.'

Ruby shakes her head. 'I want to,' she says. 'I need to, I've never told it to anyone except Owen; we didn't marry until after Harry's death. You know what this is like, you shroud something in silence and then you find you can't speak, but when you do you daren't stop.'

They sit in silence for a few minutes and Alice sees that Ruby is gathering herself together in a way that will enable her to finish the story, and she remembers both the pain and the relief that comes with the telling.

'About that time Maurice had a stroke,' Ruby continues, 'and although he recovered it was clear that he was going to need a lot of care. Freda decided to sell the hotel, and they bought a house by the beach in Cottesloe, so Catherine had no job. Actually, that's not right, she could have kept the same job with the new owners, but she said she couldn't bear to stay on there without the Bensons. So we told her to come down here for a break while she made up her mind what to do.

'It was good at first, like the old days back at the hotel, the three of us together again. It never occurred to me . . .' She stops and rests her head back against the bedhead, closing her eyes. 'It never occurred to me that it wouldn't be all right.

315

I was bored and pleased to have Catherine's company. We'd been down here a few years by then and I was getting a bit lonely. It was obvious that Harry had no real commitment to earning a living, and of course he didn't need to. So I decided to get a job. I was used to bar work, so I went down to the local pub and they took me on straight away. Harry thought it was a bit beneath him to have his wife working at the pub but I liked it.

'When Catherine arrived she said she was going to get a job too, but we both urged her to have a few weeks off before she started looking. Well, she never did start looking. She was good in the house, did some of the cooking, the washing, all that, but I don't even remember her looking at the job ads in the local paper. But the three of us enjoyed each other's company, so it didn't seem to matter.

'Then one day I wasn't feeling too well, I was dizzy and nauseous. I didn't realise it at the time but I was pregnant. It was the evening shift at the pub and it was pretty quiet so I left early and came home and that's when I found them, Catherine and Harry, here in this room, in that horrible old wooden bed. I was so naive, I assumed it was the first time, but it turned out that it had been going on since soon after Catherine arrived. Oh, I know it's not an unusual story – since then in all my years of working with women I've heard far worse. Catherine wasn't the first. I knew Harry had strayed before, but he was discreet and he always came back. I don't think I would ever have left him, because that would have meant leaving the family that was so precious to me.

'So it was much less about Harry deceiving me than about Catherine. I couldn't believe that after what we'd been through together she could do that to me. This might be hard to understand but the nuns had treated us with contempt – they called us every awful name you could think of, and they seemed always to be finding new ways to shame and degrade us. They peeled away every shred of self-esteem and each time we put our heads up it would happen again. They reduced us to nothing, but with Freda's help we'd clawed our way to a normal life, to a future and a real sense of self-worth. We'd been like sisters, closer than many sisters. I had survived the convent because of Catherine, and I think she felt the same about me. And then I walked into that room and everything I had become just seemed to evaporate. I was reduced to nothing again, and this time it was Catherine who had put me there. That was what destroyed me, that she smashed what we'd had, ground it under her heel just like the nuns.'

Ruby stops, picks up her tea again and sips it.

'It must be cold by now,' Alice says, moving to take it from her. 'I'll get you some more.'

Ruby shakes her head. 'It's still warm.'

'So what did you do?' Alice asks.

'I left here that night. Got in the car and drove to the Bensons' house. It took longer in those days – four hours, maybe more. Freda was devastated and furious with them both. She made a bed up for me, made me tea and toast. By then it was about four in the morning and she said to get some rest and we'd sort it out in the morning. But I couldn't rest, I tossed and turned and paced around the bedroom, and by daylight I felt so terrible I needed a doctor. It was a miscarriage and it seemed as though Catherine had taken everything from me, even my unborn child.

'I knew then that for me it couldn't be sorted. There was no way I was going back to Benson's Reach, nor to Harry, there was no way back for me to Catherine, not after that. She took that precious friendship and destroyed it, the thing that had enabled me to survive. I was back to being the grovelling worm child I had been in the convent – only then I'd had her, and now I had nothing.' Ruby stops, sighing heavily. 'And then twenty five years later she turned up in London looking for forgiveness.'

'*Did* you forgive her?' Alice asks.

Ruby shrugged. 'I don't know. That sounds silly but it's true. You can say, yes, I forgive you, let's put it all behind us, move on, all that stuff. But how do you know if, deep inside yourself, you've forgiven? How do you know if one day it might not all come back again, rising up inside you like some awful serpent? That's what I was battling with when I came back here – the past – all of it here, at Benson's Hotel and in the convent. Back in the seventies I did a ritual burning of everything that reminded me of it. I thought that would be the end of it, but of course it wasn't. It was just a way of burying my head in the sand. When Catherine turned up in London years later looking for forgiveness, I froze. We hadn't been in touch for all those years and there she was, suddenly, standing on my doorstep. I had no time to prepare for that, she gave me no warning. It felt like another raid on my life, another invasion that she'd orchestrated. I realised then, for the very first time, that it was typical of her. All through the years we were together I had felt I was in her debt, that she had kept me going, that I owed my life and my sanity to her. But that day I suddenly saw the other side of it. Catherine was an emotional bully and that was why we kept falling out when we got out of the convent and went to the hotel. I got a taste for independence, but she needed my dependence on her, and as that began to dissolve she would punish me.

'When she turned up on my doorstep all those years later I felt I had to invite her in. She was standing there with her suitcase, obviously intending to stay, and I fell straight back into letting her call the shots. It's ridiculous, of course, I was a grown woman in my fifties, known for being assertive, making decisions, taking authority by the throat and shaking it, and yet I couldn't say no to Catherine. So how could I really forgive her while I was still battling with that? And there was something else.

'A couple of weeks after I'd left Benson's Reach and after the miscarriage, when I was still staying with Freda, Catherine turned up at their house – it was without warning then too. Freda was out and I answered the door and Catherine insisted on coming in. She said she had to apologise, to ask for forgiveness. She talked about how important our friendship was to her, how much she loved me. And then she said, "Come back, Rube, it'll be okay, really it will. Harry and I will look after you, the three of us – we'll all be together." She was offering me a place back in my own home. *"Harry and I will look after you,"* – she wasn't moving out of my way, she was taking over. And of course Harry was just as much to blame in all this, but it mattered so much less. Catherine didn't only want my husband, she wanted my life.'

Alice shakes her head, speechless for a moment.

'I'm sorry,' Ruby says, 'I shouldn't have unloaded all this onto you.'

'No!' Alice says, 'It's not that, it's just all so . . . complex and sad. So when she left you with the controlling share in Benson's Reach, do you think she was giving you something back? Trying to make amends?'

Ruby shrugs. 'Maybe – who knows? But once again she got her own way. When I got the solicitor's letter and the will I also got a letter she had left for me. She said she was concerned about Declan being able to manage things. In her own roundabout way by leaving me the controlling share she compelled me to come here. She was still manipulating me while she was dying! She knew I'd come, she knew the only way I *could* come back would be because she had gone. She knew I'd find the journals, that I would be compelled to read them and to remember how things used to be. She knew she could reel me back in even if she wasn't here to see it.'

Dawn is just about to break when Ruby pulls on a tracksuit and slips out of the house. She has barely slept, an hour perhaps, two at the most, but she can't lie there any longer, better to get up, get some air. Each time she had drifted towards sleep the events of that night forty years ago had bulldozed their way back into her consciousness. When she'd returned to the house from the pub she could feel the strangeness of it, the silence, yet she had a sense that she was not alone. But there was no one in the kitchen, no one in the lounge, just the television flickering in the darkness with the sound turned down, no sign of Harry in his study. And then a light, a low light showing under the bedroom door, this bedroom door, and she'd opened it and there they were, in that great old family heirloom of a bed. It was as simple as that. They were so hard at it they didn't even see her, didn't even know she was there until she cleared her throat and said, with the heaviest sarcasm she could muster, 'I hope I'm not interrupting anything important.'

When she thinks back on it now – something she has managed to avoid doing for a very long time – it amazes her that she handled it so well, that she had stayed so cool and dignified, while her every cell was in turmoil. But there is, she thinks, a distinct advantage in being the one person of three who is vertical and fully clothed: it adds considerable dignity to the already high moral ground. Later, though, as she drove through the night, she had started to fall apart, and by the time Freda Benson opened the door to her she was a complete mess.

Ruby lets herself out through the back door and sets off along the track of her usual morning walk, giving wide berth to the field where the few remaining campers are still fast asleep in their tents. It's over, the festival – the carnival is over – and as she walks she hums the song under her breath. How odd, she thinks, here I am walking along, humming the Seekers just hours after I've blurted out all the stuff I was never going to tell anyone. And yet somehow it feels okay – in fact it's very okay. The irony is that she has simply done – under pressure of circumstance – what she has so often encouraged other women to do: face what happened, talk about it, drag it out from under the carpet where it was swept years ago.

Something has changed, something big. She feels as though she has shed a burden and as she walks on through the misty damp of the morning to the highest point of the sloping land behind the house, Ruby imagines it – the painful mess of the past – rolling away from her like a great boulder down the hill, beyond the house and further on, out into the road and then into the distance, until she can no longer see it. No, it's not that easy, there is more to come, more memories, more stages to go through, but somehow the power of the past to hold her captive seems defused. She sees now that there is much more to it than simply telling her story. Since that letter flopped down onto her doormat in February she has been building towards this. Coming here so quickly, staying longer than she planned, insisting on working her way through Catherine's possessions, her journals, her photographs. Has this been some sort of symbolic retribution, a posthumous raid on Catherine's life? Who knows, and perhaps it doesn't even matter. She has begun to rise from the ashes and in doing so she can see those years of friendship without the shadow of deception and manipulation. 'You knew how it would be, didn't you, Cat,' she says aloud, 'just as you knew we should change our ages, just as you knew to keep the nightdresses, the journals?'

Ruby shivers as much with exhaustion as from the morning chill. Her energy is seeping away fast now. She wants warmth, comfort, a cup of tea and perhaps another couple of hours' sleep. And now, she wonders, what about Jackson? She makes her way back towards the house along the path that weaves between the cottages. A light comes on in the kitchen – Declan probably, it's far too early for Todd.

'Ruby,' a voice calls softly. 'Ruby, it's me, Jackson. Up here.' He is standing on the balcony outside his cottage, and as she turns he runs down the steps towards her. 'Are you okay?' he asks, 'It's not even light yet.'

'I'm fine,' she says. 'I was so restless I had to get up and get some air.'

He nods. 'And now?'

'A cup of tea and then maybe some sleep.'

'Could you have the tea with me?' he asks. 'Would you?'

She follows him up the steps and into the warmth of the cottage, lit only by one small bedside lamp, and he goes on ahead through to the kitchen and switches on the kettle.

'I've been conducting a conversation with myself about the past,' she says. She looks at the chairs, which she's always thought so attractive but which now seem unappealingly low. The sort of chairs you might easily get into but struggle to get out of. 'I think those chairs look better than they are,' she says.

'Those?' Jackson says, indicating one. 'They're terrible chairs. I thought of complaining to the management. Sit on the bed. But why are we talking about the chairs?'

She shrugs. 'I don't know – it just went through my head, that's all. I'm tired, probably not very coherent.'

'You were saying something about the past,' he says, sitting down beside her.

'My conversation with the past, yes. Long, and rather painful.'

Her hand is on the bed between them and he takes it in his. 'I'm so sorry, Ruby. Last night . . . I had no idea what I was blundering into. My mouth is so much bigger than my brain.'

'You couldn't have known,' she says. 'Besides, as Alice said, it's all so long ago that it should by now have lost its power.'

'I hurt you, embarrassed you,' he says. 'Really hurt you. I'm so very sorry.'

'It's okay, really it is. In fact it's more than that, it's actually a good thing. It's like you broke open the lock on a door and a whole lot of things rolled out and away.'

'I see,' he says. 'Well, I see the shapes but not the detail. Do you want to talk about it?'

'Yes, but not now. Last night I unloaded it all onto Alice and now I'm exhausted by it. Later perhaps?'

He smiles. 'Yes, later. Sit back, put your feet up. I'll go make the tea.' And as she wriggles further onto the bed he bends down, takes off her shoes and pulls the rumpled duvet over her legs.

Ruby leans back against the stacked pillows and closes her eyes. There is so much she wants to say but she's too numb with exhaustion to begin. He brings the tea, puts it down on the table beside her, and settles alongside her on the bed. For a moment they sit in silence, sipping their tea, and Ruby's eyes begin to close.

Jackson takes the tea from her hand and puts it on the bedside table. 'There's something I have to tell you,' he says.

Ruby turns to look at him although the effort seems enormous. 'I told you, it's okay, we'll talk later.'

'No, this is different and I have to tell you now.'

'I'm listening with my eyes shut,' she says.

'The night I arrived here, something happened. I saw you and I felt as though I knew you – not as though we'd met before, but as if I'd *always* known you, in my head, and . . .' he hesitates, 'and in my heart. As though I'd always known you were somewhere in the world and had been looking for you. And it's been driving me crazy because it feels so powerful, so intimate, and yet whenever I get the chance to talk to you alone I don't know what to say.'

Ruby opens her eyes and looks into his. 'You're saying it now,' she says, 'which is a huge relief because it means I don't have to say it first.'

'You too then?'

'Me too.'

He slides further down on the bed now and puts an arm around her shoulders, drawing her to him. 'Well praise the lord and pass the ammunition. So I'm not the deranged old fool I thought.'

'Well you probably are,' she says, 'but to another deranged old fool that's very attractive.'

Twenty-four

June

*G*ordon, back in Broome after his second field trip, is having his first cup of real coffee in ten days on the deck of a small café. As he drove the final few kilometres he'd been weighing up his priorities – coffee first or, now that there's a signal, get his Black-Berry out of his backpack and check ten days' worth of messages? It was no contest, really: the coffee won hands down. It's good coffee, strong and blisteringly hot, just as he likes it. He's always surprised to find that he has survived several days on the instant variety – terrible taste, though the caffeine hits the spot – but as soon as he's within striking distance of a coffee machine and frothy milk he's like a parched man racing across the desert towards an oasis. Alongside him Bruce makes his second attack on the large bowl of water that the waitress has brought for him. Gordon finishes his coffee, orders another, and sits there contemplating his next pleasure: a long hot shower at the motel to wash away the fine red dust that seems to have become part of his skin. But first there is the phone.

As always it was pointless to take it with him, there is

never a signal, but somehow he has to have it there. He unzips the backpack, gets out the phone and switches it on to find a couple of voice messages, three texts and a stack of emails. He flicks through them: some results from the lab, an invitation to a retirement party back at the mining company, an offer from a would-be Russian bride, other work related things, cheerful greetings from the kids, advice on how to enlarge his penis and an email from Lesley. He reads everything else first, then draws in a deep breath and opens it.

It's friendly, no hostility, some confusion, a certain amount of caution. She wants to talk. This, thinks Gordon, is the big one, the big conversation about what's happened, what will happen, what should happen next. And it's serious. Lesley, to whom anything beyond the northern suburbs and temperatures in excess of thirty-two degrees, dry or humid, are anathema, is offering to fly up here to talk to him. On the other hand this is Broome, which is rather different. She'll be considering The Resort, perhaps, not a tent, not even the motel. Well it has to happen sometime, he thinks, and probably the sooner the better, but not here. Not on his territory. He loves this place, he loves this late life adventure he's having right now – the potential of the work, the freedom, the long, silent, moonlit nights in the open, pearly dawn light, and science again, science instead of the business: pure magic. No, not up here. If his marriage is about to end it will not happen here. He will go home, or wherever she is now, Margaret River again. Okay, he'll go there: a strong position, that. He'll be doing the right thing, making the effort, and he'll also be free to walk away. That's it then, he thinks, he'll email and tell her he'll book a flight. It can't be this coming week but maybe the end of the next one.

'What d'you reckon then, mate,' he says, nudging Bruce with his foot. 'Fancy a trip to Margaret River?'

Bruce jumps up with an ecstatic growl and sinks his teeth into the toe of Gordon's boot, ready for his favourite game.

'No, no, no,' Gordon says, prising the dog's jaws apart and freeing his boot. 'No fighting, no tug-of-war, this is all about negotiation. You work out what you want and then you work out what you're prepared to settle for. You have to be prepared to give a little – not that you'd know anything about that, would you, you canine terrorist.' Bruce does his odd, excited little bark and then a growl, ready for action. Gordon reaches down and scratches the top of his head. 'Thing is,' he says, looking Bruce straight in the eye, 'it would help if I actually knew for sure what I really want.'

———

As she lay alongside Jackson on his bed in the early morning, Ruby, drifting into sleep, had felt as though a great weight had been lifted from her. She would have to tell her story again, to Declan and of course to Jackson himself, but the fear that had haunted her for so long had been peeled back as she told it to Alice. Lying there, the comforting warmth of Jackson's body curled alongside hers, his words resonating in her head, she felt a delicious sensation of freedom, as though she had been made new and safe by all that had happened. Now, as she wakes just three hours later, Jackson is once again in the kitchen, this time pouring boiling water into the coffee plunger, and she stays still and silent, watching him, wishing it were she who had woken first, woken facing him, so that she could have studied him closely as he slept.

But when she shifts on the bed, stretches slowly and wriggles into a sitting position, she can feel that something has changed – awkwardness has replaced the intimacy of the wee small hours, and the awkwardness is in both of them. It's as though lying together, sleeping side by side, has moved them further along their path more quickly than is entirely comfortable. How easy it is when you're young, Ruby thinks: fall into bed, spend a night of wild sex, and ask questions later. Not that there had been sex, wild or otherwise, here, but there had been a sense of intimacy from which they now both seem to have taken a backward step.

Age, Ruby thinks, especially this much age, demands that one proceeds with caution. It requires more knowing before leaping to another level of intimacy, however small that leap might be.

'Did you sleep well?' she asks.

He nods. 'Well, but not long enough,' he says, smiling. 'And you?'

'The same.' She glances at her watch and immediately swings her legs off the bed. 'Bugger,' she says. 'I'm supposed to meet Declan and Fleur in half an hour. Better get back to the house and have a shower.'

'Can't you stay a while?'

'Sorry, no. Let's have coffee together later, or lunch perhaps?'

He shakes his head. 'The band and I have that gig in Bunbury today. We need to get sorted, load the van, and get up there to check out the venue and do a run through.'

'And you'll be back really late?'

''Fraid so. Tomorrow?'

Ruby nods, disappointed but also a little relieved. She needs time to pull herself together, think about what's happened, what it means to her. Right now she's overwhelmed by all this and by the sense of liberation from the past.

'Tomorrow, yes,' she says, 'when we've both got plenty of time,' and she pulls on her shoes, remembering how gently he had removed them, pushes some hair back from her face and stands up.

Jackson puts an arm around her shoulders and opens the cottage door. 'I thought we might take young Todd along with us today,' he says. 'Would that be okay with you?'

'Oh, he'll be thrilled. Of course it's okay.' She pauses in the doorway and they move simultaneously into a cautious, awkward hug.

Declan is sitting at the kitchen table surrounded by papers: pages filled with columns of figures, Excel spreadsheets, the accounts book for the shop and the lavender products, and the flow charts and other papers that he and Ruby have produced in preparing a business plan for the future of Benson's Reach. It amazes him that he's sitting here among all this stuff and he's not panicking. That's the Ruby effect, he thinks, she has demystified it for him, shown him how to control it rather than letting it get its anxiety inducing claws under his skin.

So he's not freaking out at the paperwork but he is feeling a bit anxious about Ruby, how she'll be after what happened last night. Why did they organise this meeting for this morning anyway? It was a ridiculous thing to do. Why hadn't they allowed for the fact that they'd all be exhausted and unable to concentrate on anything except a post-mortem of the festival? Maybe he should just knock on Ruby's door and suggest they leave it for another day. Declan pushes back his chair and is about to get up when Ruby appears in the doorway.

'Sorry,' she says, 'not enough sleep. I thought Fleur might beat me to it.'

He shakes his head. 'She rang about half an hour ago, she'll be a bit late. I told her to take her time.'

'Good.' Ruby grabs a mug, pours herself some coffee and flops into a chair. 'Do I smell croissants?'

'You do. I put them in the oven to warm.' He gets up, takes the croissants from the oven and transfers them to a serving basket and brings them to the table.

Ruby smiles at him. 'You know, Declan, you'll make some deserving woman a fine husband one day.'

'Oh I doubt that,' he says, blushing. 'Any deserving woman would run a mile if she had any sense.'

Ruby dips her croissant into her coffee. 'You will have to crack this self-deprecating nonsense, that's what would send her running. I never thought I'd say this to a man but you can afford a bit more male ego. Just a little, though – don't get carried away.'

He laughs and reaches for a croissant and their eyes meet.

'So . . .' he begins, not quite sure where he's going. 'So, last night . . .'

Ruby sighs. 'Yes, last night . . .'

'I'm sorry.'

'Don't be,' she says, leaning across the table towards him. 'It had to happen sometime. It's been the elephant in all my rooms for decades, so when I came back here I knew I'd have to face up to it one way or another. I guess Alice told you the story?'

He nods. 'I'd no idea, all those years . . . Harry, Catherine, they never said anything. Mind you, Harry had taken off before I got to the point of paying attention.'

'Of course. Catherine would never have told you anyway, but she knew that by leaving me a share of this place she would bring us together and that eventually you'd learn what had happened.'

'And you think she intended that?'

'Yes I do. It think it was her way of cleaning the slate.'

Declan leans back in his chair, half frowning. 'In what way?'

'Did you know they never married?'

'Catherine and Harry? But she was Mrs Benson.'

'She changed her name by deed poll. I suppose she thought it would look better. Harry and I were still married, you see. After it all happened I ran away. I couldn't bear the thought of divorce. It wasn't particularly easy in those days, it took ages and I just wanted to go, back to England, put it all behind me.'

Declan leans forward, resting his chin on his hands. 'But didn't they get married eventually?'

Ruby shakes her head. 'I was still married to Harry when he died. He'd taken off with a dancer by then and Catherine was still living here. He didn't leave a will so when he died Benson's Reach came to me, but I wanted nothing to do with it and I made it over to Freda Benson. By that time Maurice was dead and Freda was getting a bit frail. She moved down here and Catherine looked after her until she died.'

'I remember that,' Declan says. 'I remember coming here and Aunty Freda sitting out there on the deck with her book and her gin and tonic. She was a lovely woman.'

'She was. And by that time, of course, Catherine had turned the property into a business, planted the lavender and was starting to produce the lotions and so on.'

'So did she buy the place from Aunty Freda?'

'No! Freda left it to her in her will. Catherine told everyone that she inherited Benson's Reach and most people assumed she'd inherited it from Harry as a divorce settlement, which is what she intended them to think. But she actually inherited it from Freda. Once she owned it she could borrow against it to build the cottages, and the café and the shop.'

'So I suppose that means Freda forgave Catherine for the affair that drove you away?'

Ruby shrugs. 'I'm not completely convinced of that, at least not from the letters Freda sent me. I don't think she ever totally trusted her again, but she'd always been very fond of Catherine. Harry was dead. I was on the other side of the world. Freda had friends, but Catherine was the only person who would have felt like family to her. And I'm not a mother, but I suspect that a woman who has truly loved your son will have some sort of special place in your heart once he's gone – and whatever else I think of what Catherine did I believe she did love Harry, perhaps even from the time we all first met. Jack was just more glamorous and exciting for a time.'

They sit in silence for a moment, and eventually Declan shakes his head. 'I had no idea,' he says. 'All the years I knew her, she never mentioned any of this.'

'Pride, perhaps, or conscience,' Ruby says. 'When she came to see me in London she told me that she'd never got over the shame. I mean, we both suffered from the shame that was beaten into us in the convent, but she also lived with the shame of what she'd done to me. That was why she came. She wanted our friendship back but most of all she wanted forgiveness.'

'And did you forgive her?' Declan asks.

Ruby shrugged. 'I told her I did, but I sort of had my fingers crossed when I said it because, as I told Alice last night, I still didn't trust her. And I think she knew that.'

'I see,' Declan says, wondering if he really does see, trying to sort things out in his head. 'So when she was dying she made that will to try and set the record straight?'

'I think so,' Ruby nods. 'Half to me – the controlling interest but by such a tiny percentage, so trying to return something to me. The rest to you – returning something to the family.'

Declan rocks slowly back and forth in his chair. 'All this makes it feel as though we're related,' he says.

'Yes, it does feel as though, once again, I'm part of the family, but—'

'So sorry I'm late,' Fleur says, appearing in the kitchen doorway. 'I hope I haven't held you up.'

'No . . . no,' Declan says, forced to break out of his train of thought. 'It's fine, come on in, help yourself to coffee.' These days he's more relaxed around Fleur, although he still finds her pretty full on, but as she pours the coffee and joins them at the table he thinks she's looking a bit odd – nervous, perhaps, maybe a bit jittery.

'Croissant?' Ruby says, offering her the basket.

Fleur shakes her head. 'No thanks, just the coffee.'

Declan meets Ruby's eyes across the table and they share a look which, he thinks, connects them in a new way and is like a punctuation mark that seals what has passed between them. It feels okay, in fact it feels good, and he sits straighter in his chair, takes a deep breath and looks around for the paperwork he needs.

'Figures and plans,' he says, shaking his head, 'horrible stuff.'

Fleur gives him a wobbly smile, and he thinks she looks upset and wonders if it's his fault.

'It was good though, wasn't it,' she says, and she seems to be trying to get herself together. 'I mean, a good festival and good for Benson's.'

'Absolutely,' Ruby says. 'The feedback's been terrific, and it got us a lot of publicity. We're back on the radar again, which is why we need to talk to you.'

'We're having to rethink things,' Declan says, 'and we want to run a couple of ideas past you.'

'You mean you want to talk about *work*?' Fleur asks.

Declan smiles. 'Er . . . yes, that's why we asked you to pop in, what it means is—'

'Look,' Fleur cuts in, 'I'm sorry but I thought this was about something else.'

'We understand,' Declan begins again. 'We know you were committed to leaving but we're hoping—'

'No!' Fleur says, and Declan sees that her hands are shaking. 'No, you don't want to talk to me about this before I tell you . . .' She rubs her hands over her face then inhales deeply.

'I thought you knew, thought you'd worked it out, but you obviously haven't so I need to tell you. It was me. I got the marijuana for Catherine. She was in pain, and she asked.'

'You?' Ruby gasps, staring at her.

Declan seems to have been struck dumb.

'Me, yes. It wasn't like I was dealing, I didn't make a profit or anything, but she couldn't organise it herself. And Todd says you're worried that it was being sold to staff or guests, well it wasn't. Never, I promise you. I would never do that.

It was just a favour to Catherine, that's all. Please believe me, I would never have sold it.'

There is absolute silence in the kitchen. Ruby takes a deep breath and puffs out her cheeks. 'Well, you're the last person I would have thought of, Fleur. What made Catherine ask you? How did she know you'd be able to get it?'

'Because we'd often talked about people using it for pain. I'd told her that a friend of mine with MS uses it. So when things got very bad she wanted to try it and asked me if I could get some. I started off making her some cookies but she didn't like that, she started smoking instead.'

'And did it help?' Declan asks.

Fleur nods. 'Quite a bit, apparently. She smoked every day. But it stuffed her concentration, which is why she couldn't cope with reading, so she got Todd reading to her.'

Ruby and Declan exchange a glance across the table and Ruby looks away as Declan struggles to contain the urge to laugh out loud.

'So you're the source,' he says. 'No evil dealer fleecing old ladies and ripping off the staff and the guests, just Fleur on the mercy run.'

She shrugs, studying her shaking hands which are clasped on the table. 'If you want to put it like that. So, anyway, I'm really sorry. I should've told you straight away when you got here but . . . I don't know . . . I was upset and . . . and if you feel you have to go to the police—'

'The police?' Declan cuts in. 'Of course we're not going to the police,' and he hesitates and looks across at Ruby. 'We're not, are we, Ruby?'

'Of course not,' Ruby says. 'No, we're . . . I'm just glad you told us. It means we can stop worrying and put the whole thing to rest.'

'But you'll want me to go?'

'Go where?' Ruby says.

'To leave.'

'But you wanted to leave—'

'I did. When Catherine died I thought I didn't want to be here anymore, thought I needed a change. And of course it is different, it's actually better, but . . .'

'So are you interested in staying?' Declan asks.

'Could I?'

'That's why we asked you to come and talk to us,' he says. 'We're trying to reorganise the staffing of the shop and the lavender products, the whole thing. We were hoping we could persuade you to stay on.'

Fleur looks from one to the other. 'But what about . . . well, the other thing?'

'The grass? Well, it's sorted now, isn't it? We can destroy it. It seems to have acquired a fine coating of soot. Catherine's storage solution left something to be desired. Just, obviously, keep this to yourself.' He thinks he sounds competent, even authoritative, which is a very strange sensation. 'Don't bring drugs onto the property in future, please. And just one more thing before we get onto this work plan – do you have any idea where Paula might have got to?'

Twenty-five

t's an odd sort of week, Alice thinks, preparations for the festival have been going on for so long and now the whole thing is over everyone's spirits seem flat, besides which they're all exhausted. At Ruby's insistence Alice has retained the casual staff at the café until the end of the week to give herself a break, and although she certainly needs it she too feels strange and purposeless now the festival is over. It doesn't help any of them that Benson's looks uncharacteristically messy. The stage has not yet been dismantled; last week it looked like an invitation to a party but now its presence seems bleak and ghostly. The temporary fencing and the trestles that were used for the hot dog stall are dismantled and stacked ready for collection, and there is still a lot of litter in the field: cans, stubbies, forgotten thongs, even a couple of abandoned Eskys.

From where she is leaning on the balcony rail of her cottage, Alice sees Ruby walk out of the kitchen with Jackson. She's holding the door for him and he is carrying a tray with a coffee pot and mugs. She watches as they settle at the table and Ruby pours the coffee. They seem serious, she thinks, almost oblivious to anything but each other. And they look as though they belong together. Ruby has changed in the last

337

couple of days and Alice is pretty sure it's not only due to the relief of having broken her silence about the past.

On the other side of the property Todd is mustering his troops. Bundy and Johno have been summoned to help with the clean-up and had turned up earlier for a free breakfast at the café. Now Todd is handing out gardening gloves and black plastic sacks and delivering instructions about collecting and sorting the rubbish. Alice feels a huge rush of affection. She remembers sitting here in her first few days at Benson's, watching him wandering among the raspberry canes, wondering who he was and where he fitted in to the regime at Benson's. Now he's at the heart of the place and yet she suspects he has no idea how central he has become. He seems to have a grip on so much of what happens here, and an enthusiasm for it that is far beyond what could be expected of a sixteen-year-old. Yesterday, before he left for Bunbury, Fleur had taken him into town to open a bank account and deposit some money that Catherine had left him. His pride in being what he described as 'a man with a substantial bank account' had almost brought tears to Alice's eyes. It seems that no one here at Benson's is immune to the Todd effect – well, no one except Paula.

Paula! Alice's stomach churns when she thinks of her. It's Tuesday morning and they haven't seen or heard anything of her since the glass-smashing debacle on Saturday afternoon. Apart from the disruption of having to engage temporary cleaners, no one seems particularly concerned about Paula's absence, but Alice keeps thinking of Fleur's comments. Catherine had been good at managing her, she'd said, and Paula had been on some sort of medication. It all compounds her feeling that Paula's brash manner and her apparent insensitivity to the usual boundaries between people might be a sign of something more troubling.

'Have you tried calling her?' she had asked Declan yesterday.

'I have, and so has Ruby,' he'd said, 'and we both left messages.'

'You might have scared her off.'

He'd shaken his head. 'We agreed to keep it friendly but firm. You know – hope you're okay but we need to hear from you, please get in touch.'

'But we can't just leave it at that, surely?' Alice had said. 'She might be sick or something.'

Declan had shrugged. 'Both Todd and Fleur say she's gone to ground like this before and always come back with . . . well, not exactly with her tail between her legs but back to being the same old Paula.'

'I still don't like it,' Alice had said. 'I think we should do something. Where does she live?'

'Um . . . I think Todd said it was Wilyabrup.'

'Where's that?'

'Up the coast towards Yallingup.'

'Someone should go and see her, check that she's okay.'

Declan screwed up his face. 'Not me, I hope.'

'I'll go with you.'

He'd turned to her then, looking into her face. 'I thought you were staying within the grounds of the Benson prison farm, for fear of recognition.'

'I am, I was,' Alice had said, blushing, 'but it could be time to start taking risks.'

'Okay,' Declan had said, 'fair enough. Let's leave it another day and if we haven't heard from Paula by tomorrow morning you and I will take a ride up there.'

And this morning there is still no word from Paula and she's still not answering her phone.

⟐

Ruby isn't sure what's happening. She has been longing for this opportunity to spend time alone with Jackson, to pick up the conversation that they should have had the previous morning in his cottage. Unburdening herself of the past has energised her, left her open to possibilities. Yesterday afternoon she had thrown open the door of what had been Catherine's room and stacked the remaining boxes in a cupboard in the passage. Then she took the journals, the nightdresses and rosaries and other mementoes, into her own room and put them in the bottom drawer of the dressing table. There was a weary sort of pleasure in the realisation that the ghosts had been laid and the room that had housed them had been returned to its rightful use.

This moment ought to feel good; Alice and Declan are going out, Todd is clearing litter with his friends, Benson's is quiet and at last there is time to spare. But somehow it doesn't *feel* good as they sit here at right angles to each other on the sunlit deck. It's more than the awkwardness of the previous morning; the air seems charged with tension and it's coming from Jackson.

Ruby feels the butterflies of anxiety fluttering in her diaphragm and tries to slow her breathing to calm herself. Ignore it, she tells herself, push through it; carry on as though everything is fine.

Jackson sips his coffee and looks out towards the slope where the stage still stands deserted.

'So how was Bunbury?' Ruby asks, realising that she hasn't managed to keep the anxiety out of her voice.

He nods. 'Swell, nice little place and a great audience. Todd seemed to have a pretty good time.'

Silence again – awful, barren silence.

She grips the arms of her chair. 'We need to talk about what happened,' she says, and as she speaks he looks away again, to the stage, the cottages, the café, everywhere but at her. 'What I said yesterday morning, what you said . . .'

He turns to her now, leans forward, looks her briefly in the eye and then away again. 'I can't do this, Ruby,' he says. 'I can't get into this.'

Ruby feels a leaden weight in her stomach. 'What do you mean? You said . . .'

He sighs, turning back to her. 'I'm so sorry. I said what I felt, that when we met I felt I had known you all my life but had only just found you. It was real, it *was* what I felt.'

The blood pounds in her head and her knuckles whiten. 'It *was* what you felt – are you saying you no longer feel that?'

Jackson shakes his head. 'It was what I felt then, it's what I still feel now, but at the same time I don't have what it takes. Whatever is supposed to happen next, the next step, I can't take it. I'm not made for relationships, Ruby. Every one I ever had I stuffed up one way or another. I'm a loner and now I'm too old to change.'

Ruby stares at him in disbelief, then looks away. She folds her arms across her chest and rapidly unfolds them. 'Look,' she says, 'it was all so sudden. We have these feelings but we've had no chance to talk . . .' Her voice fades away because everything about him this morning tells her that it's hopeless. The relaxed, easygoing Jackson with his fluid movements and ready laughter has gone, replaced by someone else, someone rigid and cut off from feelings, someone hiding behind a wall. Ruby knows enough about people to realise that whatever she says now will be a sort of pleading, embarrassing and debasing. And while part of her wants to fight, her pride holds her back. A voice in her head tells her that this is worth fighting for but another tells her that holding herself together is more important. She feels she is falling apart from within but she's determined not to let him see that. But then . . .

'It's never too late to change, Jackson,' she says, and it clatters, like the cliché it is, into the space between them.

'For you maybe, but it is for me.'

'Perhaps you don't *want* to change,' she says, suddenly angry and ready now for a fight. 'Perhaps you're too selfish or too lazy.'

341

But he won't fight. Instead he just nods. 'Perhaps both,' he says.

Ruby is shocked by her own impotence. She is used to winning, and it's so long since she's had this hopeless sense of something so precious slipping away from her. How many times has she pulled back from the brink of involvement for fear of facing the abyss of loss? But this is different, now she has no choice. She wants what she glimpsed with Jackson more than she can bear, and yet it's too late, already gone. He has removed himself from the equation.

'Some risks *are* worth taking,' she says. 'Stay a little longer, give us time to see what might happen . . .' But she knows it's lost, over before it started. Tomorrow he will be gone, leaving her nothing to salvage from it but the shame of grasping at love and having it moved out of reach.

❦

'Shall we go now, Alice?' Declan calls, waving to her from outside the office.

And she gives him a thumbs-up, fetches her bag and sunglasses from the cottage and pauses to draw a deep breath.

'It's like longing to leave home but being afraid to cross the street,' the Outcare officer had told her just before she was released, 'but the feeling will pass.' It had been so much harder than she expected during those first few days of freedom, and now the fear overtakes her again. 'But it *is* different this time,' she tells herself, 'Declan will be with me, and anyway *I'm* different,' and she closes the cottage door and runs down to where Declan is waiting in the car.

'Aren't we going the wrong way?' she asks as he takes a right turn out of the drive.

'We're going into town first,' he says, 'just a little practice run. You go into a shop, on your own while I wait outside, you buy a newspaper and come out and then we walk together to a coffee shop, sit down and order some coffee and chat in a relaxed manner. As though it's something we do all the time.'

Alice, her insides churning, turns to look at him. 'We were going to visit Paula.'

'We still are,' he says, briefly taking his eyes off the road to look at her, 'as soon as we've finished the coffee. If you have the courage to go looking for Paula – something which, I have to say, I am only able to do because you're with me – then you certainly have the courage to have a cup of coffee with me. We're old friends, remember, there hasn't been much time for that recently.'

'Sometimes you really surprise me, Declan,' Alice says, smiling. 'You sell yourself short. You claim incompetence but you're actually a really good manager. You take good decisions and you're thoughtful, but you're not a pushover.'

Declan gives a short laugh. 'It must be the sisterhood effect,' he says, 'the combination of you and Ruby. It's challenging but fortifying, like that breakfast cereal that builds iron men.'

Alice bursts into laughter and then finds quite suddenly that the laughter turns to a couple of sobs.

'Shit,' Declan says, slowing down, about to pull off the road. 'What have I said?'

'Nothing,' Alice says, laughing again now, 'it's just that I'm so scared of what we're about to do – the newspaper, the café, not the Paula bit. But I suppose as I'm in the company of iron man there's really nothing to worry about.'

'Absolutely nothing at all,' he says, pulling back onto the road. 'In half an hour it will all be over and you'll be wondering what you were worried about.'

And he was right, except that it took longer, more than twice as long in fact. Not longer to stop worrying, which happened quite quickly, just longer to luxuriate in the difference, to sit there on the café terrace watching people go by. To wander back down the hill to the bookshop and browse the shelves, even longer to go into the eco shop and buy a gorgeous purple wool jacket that Declan assured her she would need as the days grew cooler.

'There's no stopping you now, is there?' he says as they leave the shop. 'You're already into retail therapy. May I escort you back to your car, madam?'

'It feels good,' she says, taking his proffered arm. 'Really good. Thank you.'

'It's an extraordinary pleasure,' he says, drawing her hand further into the curve of his arm and keeping hold of it. 'We will do it often from now on, along with other daring things, like going out for a meal, or to the cinema, or for a walk on the beach. For now, though, we'll just go and see if I can work the iron man charm on Paula.'

It takes them a while to find Paula's place, losing themselves along unmade roads and then backtracking, but at last they discover the unmarked road and reach a cluster of small weatherboard cottages dating back several decades.

'It has to be that one,' Declan says, pointing to a bright pink gate which leads up a short path of broken pavers to the white cottage with a badly painted pink door and pink window frames. 'It has Paula written all over it. Number three – there, you see, I was right.' He pulls up outside the gate and switches off the engine. 'Come on then, iron woman,' he says, 'let's do it.'

'She's not there,' Alice says as they reach the gate, and for some reason the place makes her feel uneasy. 'It's all shut up.'

'Of course it's shut up, it's a chilly day.'

Alice shakes her head. 'There's something wrong, I know there is.'

Declan runs up the three steps to the front door and knocks a couple of times. The black iron door knocker shaped like a dragon is loud in the stillness. He steps back, waiting for a response.

'She's not there, I know she's not,' Alice says.

'Give her time,' Declan says, 'she might be out the back, or in the bathroom.' He knocks again. 'Okay, she's not there,' he says, and he walks back down onto the path, jumps over a flowerbed and peers through the window of the small garage. 'No car either. I'll look round the back,' and he strides off down the drive and opens the gate at the end.

Alice knows it's a waste of time. Paula isn't there, she feels that so strongly that it hardly seems worth checking out the back of the house, but she follows Declan through into the yard and waits while he knocks at the back door. Nothing.

'I suppose that's it then,' Declan says as they stroll back to the front of the house. 'Not much else we can do. I guess she'll turn up when it suits her.'

'Hang on a minute,' Alice says.

Next door but one an elderly woman is making her way from her front door to her garage.

'Looking for Paula?' she calls.

'We are, yes,' Alice says, walking towards her. 'Have you seen her in the last couple of days?'

'Oh yes, she was there yesterday, about five o'clock. I saw her in the garden. Spoke to her.'

'Did she seem okay?'

'Oh well, you know Paula,' the woman says, 'up and down, up and down. She was having one of her grumpy days when you can barely get a word out of her. But she was there all right. Then she went out in the car in the evening. I was coming back from bridge about ten o'clock and I passed her on the lane. Goodness knows where she was going at that time of night. She'll be back later, I expect, shall I give her a message for you?'

'Could you could tell her that Declan and Alice were looking for her?'

'Dylan and Alice . . .'

'Declan,' Alice says. 'Or perhaps just ask her to call Benson's Reach.'

'Ah, that's where she works,' the woman says. 'She told me she's the executive housekeeper now. Anyway, I'll tell her you were here.'

Alice thanks her and walks back to Declan. 'Did you hear that?'

He nods. 'So shall we go?'

'Might as well,' Alice agrees, 'no point waiting here, we could be waiting all day.' But as she hauls herself up into the four-wheel-drive she can't get rid of the feeling that something's wrong, very wrong. 'I don't like this,' she says as Declan starts the engine. 'She might be inside, sick or something.'

'But the car's not there, Alice,' Declan says, 'she's out somewhere. And anyway, we can't just break in.'

'No, no we can't,' she says. 'But do you think we should report her missing?'

'But she's *not* missing. The neighbour saw her yesterday evening. Look, Paula freaked out, she yelled and screamed and started throwing things and now she feels stupid and embarrassed. That's hard for anyone but especially for Paula, who can't tolerate being in the wrong. I think she just needs a bit more time. She'll turn up before the end of the week, I bet you, and it'll all be someone else's fault.'

'But where would she be going at ten o'clock?'

'I don't know. Maybe she has a lover and went to his place for the night. She could have gone anywhere and that's really not our business.'

Alice nods. 'Okay,' she says, 'you're probably right. Let's go home.' But as Declan lets out the clutch and they make their way slowly towards the main road, she still has the feeling that something about this is far from right.

It's the police who find Paula. While Alice and Declan were knocking on her door her body was being winched up from the rocks at the foot of Wilyabrup Cliffs in a black body bag.

'She was spotted by a light plane flying low along the coast,' the police officer explains to Ruby late that afternoon when he arrives at Benson's Reach in an effort to find contact details for her next of kin.

'It would be my nan and granddad, I suppose,' Todd says, and gives him what he can remember of the address. 'But she didn't ever see them, not for years.'

'Will the cops go there or will they phone?' he asks Ruby once the officer has left.

'They'll go there and tell your grandparents personally,' Ruby says. 'They don't give people news like that over the phone.'

'I don't fancy their luck,' Todd says. 'They'll probably be drunk, they usually are.'

'Are you okay, Todd?' Ruby asks. 'I mean, Paula *was* part of your family.'

He shrugs. 'Not so's you'd notice.'

'And what about your mum?'

'Like I told the police, she's in Kuta but I don't know where.'

Ruby looks at him anxiously, searching for signs of distress. 'There must be ways of finding her if you need to talk to her.'

'The police said they'd find her.'

'But if you want to speak to her, if you're upset, I mean, we could try to speed it up.'

Todd pauses. 'Paula didn't give a rat's arse about me,' he says, blushing. 'Sorry, Ruby . . . but she didn't. In all my life she never said one nice thing to me, and she said horrible things about me and Mum *and* she tried to get me in trouble with Catherine and with Declan. I'm sorry if she jumped off that cliff because she was unhappy, but I'm not sorry that she won't be around anymore. Shall I go and tell Declan?'

Ruby watches as he goes off down the path heading for the field where Declan is chatting to the men who have finally turned up to dismantle the stage. Todd is, she thinks, far more affected by the news than he's prepared to admit. His face betrayed profound anger and hurt, less perhaps about Paula but an older, deeper hurt. Perhaps, even in their mutual hostility, there was something solid for him about her presence. His mother and grandparents have abandoned him; perhaps even as she persecuted him Paula was one fixed point of connection to his family.

As Todd reaches the group on the hill Ruby watches as Declan turns to listen to him, then draws him away from the group to sit, side by side, on some upturned packing cases. Todd, talking fast, gesticulating, stops abruptly and buries his face in his hands. Declan slips an arm around his shoulders and Todd leans in to him. He has picked the right person, Ruby thinks. Declan, robbed of his mother by death and his father by grief and depression, will instinctively respond to the complications of Todd's feelings. 'You did a grand thing with those two, Cat,' she murmurs. 'I hope you know that.'

She glances up to Jackson's cottage, sees him there on the balcony, talking with one of his musicians. Resisting the temptation to turn away she holds her ground, keeps looking at him until he stops speaking and meets her eyes across the distance, and then finally turns slowly back to his conversation, leaving her feeling rejected once again.

❦

The news travels through Benson's Reach like a flash fire. Everyone has something to say, something conditional. 'She was a pain in the neck but she had a good heart.' 'She really got on my nerves but she meant well.' 'She was so annoying and bossy but she'd have done anything for you.'

'It's my fault,' Alice says that evening as they gather around the kitchen table. 'I should have followed my instinct and gone up there yesterday.'

'It's not your fault, Alice,' Declan says. 'You would have gone but I made you wait until today. If it's anyone's fault it's mine.'

'But I should have talked to her weeks ago,' Alice says. 'I knew something wasn't right. I should've tried to connect with her.'

'I feel terrible,' Fleur says. 'I was a real bitch to her. She pissed me off so much, always nosing into things, no respect for any sort of niceties. But now I think she just wanted attention. That's all she wanted, really – attention.'

'I should have talked to her more right from the start,' Declan says, 'should have tried to involve her. But she just kept getting my back up.'

'I do feel a bit responsible,' Lesley says. 'I did use her when I was . . . when I was upset, and then she thought I had her job.'

Ruby, battling her own conscience, watches and listens. 'I didn't see it coming,' she says, 'but now I know that all the signs were there. What did I do, switch off my brain or something?'

'And I should have let her sing for me,' Jackson says, 'but you know none of this would have stopped it happening – if not now, then some other time.'

They sit on in silence, each one, Ruby thinks, crushed by the vision that Paula's death has given them of themselves as less caring, less insightful, more selfish than they had believed themselves to be.

'You may be right that none of us could have stopped this happening, Jackson,' she says crisply, 'but I guess we all know we could have done a whole lot better.'

Todd pushes his chair back from the table and gets up. 'Paula could have done better,' he says. 'Catherine said it to her all the time. I heard her – "Paula, you have to take responsibility for your own behaviour. You have to stay on the medication." So now she's done it, taken responsibility.

349

Her choice.' And he walks out of the kitchen, down the passage and they hear his bedroom door close behind him.

Declan shakes his head. 'Sometimes that boy just blows me away,' he says. 'Sixteen going on forty,' and he gets up to follow him.

Twenty-six

*L*esley is stricken with guilt. Relentlessly she tracks back over her involvement with Paula, the way she pumped her for information about Declan, the pressure she put on her to get his mobile number. She recalls how frequently she invited her into the cottage, drank tea with her and listened to Paula's tales of life at Benson's Reach and, once she was back home in Perth, Paula's efforts to help her find somewhere to stay. Most of all she thinks of Paula's persistent calls on the night before the festival – the calls she had deliberately ignored. Lesley is chilled by the memory of her own irritation at the growing number of messages and texts and how easy it had been to dismiss them simply because Paula was someone she no longer needed. It revives memories of the uncomfortable occasions when her mother has accused her of selfishness, of an inability – or was it an unwillingness? – to put herself in someone else's shoes.

'You've been too fortunate, Lesley. It's all about you. You don't have a social conscience. I don't understand it, we didn't bring you up that way.'

Lesley has rolled her eyes, ignored Dolly or made light of it, but now she can't get the words out of her head. What was it like for Paula driving that night to Wilyabrup? Just what was she feeling as she left the car and walked to the cliff edge? Had she really believed that she was to be put in charge of the shop? Could a life really hang on something so fragile? There must, she knows, be a much bigger picture, and she is clear that it was not her fault, but she is painfully aware of the role she may have played in the final days of Paula's life. Once again she is faced with an image of herself as irresponsible, as a person so fixed on her own track that she can mow others down as she follows it. It leaves her feeling shallow, selfish and ill at ease with herself.

Back in her rented house she opens her laptop and reads Gordon's message again. The weekend after next, he says, he will be here, in Margaret River. She wonders what it has cost him to do that, to detach from what he is working on and come here to talk to her. Has it all gone too far? Is he coming to tell her that he wants a divorce?

They have asked her to stay on at Benson's Reach, to manage the shop and, with Fleur, to develop the lavender business online. Their business plan is impressive. Ruby has surprised her, she is something of a dark horse. She clearly has plenty of money and is willing to invest it in the business. She doesn't talk about it herself, but Alice has filled Lesley in on Ruby's background, the Foundation in England, her DBE, her reputation. It all compounds Lesley's sense of her own self-centredness.

'I want to lead a good life,' she had said to Gordon years ago, 'a valuable life,' and she has in some ways – her children are proof of that, surely? Just the same, she has rigidly done what she wants with little thought about what other dimensions a good life might entail.

'I hope we can sort things out in ways that suit us both,' Gordon has said in his email, but that has always been his way: negotiation, compromise, listening and working through situations. It was those qualities that had condemned him to life in meetings and boardrooms, behind a desk, and in protracted negotiations, when he would have preferred to be out in the field and the lab, earning less but enjoying it more. She wonders why that seems so clear now, and at what point she actually lost sight of it.

As she struggles to remember when the malaise began she recognises that it was quite some time before Gordon retired. She had filled her time with distractions then too, but at the heart of it was an emptiness that had been hollowed out when the children began to drift off into lives of their own. She remembers the frantic search for things to occupy her – all of them pleasant and some useful, but all essentially unsatisfying. In her attempts to fill the empty space she had succeeded only in papering over it. What she wanted then and now wants more than ever is a way of being that will fill that gap. Can she find that here? Have the past few months, and now this dramatic and shocking development, taught her anything about what matters to her and how she really wants to live? She has nearly two weeks to think about that. Lesley clicks on a new email and starts to type. 'That's good,' she writes, 'ring me when you land in Perth, and let me know when you'll be here.' And then she sits for a long time wondering how to sign off a message to the man she has lived with and loved for more than thirty-five years.

———

Something inside Ruby has been extinguished – something that enables her to feel. Her energy has evaporated, her imagination is blighted, empathy is impossible and the effort required to do simple things, even to hold a conversation, is more demanding than she can bear. Lying flat on her back staring up at her bedroom ceiling on the morning following the news of Paula's suicide, she wonders whether it is going to be possible to get herself out of bed, let alone showered and dressed. The events of the previous day have left her leaden and exhausted. She is not even clear how she passed the time after her conversation with Jackson. She remembers only moving zombie-like through the kitchen and back here to her bedroom. Perhaps she slept, perhaps she just lay here, and then later, she got up and went through to the office and sat behind the desk, trying to concentrate on small things until she saw the police car making its way slowly up the drive, and a fresh faced young constable appeared in the office doorway and everything changed.

At last she drags herself out of bed and stands under the shower. As the water cascades over her she has a brief moment of optimism – perhaps, after all, it is not over. Perhaps after a good night's sleep Jackson will feel different, he will stay on a couple of days, a week perhaps, and somehow they will find their way to each other. But her mood doesn't last and by the time she steps out of the shower she is angry. Angry at herself for falling, at this age, into the oldest trap in the world. Angry at Jackson for feeding her fantasy but lacking the fortitude to risk where it might take him. And when she has dried herself and dressed, and has twisted her hair into its new clip, she studies herself in the mirror and thinks that she looks ten years older than she looked yesterday – a worn out, easily forgettable old woman, with no resources left to draw on.

The morning is about as bad as it can be in the circumstances, beginning with a number of telephone calls from radio stations and then the arrival of a reporter and camera operator from a commercial television news program. Paula's parents have called every channel they could think of, muttering darkly about workplace bullying and harassment, threatening legal action and demanding an inquest. Catherine's solicitor is summoned and consulted, and as they sit with him in the kitchen Ruby watches through the window as Jackson and his crew load their equipment and their suitcases into the van and prepare to leave.

The farewells take forever: hands are shaken, backs are patted, there are hugs and kisses, jokes and promises.

'Ruby,' he says, hugging her. 'I'm sorry. I really did . . . do . . . mean it. But . . .'

She pulls away from him. 'I know – you're just an itinerant musician too old to change.' And she turns and walks away, back into the house and down the passage to her room while the others stand outside waving as The Crowbars' van disappears down the track and out onto the road.

Twenty–seven

I t seems as though everyone is waiting for enough time to pass to allow them to feel normal again. Not liking Paula, finding her difficult, frequently obnoxious, tolerating her in order to avoid confrontation, or simply feeling neutral, seems to make no difference to the level of dismay that people feel, nor the overbearing sadness that haunts Benson's Reach. Another week passes and winter has taken hold, and Alice still carries Jacinta's dog-eared letter everywhere with her. One more week, she thinks, and that will be the right time to make the phone call. And so another week passes and Alice reads the letter again. It would be okay to ask Declan to make the call now, but something stops her. Fear, perhaps – she has so much riding on this that waiting and keeping silent seem preferable to the risk of greater hostility. She puts the letter back in her pocket.

Still shocked, and still castigating herself for what she sees as her failures in relation to Paula, she also realises that she is probably the only person to have gained strength from this. She had arrived here in a blur of misery, confusion and hopelessness, and with no sense of a future. Now there is a future, and what she makes of it is down to her. Paula, Alice believes, ricocheted between utter hopelessness and a brittle, fluctuating vision of a rescue that would lift her out of present reality into what she believed she truly deserved. But those visions were built on shifting sands and sent her always spiralling backwards into despair.

Like Ruby, Alice knows she should have seen the signs earlier. She could have reached out to Paula, talked to her, encouraged her to get help. At the very least she might have been someone for Paula to talk to. But it's easy to see this after the event, easy to talk about what one might have done, to wonder how much effort and commitment it had taken for Catherine to manage Paula for so long. Easy too to question why, knowing that she was dying, Catherine had not left any information which might have alerted them to Paula's fragile state rather than simply reacting to the difficulties of her personality. For Alice it adds up to a recognition of her own good fortune: she has survived the worst time of her life, and since the day that Declan had told her to get on the next bus to Margaret River she has been rebuilding from the ground up. There is no one simple solution, just a hard slog and slow progress. Today she is about to take another trip off the premises, this time with Ruby, who, caught short by the change in the weather, needs to buy a warm jacket, a sweater and some thick socks.

'I'd forgotten how cold it can get,' she'd said. 'When I've thought of this place it's always been as it is in the summer, brilliant sunshine and day after day of clear blue skies.'

'Ruby,' Alice says later, when they have finished shopping and are about to get back into the car, 'could we make a detour and go to the beach?'

'Redgate,' Ruby says, with obvious enthusiasm, starting the engine, 'it's just beautiful. Todd took me there some time ago. It's his favourite beach and now I think it's mine.'

They drive out of town to the coast and Ruby parks the car and pulls on the new jacket, turning up the collar. Together they walk the well-trodden path to the beach where the wind is cold and strong, whipping their hair back from their faces, making their eyes water. They stuff their hands in their pockets and press on through the soft sand towards the rocks that form a ragged boundary separating this stretch of sand from the next, and stop, searching the jagged surfaces for a place to sit.

'How are you, Ruby?' Alice asks when they have caught their breath.

'Crushed,' Ruby says quickly, surprising Alice by the speed and frankness of her reply. 'Crushed and confused. I think I've grown too accustomed to success, in all sorts of ways, large and small, in recent years.'

Alice turns to her. 'What do you mean?'

'I've had a dream run. The Foundation has gone from strength to strength, I have brilliant staff who run it and involve me when they need to. I have a home I love, a few good friends, a house full of books that I now have time to read. I have good health. Every application I've made for funds has sailed through and every person I pursued for sponsorship or to take on some sort of role for us turned to gold. But I'd become complacent. Then I came here imagining awkwardness, perhaps a difficult business partner, resentful staff – lord knows what. And of course I was fearful of confrontations with the past. But we all got on well. It was busy and challenging but we were winning. I was on cruise control. And then there was Jackson, and to my amazement I fell in love, or at least I thought that was what had happened.'

'I thought you had too,' Alice said.

Ruby nods. 'It was so sudden, so intense, and briefly it seemed that Jackson felt the same way too.'

She stops suddenly and studies her feet as she kicks at some sand.

'So what happened?' Alice asks, wondering if this is too intrusive. Ruby is a very private person and Alice suspects that telling the story of her past has, while freeing her, also left her feeling uncomfortably exposed.

Ruby shakes her head. 'Who knows? He backed off, that's all. The moment we met, Alice, I felt I'd been struck by lightning. We barely exchanged a few words before Declan turned up and took over, but it was intense and Jackson admitted he'd felt it too. He told me that early in the morning after Todd's birthday dinner. We were both exhausted and short of sleep. I'd unburdened myself to you a few hours earlier. Jackson had been pacing back and forth, flagellating himself for blowing open my past. And we had this glorious little interlude that seemed like the start of something so . . . so precious . . .' her voice trails off and Alice waits for her. 'And then I had to go, and he went off to Bunbury and when he came back he'd changed. The walls had gone up, he said he couldn't cope. You can imagine it, probably – too old, too hopeless, can't change. That was it. I could see myself sitting there, listening to him, to all that stuff, and I knew it was hopeless, and I was so hurt and then I was angry, really angry with him and with myself. How could I have made such a fool of myself? And then – well, then there was poor Paula . . .' She shoves her hands further into her pockets. 'I failed miserably there. The number of times I felt I should sit down and talk things through with her . . . but I just ignored it. I should have made the effort to get to know her better. I was angry about her wanting to get into Catherine's room all the time so when we found that bag of dope I was sure she was responsible. Now I think she probably knew what Catherine had been doing and she just wanted to get rid of the stuff to protect her. For decades my life has been about supporting women in difficult circumstances – listening to them, finding solutions. But I let Paula fall into a hole. Maybe I even gave her a little push.'

'But, Ruby, this wasn't your fault.'

'No, but I'm shocked by my negligence.'

'And Jackson, have you heard any more from him since he got back home?'

Ruby shakes her head. 'Not a word. And I won't. Look, we're two old people who had a chance and we blew it . . . well, *he* blew it. I don't think he's a bad person but I guess he was just knocked sideways by what it all might mean. We're very different people, we live on opposite sides of the world. How would we have managed a relationship anyway? I suppose it all looked too hard. Maybe that was all that he could see, or perhaps he felt too vulnerable to even explore it. I haven't really forgiven him for not being prepared to give it a go. After all, at our age we don't have all that much to lose.' Ruby sits still, slumped for a moment, and then takes a deep breath and straightens up. 'You're a great listener, Alice,' she says, putting her hand on Alice's and squeezing it. 'I really appreciate it. And what about you? How are you going?'

Alice hesitates. To speak of the strength she has gained seems callous in the circumstances and yet she suspects that Ruby will understand, and so she takes the chance.

'I'm glad,' Ruby says. 'I don't think recognising it makes you callous. It takes wisdom and insight to find strength in something like this. Sadly Paula lacked both those qualities or she might have been able to save herself. So what's ahead for you, do you think?'

The question takes Alice by surprise. She has thought about it so much she almost expects everyone else to know. 'Well I hope to stay here doing what I'm doing for as long as possible,' she says. 'Of course it all depends what you and Declan decide. I think the future for Benson's could be exciting, and I'd love to be part of that. But if it's not possible I think what I've done in the café here will be enough to get me similar work somewhere else.' She wants to ask Ruby what she's planning but, unlike Declan, she is an employee. Despite the fact that they are speaking as friends this seems to Alice to be a boundary she shouldn't cross.

Ruby nods. 'You've done a terrific job, Alice, any employer

would be lucky to have you. If I stay in the business I'd certainly want you to stay on. I can't imagine the place without you.'

'I've been incredibly lucky, Ruby, Declan asking me to come here, both of you involving me the way you have, and giving me the space to sort myself out. You've both made a sort of investment in me, I suppose, and because of that I feel I have an investment in Benson's Reach. It feels like home. And I think Declan and I . . .' she hesitates, 'we trust each other. I think if I left . . .'

'He would obviously be devastated.'

'Yes.'

'But you have to decide what you want for yourself, Alice. I know you feel Declan rescued you when you needed it most, but you shouldn't feel that you have to spend your life rescuing him. In fact I don't know about you but I think Declan's grown enormously in the last few months. I don't think he's going to fall into a hole anytime soon, and anyway, if he does it's not your responsibility.'

❧

Todd is in his room browsing for information on sound engineering courses when the phone rings, and he gets up from the table and goes to the kitchen to answer it.

'Todd darlin'? Is that you?'

Todd's heart lurches in shock at the sound of his mother's voice, and what rushes immediately through his head is that he hopes beyond hope that she's not coming home.

'Mum?'

'Happy birthday, baby.'

'Thanks.' He wishes she wouldn't call him 'baby', although that's what she calls most people. 'But it was three weeks ago.'

'I *know*,' she says. 'I'm so bad with dates, but I was thinking of you, hon. Sixteen, eh! Independent now!'

'That's me,' Todd says, remembering with sudden relief that he really is free to live a separate life. 'Where are you, Mum? Are you okay?'

'I'm fine, Todd. It's lovely out here, you should come and join us. Get yourself a passport. I can ask Stanley to send you a ticket if you like.'

Todd is almost reeling with horror at the prospect of being with his mother and the awful Stanley in Bali; a deep flush floods his face and neck. 'I'm thinking of going to college,' he says, 'so that wouldn't work for me right now. Anyway, why are you ringing?'

'About Paula, baby. You know we weren't that close, in fact she hated my guts, but she was my sister and your aunty. The Aussie police rang the local guys here and they found me and gave me this number. Just wanted to see if you were okay.'

'I'm fine, Mum. Paula and me . . . we didn't get on.'

'Tell me about it! She never really liked us, Toddy, she was such a party pooper. Always going on about me having a drink or two. Has she been buried yet?'

'Cremated,' Todd says.

'That's nice. Who paid for it? That Catherine woman, is it?'

'Catherine's dead too, Mum,' Todd says, suddenly finding this is just too hard, and resenting the fact that his mother knows and cares so little about what's happening in his life. 'She's been dead for months. Declan and Ruby own the place now and they're looking after the cremation.'

'Declan who?'

'Look, it doesn't matter, does it? You don't know them anyway.'

'And are they looking after you all right too, baby?'

'Fine,' he says, 'really good.'

'Righty-oh then,' she says. 'D'you want to write my number down in case you need it?'

Todd writes the number onto a pad as she reads it to him.

'You can always ring, you know. I don't know why you never get in touch.'

Todd starts to feel physically sick. 'I didn't know where you were. You changed your mobile number. Just sending a letter addressed to you in Kuta wouldn't be much good, would it?'

'Oh well, darlin', you've got it now. Take care of yourself, Todd, won't you?'

'I will. But Mum, about Paula—'

But she's already hung up.

Todd puts the phone down. He takes a few steps out of the kitchen into the passage and leans back against the wall.

'Was that for me, Todd?' Declan calls coming through the back door. 'I heard it ring but I just had to sign off on some deliveries.'

Todd hears what Declan says, but he can't respond, not just yet.

'Todd,' Declan calls again. 'Todd, are you there?' And he sticks his head around the door to the passage. 'Jesus, mate, are you all right? You look terrible.'

And as Declan strides across the passage towards him Todd slides slowly down the wall until he is sitting, knees bent, on the tiled floor.

'What's wrong, mate? What's happened?' Declan sits down beside him.

Todd shakes his head. 'Nothing,' he says eventually, 'just, my mum rang . . .' he pauses, 'for my birthday. She's such a loser, she never gets it right.' And he pushes the heels of his hands into his eyes to stop himself from crying.

━

Lesley hadn't counted on the dog; in fact she'd forgotten he even existed. She much prefers cats but has never wanted to own one: hair everywhere, snagged threads on the uphol-stery, furry bodies sneaking onto the beds are not her thing.

So when, as soon as she opens the door, Bruce gives a short bark and looks up at her, head tilted to one side, it comes as such a shock she barely notices how Gordon looks.

'Oh!' she says, stepping back from the open door. 'I didn't realise . . . well, I wasn't expecting . . .'

'He's very well behaved,' Gordon says. 'And I hadn't anyone to leave him with.'

Bruce wags his tail and Lesley has the uncanny feeling that he is smiling at her. 'Well then,' she says, 'you'd better come in – both of you.' And he darts past her and begins a tour of the house, sniffing cupboard doors, inspecting chair legs. 'He won't . . .?'

'No,' Gordon says, 'he has impeccable manners. Whoever trained him did an excellent job,' and he steps inside and puts his bag down on the floor.

Now, as they stand facing each other, Lesley sees that Gordon is as confused as she is about what comes next. Should they kiss each other? Hug? It would be ridiculous to shake hands. Best perhaps to avoid the hazards of physical contact, and so she falls back into her characteristically brisk manner with visitors, urging him further in and closing the door.

'You must be tired . . . the flight and then the drive,' she says. 'Cup of tea? Glass of wine, or would you prefer a beer?'

'Tea, please,' he says, following her through to the kitchen, looking around approvingly. 'This is a nice little place. How did you find it?'

'Someone told me about it,' she says, filling the kettle. 'The owners very rarely use it.'

'All right if I have a look around?'

'Of course,' she says, and he wanders through the living room, across to the glass door that opens onto the little courtyard, and then down the passage to the bathroom and the two bedrooms.

Lesley pours the tea and puts the mugs onto a tray alongside slices of carrot cake, wondering, as she carries it to the coffee table, how they will move on from this awkwardness, which of them will be able to take the first step towards normality.

'You must find it very small,' Gordon says, coming back and sitting in one of the two armchairs. 'I mean, it's a lovely place but . . .'

'I like it,' she says, 'it feels cosy, and it's easy to look after, not much housework.'

He nods and takes the tea from her. 'Thanks. Is that carrot cake? Excellent, my favourite.'

It's only then that she really looks at him – his hands first, as he reaches for the cake. They are dramatically changed, roughened and scratched, his nails neat but ingrained with red earth, so different from the smooth, manicured hands that emerged from the cuffs of his shirts as he set off each day for the city. His face is different too, quite weathered, and his hair is longer and lightened by the northern sun. It suits him, as do the jeans and the dark blue shirt, neither of which she has seen before.

Bruce has finished reconnoitring and stands between them, looking from one to the other as though deciding which side to choose. Then he moves swiftly to Gordon and flops down by his feet.

'Does he need anything?' Lesley asks. 'Water, perhaps?'

Gordon looks at Bruce. 'He probably does.'

She moves to get up but Gordon puts up his hand to stop her. 'It's okay, I'll do it. I brought his bowl, it's with my bag.' He gets to his feet and crosses to his bag which is still standing just inside the front door, Bruce's red plastic bowl on top of it. He fills the bowl from the kitchen tap, sets it on the tiled floor and Bruce, who has followed his movements attentively, jumps up and starts lapping noisily.

'He *is* rather sweet,' Lesley says, watching from the lounge.

'He attached himself to me when I was on a bike ride by the river. Picked me up, really. I couldn't trace the owner and I was going to take him to the pound, but somehow I just couldn't part with him. He looks a bit of a scruff but he's big on personality.'

She nods and there's that silence again. She takes the plunge. 'I'm glad you came.'

'Me too,' he says. 'I missed you, and this feels very strange.'

'Doesn't it! It'll get better . . .'

'I hope so!'

'It just takes time, I suppose.'

In fact it takes about an hour, an awkward hour. They talk about the children and the grandchildren, and specifically about Simon and Lucy, whose lease is up, requiring them to move out of their current house. They talk about Lesley's mother, and about the message they've both had from Karen, who is keeping an eye on the house and is concerned about a section of fence that has been damaged.

'So tell me what you're doing,' she says eventually.

And he kicks off his shoes, swings one leg over the arm of the chair and begins to explain about his relationship with the Land Council and a group of Indigenous people who are preparing to take on a mining company.

'Which company?' she asks.

He grins and she laughs. 'No – not really?'

'Really,' he says. 'They're not happy. I pointed out that the fact I worked for them for so long didn't mean they owned me for life. But they're not amused.'

They both laugh then, a lot, and Gordon gets to his feet and comes to sit beside her on the sofa. 'I've missed you,' he says, taking her hand. 'I really have, but I can't go back to how it was.'

She shakes her head. 'Me neither. I can't . . . I mean . . . I don't want to do all those things we talked about. I want a different sort of life.'

'I know,' he says, 'so do I. So now that we know that, maybe we can start to talk about what we do want, and whether any of it fits together.'

Lesley nods. 'The great negotiator,' she says, smiling.

'That's me,' he says, 'but negotiation works best if both parties want it to succeed.'

'Well then,' she says, taking a deep breath, 'we're probably going to be okay.'

———

Paula's death has affected Declan in ways he could never have imagined. One morning he wakes at dawn. Troubled by dreams he can't recall and too restless to sleep any longer, he gets out of bed, pulls on a tracksuit and drives to the beach. It's cold but as he walks onto the sand the first shafts of sunlight appear and the waves crash on the beach, exploding in clouds of sparkling white foam. Declan pauses for a moment, watching, listening to the roar of the ocean, allowing himself to taste the salt wind and marvel at the beauty of the waking landscape. Then, hands in his pockets, deep in thought, he walks on, along the firm ridge of damp sand, contemplating his sense of no longer being alone.

For most of his teenage and adult life he has been a loner. The fractured nature of his family relationships was not conducive to closeness, and as he moved from his late teens into his twenties it was Catherine who became the fixed point in his life. But as time went on he had distanced himself from her. The effort of hiding the extent of his drinking and drug use was just too hard to handle. At thirty he had fallen in love with Shona, whom he met on holiday in Byron Bay. She was a veterinary assistant, rather serious, deeply into natural remedies and healthy living, and in the novelty and passion of their first few months together they had married, only to part three years later. It took much longer for Declan to realise that he had thought she would rescue him from himself. Shona had believed him when he'd promised to give up the drink and drugs, but he had spectacularly defaulted on that promise. By this time his visits to Catherine had become occasional, replaced largely by awkward phone calls, post-cards and, later, emails. It wasn't that he had stopped caring about her but she had become the face of his moral and social conscience and that wasn't something he wanted to confront any more than necessary. His addictions had isolated him, too, from friends who found his behaviour tedious and frequently embarrassing. By the time he had quit the drugs and finally the grog they had all drifted away. Only Alice, by then his AA sponsor, had always been there when he needed someone to talk to, but then she too was gone, into custody for five long years, and he was on his own.

In many ways he had grown comfortable with his aloneness, although he regretted his failure to attract women, and particularly to establish a meaningful long-term relationship, but eventually, being alone became safe and comfortable. No tense silences, no making concessions, no negotiations over where to go for dinner or for holidays, no arguments about money or the lack of it, no sulking, no emotional tugs-of-war, no being accountable to someone who knew him uncomfortably well. But Catherine's death and his resulting guilt and suppressed grief had torn at the seams of Declan's isolationism and they have been fraying ever since.

When he saw the conflicting emotions that flickered across Todd's face when he broke the news about Paula, Declan wanted to absorb all that confusion, the hurt and the anger, and he despaired at his own uselessness in the face of such emotional turmoil. Todd might have played it cool with Ruby and later with others, but with Declan he had been unable to hide his emotions. And when he had found Todd sitting on the floor of the passage, Declan knew that his own emotional immunity was gone for good.

'Okay, mate,' he'd said eventually, 'd'you want to talk about it – about your mum, I mean?'

Todd shook his head, and as they sat there in silence Declan remembered what this was like – being a boy, being scared and lonely, longing for comfort but struggling not to reach out, not to cry, not to make any move to touch or be touched. He could feel the struggle going on, and knew that all he could do was wait until Todd was ready and able to talk.

'I hate her,' Todd said finally. 'She doesn't care what happens to me as long as she doesn't have to do anything about it.'

It was a long and very difficult conversation that followed, Declan trying to prise out more and Todd saying very little.

Ruby turned up at one point, hovered in the doorway and slipped quietly away; the phone rang again and rang out; Alice came into the kitchen and at the sound of their voices popped her head around the door, raised her eyebrows at Declan and when he shook his head disappeared back to the café. Todd picked up a sheaf of paper that he had dropped onto the floor beside him.

'I was looking at these,' he said. He was quieter now, exhausted probably, Declan thought. 'Just before she rang I was looking at these and thinking how cool if I could do one of these courses, be a sound engineer.' He dropped the papers again. 'But I can't because I can't do it all on my own. Paula was always horrible to me, but I suppose I thought that if I was ever in real trouble she'd help me. I knew I had a family. Now Catherine's gone and Paula's gone, and Mum . . . I haven't got anyone. I can't do anything.'

'Hey,' Declan said, 'you've got a bigger family now, don't you know that yet? What you're feeling now is awful, but you're not on your own. Look, you, me, Alice and Ruby, we're not related but in the last few months we've become like a family. There are people here who really care about you, Todd.'

'But that'll all be gone soon,' Todd said. 'Ruby's going home, you don't have to look after me any more, I'll have to go back to the caravan. And, anyway, you might just sell it all and go away.'

Declan leaned forward and grabbed Todd by the shoulders, turning him to face him. 'I thought we were mates,' he said.

'Yeah, but . . .'

'No buts. You and me, man, we're a team. We stick together. We stay here, or we go, whichever way it works out we do it together and that's how it'll be for as long as you want. And when you're ready to move on, wherever you go I'll still be looking out for you. And I'll want to know that when I'm a much older and an even more boring old fart than I am now, you'll be there looking out for me. This isn't the end of things, Todd, it's just the beginning, and it has rewards and responsibilities for both of us. I don't have a son, and I don't know how to be a father, but years ago, before I stuffed up my life, I knew how to be a friend. Now you can help me learn that again. We stick together, we learn from each other, look out for each other. Got it?'

When Declan thinks back now the enormity of that commitment frightens the life out of him, but he doesn't regret it. He pauses and takes a deep breath to calm himself. He could see what it had meant to Todd, and one day, he thinks, Todd will come to understand how important this is for him too, this chance to reclaim a part of himself which has for so long been lost. If he wants his life to change he has to open himself to responsibilities that are greater than just restoring and running a business. He was thrown together with a group of strangers who have crept into his heart in different ways. Now he must work at keeping them there.

Declan walks on up to the end of the sand and back again, taking a last look behind him at the beach, which is now bathed in sharp early sunlight. It's the third week in June, long past the time that Alice's daughter and her family were due home.

'I'm giving them time to settle back in,' she'd said ten days ago when he'd offered to make the call.

But Declan knows there's more to it than that. While she does nothing there is still hope; she has too much invested in this to risk the first step.

Back home he parks the car and walks swiftly up the hill to her cottage. Alice is sitting on the balcony, a blanket around her shoulders, with a mug of tea.

'Can I come up?' he calls.

'Of course you can,' she says. 'Do you want tea?'

He runs up the steps. ' No thanks, I'm going back to the house to make a big pot of coffee. I'll need it because this is the day we're going to make the call.'

She puts down her cup. 'Well, I don't know . . .'

'Yes, Alice,' he says, 'you *do* know. It's time, really it is.'

She sighs and looks up at him and he can see the fear in her eyes. 'It is,' she says, nodding. 'Yes it is.'

―✦―

Gordon hates having to send Bruce down into the hold but there is no alternative. If he's going to travel back and forth more regularly he really will have to find someone up there who'll look after the poor little devil, it's not fair to him. Bruce looks up at him through the grid of the travel crate – a picture of misery.

'Not long, mate,' Gordon lies, scratching the dog's head through the bars. 'Home before you know it.' And he hands Bruce over to the man at the desk and strides off to the passenger terminal without looking back.

A little over an hour later, as he loosens his seatbelt and reclines his seat, he closes his eyes and concentrates his mind on Lesley in her little rented house, furnished in a way that she would never choose for herself. But maybe she *would* choose that now, he thinks, the simple, almost Scandinavian décor seems to suit her. Something, many things in fact, have changed, changed so much that he's still trying to work out just what of the old Lesley remains. But he's not trying too hard because this Lesley seems to have emerged from the last few months more open minded, less controlling, and with rather different ideas from the one who stormed out of the house earlier in the year. She is, in fact, more like the woman he married.

'But I'm not that person,' she said when he'd told her that. 'I'm older and hopefully a bit smarter. When we met I was a blank slate, I had no ideas of my own other than that I wanted to be married and have a family. You, and then the kids, shaped me. I became the person who could be the wife and mother and who could cope with your absences, and the times when you were present but disengaged . . .'

He'd opened his mouth to protest then, but she'd stopped him.

'That isn't a criticism, Gordon, it's a fact of life. You *were* frequently away, and often when you were there in body your mind was elsewhere. You were focused on solving some work or scientific problem, preparing for difficult meetings, or deals that had to be made. I know you had to do it, and that you were doing it for us, but just the same for a lot of the time you weren't present, and I had to fill the gaps for myself and the kids. Now I have to learn to be different. I need to stop pretending the gaps aren't there, and learn to fill them with something that's important and satisfying.'

She was right, and although at the time he'd felt he hadn't any choice he can admit now that for some of the time, at least, it had been easier to be swept along by the pressures of corporate life than to focus more on the messy, volatile and less predictable demands of domestic life. Lesley wanted security and comfort, the comfort and the choices that came with a good income. She was needy rather than greedy and the neediness was for approval. She couldn't cope with being in the wrong.

Gordon has, over time, come to understand what he had not understood in the early days of their marriage – that

Lesley has an old fashioned sort of class awareness. She came from hard-up, hardworking parents, but in marrying him she felt she had moved up in the social scale and is always anxious about slipping backwards. Her constant attention to how she – how all of them – appeared to others frequently determined the way she sculpted their family life. Gordon thinks that this weekend he saw a woman less concerned with external appearances than in discovering who she had really become.

'I don't want to go back,' she'd said, 'not to the house, not to the way we were. I feel as though when the kids started to leave home I panicked. I tried to fill up the spaces but I didn't have a plan or a passion, I didn't think about what I really wanted. I convinced myself I was doing fine – keeping busy like I always had . . .'

She'd hesitated then and he could see that she was bordering on tears.

'Raising a family is exhausting and often frustrating but it has huge rewards. In a way seeing them leave and have successful lives of their own is part of that reward but it also . . . well, it left me feeling redundant. I was still busy but I wasn't working towards anything, I was just treading water. Does any of this make sense?'

He nodded. 'Of course it does, complete sense.'

'And then, quite suddenly, you were there, full on all the time, and I suppose I resented it. Just by being there you were demanding some sort of change. I felt I was being pushed to fit in with you again and I resented it, but at the same time I didn't know what I wanted.'

'Something to eat, sir?' the flight attendant asks, bringing the trolley to a standstill alongside him, and leaning over to let down his table. Gordon returns his seat to the upright position, takes the tray of food and asks for a sparkling mineral water. As he unwraps his food he thinks how much easier everything would have been if they could have talked about it earlier.

'I thought I was doing the right thing,' he'd said, 'retiring when I did. I thought you'd put up with the job for long enough, that you were waiting to do all those things we talked about when the kids were small.'

She'd nodded then. 'I know. The trouble was that we never revised that, did we? We talked about all that when we were younger, but we never thought that what we'd actually want might be something different. I want something totally different now and I think you do too.'

Gordon picks at his meal and ends up eating just the dreary little salad and the bread roll and finally triumphs over the stubborn plastic that seems melded to the rectangle of cheese. He wonders about Bruce, down there in the cold dark of the hold. Taking him along had been a sign of how he too had changed. He wonders whether it had also been more than that, whether he had been testing Lesley, testing her willingness to compromise. This morning, as he came out of the shower, he had heard her talking to someone.

'No,' she was saying, 'you've had the last one, but I could make you a piece of toast, would you like that?'

Gordon, a towel around his waist, had walked to the kitchen door. Lesley was standing by the toaster and Bruce was looking up at her, head on one side. He gave one of his short little barks and wagged his tail.

'Okay then,' Lesley said, 'toast it is.' And then she'd seen Gordon standing in the doorway. 'He's eaten the last banana,' she said. 'Helped himself to it from the basket in the pantry.'

'Sorry,' Gordon had said, 'he does have a weakness for bananas.'

'So I'm making him some toast. Next time I'll get proper dog biscuits.'

Of all the good things that had happened over the weekend, this seems to Gordon to be particularly significant.

Twenty-eight

July

'I don't suppose I'll be gone long,' Declan says, getting up from the table and reaching in his pocket for the car keys. 'So just sit tight, have another coffee and try not to worry.'

Alice nods and forces a smile. Her insides seem to have turned to water, her legs are shaking and she wonders whether she will make it to the toilet in time if she needs to vomit.

'We'll be fine,' Ruby says reassuringly. 'You just go, and remember to pay attention to everything.'

'Yes,' Alice says. 'How Jacinta looks, and Jodie, and the house, everything.'

'I know,' he says, putting a hand on her arm. 'You've told me several times. I'll do everything short of interviewing her and taking notes.'

They have already driven twice past the end of the street but he drew the line at driving past the house. 'Jacinta might see us, then when I go back and knock at the door it won't look good. It'll look as though you were spying on her.'

'If only I could,' Alice had said, 'but okay, I see what you mean.'

'Shall I order you more coffee?' he asks.

Ruby shakes her head. 'You go,' she says, 'I'll get the coffee.'

'Thank you, Declan,' Alice says, grasping his hand. 'Thank you so much for doing this.'

And he smiles and squeezes her hand and they watch as he walks away from the café, starts the car and drives off down the street in the direction of Jacinta's home. The phone call had been simple and businesslike. Jacinta, Declan had said, was helpful when it came to fixing a date and time. There was a suitcase and several quite large boxes, she'd said, so when he arrived at the house he should reverse into the drive and they could lift everything into the boot.

Alice knows that he would have preferred to go to Mandurah alone, but her own need to be close to the house while he is there was too overwhelming for her to back down. 'Please,' she'd said. 'I need to go with you, really I do. I'll go insane waiting here till you get back.'

'I'll call you as soon as I leave the house,' he'd said. 'I'm not comfortable with you waiting around in Mandurah on your own, chewing your fingernails down to stumps.'

'Why don't I come too then?' Ruby had suggested. 'You can drop us off at a café somewhere nearby and then pick us up when you've seen Jacinta.'

It's the first time, with the exception of Paula's funeral, that they have all been away from Benson's at the same time. That day they had organised a small wake in the café and while a few of the staff had wanted to be at the funeral others had volunteered to stay behind and get everything organised for when the mourners arrived back. Alice thinks of it now as she sits alone at the café table while Ruby goes inside to order more coffee. It was, she thinks, a remembrance that Paula would have liked, though perhaps not as flashy as she would have wished. They had decorated the café with pink and white flowers and ribbons and Todd had mixed some of her favourite music to play continuously in the background. Even Paula's parents had turned up on time and almost sober, presumably having realised that there was nothing to be gained by trying to apportion blame. The number of people who attended seemed to surprise everyone and conversations revealed the same themes: 'I should have tried harder', 'We ought to have reached out to her', 'I feel so guilty'. Alice couldn't help thinking that had it been her funeral the mourners could have been counted on the fingers of one hand, and there would be a complete absence of relatives. She wonders whether she will live long enough for that to change.

'I'm so glad you came with us,' Alice says when Ruby gets back to the table with fresh coffee. 'Declan was right, it would have been awful to be waiting here alone.'

They sit for some time, talking sporadically, looking out across the neat lawns and trees on the esplanade through to the water of the inlet sparkling in the winter sunshine. Alice feels each minute as though it were an hour.

'It's going to be hard to leave here,' Ruby says eventually. 'I didn't want to come back to Australia – too many bad memories, too much sadness. Not just the stuff with Catherine and Harry, but all those years in the convent. But being here has given me back the good memories, the things that my bitterness had allowed me to forget.'

'So what happened when you went back to England?' Alice asks. 'I mean, didn't they tell a lot of the child migrants that they had no families or the families were dead?'

Ruby nods, sipping her coffee. 'A lot of us were told that. Catherine was and she believed it, but I never really knew why. She'd never talk about it, even as an adult. I was thinking about that as I went through her journals, but there's no explanation there either. I wonder now if she had had a hard time at home and thought she was escaping it. But of course what we went to would have been worse. I always felt that my mother was alive. After the bombing, when I was dragged out of the rubble, I knew she was there but no one would listen. And I knew that my father was somewhere overseas. I never, ever, gave up believing that I would find them one day. And I was right. Well, partly right.'

'So you did find them?'

'I found my mother. She'd remarried and changed her name, so it took some time, a lot of trawling through records. An awful lot of people were injured when that doodlebug fell, and a number of them died. Those with minor injuries, like me, were taken to a hospital further away, to lessen the load on the nearest one. It was just a terrible muddle, I suppose. Mum was quite badly injured. She was in a coma for several days. By the time she came to and started asking for me no one knew anything about it. You see, when it happened we weren't close to home. Mum had taken me to visit a friend whose husband had been killed in action. We were right on the other side of London and we were on our way home. I suppose if we had been in our own street when the bomb fell someone might have recognised us, made a connection, but no one knew us there.'

As she listens to Ruby's story Alice is reminded, once again, of how obsessively she has focused on her own situation, the schism in her own family, her own sense of being detached, cut off from the people to whom she should be closest. Right now Declan is a couple of minutes' drive away talking with her own daughter to whom she can't speak, but he too comes from a family fractured by his mother's early death and his father's depression. They're all aware now of Todd's sense of abandonment and disconnection from his family. How strange, she thinks, that chance has brought the four of them together.

'What was it like,' she asks, 'finding your mother, seeing her for the first time after all those years?'

'It was shocking at first and then, well, perfectly wonderful. I'd always imagined Mum the way she was when

I last saw her. I suppose I had some sort of filmic vision of us, not exactly running towards each other through fields of waving corn, but something beautiful. But by the time we met she had just turned seventy and was widowed for the second time. She had very low bone density and had had a number of falls and although she could walk a bit it was very painful and she spent most of her time in a wheelchair, and never ventured far on foot and never outside. She was in a residential care home, quite nice but a home none the less. In my mind I had never allowed her to grow old – I always expected to see her as she had looked that night, so it was a shock. We didn't know what to say to each other at first, but then she just took my hands in hers and she said . . .' Ruby hesitates and her eyes fill with tears. 'She said, "I was waiting impatiently to die, so that I could see you again, but now I want to live forever."' She stops briefly, catching the crack in her voice, swallows and goes on. 'We took her to live with us, Owen and I, and she lived another eight years and every one of them seemed like an incredible gift.'

'And your father?' Alice asks.

'He was killed. I thought he was in the army, but he was actually in the air force – Bomber Command. The plane was limping home with engine trouble after a raid but didn't make it.'

Alice stares out across the water, imagining Ruby's mother losing first her daughter, and then her husband. How, she wonders, does a person cope with such loss and still carry on? Did she feel rage when she discovered the truth about her daughter, or was it enough just to get her back after all those years?

They wait on in silence once more, each lost in her own thoughts, and Alice thinks it is rare to be able to share such silence without tension, without feeling the need to fill it with words. She studies Ruby's hand lying close to her own on the table. There are about ten years between them but Alice's own skin is comparatively firm, whereas Ruby's seems thinned and is scattered with age spots. Do you see that happening? she wonders, or do you just wake up one morning and find that your skin has changed, that veins are more prominent, the knuckles slightly enlarged? How will it feel to grow old with no one around to share the pleasures or the fears? Ruby seems to be managing it, but then she's that sort of person – one who takes things in her stride. Alice wonders if she can become that sort of old woman – self-contained, competent, always clambering back onto her feet ready to start again.

Ruby clears her throat. 'Declan's back,' she says, 'look – there, pulling into that parking space.'

Alice's heart leaps. Listening to Ruby had distracted her for a while but now her earlier anxiety returns, multiplied several times, and as Declan pauses to wait for the traffic to clear before crossing the street and then runs up the steps to join them, she feels weak enough to faint.

'All done,' he says, flopping into a chair beside her. 'I collected everything and it's all in the car.'

'And . . . and what else?' she asks, frantic now for more, for even the slightest fragment of information.

'Well, Jacinta was very pleasant,' he says. 'Nervous, I think, but definitely not hostile. She was curious about you, why you were at Benson's, why you went there in the first place, what you do there. She seemed concerned about . . . well, about your welfare, I suppose.'

'And you told her . . .?'

'I told her exactly what we agreed, about us being friends, my offering you the job, what you've done with the café, all that.'

'And Jodie?'

He smiles. 'Jodie is an absolute sweetheart – it's easy to see she's your granddaughter. She was friendly and very curious about you. I had to tell her what sort of dishes you make in the café. And she asked if I had a picture of you.'

'I never thought about that,' Alice says. 'It never even occurred to me – I never imagined they would *want* a picture.'

'Well, I did think about it,' Declan says, 'and I didn't mention it to you, but I took along one of the photos from Todd's birthday dinner – you with Todd and Ruby. When Jodie asked I didn't know quite what to do but Jacinta just nodded and sort of shrugged and so I gave it to her. Jodie couldn't stop looking at it. She wanted to know who the other people were, how old Todd was, all that. Jacinta was looking at it too, but then she seemed to get a bit uncomfortable, so I stood up to go, and Jodie asked if she could keep the photo and I said she could. And then I left. But as I was going, Jacinta gave me this.'

He reaches into the inside pocket of his jacket and hands her a stiff white envelope with her name on it: 'Alice', not 'Mum' or 'Nan', just 'Alice', and Alice feels sick again at the thought that her daughter can't bear to acknowledge their relationship.

'What is it?'

Declan shrugs. 'I'm just the delivery boy.'

Alice looks at him and then at Ruby. She is paralysed by the prospect of what it might contain. Her body is tense as steel, her heartbeats drumming through her head. She fumbles with the envelope, tears it open and pulls out the contents. And suddenly she is looking at them, Jacinta and Jodie, side by side, and behind them, Alan. A coloured photograph in a cream cardboard mount, and in that moment Alice feels she holding the world in her hands.

❦

It's a very quiet Friday at Benson's and for Lesley, being left in sole charge of the shop and café is not much of a challenge. The trickle of customers into the café is easily dealt with by the staff – all she has to do is keep an eye on things – and the shop is even quieter. An easy day, but it feels like an important one. Whatever happens over the ownership of the place in the next few months, it's obvious that both Ruby and Declan want to see it grow. She and Fleur are to expand the retail side by refitting the shop, diversifying the range of merchandise and increasing the volume of the lavender products to service an online business. Fleur will train Todd in production and he will also learn to manage the online accounts, and deal with the postage and packing, until he can enrol in the sound engineering course next year. As she sits at the computer in the shop searching for local craftspeople whose work might enhance the range of merchandise, Lesley relishes the fact that she has a significant role in how Benson's will develop.

'I can't see how it can fail,' Gordon had said. She'd shown him around when she knew Declan had taken Todd to a football match in Busselton. 'I can see why you're so excited about it, but won't it bother you to be away from the kids and particularly the twins?'

'I've already been away a lot this year,' she'd said. 'Karen's still a bit prickly with me but everyone else seems fine. They're managing perfectly well without me, which, while being a bit of a blow to my ego, is probably a very good thing. Besides, it's only three hours to Perth and I've explained to Declan and Ruby that I'll need to go back and forth.'

'Then you should sign the contract and stay,' he'd said. 'You might even be able to get a long rental on this house. You seem to like it here.'

'I can have it for twelve months,' she'd told him. 'It's what I want to do, but I need to know what you want.'

He'd explained to her then about the work he was doing in the Kimberley. 'It will take another year at least,' he said, 'and I'd really like to stick with it. But I don't have to be there all the time. I could come here for breaks, long weekends, a couple of weeks, sometimes a bit more when there's a lot of paperwork to do. So how would you feel about that?'

'I want us to stay together but I'd like to try some time living alone and doing my own thing,' she'd said. 'I could visit you in Broome – I've never been there.'

They were in the kitchen where she was making soup and Gordon, who had just opened a bottle of wine, set it down on the table and came over to hug her.

It was the first real physical contact since he arrived the previous afternoon, and that in itself was a relief. Lesley had been unsure about the sleeping arrangements and she had assumed Gordon would also feel cautious after so much time apart, so she had made up the bed in the spare room. But he had assumed that they would sleep together and she had decided not to challenge that. The night was awkward; the familiarity of decades had been ruptured and Lesley had kept as close as possible to her side of the bed, lying there tense and anxious about what might happen and how she would handle it. But it didn't take long for her to realise that on his side of the bed Gordon was doing exactly the same thing. She had relaxed after that and fallen asleep. When she woke she was still firmly on her own side, the space between them as wide as physically possible in a queen size bed. But this had been a good day, and Gordon's hug cut through the physical barriers.

That night they had lain close, talking, touching, eventually making cautious moves towards intimacy and finally making love, slowly, thoughtfully, knowing that this could either seal or destroy the reconciliation to which they had edged closer during the day. Lesley, remembering the surprising difference and the comfort of Declan's body, wondered whether she should confess, but it occurred to her that Gordon might be contemplating a similar dilemma. In that moment she realised that if this was the case she would rather not know and so the metaphorical sleeping dog or dogs were left to sleep just like the real one stretched out on an old blanket by the warmth of the wood stove.

Now Gordon is back in Broome and they are apart again, but this time it feels right – at least for now.

'I've closed the office for an hour and put a notice on the door that I'm over here,' Fleur says, appearing in the shop. 'Declan just called. They've collected Alice's things and they're going to have lunch and mooch round Mandurah before heading back, so I thought you and I could have lunch over here.'

There are only half a dozen people in the café so they pick a table from where they can see through into the shop.

'I'm really pleased we're in this together,' Fleur says. 'In all the time I've worked here it was only Catherine that I had much contact with. And then Todd, of course. I'm a bit of a loner but I regret that now. It's really why I felt I needed to leave once Catherine had gone – it was just a job after that, but this is different.'

'I'm pleased too,' Lesley says. 'I think there's a great online market for the lavender products and I've been making a list of local craftspeople we could talk to about bringing their products into the shop. But I need to ask you about the soft toys, the ones that we sell for charity. We're out of stock, and I also need to know what to do with the money. I asked Declan and he said you'd explained it to him but with everything else to think about he'd completely forgotten.'

Fleur nods. 'That's one of the things I wanted to talk to you about too. Catherine started it but when she got sick she just let it go. There's a group of volunteers who make things with dried lavender – the neck and eye pillows, and the soft toys. Benson's provides the lavender and some of the fabric. The rest of the materials come from local people and businesses who give us offcuts and remnants. And Catherine knew various people in Perth so every time she went there she'd come back with bags of leftover fabric. The volunteers make up the toys and the pillows at home. At least they used to.'

'Used to?'

'Yes, when I explained it to Declan I could see it was going in one ear and out the other and I was worried that there might be big changes and it would just get ditched. So I gave the bags of lavender to one of the volunteers, together with all the fabric, and asked her to distribute them to the others, and keep making the toys until we knew what was happening. I should probably have told Declan and/or Ruby, but I thought I'd just wait and see how things panned out.'

'So what's the situation now?'

'There's a stack of products all ready to go, they just need collecting, labelling and pricing. So I'm thinking I should talk to Ruby and explain it. I think she'll go for it in a big way, and we could get them into the shop with a really nice display and maybe promote them online too. But I need to know how you feel about that.'

'I think it's a great idea,' Lesley says. 'But I don't know where the money goes.'

'They go to producing these,' Fleur says, reaching into her bag and putting a small plastic package on the table. 'Open it up, have a look.'

Lesley opens it and takes out a folded black plastic sheet, a tiny tablet of soap, two fine latex gloves, a scalpel blade sealed in cellophane, three lengths of white cord, and some squares of gauze. She lines them up in front of her on the table, looks at them again and shrugs.

'It doesn't look like much to me.'

'Exactly, but it's a lifesaver, literally,' Fleur says, smiling. 'It's a birthing kit.'

Lesley shakes her head. 'Sorry,' she says, 'you're going to have to explain that.'

'Okay. Hundreds of thousands – well, actually millions – of women in developing countries like in Africa and Afghanistan give birth alone in non-sterile conditions and every year almost four hundred thousand of them die from preventable infections, and so do their babies. This little kit provides the six clean items they need for a safe, sterile delivery.'

'No,' Lesley says, picking up the plastic. 'Really? How can it? I mean, it's so simple, when you think of all the sterilising and stuff that goes on in hospitals.'

'It works, Lesley,' Fleur says, 'it really does save lives.'

Lesley looks again at the contents of the kit. 'Bits of cord, gauze, some plastic – it doesn't seem possible,' she says, and it's hard to say it because the very simple, personal nature of it touches her deeply. 'What does it cost for one of these?'

'Two dollars for the contents and then lots of hours to put them together. There are assembly days when women volunteer to spend the day making up the kits and sealing them into the bags.'

'Two dollars! So if we sell an eye pillow for ten or one of those little pram toys for twelve . . .?'

'Exactly – five or six kits.' Fleur grins. 'I couldn't believe it when I first heard about it. So I'd really like to get this going again, and give it a boost, make a feature of it. And I think it'd be good for Benson's too. The other thing is,' she pauses, leaning forward across the table, 'I think we're all feeling pretty bad about Paula, you know . . . feeling we let her down. Well, it was Paula who told Catherine about this and persuaded her to get involved. Paula used to volunteer for the assembly days, and she gave something to the birthing kit project every month. I know it doesn't sound a bit like Paula, but she did. She never talked much to me, mainly because I couldn't be bothered to listen, but I do remember her telling me that it made her feel she was making a personal connection with a woman in another country. So I want to get this going again, because it's a brilliant project and because . . .' She blushes, looking down at her hands and then up again at Lesley. 'Well, because I want to honour Paula now in a way I failed to do while she was alive. And before I go and talk to Ruby and Declan I want to know if you're with me on this.'

Twenty-nine

R uby hesitates outside Todd's door. He's been in there for ages and while it's more than a month since Paula's death and then the phone call from his mother, she's still concerned about how he's coping.

'It's Ruby, Todd,' she says, tapping on the door. 'May I come in?'

'Sure,' he says, 'come on in, I want to show you some stuff.' He gets up from the desk and moves a pair of jeans off the armchair to make space for her. 'Look at this,' he says, handing her half a dozen printed pages. 'I thought I could do one of these courses before I go on the sound engineering thing. I could use some of Catherine's money.'

Ruby puts on her glasses and leafs through the information. 'Looks good,' she says. 'Which did you have in mind?'

'Well, I thought Bookkeeping in Excel would be useful, although it'd probably be pretty dull. And there's one called Basic Principles of Management, and another about marketing. They'd be useful, wouldn't they?'

Ruby smiles. 'I'm sure they would. You need to have a look at all the elements of the sound engineers' training course and see which you think fits best with that.'

'That's exactly what Jackson said,' Todd says, 'see what matches the curriculum.'

'Jackson said that?'

'Well, he emailed it. I forwarded this stuff to him late last night and there was a reply when I got up this morning.'

'Well that's good,' Ruby says. 'He's an excellent person to get advice from on this.' It's hard for her to speak at all as she reels with shock at the news of Todd's correspondence with Jackson. She hasn't heard from him at all since he left, not that she'd expected to – just the same, the fact that he's corresponding with Todd gives her a jolt. She gathers herself together in a long breath.

'The other thing you could do,' she says, forcing herself to concentrate on Todd, 'is to choose a course simply because it's something that you'd really enjoy. You'll be doing some bookkeeping and other things with Fleur, so you could pick something you're interested in just for itself.'

Todd cocks his head on one side. 'Like what?'

'Well, I was thinking about all the reading you were doing with Catherine, and what you've read since then. You might want to think about a course that would put those books or books like them in a historical and social context for you, that would explain the issues in them and why they were important to the authors, and what the authors were actually trying to achieve in them.'

He looks puzzled. 'They were trying to write stories, weren't they?'

'Yes,' Ruby says, 'of course they were, but why those stories at those particular times? What did the authors want to say about the times and the places in which they lived, what influenced them? Because those books are much more than just good stories, they tell us a lot about what life was like, and what was important to the authors.'

Todd is silent for a moment, and Ruby could kick herself for boring him, for taking what is his pleasure and turning it into something else, something that probably sounds like the dreariest of lessons that he was thankful to abandon when he left school.

'That sounds cool,' he says. 'What would it be called?' And he turns back to the computer and opens another window.

'Well, probably something like understanding literature, or reading the classics,' Ruby says. 'I'll help you look for it in a minute but I want to talk to you about something else first.'

He turns back to her, nodding.

'I know Declan's talked to you about the future,' she says, 'but I want to do that too. You know I'm leaving here soon?'

Todd nods again. 'I wish you wouldn't,' he says. 'I'm going to miss you.'

'Me too, Todd, and that's why I need to tell you this. If, at any time, you need help and Declan's not around, then I want you to know you can come to me. If you need money, or help in some other way, you can call or email. The other thing is that if you decide to go on the technical production course or do a different sort of training course, I'll pay for it.' She leans forward, her forearms resting on her knees. 'I don't have any children, Todd, and so obviously I don't have any grandchildren, but if I had a grandson I'd be enormously proud if he was like you. So I want to be there for you if you need it in the future.'

Todd rocks back and forth on his chair, arms clasped around his body. He looks awkward, unnerved, and he shakes his head.

'Everyone's so kind,' he says, his voice thick with emotion. 'I don't know why but it's like everything changed for me. First Catherine, then you and Declan, and everyone else. I don't understand . . .'

'It's because of you, Todd, because of the sort of person you are. As for the kindness – well, we're really not *that* kind because none of us helped Paula. We all looked at Paula and saw a problem or a nuisance. None of us took the trouble to look beyond that to what was happening for her, to see what she needed, or question why she behaved as she did. So, don't start to think too well of us. Now let's have a look for some literature courses.'

Side by side they sit at the screen, and Todd prints out their findings to read later.

'Okay, time for me to get on with the dinner,' Ruby says eventually, getting up from her chair and heading for the door. 'By the way,' she says, turning back to him, unable to help herself, 'how *is* Jackson?'

'He's cool,' Todd says. 'He's going to Canada next week. Just him, not The Crowbars, it's not like a festival or concerts or anything, just something for the university.'

Ruby nods. 'Good,' she says. 'That's nice. I'm sure he's really good at that. Well, say hello to him from me when you email again.'

In the kitchen she opens the fridge and stares at the contents without seeing them. She holds the door open for so long that the alarm starts to beep and she closes it. And still unable to think about whatever it was she was going to cook, she sits down at the table, remembering the moment she first saw Jackson, how that felt – visceral, certainly, but also so much more, the sense of a deeply intimate connection. Was he lying when he'd said he felt it too? Was it all just a figment of the florid imagination of an old woman grasping at youth, a desperate last attempt to find something that had eluded her for so long? She feels shamed by her self-delusion, shamed when she remembers standing naked in front of the mirror, shamed by the erotic dreams, and shamed most of all by the way she still can't quite let go of it.

Oh, she'll be all right, she knows that. And coming here has helped her to reclaim her past, and to make new friends. But she had briefly allowed herself a glimpse of other possibilities, and the more she thinks back on it the less clear she is about what was real and what was mere imagination.

It's time to leave. Time to take up her old life once again, and the sooner she does it, the better.

───

Ten days later she is home again. Islington in August is mild and pleasantly green, but as she walks through Highbury Fields, sits on a bench watching the joggers with their iPods and mothers strolling with their toddlers in pushers, Ruby struggles to find her place.

'Perhaps this is how astronauts feel,' she attempts to joke with Jessica, 'totally disorientated and struggling with re-entry.'

'That's a good way of putting it!' Jessica says. 'A few more days and you'll be through the jetlag and back to normal. And you don't have to go back again, you know. When you've decided what you want to do about Benson's Reach you can let them know in writing or send someone else. I can go for you if that helps.'

But Jessica doesn't know how it was to be there, to be in the house where she had once lost everything, and then to think she had found it again. And Ruby can't begin to explain the magic of four such different people, each with their own problems, connecting in such a profoundly satisfying way. Why couldn't you have been satisfied with everything else that happened? she asks herself. You found love with them, why did you have to run after another sort of love as well? It should have been enough but she had wanted more, and in that wanting she had deluded herself. Well, she has lost love before, through war and politics, through death and deceit, and she has recovered, so she supposes she will also recover from this.

Think how fortunate you were, she tells herself, remembering the pleasures and satisfactions of the last few months. Think of Paula, who had so little and lost it all. Get up, get back to work, get on with your fortunate life – you've done it before and you can do it again. But she knows that this time it will be harder because what she has lost is a dream and one can only lose so many dreams in a lifetime.

But time does work its old magic and in the weeks that follow she feels she is waiting, waiting for it to be time to go back, to tie up the loose ends. Catherine had asked for a year, but what difference will a few months make? To distract herself she employs a builder to fix the roof and add a small conservatory at the back of the house, which she has planned for years. At least one item can now be crossed off her bucket list. And over and over again she ponders her plan for Benson's. But most of all she thinks of the future and what it means to be old: to be a woman who had learned to be entirely comfortable alone but who stumbles and injures herself while grasping at the chance to feel young, to be wanted, to be precious, to come first with someone once again. Old age looks different, less attractive, today from the way it looked a year ago.

And then early one morning in late October she stoops to collect *The Guardian* from the doormat and reads that next month the Australian prime minister is to move a motion in parliament to apologise to the child migrants for the hardship and neglect they suffered in Australia. Ruby has to grasp the back of a chair to steady herself. Finding her mother and discovering the truth of what had happened all those years ago had resolved only part of her story. The greater story of the ruthless and unlawful removal of thousands of children – the horrors perpetrated on them, the misery, the humiliation, the shame – remains. The lies and denials, the defensive rationales, have all raged back and forth against the background of increasingly poignant and painful personal stories. At last, after all this time, there is at least to be acknowledgement, validation; someone is finally willing to say sorry.

Restless with a churning mix of emotions, Ruby puts aside the newspaper, pulls on her old anorak and boots and goes outside to burn off some of her nervous energy in the garden. And with little awareness of what she is doing she pounds back and forth, digging, hoeing, clipping, dumping and finally, as she rakes leaves from the lawn, she comes to an abrupt halt.

'Sorry, Cat,' she says aloud. 'I've done my best, and I need it to be finished now. I need to let go of the reins. They don't need me to sit on my hands for the next few months.' And she drops the rake, goes back into the house and books a flight to Perth.

In the arrivals hall Alice pushes her way through the waiting crowd to the barrier. The drive took longer than it should have and Declan has dropped her and gone to park the car. For the last half-hour, as they seemed to catch every red traffic light and get stuck behind truck after truck, she had thought they weren't going to make it in time. As Alice weaves through the crush she can feel the impatience of the people waiting for the appearance of the first passengers. Relieved to have made it in time she takes a deep breath and positions herself close to the barrier from where she can see both exits from the customs hall.

'Can you book me a car, please?' Ruby had asked in her email. 'I'll drive straight down from the airport.'

'Do you think something's wrong?' Declan had asked when he showed Alice the email. 'She said she wouldn't be back until February.'

'What could be wrong?' Alice had asked. 'She's probably just decided to sort things out sooner. Or maybe she wants to escape another English winter. In any case, what difference would another few months make? The year was only Catherine's idea.'

But Declan is obviously worried by this sudden change of plan. For her own part Alice is longing to see Ruby again.

She realises now how firmly but discreetly Ruby had taken charge when she first arrived, and then how carefully and respectfully she had slowly released control to Declan, and then to herself. By the time Ruby left, although they missed her company, they were managing the place between them. This, Alice suspects, was always Ruby's plan – a way of supporting Declan and encouraging her to think beyond the café and broaden her understanding of the business. It worked, and now she wants to show Ruby the changes they've made: the different reservations system, the reorganisation of the shop with its new range of merchandise, and the decision to abandon the berries and replace them with more lavender to meet the anticipated demand of the online business. It's good, she thinks, that Ruby will see it all at the start of the season rather than the end.

The doors open and the first passengers begin to emerge. Lone men in crumpled business suits hurry purposefully out, scanning the small cluster of drivers holding up name cards. Young couples, old couples, exhausted parents with fractious children, are greeted with whoops of delight by families and friends and block the exits with their trolleys piled high with luggage. And then, behind a huge man with an equally huge suitcase, there is Ruby. Looking older, Alice thinks, and tired.

Ruby hesitates, seeking the easiest route through the crowd.

'Ruby!' Alice calls, waving. 'Ruby! This way, over here.'

Ruby looks into the crowd, her face lights up and she does a swift manoeuvre with her trolley and slips through a gap to reach her. 'You shouldn't have come all this way,' she says as Alice hugs her, 'but I'm awfully glad you did. What a lovely surprise.'

And Alice can see that there are tears in Ruby's eyes. They edge out through the crowd to the exit where Declan is waiting.

'You too,' Ruby cries, 'how lovely of you both to come. I feel so spoiled being met.'

In minutes they are heading out of the airport to Fremantle for lunch before the long drive south.

'I've something to show you,' Alice says when they have found a table and ordered their meal. She reaches into her bag and takes out a postcard with a picture of dolphins and hands it to Ruby.

'Hmm, what's this then?' Ruby asks, smiling as though she's already guessed.

'Turn it over,' Alice says, 'read it.'

Ruby turns the card over. 'From Jodie?' And she reads the carefully written message, looks up, smiling, and grasps Alice's hand. 'Alice, how wonderful, you must be over the moon.'

Alice nods. 'I could hardly believe it. She was on a school camp in Exmouth. Isn't it amazing? The photograph and then this – it makes me feel so . . . well, so hopeful.'

'She's been a different woman since it arrived,' Declan says. 'I think it's a really good sign, don't you, Ruby? Another step forward. I know it's only a small one but it's important.'

'Absolutely. It'll take a while, Alice, but I think you have plenty of grounds now for optimism.'

The waiter brings cutlery and glasses to the table and they settle back in their seats, but Alice can feel the tension and she knows this is not going to be an easy ride. Declan is bursting with questions, and she too is anxious to know what the future holds for both of them and for Benson's. But Ruby is a person who cares about process: whatever her decision means for all of them she won't want to discuss it at a restaurant table, nor in a moving car. It will happen later, at the big table in Benson's kitchen where the other decisions about the business have been made. The tension weaves its way through the conversation, causing abrupt silences and nervous laughs, and it lessens only when they are on the road and Ruby tilts her seat and closes her eyes. She is asleep in minutes and Alice leans forward from the back seat to put her hand on Declan's shoulder.

'It's going to be okay,' she says. 'I'm sure it is. It won't be long now.'

And he smiles at her in the driving mirror and nods, and keeps on driving as though his life depends upon it.

Thirty

Mid-November 2009

I t's clear that Ruby notices it the minute she walks into
the shop. She stops, looks around, waves hello to Lesley,
who is handing a credit card back to a customer, hesitates and then goes straight to the big display by the window.
Lesley puts the customer's purchases into a Benson's carrier
bag and comes out from behind the counter.

'Hello, Ruby,' she says, 'great to see you back again.'

Ruby looks up, smiling. 'Hello, Lesley. These are just beautiful,' and she picks up a small, lavender-scented elephant
made of purple corduroy. 'This display is terrific and you've
completely transformed the shop.'

'Well, Fleur and me together,' Lesley says, delighted at
Ruby's evident appreciation. 'And we are pretty happy with
it. And the toys and pillows and the lavender bags are selling
really well. We think they'll do even better as we get closer to
Christmas. They make lovely little gifts.'

Ruby keeps hold of the elephant and picks up a floral cotton hippo. 'They're gorgeous – do you think you're charging
enough?'

'We talk endlessly about that,' Lesley says with a laugh.

'We might raise the prices a bit, but we're very caught up on the idea that every ten dollars means five birthing kits and if people like them and they're appropriately priced, they'll come back for more.'

Another customer arrives and she leaves Ruby to browse, thinking that she looks worn out and a bit fragile, unlike her usual robust, energetic self. There is a series of customers now, but Ruby continues to move around the shop looking closely at the new range of silver jewellery, the locally made beads and scarves, the novelty bottle openers, the handwoven baskets and boxes, chopping boards, bowls and mugs. And she stops even longer to check the lavender products with their new, more elegant containers and labels.

'I really like the way you've developed that separate range for men,' Ruby says when Lesley is free again. 'I know they're not all new products, but they got lost among the others and differentiating the packaging makes a big difference.'

Lesley nods. 'Yes, and Fleur's working on baby products now, nappy cream, powder – we could have another complete range. The online business is shaping up well too. I can talk you through it later if you like. Fleur's actually away for a week, having a break in Bali.'

'Good, I'm sure she can do with it. I'm very glad that we were able to encourage her to stay on. And what about you, Lesley? You've been through a bit of a rough time.'

'I have but it's a lot better now. Gordon and I are working things out. I think we're going to be fine. Things have changed for me, Ruby, and I've changed. It's not just working here, I've got involved with the women's group in Bunbury – it was through someone there that Paula first heard about the birthing kits. It's Zonta – you know all about them. I'm really enjoying it. This probably sounds really silly but I honestly think that coming here has helped me to grow up. A bit late – I should have grown up decades ago.'

'It doesn't sound silly at all,' Ruby says, putting the things she's holding down on the counter. 'I'm much older than you and right now I'm battling with a serious bit of growing up myself. Perhaps it never stops. One can only hope it's a continuing state of improvement, but sometimes it just feels like a mammoth pain in the butt.'

***

'I got you a present,' Todd says, and as he hands over the carefully wrapped parcel he is suddenly crippled with embarrassment. 'It's only small, and you've probably got it already, but . . . it looked sort of special.'

Ruby takes the package from him and begins to unwrap it. Thankfully she doesn't say anything like 'Oh, you shouldn't have', or 'You didn't need to buy me a present', which is the sort of crap adults do all the time. Everybody likes getting presents, even old people. In fact, Todd thinks, they must like it more because they probably get fewer presents as they get older.

Ruby discards the wrapping and turns the book over to read the title. 'Oh, Todd, it's beautiful,' she says, and he can see from the way her face is all lit up that she's really pleased. It's a copy of *Madam Bovary*, bound in navy blue leather with gold lettering, and gold edges on the pages that are thin as tissue and light as silk. He'd never seen pages like that before.

'It's not new,' he says, blushing. 'I got it in the second-hand bookshop. I liked the cover, and the gold bits. I thought you'd like that too.'

'I love it,' Ruby says, and she hugs him. 'I shall treasure it.'

'Have you got it already?'

'I did have,' she says, 'but I lent it to someone and never got it back. And this one is so much nicer. Did you read Catherine's copy?'

He nods. 'Yep.'

'And did you learn something about women, like she said?'

'I think so,' Todd says cautiously, 'and I learned something about writers.'

'Really?'

He turns around and takes Catherine's copy down from the shelf. 'I actually learned it in the introduction – it's by Anita somebody.'

'Brookner.'

'Yes, Brookner, that's right. You see here,' he says, pointing to the first page of the introduction, 'she says that Flaubert said, "*Madame Bovary – c'est moi!*", which means "Madame Bovary – that's me!" and she sort of explains about how writers identify with characters, like get inside them and tell stories through them. I never thought about that before. And you know, the subtitle is "Life in a Country Town". And Alice said to me that it could be like Margaret River, and once you know that you can just go and sit outside one of the cafés in town and you can see all the characters going past. So we did it one day, me and Alice, we sat on that seat near Target and watched, and we said that could be Emma, and that man looks like Charles or Rodolphe. And it made me think all those people could be in stories too, they *have* stories. Like you, Ruby, you have a story that Flaubert could have written . . . you and Catherine and Declan's Uncle Harry . . .' He stops abruptly, shocked by what he's just said. 'Sorry,' he says, blushing, 'sorry, I shouldn't have said that. I didn't mean . . .' He wishes he could just sink into the ground and disappear.

'It's okay,' Ruby says. 'Catherine and I – we had a long story and it ended really badly and for a very long time I couldn't forgive her. For years and years she was the most important person in my life but I was so hurt by what happened here that I chose to bury the good and remember the bad. And you're right, it *is* a story that Flaubert could have written. Thank you so much for my book.'

Todd nods, relieved that he got the present right, and that perhaps what he'd said wasn't too bad after all. 'You're not coming back again after this, are you?' he says abruptly.

Ruby looks taken aback. 'Who told you that?'

He shrugs. 'No one, I worked it out. You came back now for the prime minister's apology, to be here while it happens. It's like an ending.'

He sees Ruby swallow and she seems to be struggling for words. 'You got it in one,' she says eventually. 'How did you get to be so smart?'

He grins and shrugs. 'Must be mixing with all you olds all the time,' he says, and suddenly he feels as though he's crumbling, and he stumbles over to her and she opens her arms and grabs him. 'I love you, Ruby,' he says, 'I wish you'd stay.'

'I know, Todd,' she says, hanging on to him tightly. 'And I love you too, but we'll see each other again. Not for a while yet, but I'll come back here as a visitor. And you'll come to London, I know you will. I'll show you my big untidy house, and introduce you to my friends, and I'll take you to see all the places you need to see in London. In fact we can make a plan before I leave. You should come next June, when the English raspberries are in season. You've never really tasted raspberries until you've picked from the canes at the start of an English summer.'

Todd nods, rubbing his eyes on the sleeve of his sweatshirt. 'Cool,' he says, 'that'd be cool. But it won't be the same.'

'No,' she says, 'no it won't, but it might be even better. All your life, Todd, people will come and go, and it will be wonderful and it will be awful, and when you get to be ancient like me, all those people and their stories, good and not so good, will be part of who you are. We'll all be talking to you from the past, making up a big jigsaw of your life. I want to be a part of your jigsaw, so we *will* see each other again, many times, I think, and we'll make many more pieces of the jigsaw.'

It's early evening when they finally sit down together at the kitchen table. Declan doesn't know how he's got through the day because, despite her reassurances and the fact that he knows that Ruby believes he's put his heart and soul into Benson's, he has continued to feel as though he's on probation. Perhaps it's the legacy of his past work failures and disastrous lifestyle choices together with his chequered relationship with Catherine, but in many ways he feels he doesn't have a right to the place and that to lose it now would be the sort of punishment he deserves. If Ruby wants to sell it's most unlikely he could borrow enough to buy her out, and he dreads the prospect of a new partner – one who would have Ruby's controlling share.

'Somehow this feels rather formal,' Ruby says. 'That's not what I intended, but I do think this is pretty important to all three of us so perhaps it's as it should be.'

'Shouldn't it be just you and Declan?' Alice says. 'It's between the two of you, you're the partners.'

Declan opens his mouth to say something but his throat is so dry with nerves that he just starts coughing. What he wants to do is beg her to stay, to be here with him through whatever it is Ruby has to say, but now he can't stop coughing. Alice gets up to fetch a glass of water and puts it on the table in front of him.

'Okay?' Ruby asks, looking at him with concern. 'Are you okay? If not we can do this later, or tomorrow . . .'

'No,' Declan gasps, and gulps at the water. 'No, no, let's do it now, and, please, Alice—'

'Alice, you need to stay,' Ruby cuts in. 'We both need you to stay.'

And Declan nods furiously as he always does when nervous, and he swallows more water.

'Good, well I'll keep it simple,' Ruby says. 'I have a plan that I want to put to you. I'd sort of come to this position before I left but I felt we should all take a bit more time before making the final decisions. I'm absolutely clear about my preferred solution for dealing with my share of Benson's.'

Declan coughs again, and Alice refills his glass.

'So the first thing is, Declan, that I am going to transfer enough of my share to you to bring your share up to fifty per cent.'

Declan is shocked. Obviously this is good – or is it? It probably means that Ruby has decided to sell, but then at least he'll own half instead of less than half. He tries to say something but the cough gets him again.

Ruby smiles at him. 'I know this is torture for you, Declan, but hang in there, the rest is quick and easy. That leaves me with fifty per cent and so I have a choice of either holding on to that and keeping it as an investment, or looking for a buyer whom you, Declan, would obviously need to approve, and feel you could work with.'

Declan nods in dismay. Keep it, Ruby, keep it, please, echoes a silent scream inside his head – please, please keep it.

'But there is another alternative and it's the one I prefer. You see, I feel I've done what I came here to do. I've kept faith with Catherine, I've helped to get the place up and running again, I've helped to put the business plan together so there's a strong sense of the future. And I've also come face to face with the past and laid a few ghosts. All of that is good, but now I feel it's time for me to butt out and hand over to someone whose future is here rather than on the other side of the world and whose commitment to Benson's can't be questioned. So, Alice, I would like to transfer my fifty per cent to you, if you'll accept it.'

Declan lets out something between a gasp and a whoop of joy and doesn't cough at all. He feels as though his body has been set alight as sweat runs down his neck, 'Yes!' he shouts. 'Yes, Ruby,' and he grabs her hand and as he does so he realises that she too is flushed with emotion, but she's looking anxiously at Alice, who has gone a ghostly white.

'Alice?' he says. 'Alice, this is wonderful, isn't it. Isn't it wonderful?'

'Give her time, Declan,' Ruby says, grasping his hand now with both of hers. 'She needs time to think.'

'But of course she—' Declan begins.

'Declan, stop!' Ruby orders him and she turns back to Alice. 'Alice, I really hope you'll accept this. You deserve it, you've made a huge contribution here, and you're really committed to the place. You've also got a fine head for business and an amazing work ethic. I think you're the best business partner Declan could possibly have. But there may be reasons why you don't want to accept, so I promise you that if you say no, I will not sell. I'll bring Declan's share up to seventy-five per cent and retain the rest. And of course you don't need to make a decision now – you may need time to think about it. And no pressuring her, Declan!'

Declan drinks more water and looks back and forth between the two women. Much of the tension has evaporated now he knows he can stay here, carry on with what he's doing, learn to do it really well. Just the same, he wants it settled. He wants Alice here. Without Ruby his responsibilities will be greater and Alice – well, it seems unlikely but Alice might just decide to leave and what then? His insides churn uneasily at the mere thought of it. He knows it's wrong, unfair, to try to persuade her but it's agony to hold back. He wants her to see it as he does, as the perfect solution. They are already a team and this way they will be even better, and she – well, she'll be here, always, stay here with him, and he wants that just as much or more even than he wants to keep running Benson's.

'But why?' Alice asks. 'I can't really get my head around it. Why do you even want to give away your share? And why not give it all to Declan?'

It's later, much later, almost ten o'clock. Alice, sitting on the balcony in the dark, had seen Ruby walk out onto the deck at the back of the house. She'd waved, and Ruby waved back.

'Could we talk?' Alice had called, and Ruby had nodded and made her way across the stretch of lawn and up the steep path to the cottage.

'Look, Alice,' Ruby says, 'it's less about me wanting to give it away than about what I want for this place. I want Declan to be able to stay here. He has a right to it and I believe he's good for the place and it's good for him, it's the making of him. You can see that yourself, I know you can. But I'm not convinced that full ownership would be very good for him, nor that he would want it. It would be a daunting prospect for him. He needs to work with a partner but it has to be someone he gets on with, so who better than you? And you say I'm giving it away, but it doesn't feel like that – after all, I never really had it except on paper. That happened once before, when Harry died and I inherited it. Back then I made it over to Freda Benson because it felt like the right thing to do. This feels like the right thing now, as though it was only ever on loan. This is not my place and I don't really want the responsibility. I'm getting old and I don't want to make an arrangement that will fall apart if I die within the next couple of years. I'd prefer to leave here knowing that you and Declan can keep it going, build it up, and that he feels secure. And frankly I think security is important to you too.'

Alice stiffens with a sense of resentment. 'Look, I don't want to offend you, Ruby,' she says. 'I appreciate the enormous generosity of your offer, and the opportunity it gives me, but you've spent your life rescuing women. I'm sure you chose to do that because of what happened to you as a child, and I admire it enormously. But I don't need you to rescue me.'

Ruby smiles. 'Well said. And I'm not. If I thought you *needed* rescuing then I wouldn't be doing this. I think you're perfectly capable of rebuilding your life anywhere you choose, Alice. You don't need me or anyone else to rescue you. Nor do I want you to rescue Declan. I just think you're an excellent partnership.'

Alice sits for a while, silent, contemplating what Ruby has said. She can see it makes sense, but she is also trapped in the feeling that it is too much to be given this. She feels unworthy of such good fortune.

'And by the way,' Ruby says, 'I don't think you have to go on paying for what happened for the rest of your life. You served a sentence that most people think is excessive, you lost your granddaughter and in a way you lost your family too. You've paid the price. It's time to stop limiting your expectations, Alice. Of course you can't forget it and you don't want to, but you need to cast off the feelings that make you think that you can only be viewed as someone who might need rescuing.'

Alice watches as Ruby makes her way carefully back down the path to the house. She tries to imagine how it would feel to be the joint owner of this place with its beautiful old house, the cottages, the gorgeous sloping fields of lavender, the shop – all of it; to be able to make plans and decisions for its future, and to do so with Declan, whom she trusts more than anyone in the world. You'd be a fool to say no, she tells herself, anyone else would jump at it. She imagines moving into the house, reorganising some of the rooms, taking ownership simply by her presence there. She thinks of the room that they would keep for Todd so that he always has a place to come home to, of where Jodie might sleep if she were ever allowed to come and stay, or perhaps came sometime in the future when she is old enough to make her own decisions. She imagines Ruby coming here for a holiday and to see what they've done.

But most of all she thinks of Catherine – about whom she's heard so much but knows so little. A woman who had struggled on here for years after the errant Harry fell into the arms of someone younger. A woman whom many people might say got no more than she deserved. To Alice Catherine is both larger than life and almost transparent. It seems impossible to grasp who she really was, but it's clear that she wanted Declan to stay here and felt that Ruby was the key to that. What Alice has to decide now is whether she wants this extraordinary gift with its burdens as well as its rewards.

Quarter to eight on Friday morning and they are there in front of the television, Ruby, Declan and Todd, no sign of Alice yet.

'She might've got mixed up with the time and forgot that eleven o'clock in Canberra is eight o'clock here,' Todd says. 'I could go and get her.'

He is sitting on the floor leaning against the couch and Ruby reaches forward and puts a hand on his shoulder. 'Alice won't forget, Todd,' she says, 'she'll be here in time. It's not starting yet.'

They watch as the camera pans across the Great Hall of Parliament House where hundreds of people are settling into their seats. They are almost four thousand kilometres away but Ruby feels she is a part of it, she feels the tension, and the anticipation, senses the agonising reliving of painful memories, sees it in the shots of clasped hands, in the anxious, desperate expressions. So many years, so much misery, cruelty and neglect, are contained in those faces. She hadn't expected it to feel quite like this, the past rising up within her like a thunderbolt of outrage ready to break out and scorch everything and everyone within reach.

Lesley pops her head around the door. 'May I join you?'

Ruby nods, unable to take her eyes off the screen.

Declan shifts closer to her on the sofa to make room for Lesley and takes Ruby's icy cold hand in his. She squeezes it and hangs on, watching and waiting.

Todd gets up and crosses to the window. 'She's coming,' he calls in relief. 'Alice is coming down the hill now.'

'Sorry,' Alice says, breathless, and she slips across the room and into the seat on the other side of Ruby. 'So sorry, I lost track of time, so much to think about.'

Ruby glances at her and then at Declan. The weight of what he has hanging on Alice's decision is written across his face, but Ruby can't think of that now because all she can concentrate on is all those people with whom she shares so much. And they are just a fraction of the whole, the others sitting, like her, in front of screens around the country, maybe around the world, all of them linked by their painful history. Could some of them have been on the same ship as her and Catherine? Were any of those women at the same convent, sleeping perhaps in the same dormitory? She leans forward, studying the faces, the clasped hands, the tense profiles, searching for recognition, and she finds it in every face because each is inscribed with the grief, the loss, the shame and desolation that is in her own. She can feel the tension and the longing to hear at last what they have been aching to hear for decades: a thought, an acknowledgement, in just one word – sorry.

And then it begins. The prime minister steps up to the microphone, his face strained with emotion.

'We come together today to deal with an ugly chapter in our nation's history,' he begins. 'And we come together today to offer our nation's apology. To say to you, the Forgotten Australians, and those who were sent to our shores as children without your consent, that we are sorry.'

He talks of physical suffering and emotional starvation, of childhoods lost, of the repetitive drudgery of menial work, of abuse, humiliation, violation and cruelty. 'We look back with shame,' he says, 'at how those in power were allowed to abuse those who had none.' And so it goes, each word, each sentence freighted with the horrors of their collective history, there in Parliament House and around the country, as those whose stories are being honoured wrestle with the hurt of a lifetime and the relief of acknowledgement.

Ruby watches through the prime minister's speech, and the leader of the opposition's, she watches as they step down to shake hands, to listen and acknowledge the people, each of whom represent so many more. It is almost unbearable, but she watches on, the tears pouring down her face, Declan and Alice on either side of her, holding her hands, Todd on the floor with his warm back resting against her legs.

'I am so lucky,' she says eventually, her voice breaking with emotion. 'I am just so lucky.'

Eventually the coverage ends and one by one they get to their feet, silent, awkward, still reeling with the emotion of the occasion, unsure how to move from that into a normal day. Lesley slips quietly away back to the shop.

'Who wants a cup of tea?' Todd asks, and they smile and nod with relief and he shoots off to the kitchen and they hear the water running into the kettle and the sound of cups being taken from the cupboard.

'Who wants a decision?' Alice asks, and they turn to her.

Ruby is close to holding her breath.

'I've wrestled with this all night,' Alice says. 'I've put up every argument I can think of, and talked to both of you, and despite the murmur of voices that keep telling me I shouldn't have this I've decided to celebrate my good fortune and accept your extraordinarily generous offer, Ruby. I feel honoured by your trust and I'll do everything I can to make this work.'

Ruby closes her eyes and sinks back onto the sofa. 'At last,' she says, 'a day of endings and beginnings. At last.'

They are laughing now, and crying, hugging and congratulating each other. Relief is palpable, emotional exhaustion and the anxiety of waiting replaced by the need for celebration.

'What's happened?' Todd asks, appearing in the doorway with a tray of tea. 'I thought everyone was upset.'

'Todd,' says Declan, taking the tray from him, 'please meet my new business partner,' and Alice steps forward and does a little curtsy.

'Really?' Todd says, looking from one to the other. 'That's awesome. It means you'll both have to be here forever.'

Thirty-one

Islington, late November 2009

'You're kidding,' Amanda says, standing behind Ruby and talking to her reflection in the mirror. 'All of it? You want me to cut all of it off?'

'I do,' Ruby says. 'I don't want to be bald, not a number two or anything like that, but I want it short, and sort of spiky, and as a young friend of mine says – mega cool.'

'I've been doing your hair for more than twenty years and all that time I've been begging you to let me cut it and you've been insisting that you'll never have it cut.'

'So, times change, people change, I've changed.'

'You said it was important. Symbolic.'

'Well, what's important and symbolic now is having it cut. So get going before I change my mind.'

She watches as the locks of grey hair slip to her shoulders and then to the floor, and the strange process of transformation begins. Almost immediately she sees that she will look younger. It's not an effect she had sought but it's not unwelcome. And it *is* symbolic: as Amanda shapes the cut to frame her face and chips into the crown to give it height and movement, Ruby feels that more than just the hair is dropping

413

away from her. The past lies bedraggled on the salon floor, ready to be swept away by the first apprentice with minutes to spare between shampoos.

'You okay, Rube?' Amanda asks.

'I'm absolutely okay,' she says. 'It's going to be very different. I think I'll like it.'

Amanda works some product into Ruby's hair, fluffs it up and picks up the dryer.

You're not a bad looking old dame really, Ruby tells herself. Perhaps there *is* a touch of Dame Judi there. Shame you didn't get her eyes and jawline, but all round not a bad look.

'So what do you think?' Amanda asks, holding the mirror up so Ruby can see the back of her head.

'I like it,' Ruby says. 'A lot. And it feels good. You've transformed me. What do you think?'

'I love it,' Amanda says. 'Should have done it years ago.'

'I wasn't ready years ago. This is my moment.'

It's bitterly cold outside and as she walks back along Upper Street, negotiating the icy patches on the pavement, Ruby realises she will now need to buy a hat for the cold weather, and dig out some scarves for her newly naked neck. It feels right to have done this now, although it's still a shock each time she catches a glimpse of her reflection in a shop window.

'So what's next?' Jessica had asked her yesterday evening when they got home from the airport. 'Are you coming back to work?'

'You seem to have managed rather well without me,' Ruby had said. 'Which is good, and while I obviously don't want to give up, I'm thinking I might cut right back. I'm going to cruise for a while, wake up in the mornings and see how the mood takes me. Maybe I'll get to read all those books I've started but never finished, perhaps do something new and different. And I really am going to start writing that history of the Foundation, but first I thought I might have a rest.'

'Rest?' Jessica had said, laughing. 'That's a word I've only ever heard you direct at other people.'

'Well there you go,' Ruby had said with a grin, 'I'm full of surprises.'

So what *will* I do, she wonders now, turning onto the path that runs alongside the park. I'm convincing everyone else that I'm reinventing myself, but how do I convince myself? It's not so windy here off the main street, but the trees are stripped bare of leaves, their branches silhouetted like gnarled fingers against the leaden sky. By a bench at the side of the path a young man stands on one foot, the other resting on the edge of the seat. He is wearing an old army greatcoat, a Dr Who scarf wrapped around his neck, and gloves with the fingers cut off to the big knuckle, and he's playing the fiddle. Irish tunes, she thinks, although she can't remember the names, but the melodies float out in the chill air over the heads of the pedestrians up into the old branches. Ruby stops to listen and feels, in the stillness, as she had felt the morning after she had told her story to Alice. Then the great burden of the past had rolled away down the hill; now, the final vestiges have been swept away with the strands of her hair. The fiddle player begins another tune and Ruby digs in her pockets for coins, drops them into the open fiddle case at his feet and walks on, head down into the wind towards home.

It's only when she's almost there that she looks up and sees him, standing on the top step, hands in his pockets, a backpack looped over one shoulder, watching her, waiting. Ruby stops, narrowing her eyes to make sure she isn't imagining things. But no, it's him all right. She walks on to the bottom of the steps.

'Jackson?'

'Ruby,' he says. 'Todd said you'd be back by now. Great hair.'

She narrows her eyes again, this time with scepticism. 'Why are you here?'

'I think you can guess why.'

'I don't have the time or the inclination for guessing games.' She hears herself as haughty and dismissive, and is glad of it. 'What is it that you want?'

He looks around as though searching for someone to rescue him then draws a deep breath. 'You, Ruby,' he says, 'you and me. I want us.'

She looks at him, saying nothing, struggling not to let him see the inner turmoil. 'You said something like that once before,' she says, 'and then you backed off faster than lightning.'

Jackson nods, looking down at his feet in obvious embarrassment, then up at her again. 'I ran away,' he says. 'I'm an old man, seventy-two years old, but I got scared. I didn't know how to do it all again . . . relationships, companionship . . . love. Most of all love, but I found I couldn't stop . . . thinking . . . hoping . . .' His voice trails away.

Ruby gives him another long look and walks up the steps to join him at the top. She shakes her head, reaches into her pocket and takes out a crumpled piece of paper, unfolds it and looks at it intently. 'Your name does not appear on my bucket list.'

He hesitates and she sees the expression in his eyes change, and one corner of his mouth twitches into the start of a smile.

'Well maybe I could audition for a place?'

'Catherine did this once,' Ruby says. 'Ambushed me on my own doorstep. It wasn't a good move,' she sighs, 'but this . . .'

'This?'

'. . . is different.' She turns away to unlock the door, pushes it open and walks in, turning back to hold the door for him. 'Not much luggage, I see. I'm not sure that a backpack indicates any level of commitment, but then I suppose that's appropriate for an itinerant musician. Come on in. The audition starts now. I think you'll find it won't hurt a bit.'

Acknowledgements

I am grateful to Peter Sirr, Executive Director of Outcare Western Australia, his explanation of the prison system was invaluable. My thanks too to Richard Utting for advice on sentencing.

Thanks too to Bev Ainsworth of Cape Lavender in Margaret River for taking time to tell me her story of starting her lavender farm. Benson's Reach is not Cape Lavender but Bev's experience and knowledge was most valuable. You can find out about Bev and Cape Lavender at www.capelavender. com.au.

I am grateful to the women of the Zonta Club of Bunbury for their hospitality and for introducing me to the Birthing Kit Project. Zonta is a proud supporter of the Australian Birthing Foundation and its members raise funds and work as volunteers to assemble the kits. The impact of these simple, inexpensive kits on the lives of women in developing countries is remarkable, and you can find out more about it at http://www.birthingkitfoundation.org.au/.

As always my grateful thanks to my friends and colleagues at Pan Macmillan: my publisher Cate Paterson, editors Emma Rafferty and Jo Jarrah, and to the many other people who work so hard to turn a manuscript into a book, publicise it and get it onto the shelves in bookshops. It is a pleasure and a privilege to work with you all.

MORE BESTSELLING FICTION FROM LIZ BYRSKI

Gang of Four

She had a husband, children and grandchildren who loved her; a beautiful home, enough money. What sort of person was able to feel so overwhelmed with gloom and resentment on Christmas morning?

They have been close friends for almost two decades, supporting each other through personal and professional crises – parents dying, children leaving home, house moves, job changes, political activism and really bad haircuts.

Now the 'gang of four', Isabel, Sally, Robin and Grace, are all fifty-something, successful . . . and restless.

Food, Sex & Money

It's almost forty years since the three ex-convent girls left
school and went their separate ways, but finally they meet
again.

Bonnie, rocked by the death of her husband, is back in
Australia after decades in Europe, and is discovering that
financial security doesn't guarantee a fulfilling life. Fran, long
divorced, is a freelance food writer, battling with her diet, her
bank balance and her relationship with her adult children. And
Sylvia, marooned in a passionless marriage, is facing a crisis
that will crack her world wide open.

Together again, Bonnie, Fran and Sylvia embark on a venture
that will challenge everything they thought they knew about
themselves – and give them more second chances than they
could ever have imagined.

Belly Dancing for Beginners

Gayle and Sonya are complete opposites: one reserved and cautious, the other confident and outspoken. But their lives will converge when they impulsively join a belly dancing class.

Marissa, their teacher, is sixty, sexy, and very much her own person, and as Gayle and Sonya learn about the origins and meaning of the dance, much more than their muscle tone begins to change.

Trip of a Lifetime

How do you get your life back on track after a sudden and traumatic event? This is the question Heather Delaney constantly asks herself as she eases herself back into her busy job.

Heather is not the only one who is rocked by the changed circumstances – reverberations are felt throughout her family and friendship circle. And then along comes Heather's old flame, Ellis. Romantic, flamboyant, determined to recapture the past and take control of the future, he seems to have all the answers. But can it really be that easy?

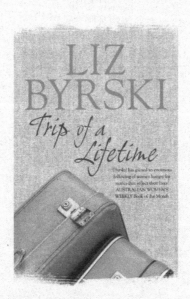